To Jon – I love you.

BOOK TWO
A LOSANTIVERSE NOVEL

TO DIE
IS
GAIN

JAYE POOL

TARTANIUM
PRESS

TO DIE IS GAIN

Cover design by GetCovers

Published by Tartanium Press
PO Box 33113 | Cincinnati, OH 45233

ISBN: 979-8-9923291-3-1 (eBook)
ISBN: 979-8-9923291-4-8 (Paperback)
ISBN: 979-8-9923291-5-5 (Hardcover)

Library of Congress Control Number: 2025906788

First Edition: May 2025

10 9 8 7 6 5 4 3 2 1

BOOK TWO
A LOSANTIVERSE NOVEL

TO DIE
IS
GAIN

JAYE POOL

TARTANIUM
PRESS

TO DIE IS GAIN

Copyright © 2025 by Jaye Pool.

Cover design by GetCovers

Published by Tartanium Press
PO Box 33113 | Cincinnati, OH 45233

ISBN: 979-8-9923291-3-1 (eBook)
ISBN: 979-8-9923291-4-8 (Paperback)
ISBN: 979-8-9923291-5-5 (Hardcover)

Library of Congress Control Number: 2025906788

First Edition: May 2025

10 9 8 7 6 5 4 3 2 1

You can't go back and change the beginning, but you can start where you are and change the ending.

Unknown

THE END
June 25, 2023

The straw-hued strands gave a rough feeling a the fingers.

This should at least be quick.

A man sat nude on the queen-sized bed by the window, staring painfully at the weathered oak desk next to the plush bed. On top was a small laptop, alone and shut off. Nothing else remained, not a lamp, not a book, not a notebook, not even a piece of mail or stray scrap of paper out of place. The stark wooden chair was next to the desk, pulled out.

He turned to the open window to view the dark, dense neighborhood lined with small, two-story apartment buildings and bungalows. The street was eerily quiet as the children of the block were settling into bed, as were the adults, readying themselves to begin yet another routine week of work. The deafening silence reflected much of the man's miserable life, including this night.

◆◇◆

Several hours earlier, the sun shone in the man's face as he opened his eyes and peered at his smartwatch.

Eleven AM. Shit.

Slowly, he arose, clad in navy blue boxers and a tee shirt, and turned around to fastidiously make the bed nice and neat. He carefully folded in each corner of the navy sheet military-style, as he had been taught as a child. Then, he laid the stark white comforter over it, each side evened up just so. The two pillows were neatly fluffed and shaken, with the pillowcases smoothed, and set on each side of the bed. After having checked it three times, he let it be and headed to the bathroom on the other side of the small hallway. His cell phone rang.

He breathed in fully. *It's Mom. I better pick up.*

"Hi, hun, how are you?"

"I'm okay. It's a little early for me, though."

"Sorry dear, I forgot. Anyway, you sound better than you have been. Hopefully, you've been sleeping better?"

"Yes, I stopped drinking caffeine like you told me to."

"Well, I said it would work. As I've been saying to you, it's going to interfere with your medication...now Luke, you *have* been taking your medication, right?"

"Yes, Mom – I'm taking my daily pills. I suppose not drinking coffee before bed has cut down on the insomnia."

"As you know, your mother knows best."

"I guess so," Luke muttered.

"Of course. Anyway, I'm calling to remind you supper tonight. Remember your brother's in town from San Francisco and he's got Sandy and the kids with him this time. They're over the house. And your father wants you there too. We've always wanted you and your brother to be closer, for you to be in your nephews' lives."

"I know, Mom."

"Well, we're eating at six o'clock. Don't be late."

"I never am, Mom."

"Of course, dear," his mother responded softly.

Luke had errands to run before family supper. He stopped by the neighborhood Lovett's, the local grocery store, to pick up a sack of Yukon gold potatoes, butter, and heavy cream for making mashed potatoes, the side he would bring to Sunday supper. Afterward, he visited two stores to purchase toys for his nephews: a special edition Golden Ghost action figure for the younger one, Braiden, and a mint green Yamaha electric guitar for the oldest boy, Shane. He then stopped by Champs Hardware before heading home, where he found the item he had in mind, in extra strength.

He arrived home and got to work making a side dish for Sunday supper, whipping up mashed potatoes from scratch. His mother taught him the recipe as a child, but he possessed a special touch that made the dish extra creamy and delicious. His family would rave about his mashed potatoes, but he had not made them in years. These days, it was hard to summon the strength to make anything for Sunday supper. Getting there was difficult enough, but this time, Luke was up for it, and it would be a nice surprise for the family. It was the one thing he could do that pleased them.

It was ten minutes before six, and Luke arrived at his childhood home. *I don't wanna stay any longer than I have to.*

The brick, 1920s colonial-style house was located in Denbytown, a cozy, middle-class, bedroom suburb just outside the southwestern Ohio city of Losanti. The street was lined with other homes similar in age, with manicured lawns and beautiful floral landscapes. He recalled his father, a strict Marine veteran, always saying, "If you're on time, you're late." Even as a man of forty-three years of age, no way would Luke dare be late to Sunday supper.

He parked in the half-circle driveway near the painted green front door and retrieved the potato dish and the gifts from his car. The door opened, and a solid-bodied, ruddy-skinned man strolled outside to greet him. Peering down at his younger brother, and then the covered Tupperware dish and the giant bag, he quipped, "Asshole, *that's* what you chose to wear? An undershirt and jorts? At least you brought something."

Luke rolled his eyes and spoke pointedly, "Hi to you too, Trey. Long time. No see."

A grey-haired, diminutive woman with alabaster, slightly wrinkled skin rushed outside. After greeting Luke, she took in the tension between her two sons and pointed her withered index finger at them. "Luke Carter Phillips, Gerald Cameron Phillips the Third, be nice."

"Yes, Mom," Luke mumbled.

"Alright, Mom," Trey grumbled.

She then took the food container and stepped back inside the house. As they followed her indoors, the brothers gave each other smug glances.

The scent of citrus incense filled Luke's nostrils as he shuffled into the beige and white wallpapered foyer. To the right in the living room, a young boy with a white printed tee shirt could be seen jumping up and down on the tan felt Davenport, his straight blond hair bouncing with every hop.

"Get off the couch, Braiden!" scolded a slightly pudgy, mousy-haired woman sitting on the matching loveseat with knitting needles in her hands.

"But I'm so bored!"

"You're fine, honey. Come here." Braiden slid off the couch onto the polished hardwood floor and sat with his mother, who put her arm around him. She looked up and saw Luke standing in the foyer.

"Hi, Luke! It's lovely to see you!"

Luke turned his head as he heard his name called. "Oh – hi, Sandy! It's good to see you too. And wow, that's Braiden? You've gotten so big!" He placed the gifts against the foyer wall as he walked into the living room, gave Sandy a hug, and sat on the couch. "You might not remember me," he said to the child. "I'm your Uncle Luke."

"Hi!" Braiden said.

"How old are you now?"

"I'm seven." He held up all five digits on his right hand and two on his left.

"More like seven going on seventeen," piped Sandy.

Luke looked at his sister-in-law astonished. "How long has it been since you've been out here to Ohio?"

"Oh, I want to say it's been at least a good five years or so?"

"Yeah, I believe it was 2018."

"Figured as such...you were still married back then, and it was before Trey became the dean of the applied sciences school. That keeps him so busy, you know?"

"Of course." Luke turned back to Braiden. "You were a baby the last time I saw you."

Sandy looked up from her knitting project and peered at her brother-in-law earnestly. "Have you thought about taking a trip out to the Bay?"

Trey had lived in San Francisco for at least two decades, but in that time frame, Luke never visited. *Reasons,* he thought to himself.

"Eh, I don't know, Sandy. Haven't had a chance to, but maybe I should one day."

"You should. The boys would love it, and whether your brother admits it or not, he would like that too."

Growing increasingly uncomfortable, he changed the subject.

"So, what are you knitting?"

"Oh, it's a beret I'm making for your mom."

"It's kind of warm for that, isn't it? I mean, it's gonna be the Fourth of July in a little more than a week."

"True, but how often are we out here? And besides, it keeps my hands busy."

"Fair."

Luke's mother entered the room. "Supper is ready. Luke, could you come help me set the table? Trey and Sandy are visiting, I'm not going to make them do any work."

"It's no trouble at all, Libby," Sandy called out as she was in the midst of standing up.

"No no, Sandy. Relax – I insist. Luke can help."

Luke stepped into the dining room and opened the oak china cabinet. He carefully counted seven delicate ivory plates.

One, two, three, four, five, six, seven.

One, two, three, four, five, six, seven.

One, two, three, four, five, six, seven.

Okay, good. Didn't want tonight to be a disaster.

Having reassured himself he had the correct number of plates for supper, Luke carefully lifted the stack of dishes from the cabinet.

"Be careful, don't drop the china!" Libby said curtly.

"I'm not going to drop the china, Mom. Have I ever dropped the china?"

Libby cut her eyes at her son but did not respond.

"No, Mom. No, I haven't. Goddammit..."

"Don't get fresh with me, Luke."

With no will to snap at his mother, he sighed and quietly set the delicate plates onto the walnut table, which matched the cabinet, and brought out the accompanying silverware and wine glasses. Libby removed a green runner from the china cabinet drawer and laid it in the middle of the long table lengthwise. She added a gold candelabra to the middle of the table, placed plain white candles atop, and lit them with her metal lighter.

"Your father's coming down in a moment. Let's set supper on the table," she instructed him.

Mother and son brought out the spread, which included a glistening honey baked ham, green bean casserole, golden dinner rolls, and Luke's homemade mashed potatoes. A one-and-a-half liter bottle of Merlot and Riesling accompanied the food, along with a carafe of ice water. As the final items were brought in, heavy footsteps could be heard lumbering down the stairs. In the kitchen entered an imposing man with silver hair, steeled jaw, shaved face, weathered skin, and midsection paunch. He took his rightful seat at the head of the table.

"What would you like, Cam?" Libby said to the steeled old man.

"Merlot."

"We have Guinness in the fridge, nice and cold just like you like it."

"Lib, I want Merlot. Tonight is a Merlot night."

"Certainly, dear," she quietly replied. She turned to her youngest son. "Luke, call everybody to the table."

Luke stepped into the living room, where Sandy was waiting along with Braiden. Trey was seated there as well, wearing a short-sleeved polo shirt with his university's logo adorning the left chest. "Supper is ready," he called to them.

"Is Dad seated?"

"Yeah, he's sitting down and ready to go."

"Of course," Trey rolled his eyes.

"Sandy, where's Shane?"

She sighed. "He's in the back bedroom, being his normal moody self. You know, teens are like that. Ever since he started high school..."

Trey shot a look at her. "Don't start."

"You know how he i—"

"I mean it, Sandy. Don't start," he admonished her through gritted teeth. He stood up and headed towards the first floor hallway. "I'll go get him."

Everyone filed into the dining room and took their seats. Each time the Phillips family reunited, family members sat in the same exact chairs based on how close the patriarch felt to each of them, and this time was no exception. Dutiful wife Libby sat to Cam's left and favored son Trey to his right. Sandy sat on the other side of Trey, with Braiden on the right side of her. Shane, a gangly young teen with wavy dark hair in his face, trudged in at his father's behest, and placed himself next to his dear grandmother. Between Shane and Sandy, furthest away from the head of the table, Luke took his position.

"It's time to say grace," Libby said.

Her husband prayed aloud. "Dear God, we thank you for the food we are about to receive. And I thank you for our children and grandchildren being here with us tonight, as we now eat as a complete family. In the name of Jesus, Amen."

"Amen," the Phillips clan chanted.

Everyone passed around the food, and all began to eat.

Trey spoke up. "Braiden is doing very well at his Montessori school. His last report card was great, and he's really excelling."

"Ah," said the proud grandpa. "Papa loves hearing those great reports, Braiden. Very nice. Keep going, kid."

"What do you say, Braiden?" Sandy prompted her youngest boy.

He looked up at his grandfather. "Thank you, Papa."

"You're teaching him well, Sandy. I see why my boy married you."

Sandy blushed. "Thank you, Cam." Trey gently rubbed his wife's back and smiled, feeling the comment his father made towards her was a positive reflection on him.

Libby then commented, "I hear Shane's really got an ear for music."

"Oh, is that so?" Cam said.

Trey pointed out, "Yeah, but as I'm sure you know, Dad, music doesn't pay the bills."

"True, it is hard to make a living that way, but music does soothe the soul," Sandy responded.

"So, Luke, what have you been doing?" Trey inquired with a glint in his eye.

Shit. "You know, a little bit of this and that."

"He's working down at the Dairy Union in Marydale. The one near his apartment," Libby said of Luke's job at the local convenience store chain.

"He's a clerk. Overnights." Cam added with an undercurrent of disappointment in his voice.

Luke stared down at his plate, his eyes moistening with emotion. He hardly touched anything. Not that the food was bad. The spread was satisfactory overall, but the direction of the conversation made it quite difficult for him to force down each bite. Nevertheless, he kept eating to not disappoint his dear mother.

Cam scooped a heap of mashed potatoes onto his fork and took a bite. He cracked a smile. "You know what? These are incredible."

Libby informed him, "Luke brought those over."

The patriarch looked over to his younger son. "You know I love these. It's been so long. These are like magic."

Sandy's eyes checked Shane's plate. He had eaten everything except the potatoes. "Take a bite of them, Shane."

The young teen whined to his mother. "Mom, you know I don't like mushy things."

"Bud, you know we try things at least once."

Luke spoke up. "It's okay, you don't have to."

Sandy interjected, "He does. It's the right thing to do."

Shane poked at the potatoes and took a small taste. After a moment, he heaped a second portion onto the fork and ate the rest. "These are, like, solid, not weird like normal mashed potatoes. Unc, these are really good."

"Thanks, Shane," Luke responded with a small grin.

After supper and cleanup, the family sat in the living room. Cam sat in a brown leather recliner, drinking a Guinness beer and watching the news. Libby and Luke sat on the sofa. Trey and Braiden sat on the floor playing checkers. Sandy sat on the love seat continuing to knit, while Shane sat on the floor in front of the loveseat on his cell phone.

Luke rose from the couch. "I've got to take off. I need to make sure I get my rest for work tomorrow."

Trey then called him out. "You work third shift, Luke. Don't you sleep during the day?"

"Yeah, but I didn't sleep much this afternoon."

"You're so full of shit."

"Watch your language, Trey!" Libby admonished him. "Is that how they speak in front of their elders in California?"

"I'm sorry, Mom."

"Luke, don't you want to at least give the boys the presents you got them before you go?"

"Sure." He gave the Golden Ghost action figure to Braiden. "Push the red button on his chest," he instructed his nephew.

He pushed the button accessible by a hole cut out in the clear plastic packaging. The yellow plastic man bellowed, "I am the Golden Ghost, the guardian of the great beyond!"

"This is awesome!" the young boy exclaimed while opening the box to release the toy from its cardboard display casing.

"What do you say, dear?" Sandy reminded her younger son.

"Thank you, Uncle Luke!" he replied as he hugged his uncle.

"You're welcome."

Luke then turned and gave his older nephew a black case. Shane opened it and scanned the guitar inside. His eyes opened wide like saucers as he carefully lifted the instrument and marveled over it.

"It's a limited-edition Squier Sonic Stratocaster. This is so cool! I've been asking my parents for an electric guitar for a while, but they kept saying 'no.' Thanks so much, Unc!"

Trey sat on the floor, annoyed. "Shane, since your uncle got that for you, I fully expect you to learn how to play it. If we sign you up for lessons, we don't want you to get bored and quit part of the way through. You give up way too easily, especially when things are hard. I don't want the guitar to be a waste."

"Trey, stop..." Sandy pushed back.

"It's true. Remember when we signed him up for art classes last summer? Or when he was in grade school and we put him in piano lessons?"

"Look, if Shane ends up not being into it, that's fine, don't worry about it," Luke interjected.

"No, Luke, it's not. I don't want *my son* to be a quitter. I want him to actually finish what he starts."

Ouch.

Shane tried to reassure his doubtful father. "Dad, I've wanted to play for a long time, and if I learn, I can play with my friends. I won't quit, I promise."

Trey relented. "Okay, we'll go ahead and sign you up for lessons. But I'm serious...you better not quit."

"Thanks, Dad!" Shane responded.

Sandy smiled at Luke. "Thanks for thinking of the boys like this, Luke. That was very nice."

Despite the tension of the evening, he was thankful to have made it to Sunday supper – this supper – one last time.

———◆———

Shortly after nine o'clock in the evening, Luke trudged through the entrance of his claustrophobic one-bedroom apartment in the older, working-class neighborhood of Marydale, just north of downtown Losanti. The synthetic pine-clad floors were immaculately polished, and his futon was worn yet neatly covered in a woven blanket that came from his travels in the American Southwest. *Better times.*

After removing his loafers and placing them by the door, Luke poured himself a glass from the half-empty bottle of Cabernet in his otherwise barren refrigerator. He took a sip from his clear tumbler and slowly reclined on the beige futon. He carefully placed the glass on the cheap wooden coffee table and sat in complete silence. Contemplating his next steps, he found himself spiraling.

I can't live like this anymore.

He went to the tiny, plain bathroom down the hallway and used the toilet. Once he was done, he stood up, flushed, and faced the sink and mirror situated above it. He peeked inside the medicine cabinet behind the mirror, avoiding the view of his face as he did so. He scanned the multitude of pill bottles on the shelf.

Lexapro. Lamictal.

Half a dozen containers, all filled to the brim but never opened.

He then closed the cabinet door but inadvertently caught his reflection. He could not help but notice his scraggly grey locks thinning, the wrinkles beginning to form on his ivory-toned skin. But despite the changes that had come with age, his pale blue eyes, which often reflected the shades of the world around him, remained the same.

Luke shied away from the image and stripped his clothing. First his green pullover and white undershirt, then his khakis, and lastly his boxers and dress socks. He stepped into the tiled walk-in shower. He bent over and turned on the faucet, and slid it to warm, closer to hot.

The steamy water glided over Luke's stubbled face and hirsute body. He squeezed out a portion of musk-scented men's soap cum slathered himself with it from neck to toe.

Should I write a note? No, it's pretty damn clear as to why.

I'm a failure and they know it. Everybody knows it.

I'm a complete failure, and there is no coming back from this.

After ten minutes, he stepped out of the shower, dried himself off with a white towel, then fastened it around his waist. He entered the living room and chugged the last of his tumbler of wine. Once finished, he wiped down the coffee table, washed the tumbler, dried it, and placed it back inside the cabinet. He then clutched the small plastic bag he left behind when he went to family supper.

He slowly yet determinedly headed into his bedroom, a plain white-walled room, much like the rest of the apartment unit. His bed sat next to the window, and his desk next to it. Opposite the bed and desk was a matching chest of drawers. His clothing was folded perfectly inside each drawer. On top was a picture of himself, his parents, and his brother, from when he and Trey were both children. Next to it sat a small pine box full of photos Luke kept there but rarely ever opened.

He opened the box and focused on the snapshot at the very top of the pile. *I miss you so much...God, I wish things had been different. I wish I hadn't ruined things between us.*

Once he closed back the box, his eyes lifted towards the sole item hung on the wall: a framed bachelor of science degree from the University of the Great Lakes, a highly-rated public institution in mid-Michigan.

I majored in chemistry and minored in journalism. Summa cum laude. Working at the Dairy Union is all I have to show for it. Failure.

Luke pulled off the towel and carefully placed it in the wicker hamper next to his door. He slouched on the side of the bed by the desk and opened the bag. Out came a length of thick beige rope.

He lifted his head upwards and carefully inspected the exposed structural beam above him running the length of the room from the back of the desk to the door. Methodically, he created a hangman's knot on one end of the rope.

Boy Scouts really came in clutch. Having a military dad helps too. Thanks, Dad.

Luke stood up then lifted himself onto his desk chair, tying the other end around the I-beam. He shifted his weight onto it to make sure it was secure.

It's go time.

Luke held the noose with both hands, readying himself to slip his head in.

Ring!

Luke's cell phone, left on his desk from the morning, was going off.

Shit. I thought I turned off my ringer. Whatever.

The phone continued to ring.

Wait a second...

A distinct ringtone wailed that had not emitted from the phone in quite some time. He stopped what he was doing and climbed down from his chair. He picked up the phone.

"Hello?"

"Hi, Luke! It's Paul."

In his despair and hopelessness, he was relieved to hear a familiar, friendly voice. "Paulie! What's going on?"

"Nothing much, life's good. How are you?"

Luke sat back down on the side of his bed. "Eh...I'm doing alright."

"Hope I'm not calling you at a bad time," Paul responded with a little regret.

"Uh...uh, no, you're fine. Just getting ready to relax."

"That's good. Listen, I'm gonna be in town tomorrow and I wanna hang out. Maybe we can grab a bite to eat or something. When are you off work?"

"Oh...uh...I'm off tomorrow. I'm free whenever."

"Okay, cool. Maybe we can go over to Uno near downtown. I heard it's supposed to be really good, like great Reubens."

"Sure, sounds great. That's not too far from me."

"Oh, okay. What part of town are you living in now?"

"Marydale."

"Oh...wow, that area's pretty run down, isn't it?"

"It's not too bad. It's come a long way since the riots twenty or so years ago. My block's pretty quiet."

"Alright, that's good to hear. Anyway man, can't wait to see you."

"I can't wait either."

Paul took a short pause. "I missed you, brother."

"Ditto, Paulie."

Once hanging up, Luke leaned back on his bed and freed a torrent of feelings. He wept harder than he had in a very long time. He still felt deeply depressed, but his friend was a lifeline in the darkness.

After an hour curled up in bed, he stood up and took the noose down from the rafter, placing it in the bedroom closet. He returned to the bathroom, picked up the towel, and threw it around his waist. He walked into the living room, opened the window, and sat on the futon, breathing in the warm June air and watching the cars drive by.

EVEREST
June 26, 2023

"Welcome to Uno! Can I start you off with something to drink?" asked the bubbly waitress with rows of pins affixed to her black smock.

"I'll have a Coke," said Paul.

"And for you, sir?"

Luke asked, "Uh, what do you have on tap?"

The server pointed to the list of draft beer selections printed on the menu.

"Um...I'll have a Miller Lite."

"Certainly!" She left to enter the order.

"Paulie, you look great! Hittin' the gym?"

"Yeah, something like that. Between working out and living the Florida lifestyle, I've lost, eh, around thirty or so pounds since the last time you saw me."

"Wow, maybe I need some of that."

"You still look pretty good, man. Not bad for forty-three," Paul responded encouragingly.

"I'm alright...but underneath this shirt, it's average at best. But look at you – you still have a full head of hair!"

"Sure, but see this grey? Father Time is undefeated."

The friends thumbed through their menus.

"So, what brought you back to town?" Luke asked.

"Good question. I was thinking it's been a really long time, and the weather's been holding up, so I decided to drive on up."

"Your parents moved to be closer to you, right?"

"Yeah. It really made sense for them. I was already living down in Jacksonville, this was back when I was still with Alyssa, and the kids were young, so they wanted to be close to where we were."

"It sure helps that Florida is paradise for retirees."

"True."

After they received their drinks, they placed their food orders. While waiting for their meals, the greying men engaged in more conversation.

"So, what have you been up to these days?" Luke asked.

"I've been working. Jacksonville is like a lot of places, always under construction. As long as there's construction, there's always a need for building codes. It's been good, though."

"Looks like it. I'm always seeing you out on the open water."

"Oh, on Facebook? Yeah, it's beautiful. It's nice. The ocean is the best thing. It can get a little dicey sometimes during hurricane season, but you get used to it, I suppose. But man, I wouldn't have it any other way."

"Yeah, sounds like quite a nice life."

"Sure...I'd say I'm pretty happy. But it took a lot to get there, and honestly, I've made my share of mistakes."

"I hear ya. So, how are the kids?"

Paul took a slurp of his Coke and sighed. "From what I've heard, they're doing okay."

"From what you've heard?"

"Yeah...they're grown and living their own lives."

"What are they doing?"

"So, Bella's in college up in Michigan."

"What school?"

"U of M."

"Michigan...we're from Ohio, but I've gotta admit, that's an excellent school, and Ann Arbor's a beautiful little town."

"For sure. Her mother wanted her to go to a Christian college, but Bella had other ideas. She's stubborn, so what she wants, she gets."

"Makes sense. What's she studying?"

"Journalism. Dean's list. She's smart as hell. I'm really proud of her."

"That's great. Journalism's a good major. And how's Danny?"

Paul paused. "I think he's doing okay. He's more the free spirit, figuring things out. Last I heard, he decided to join some commune in Oklahoma."

Luke grew concerned. "That's...weird. You're not worried about him?"

"Kind of. But what can I do? I usually hear about the kids from Alyssa. Neither of them really talk to me."

"They're young, I'm sure they'll come around."

"Maybe, but if they don't, I can't be mad. It's my fault."

Luke furrowed his brow. "What do you mean...shit, I'm sorry I shouldn't have asked."

Paul shook his head. "No, it's fine. You know I'm an open book. I guess I'm the same as I was back in the CK days, at least in that way. That hasn't changed."

The longtime friends were members of Christian Kingdom, dubbed "CK," while in college at the University of the Great Lakes in Upper West Osceola, Michigan. Christian Kingdom was an evangelical Christian campus ministry with chapters at colleges and universities worldwide.

"Yeah," Luke said, laughing. "I remember back when we were in college, you couldn't keep anything to yourself! Like that time you confessed at CK large group altar call that you jerked it the night bef—"

"Bro!"

"That was a bit TMI, wasn't it?"

"Uh, yeah...but you know what, though? I always admired your honesty. You were so transparent, and a part of me wished I was more like that. I had a lot more shame. Still do."

"I appreciate that, but I've done more than my share of things I'm truly not proud of. Especially after college. My kids are still pissed at me, and if I'm honest with myself, they have every reason to be."

"Why?"

Paul hung his head. "It's a long story."

"If you wanna share, I'm all ears."

———◆○◆———

June 2002

A young Paul stared into a full-length mirror, combing his short jet black hair back. "I can't believe it. I get to marry the girl of my dreams," he voiced softly, while Luke straightened his bow tie.

"So happy for you, Paulie," Luke affirmed.

Craig Dombrowski, a slightly older gentleman who served as Paul and Luke's staff leader while they were members of Christian

Kingdom, entered the room. He approached the preparing young men and lovingly placed his large, manicured hand on the groom's shoulder.

"Paul, I'm so happy for you. This is such a blessing from the Lord, that he brought you and Alyssa together."

"Yes...but, I'm scared."

"Why? What is there to be afraid of?"

"I mean...I wanna be a good husband, a good provider. I wanna do right by Alyssa, but a part of me wonders if we should've lived more life before getting married. We're only twenty-two...what if we get older and we aren't truly compatible? I don't know what I'm doing...I hope I'm not making a big mistake..."

Craig took a deep breath. "Well, son...you're both going into this pure, and that's the way God intended it. Remember, she doesn't know what she's doing either. But you'll learn together – how to live together, how to show intimacy, how to be husband and wife. You will learn how to be a great provider, and she will learn how to be a great helpmeet."

"Yes."

"And remember, there will always be three of you in your marriage – you, Alyssa, and Jesus Christ. You're still young, too, so plenty of time to be fruitful and multiply. And as you grow your family and you parent your babies, you and Alyssa will grow closer. I'm sure of it."

"Thanks, Brother Craig."

"Anytime, Paul. I'm gonna head into the sanctuary. I'll see you out there soon. Luke, take good care of him."

"I will."

Once Craig left the room, Paul turned to his closest friend. "Luke, can I tell you something?" he whispered.

"Yeah – you can tell me anything."

"Swear you're not gonna say anything to Brother Craig."

"Of course. Why would I do that, Paulie?"

"Ugh...I know you won't, but this has been weighing on me for a while."

"You can tell me anything. What's up?"

"Brother Craig doesn't know, but Alyssa and I aren't going into our marriage pure."

"What d'you mean?"

"Ugh...Alyssa and I...well..."

"What is it?"

"We fell into sin."

"What? How?"

"We made the mistake of hanging out by ourselves, and we slept together."

Luke's eyes widened. "What? When was this?"

Paul sighed regretfully. "It started back in December before we all went home for winter break."

"After the CK Christmas party?"

"Yeah. When I walked her back to her dorm, I stayed to hang out like I always would. We thought it would be fine...nothing happened before, but her roommate was usually in there too. This time, she went home early for winter break, so we were in there by ourselves. Well, one thing led to another, and we went all the way."

"Wow. Was that your first time?"

"Yeah. It was the first time for both of us. But I'll be honest, sex feels amazing. We kept doing it. Then, a few weeks ago, Alyssa told me she's pregnant."

"Oh…"

"Yeah. That's why we're getting married so quickly. I needed to be responsible and do the right thing."

"Paulie, I had no idea this was happening. Why couldn't you tell me sooner? We could've prayed about it and maybe y'all could've gotten back on the straight and narrow before you got into this situation. That's what we're supposed to do. Iron sharpens iron."

"Yeah, I should've told you. I really should've, but I dunno. Once we started down that path, we just couldn't stop. Our flesh just took over; it's crazy how quickly that happened. I've never felt so horrible, so guilty, in my entire life. But not enough to stop, or to confess to anyone who would tell us to stop."

"Sin is like that."

"Yeah. We were hoping we could keep it secret and discuss the future of our relationship after graduation. But then, when she got pregnant, that changed everything. I'm ashamed to say that I thought about, you know, telling her to get an abortion."

"Ooh…"

"Yeah, I know that's bad. But then, that would just make us even more out of step with God, and Alyssa had already told her parents and her pastor she was expecting."

"Shit."

"Yeah, I know. At that point, there was no going back. Her parents reached out to my parents, I had to propose marriage to 'make things right,' and so here we are."

The best man patted the groom on the back. "You'll be okay, Paulie."

Just then, Alyssa's hometown pastor, a bookish man in his fifties, strolled into the room, worn Bible in hand. "We're ready for the ceremony. It's time."

Paul sighed. "Thank you, Pastor Jim." He then turned to Luke. "Let's go, Best Man."

The three men walked into the small, quaint sanctuary and stood in front of the altar, along with a childhood friend of Paul's, Conor Hayes. Paul's family was sitting on the right side facing the altar, while Alyssa's family, which was slightly larger, filled the pews on the left. The couple's friends, including those they knew from Christian Kingdom, dotted both sides.

It was sweltering hot inside the church, the dark paneled interior served only to trap the incredible heat on that hot early summer day. But Paul and Alyssa's friends expressed their excitement nevertheless, focused on their friends stepping into a new phase of life. Paul and Alyssa had just graduated from the University of the Great Lakes in central Michigan, as had Luke and a few of their other campus ministry and school friends.

After several minutes, the speakers blared with the sound of "The Bridal Chorus," from the Wagner opera *Lohengrin*. A young woman slowly slinked down the aisle, her wavy brunette hair with blonde highlights flowing down her back. Her snow-colored empire waist dress sparkled as it skirted the floor with each step, and a small tulle veil shrouded her face. Her floral-laced arms held her full, stark white rose bouquet.

Behind the bride were two young ladies in simple, forest green knee-length A-line dresses with cap sleeves. One of these women was her younger sister and maid of honor, Karin, whose crinkled mane, beaming smile, and hourglass curves were very similar to the bride. The other was Megan Tsong, Alyssa's friend from Christian Kingdom and a bridesmaid, with pin-straight hair, dark brown eyes, and a slight, slender figure.

Paul's smile was broad and bright as he stood at the altar in an all-white tuxedo, waiting on his gorgeous bride. His dark hair was cut into a neat fade. Next to him was Luke, in a black tuxedo and white floral boutonniere, with neatly trimmed mushroom-cut brown hair. On the other side of Luke stood Conor, also clad in a black tuxedo, with his long blond locks in a slicked ponytail.

Alyssa took her place on the other side of the officiant with her party standing beside her. The ceremony began.

"Good morning," proclaimed Pastor Jim. "We are all gathered here today in the presence of Father God to witness these two dear children in Christ, Alyssa Van Hooten and Paul Chu, brought together in holy matrimony. Let us start with the Source, the center of our lives, the Creator, the One with many names – Yahweh, Jehovah Jireh, Elohim, Adonai. Let us go to him to bless this ceremony, let us pray."

After the prayer, the pastor called up Brother Craig to read a passage from the Bible.

"From the King James," Brother Craig announced in a deep, commanding voice. "1 Corinthians 13:4-7. 'Charity suffereth long, and is kind; charity envieth not; charity vaunteth not itself, is not puffed up, Doth not behave itself unseemly, seeketh not her own, is not easily provoked, thinketh no evil; Rejoiceth not in iniquity, but rejoiceth in the truth; Beareth all things, believeth all things, hopeth all things, endureth all things.' Amen."

The ceremony continued with the definition of commitment and then, vows.

The officiant asked, "Do you, Paul, take Alyssa to be your wedded wife, to have and to hold from this day forward, for better and for worse, for richer and for poorer, in sickness and in health, to love, honor and cherish, as long as you both shall live?"

Paul stared into Alyssa's eyes and declared, "I do."

The pastor then turned to the bride. "Do you, Alyssa, take Paul to be your wedded husband, to have and to hold from this day forward, for better and for worse, for richer and for poorer, in sickness and in health, to love, honor and *obey*, as long as you both shall live?"

Alyssa gave a small smile. "I do."

After the wedding rings were exchanged, Pastor Jim announced, "Alyssa and Paul, because God has brought you together, and you have vowed to remain married for as long as you both shall live, I now pronounce you husband and wife. Paul, you may now kiss your bride!"

Paul lifted the veil from Alyssa's glowing face and kissed her tenderly.

———◆◯◆———

"This burger is amazing!" Luke exclaimed after taking a couple of bites from his gourmet craft burger while at Uno.

Paul dabbed the corner of his mouth with a paper napkin. "Man, if it's anything like this Reuben, I'm sure it is!"

"I remember when you and Alyssa got married, that was a hell of a wedding, and I was really happy for you. Then you moved down to Florida, had the kids, and it seemed like you were doing well there. Then I got married and I started living my life and we kind of lost touch. All I know is that things didn't work out between you and Alyssa. Not trying to pry too much, but what happened there, bud?"

"Ugh, yeah, come to find out, I never quite figured out the whole marriage thing."

"I get it."

"See, I thought I did at first. Had a rising career making great money...this was before I started working for the city. I thought we were happy. I thought that if I made sure she and the kids lived comfortably, she had anything she wanted, and the kids could go to the best schools and join whatever sports and clubs they liked, everybody would be happy."

"That's fair. It's the American dream."

"For sure, but the problem was, my work kept me away from them. My parents were kind of the same way when I was growing up. My dad really worked his ass off and Mom did her best to support him."

"Makes sense...being immigrants, I can respect it. They worked hard for their piece of the pie."

"They did...and I guess in my own way, I tried to live up to that."

"Yeah, I get that. You know how my dad's former military, Marines?"

"Oh yeah, for sure. I remember him, and how hard he was on you."

"Yeah, that's how he was...still is. We never wanted for anything, union job after coming back from Vietnam...but he would always say he wished he had gone to college and made something of himself, that's how he'd put it. Wanted to redeem himself through his kids.

My brother knocked it out of the park." Luke shrugged. "One out of two ain't bad."

Paul shook his head at his friend's comment.

"I'm sorry things didn't work out, Paulie. Sometimes we think we're doing the right thing, but it doesn't end up that way."

"See, that's the thing Luke. The work made things hard, but the work wasn't what ended our marriage. I mean, not exactly."

November 2017

It was a quarter to eight on a sunny Wednesday morning. Thirty-seven-year-old Paul, suited up in navy blue, freshly showered and ready to face the day, stepped out of the elevator and onto the thirty-second floor of the Bank of America Tower, the tallest building in Jacksonville.

John Cunningham, a tall, commanding gentleman, strolled up to Paul with a broad smile. After the men greeted each other, Paul noticed a small binder in his supervisor's hand. "You got something for me?"

"I sure do!" John firmly placed the binder into his subordinate's arms. "Happy birthday, Paul!"

"My birthday's not for another month..."

"Think of this as my early birthday and Christmas gift wrapped up in one. You're on the Niehaus project!"

He looked up, stunned. "Oh, wow John, this is the biggest project in the city! We won it?"

"Hell yeah, it sure is. And yes, we sure did. Their CEO saw your work and asked for you by name. This is huge for VYNE Engineering. I believe in you, son. You got this!" John patted Paul's shoulder with his strong, weathered hand, and walked away.

Paul went to his desk, fired up his laptop computer, and scheduled a meeting for his full team of building engineers at one o'clock to discuss the new project.

"What's this meeting for, Paul?" asked a female voice across from him.

"I was wondering the same thing," a male voice next to his desk concurred.

"Bianca...Dean...you'll find out at one, along with everybody else, but make sure y'all aren't late. It's very important."

"Ooh, I wonder if we won Niehaus," Dean guessed.

"Not gonna say," Paul emphasized. "But it's only a few more hours until the meeting. Just be on your 'A' game."

A few minutes before the meeting began, the team filled in the paneled boardroom and took their seats. Paul, the head engineer on the project and civil engineer by training, took off his suit jacket to reveal his sky blue dress shirt and silken navy tie, and placed it neatly on the back of the chair at the head of the table. He then pressed a few buttons on his laptop to begin projecting on the screen behind him.

"As some of you probably figured out from the meeting invite, our team has been selected to work on the Niehaus Building."

"Knew it!" Dean, the plumbing engineer, blurted out.

Paul continued. "So, we got the design drawings from the architect, we're talking about a building spec'd at 589 feet high, fifty stories, 660,000 square feet of commercial space."

Bianca, the electrical engineer, spoke up. "Hey, Paul...looks like the client wants this LEED certified. Are we gonna be bringing in a green building consultant for this?"

"Good call-out. Yeah, we're bringing in a consultant, J. Martinez. Supposed to be the best one they've got over at the Viburnum Consultancy. He should be arriving any minute now."

He heard a knock at the solid oak door. "Speaking of, I think that's him." Paul walked over to the door and opened it. There stood a young, zaftig woman with a smooth ochre complexion and silky brown hair tied up into a smart bun. He stared into her deep brown eyes and hesitated.

"Uh, hi," said the woman, "I'm sorry to bother you. I was told by reception that this is where the Niehaus meeting is."

Paul finally found his voice. "Uh, yes...are you from Viburnum?"

The woman responded, revealing a warm smile. "Yes, I'm Jenny Martinez, and I'm assigned to your project. You must be Paul Chu...heard a lot about you. It's nice to meet you." She held out her manicured hand. After a moment, Paul shook it.

Jenny headed over to the empty seat between Steve, the architectural engineer, and Manish, the mechanical engineer. Everyone at the table nodded to the new arrival in acknowledgment – everyone except Bianca, who rolled her eyes, then crossed her orange-tinted arms and stared smugly at the projector screen.

The lead engineer returned to the front of the room, waking up his computer. "Yes, now where were we?"

After working until a quarter after five in the evening, Paul stepped into a nearby garage and got into his red metallic 2017 Tesla S. He started the car, and as he approached the exit, brought down his tinted driver-side window to scan his parking pass.

Fifteen minutes later, he arrived at a three-story condominium in the historic neighborhood of Avondale. Once he climbed the stairs to the top floor, he grasped his lanyard from his pants pocket and used a copper key to open the pine-paneled door and let himself in.

Inside, it felt cozy, with dark beige walls and an open concept kitchen to the left. A red scented three-wick candle was burning on the kitchen island, the smell of coffee and cookies wafted in the air. The clock on the kitchen countertop read "5:34P." He slipped off his shoes and placed them next to the door, took off his tie and laid it on the chair next to him, and loosened his shirt buttons.

"Baby, where are you?" he called out.

"I'm in the bathroom," a disembodied feminine voice yelled back. "I'll be right out."

Paul walked over to the maroon felt couch, swiped the remote from the glass coffee table, and turned on the television. He flipped through the stations and settled on a pro basketball pregame show on ESPN. The Orlando Magic were on the court preparing to play the Detroit Pistons.

The bathroom door opened. "Baby," Paul called out, "I put fifty bucks on the Magic tonight."

The voice sighed. "That sounds great."

He looked up. "Oh, what's wrong Bee?"

Bianca, who had changed into a white cotton tank top and blue plaid lounging pants, sat next to Paul on the couch. She was drying her bobbed auburn hair. "Nothing."

He looked at her sympathetically. "Bee, I know it's something."

"I saw how you tripped all over yourself when that girl showed up at the Niehaus meeting earlier," she snarked.

"It was nothing. I was just a little off my game. This is such a huge project, probably the biggest project I've ever been involved in, and I'm the head of it." He turned to face her, held her hands, and looked earnestly into her soft hazel eyes. "Bee, you have absolutely nothing to worry about." He then got up and grabbed Bianca's hand to pull her up and gave her a sly smirk. "You know what I'm in the mood for?"

She smiled wryly. "You're always in the mood for that."

He then stood up and led her by the hand into the bedroom. Once inside, they began to kiss and embrace. She finished unbuttoning his blue shirt and cast it aside, along with his white undershirt, while he took off her tank top and tossed it on the bed. She wriggled out of her pajama bottoms, while he unbuckled his slacks and took them off, along with his briefs. As they continued to embrace, she sat on the dresser behind her, gliding her hands across his smooth, well-toned pectorals, then moving them up to his defined shoulders, where her soft arms rested.

"You're a goddess," he whispered, kissing her strong neck and placing his hand on the bend of her back. "I just wanna please you."

"Paul, you're so good, you make me feel so good."

"Are you ready for me, my goddess?"

"Yes, I'm ready and willing."

He then gently entered her ample body, immersing himself deeply.

She whimpered sensually. "Oh Paul, oh, oh my God!"

"You're amazing, my goddess. So amazing," he continued to voice quietly, while staring into her fine hazel eyes.

A few minutes later, the action transitioned to the plush, ivory bed, where Bianca climbed on top of Paul. She motioned back and forth slowly while he carefully caressed her bosom, seductively humming.

"Fill me up, oh, fill me," she groaned.

"Your wish is my command."

After over a half hour of passion, the two found themselves dozing off in the soft, plush bed.

Two hours later, Paul's cell phone buzzed. He rolled over and checked the screen. "Oh shit! Bee, I gotta go."

"It's about that time?" Bianca, lying next to him, turned to face him.

"It's, like, past that time. Kinda screwed up there. I'll just tell Alyssa I partied too hard with the boys after getting the Niehaus project."

"You didn't even have anything to drink."

"Shit, I know," he responded as he was pulling up his pants over his white briefs. "But it'll be fine, don't worry about it. It's not like she'll question me."

"Okay, good luck." Bianca slid her tank top back on while still in bed. "You know, Paul, you don't have to live like this."

Paul sighed as he was buttoning up his dress shirt over his white sleeveless undershirt. "Bee, we've talked about this. When the kids are grown, I'll divorce my wife, and you and I will be together, officially. It won't be much longer. " He leaned over and kissed her tenderly. "I love you, Bee. Just be patient with me."

She touched his cheek lightly. "I love you, too."

Twenty minutes later, Paul pulled up to a posh gated community in suburban Jacksonville. He slowly rolled into the driveway of a newly developed two-story grey stone McMansion, complete with manicured lawn and professionally landscaped flower patch. He clicked the garage door opener and entered the two-car garage. The electric vehicle was placed next to a silver 2016 Acura MDX. After plugging in the car and grabbing his plain black computer bag from the passenger seat, he slithered through the door connecting the garage to the attached home.

"Hun, I'm home!" he yelled into the house, his voice echoing slightly. He barely had a chance to remove his shiny black dress shoes at the door when a ball of energy quickly flew in his direction.

"Daddy, I need you to sign this permission slip." Paul's daughter Bella told him, piece of paper and pen in hand. "The band is going to be marching in the Thanksgiving Day parade downtown. Please?"

"Whatever happened to 'hi?'" He took the paper and pen from Bella, scribbled on it, and handed it back to her. "Here you go."

"Thanks, Daddy!"

"Of course, Bella Donna."

"Oh – I got invited to Nevaeh's birthday party on Saturday. It's at the Sportsplex and we're going ice skating. Mom says I have to ask you."

"What time's the party?"

"It starts at two, but we're gonna hang out at her house afterwards."

"Will boys be there?"

Bella gave her father a sheepish look. "Yeah."

"Then you need to be home by nine."

"But there's gonna be a sleepover."

"You're fourteen. You aren't even allowed to date yet. You're definitely not going to a sleepover with boys."

She sighed and mumbled, "Okay."

"Oh, where's your mom?"

"Um, she's in her room." Bella walked away, then stopped for a second and turned back around, her long, straight brunette hair whipping around. "Daddy – your dinner's in the microwave. We had goulash and fries. Danny's out."

"Where is he?"

She shrugged. "I dunno. He didn't come home from school, but he'll be back later, I think." She then headed to her bedroom.

Paul set his bag down on the blue suede chaise, quickly ate from his dinner plate, and trudged up the curved staircase. He passed by the hanging Jesus portrait on the wall and headed down the hallway to the bedroom he shared with his wife. As he was walking past his son's room, he noticed him sitting at his desk, immersed in *The Sims 4*.

"Hey, Danny! Bella said you were out."

"No, Dad," the boy responded, his chestnut eyes fixated on the monitor. "I got home a bit late after school, I was hanging with Emma and Maddie and we were working on a project for the eighth grade science fair. I guess she didn't see me come in. I don't think Mom did either."

"Oh, okay. Danny?"

"Yeah?"

"Next time you stay out after school, make sure you tell us where you're going and when you'll be home."

Danny paused and turned to look at his father. "Okay, sure Dad."

Paul opened the door to see his wife relaxing on the bed wearing dark skinny jeans and a linen flowing shirt, her hair tied up in a large bun against the nape of her neck. She looked up from her book.

"Hi Paul! You're kind of late getting home," Alyssa noted.

He closed the bedroom door and began to take off articles of clothing. "Hun, I'm sorry. I was out with the guys from work. You know how I texted you earlier about the new project?"

"Yeah, I saw that...but you didn't tell me you were going out with your coworkers."

"Sorry – it was spur of the moment."

"Where's your tie?"

"Oh...yeah...I probably left the tie back there at the bar. I remember taking it off because it was hot in there. I'll call them to see if they found it."

"Don't worry about it."

"No, I'll call them, probably tomorrow since I don't wanna go back out. It's important – you gave it to me for Christmas last year."

"You can if you want to. By the way, did Danny come home yet?"

"Yeah, he's been back awhile, he told me. He's in his room playing video games. I told him to start telling you where he goes after school and when he'll be home."

"Thanks. He'll probably do it since you're the one who told him."

"Hopefully so. He should be listening to you too, though. You're his mother. I'll talk to him about that."

"I appreciate it."

"Anyway, this new project at work — it's a huge deal, it'll be the biggest commercial tower in the city. Since it got assigned to me, I took the team out to celebrate."

"Paulie, wouldn't you celebrate *after* you're finished with the project? Aren't you jumping the gun a bit?"

"Yeah, but you know honey, think positively. As the Good Book says, 'call things which are not as though they were.'" He gave her a quick kiss, then headed towards the bathroom for a relaxing, hot shower.

"The hell?" Luke nearly choked on his lager. "Bro, I had no idea."

"Man...I know, right?" Paul stroked his peppered goatee. "Thing is, no one did. My family, my friends, my church. Can you believe I kept that shit up for over ten years?"

"Ten years...Jesus Christ."

"Yeah, I know."

"I must ask...what got the ball rolling?"

"On the affair?"

Luke nodded.

"Hate to admit it, but it was easy. Bianca and I met at work, and after some time working together, we hit it off. Thought nothing of it, she was just a coworker, and Alyssa and I were happy. Bianca didn't even catch my eye at first. But the nature of my job meant that over time, I spent more time there than I did at home. And it was just one night and one thing led to another, and it was like a switch flipped."

"Damn, Paulie. Did Alyssa know?"

"At the time, I didn't think so. At least that's what I told myself. I did my best to keep it from her, but a part of me just knew she must've known."

"What made you think that?"

"As I continued stepping out on her, our relationship changed. It was like a light went out. The bedroom was kind of dead, you know what I mean?"

"Yeah, I do."

"When everything was over, you know, after the divorce, I realized it was the guilt, the paranoia. But when I was in the thick of it, I convinced myself that she let herself go, she stopped caring, and she was pushing me away."

"I get it, bro."

Paul sighed. "Luke, things were rough for a long time, and I kept it all to myself. And here's the thing about keeping secrets like that – the cheating, the gambling, especially the cheating. When you do it for long enough, you feel invincible. Like you can do anything...like you can climb Mount Everest without the sherpas. Anything. It's a high in and of itself. Then you get sloppy."

FACE
June 26, 2023

Paul stared out the pane glass window wistfully while conversing with Luke at the restaurant. "You know what's wild about that time in my life?"

"What?" Luke asked.

"I would be singing 'Here I Am to Worship' on a Sunday morning and then I'd be at my mistress' condo fucking her brains out that same night. Hell, either that or putting a payday's worth of cash on the Jags or the Magic. Sometimes both."

"Oof. I remember back when you would tell everybody everything, and more than we really wanted to know. Didn't know you had it in you to keep all that in."

"Yeah, it was insane. I surprised myself, honestly."

"Why?"

Paul raised an eyebrow. "What do you mean?"

"Why did you do it? I mean, gambling is one thing – y'know, everybody could use more money. But why'd you cheat on Alyssa? Not judging, I got my own problems, but from what I remember, she was cute. When you first got married, you seemed to really wanna be a good Christian and a good husband. What happened?"

"Honestly? It was the guilt. It was easy for me to be this hardcore model Christian when everybody and everything surrounding me was Christian. My family was Christian. I was in Sunday school and then youth group at my family's Korean Christian church. Went to Catholic high school. Campus ministry in college. And then, I gave in once, just *once*, and then all of a sudden, I found temptation everywhere."

February 2017

It was a rainy February night in Jacksonville, and the Niehaus project, which was chugging along in the engineering phase, called for a long night of intense work.

"Hun, tonight's gonna be a late one. I'm working with the green building consultant to make sure the Niehaus building is energy efficient," Paul told his wife over the phone.

"Okay, that's fine," Alyssa replied softly. "Dinner will be in the fridge. I'll probably be asleep by the time you get home. Love you, dear."

"Love you too, hun." He hung up his phone and sat it on his desk. He then took his computer into a corner meeting room. He walked through the clear door and noticed Jenny was already sitting on a tall bar-style seat at the raised white desk, computer on the table. He sat down opposite her and opened his laptop.

"Okay, so where were we?"

"Yes, so we were looking at how we want to spec in some products that would make this right here more efficient. Come here, I'll show you."

He came over to Jenny, and she pointed to where she had a list of potential products on the left-hand side of her screen. "So, this is what we want to consider when building the foundation," she noted. "We want to make sure this is secured properly on bedrock and ensure it won't go anywhere in case of high winds and intense flooding."

"Of course."

"But we want to also keep energy efficiency and conservation in mind. There are tax breaks that come with those efforts, so that's why the client brought me on, to make sure we aim for those incentives."

"Yeah, that makes sense. Uh, we're gonna be here awhile and I think I'm gonna grab myself something to drink from the break room. Do you want anything?"

"What's back there?"

"We have Coke, Diet Coke and water, and we have beer too. I think we have Bud Light, Corona, Bay Beer, Bromosa and some wine, I think a Cabernet and a Chardonnay."

"Wow," Jenny looked up, surprised. "That's a lot, I'm surprised you have so many 'drink' drinks. Never seen that at an engineering firm. What is this, 'Mad Men?'"

Paul chuckled. "You'd think. But no, it's not like that. We just work hard and play hard, you know what I mean?"

She nodded.

"Anyway, I'm getting a Bay Beer. It's great. What sounds good to you?"

"I'll have a Bromosa. What's that, an IPA?"

"Yeah."

"Perfect."

He left for the break room and returned in a few minutes with two cans of unopened beer. He slid Jenny over her beverage of choice.

"Thanks!" She opened her can, and he opened his.

The two continued to collaborate through the evening, periodically reaching out to all teammates virtually over Zoom. Then, two hours into the work session, Paul's phone vibrated. He picked it up and engaged in a text conversation:

> **Bianca: You better not fuck that girl Paul istg**

> **Paul: Bee I won't.**

> **Bianca: I saw how you looked at her**

> **Paul: I swear I won't sleep w/her. Trust me. This is work.**

> **Bianca: Call me when you're heading home**

> **Paul: K**

He then placed the phone on silent mode.

The two worked in earnest for another thirty minutes. Then she closed her laptop and stared back at him. "That should be more than enough work for one night, I think."

He subtly licked his upper lip and shut down his computer as well. "I'm with you there. Let me help you get your things bagged up and we'll head out."

Paul walked over to her side of the table and stooped down to unplug Jenny's laptop cord, when she gently placed her soft hand over his fingers. He looked into her intense eyes, and her eyes locked onto his. Then she went in for a kiss, a kiss he was dying for. They began to make out passionately, then his hands went to her skirt, and he brought down her silk panties. He then unbuckled his khaki pants and opened his fly to reveal he was more than ready. They embraced as he held her against the wall and began to thrust deeply. She moaned softly with every plunge.

They then migrated to the floor, Paul unbuttoning Jenny's white blouse to reveal a smooth beige bra trimmed in ebony lace. He slid his hands underneath the undergarment to feel her ample breasts and touch her protruding nipples. They continued to lock lips as he drove himself further inside her.

After the brief encounter, the two straightened up, packed up their work materials, and left the building together without saying a word. Jenny entered her own car and departed, while Paul got into his car to drive home to his wife and children. On his way home, he used his car speaker phone.

"Hi, Paul!"

"Hi, Bee! I'm calling like I promised. I'm on my way home."

"I'm glad you called me. I love hearing your voice."

"You know that makes me feel amazing, Bee. You always make me feel amazing."

Paul arrived home and quietly crept into the house, as to not wake up a fast asleep Alyssa. He looked at the clock and it was half past midnight. He slipped off his shoes and headed towards the bedroom he shared with his wife. As he walked through the living room to the staircase, he glimpsed in the darkness, noticing a pair of eyes staring at him.

"Oh fu—!"

"Daddy," Bella said quietly, "that's a swear word."

Relieved, he calmed down. "I know. Bel, you scared me. I didn't see you sitting there. What are you doing up? You have school to-morrow."

"I know. I'm just waiting up for you."

Paul sat on the edge of the recliner and leaned forward. "Bella Donna, what's wrong?"

The teen sighed. "Daddy...are you and Mom getting a divorce?"

He sat back for a moment, shocked. "No. No, Bella. Why would you think we're getting a divorce?"

"Mom's always in her room crying, and you're home late all the time. Soon, you won't be here at all."

"Sometimes, I have to work long hours, especially when I'm working on big projects. That's all."

"Okay," she whispered.

"Now, you said, "Mom's always crying.' What's that about?"

"Yeah. Maybe not always, but more lately. She's tired when she's not in her room, but she's in her room a lot, even more than normal. Every time I come home from school, or band practice, or hanging out with my friends, she's in her room and I hear her crying. At first, I thought she found out that Danny's ga—" Bella caught herself. "Oops, forget I said that. I hope I didn't get him in trouble."

Paul looked at her sideways and sighed. "No, I already knew that. Stevie Wonder could see that. C'mon. The only one I'm sure doesn't know is your mother. I love Danny just like I love you. It's fine. So, you were saying..."

"Yeah, so I heard Mom talking to Nan on the phone, and she was saying you might leave her for somebody else. Why would you leave Mom?" Tears welled up in the girl's eyes.

"No, darling." He moved to the sofa and sat next to his daughter. "Come here." He hugged her tightly. "I'm not going anywhere. I love you. I love Danny and I love your mother very much. I'm not going anywhere."

"Okay, Daddy."

"Now head to bed, Bel."

Bella stood up and began trudging up the stairs. When she was halfway up, she turned around to look at her father, who was still sitting on the couch. "Um, Daddy?"

"Yes, Bel?"

"You should wash your face."

Paul rose and took a glance in the mirror above the fireplace. Seeing his reflection, he then noticed splotches of dark magenta lipstick smeared on his face and neck. *Shit.*

Luke smirked. "Oh...that had to be awkward."

"Yeah, it sure was," Paul concurred. "I was embarrassed. Even my daughter caught on to what I was doing. I was supposed to be her first example of what a man's supposed to be like, and I was out here hurting her mother. The guilt weighed on me for sure, but I just couldn't stop. Then, things got worse."

February 2018

The morning after his late-night work session, Paul returned to the office, working normally at his desk. An hour after his arrival, John came by and tapped him on the shoulder. "Paul, lemme talk to you for a second."

Paul stood up and followed his supervisor to his corner office, which was partially enclosed in glass on the other side of the floor. John sat down, and when Paul walked in, he asked, "Could you go ahead, close the door behind you and have a seat?"

The nervous employee shut the door and sat in the chair in front of a glass desk.

John, behind the desk, began speaking. "This is going to be really quick. I absolutely love what you're doing on the Niehaus project. I've been seeing the work you and the team are putting in. I'm thrilled at the progress, and the clients are as well."

"Thank you, John, I...I really appreciate that."

Then John took a deep breath. "I will say this one thing, and I'm only going to say this once." His right arm rose, and he pointed to a discreet black box in the top corner of his office, as well as one that could be seen on the main floor outside the glass walls of his office. "These are in every room, Paul."

Paul blinked, having not previously noticed the inconspicuous cameras around the office.

The manager then gave him a stern warning. "Don't put your dick in your wallet. Understood?"

"Understood."

"That's all. You're doing great on Niehaus, keep up the excellent work. Thanks, Paul." Sufficiently chastened, Paul wandered back to his desk in the open plan office.

Bianca, sitting across from him, noticed the meeting and the unnerved expression on his face. "Paul, what's up?" she asked quietly. "Everything okay?"

"Um...yeah Bee, everything's fine. It's perfect, as a matter of fact." He regained his composure. "John said our project is going very well and the client is loving it."

"Oh wow, love hearing that kind of feedback. It's really coming along, um..." Bianca, her skin turning a bit pale, rose from her office chair fast and sprinted to the restroom. After a few minutes, she returned and sat back in her seat.

"Are you okay?" Paul inquired, concerned.

"Yeah, I...I'm good. I think it might've been the eggs I ate this morning. Didn't settle in my stomach properly. It happens." She took a stick of gum out of her desk drawer and placed it in her mouth. "I feel better already."

———◦◇◦———

March 2018

The winter rains gave way to vernal bloom on a brilliant Saturday. On that day of the week, the children typically took part in activities such as soccer, band, cheer, and chess club. Alyssa and Paul's role was to shuttle them to and from these events and provide in-person support. The proud father was often there with cell phone camera in hand to record the special moments of his offspring for posterity. While he loved his work at VYNE, he insisted Saturdays were reserved for family time.

This particular March morning was the odd one where there was nothing planned for the kids. Along with the rest of the Chu family, Paul decided to sleep in. His cell phone, which was sitting on the nightstand, audibly vibrated, so he rolled over in bed to glance at it. He received a text message, and he knew he needed to respond:

Bianca: **I know you're busy but we need to talk.**

Paul: **Why? I spend Saturdays w/the kids. What's up?**

Bianca: **It's important. Starbucks on Main?**

Paul: **I'll just stop by your place**

Bianca: **No. Not a good idea.**

Paul: **I can be at Starbucks in 30 min. Is that ok?**

Bianca: **Yes**

Donning a burnt orange hoodie, loose heather grey sweats, and old gym shoes, he arrived at Starbucks at a quarter after ten. He spotted his lover sitting at a corner table, wearing a black fleece jacket and matching stretch workout pants, holding pink liquid in a clear cup. He ordered himself a caramel latte, and once it was ready, he took his cup and sat at her table.

Annoyed, he said, "Bee, Saturdays are a bad day for me, you know that. I was lucky to be able to get this time right now. The kids usually have their sports and stuff. What was so important that it couldn't wait?"

"Paul, I'm pregnant."

"Really?" He paused, looking up and out the window but incapable of focusing on anything. Then, he took a deep breath and removed his cell phone from his pocket. "Alright...Bee, I'll Venmo you the money like I did last time for you to take care of it..."

"I'm keeping it."

"No, you're not."

"Paul – I need you to hear me. I am keeping this baby. It's not like last time or the time before that. I'm thirty-six now. I'm not getting any younger. I have always wanted children. I want this baby. I'm keeping it."

"But...what am I gonna do about my family? My wife? How am I gonna tell my wife about this kid?"

"How were you going to tell your wife you were leaving her once your kids were grown?"

He sighed.

Bianca told him bluntly, "The baby is coming. It's due September 8th. Figure it out."

She stood up from the table, cup in hand, and left the coffee shop. Paul was shaking, stressed, and alone.

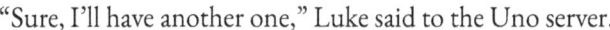

"Sure, I'll have another one," Luke said to the Uno server.

"And sir," she turned to Paul, "would you like another Coke?"

"Ah, no. Could I have a Sociopathy?"

"Please?"

Paul paused for a second, "Um, a Sociopathy." He took a drink menu in his hand and pointed out the Hoppy Bear Sociopathy India Pale Ale listed under "Craft Brews" to the server.

"Oh yeah, sure!" The server responded and walked away.

"Man, it's been so long since I've heard anybody say 'please' instead of 'what' or 'excuse me.'"

"Well, Paulie – welcome back to Losanti!"

"Home sweet home, brother."

"So yeah, about that situation...what happened? That must've been the last straw for Alyssa, right?"

"No. Believe it or not, it wasn't."

"Really?"

"Nope. Now don't get me wrong, it was really, really rough. It truly was. She was seriously thinking about leaving me."

"Oh, boy."

"I mean, at this point, it was out there, she couldn't bury her head in the sand. But, you know, she's a God-fearing woman. The pastor talked us through this, uh...speedbump."

"That's a bit of an understatement. What did he say?"

"He explained to her how to best meet my needs as a man, like improving her attitude and keeping herself up physically, and he talked me through how to be faithful to her, like not meeting with other women alone, not talking to them on the phone or texting them, things like that."

Luke rolled his eyes. "Huh...that's a take."

"It is. I didn't realize how that may have hurt her until much later on – after everything was said and done. It didn't have anything to do with her, but at least in the church, we're expected to rely on our wives to keep us in line."

"I guess they believe we can't control ourselves, and women drive us crazy."

"I mean, for some of us, they kind of do...but at the end of the day, choices, man. Choices."

The server came back with the second round of drinks. "Here you go!"

After the waitress left, Paul took a sip of his IPA. "Anyway, you know the hardest part of all this?"

"What?"

"After my daughter Gracie was born, we had to figure out how to integrate her into the family. I mean, at first the kids didn't take it well at all. Bella was especially angry with me."

"Understandable. How did Alyssa take the news? Was she upset?"

"I dunno. I'm sure that Alyssa had to be hurt by a reminder of my infidelity just running around in front of her face. But to her credit, she handled it with such grace. Of course, Bianca and I had to end things, but we made co-parenting work."

"Wow, that had to be tough. How did your parents feel about Gracie? Did they have a problem with what happened, or were they happy to have another grandkid?"

"Well, my parents couldn't understand why I even acknowledged her. They're traditional in that way. They looked at the fact that I got caught cheating and I had an illegitimate child as shameful. So, they'd rather not even think about it or even see the evidence of it."

"Oof, I'm sorry to hear that."

"I'm sorry too. It's not her fault."

Luke took a sip of his beer. "So, what finally ended your marriage?"

"Well, I lost my job at VYNE."

"Oh no...I'm sorry."

"Eh, it's a part of life."

"How did that happen?"

"Well, our work on the Niehaus project was successful, and it did eventually go up. Beautiful building. But the excitement didn't last long, and I got let go shortly after the project ended. They said 'economic dip,' 'budget cuts,' all that. But I heard through the grapevine that it was because of my extracurriculars."

"Really?"

"Yeah...you know, it was a bit obvious when Bianca had the baby, and she never talked about having a husband or even a boyfriend while working there. Those newborn baby pictures she emailed to everybody at work while she was on maternity leave...damn, I guess those monolids gave it away."

"Monolids? What?"

Paul pointed to his angular-shaped eyes.

"Oh."

"Yeah, the writing was on the wall at that point."

"That sucks, man."

"It did. The thing that scared me so much, after embarrassing my wife already with my cheating, was embarrassing her even worse by losing my job. I mean, a man is supposed to provide. I was always taught that. My family, the church, even CK. And at that point, I couldn't even do *that*. I felt like a failure."

I understand that feeling.

"Then, I found a way to make things worse."

<hr />

February 2019

"Hun, I'm going in to work." Paul kissed a half-asleep Alyssa on the forehead. "I'll call you when I get there."

"Okay, sounds good, dear. Make sure you pick up the mail on the way home. Karin is supposed to be sending me an invite to her baby shower."

"Will do, hun. Love you."

"Love you too, Paulie."

Paul walked out the side door to his Tesla, turned on the car, opened the garage door, and drove off.

His first stop was to the local fitness center. *Gotta get in a good workout to face the day.* He stepped on the elliptical machine and cycled for forty-five minutes, then performed thirty minutes of deadlifts and kettlebells. Afterwards, he took a nice shower, changed into a grey business suit he brought with him in a dry-cleaning bag, and left the gym.

Several minutes and a few turns later, the car pulled into a parking lot. Paul grabbed his computer bag and exited the vehicle. He proceeded to walk through the door of the building next to the lot. He stopped for a moment to look around.

"Hi, sir!" the middle-aged woman at the desk greeted him. "Welcome to the Jacksonville Public Library. Can I help you find something?"

He hesitated. "Uh, no thanks, not right now."

"Sounds good! Let me know if you need anything."

He found a carrel in the corner of the library and set up his personal MacBook. Once he was connected to wifi, he began searching for jobs. Thumbing down the list of open civil engineer and lead engineer roles on Indeed and LinkedIn, he picked out a few postings and began to fill out applications.

Why do these people need me to type the same damn thing that's already on my resume? It's so ridiculous and a waste of time. But whatever.

After a few hours of job hunting, his phone vibrated. He looked down to see an alarm had gone off. *Shit, it's 2:15, I need to get to this interview.* He packed himself up and left the library to head to his scheduled job interview.

Paul arrived in downtown Jacksonville and found a nearby parking structure. He then grabbed a folder holding his resume and walked over to the eleven-story office building.

When he made it to the engineering firm on the ninth floor, he entered through a heavy timber door. The room was adorned with wood paneled walls, felt orange chairs in mid-century modern style, and a floating staircase that appeared to be made of polished dark planks. He breathed in the air smelling faintly of moth balls and approached the front desk. *Okay great, ten minutes early.*

"Good afternoon, sir," greeted the receptionist in a thick Georgia accent. "How may I help you?"

"I'm here for an interview at two o'clock with Tom Harlan."

"Okay," she looked down at what appeared to be a written schedule. "You're Paul, um, Paul *Cheew?*"

"Yes, Paul Chu."

"Okay, have a seat right over there. I'll let Tom know you're here."

The interviewee took a seat in the spacious lobby. It was conservatively decorated with blue upholstered seats, thin beige and white carpet, and cream walls with framed painted portraits.

After a few minutes, he heard a slightly weathered voice. "Paul?"

He looked over and saw a tall, stocky man with grey hair waving him over. He stood and held out his hand, which the man shook with a noticeably firm grip.

"Hi, I'm Paul Chu."

"Thrilled to meet you, Paul. I'm Tom Harlan. We'll just go over here to my office."

The walk felt long, as they continued down a dark brown paneled hallway where very little light penetrated. The men arrived at a maple door, which Tom opened. Paul followed him into the room.

"Have a seat right here, Paul." Tom motioned him to a seat in front of a giant desk. Another man and a woman sat to the side, and he took his seat at the stately desk.

"This is my partner, Jim Slade, and my personal secretary, Peggy Smith." After shaking their hands, Paul returned to his seat.

The interview began in earnest. The interviewer scanned the resume of the prospect in front of him. "Huh, so you went to the University of the Great Lakes up in Michigan. Excellent engineering program, stellar reputation."

Paul nodded. "Yes."

"Oh yeah, it's great if you can stand the cold. I can't imagine, you know. I'm a Florida man through and through. Born and raised here. You sound very American. Did you grow up in Michigan?"

"No, just down the road though, I'm from Ohio originally."

"Oh? Where at in Ohio? Jim right here is from Ohio."

"Yeah," Jim spoke up. "I grew up in Cleveland, but I've been down here in Jacksonville for around thirty years."

"Oh, okay. I'm from the other end of the state in Losanti, but I moved down here back in '02," Paul shared.

"Losanti...y'know, the Green Sox are in a rebuilding year, but I heard y'all got some nice pitching prospects comin' up from Triple-A."

"Yeah, definitely. Keeping an eye on that, though these days I follow the local teams a bit more. Now Cleveland — Cleveland's looking really nice as of late. I'm sure you're thrilled about that."

"Oh yeah, no doubt. Y'know, no matter how many years I've lived here, my heart will always be stamped with Chief Wahoo's face."

The interview continued.

"Now, Paul, looking at your resume, I see you were lead engineer on the Niehaus Building."

"Yes, I was."

"Nice project, the jewel of Jacksonville, envy of the town. We here at Harlan and Slade put in a proposal for that one, but we came up short. That turned out very nicely, kudos to you. It looks like you got a lot of industry accolades for that too. Definitely something to be proud of."

"I am. It was a pretty complex project. A lot went into it, and I led a great team."

"That's fantastic. It's the kind of experience we love seeing in a lead engineer candidate. So, Paul, it looks like your employment ended at VYNE Engineering not long after your part in the project was over. What happened there?"

Paul hesitated, then took a deep breath. "Working at VYNE was a fulfilling experience. I received a lot of great opportunities, which I took advantage of and succeeded in. My clients were extremely satisfied. All in all, I can't say enough about that period in my career. But at the end of the day, all good things must come to an end, and it was time for me to seek new opportunities."

Tom nodded, as did Jim and Peggy. The secretary took furious notes on her white legal notepad.

After a few more questions from the partners, and once the candidate asked questions of his own, the interview was over.

"We're going to do a quick employment and reference check, and you'll hear back from us within the week. And Paul, if we bring you on, I would love for you to come over to my house so you can meet my wife Daiyu. She's from China, Shenzhen, I'm sure you're familiar."

Paul smiled but was otherwise quiet.

"She really loves cooking her delicious dishes, which were handed down through the generations. Her seafood hot pot is the best. Believe me, it'll be a scrumptious taste of home."

He chuckled and nodded graciously. "That sounds wonderful. Thank you Tom, Jim, and Peggy for your time, and I hope to hear from you soon." After shaking hands with the interviewing team, he left the building and set out for home.

Due to very heavy traffic at this time of the day, it took an hour – half an hour longer than usual – to return home. Once he arrived at the open gates of his subdivision, he stopped by the cluster box unit to retrieve the mail. *Hmm, nothing. That's weird. I'll have to tell Alyssa the invite isn't here yet.*

Paul pulled into the garage and shut off his car. He decompressed for a moment in the driver's seat, checking his email inbox on his cell phone. He noticed an email had just arrived from Harlan and Slade. He opened it and read:

Dear Mr. Chu:

Thank you very much for taking the time to interview for the position of Lead Engineer at Harlan and Slade Engineering, LLC. Unfortunately, you were not selected to continue in the hiring process. We have decided to move forward with other candidates who more closely align with our position requirements.

Sincerely,

Thomas J. Harlan, PE

Harlan and Slade Engineering

Motherfucker, I'm Korean!

Seething, he flipped his phone into the passenger seat and smashed his hands against the steering wheel in frustration.

"Ow! Ow, fuck!" he exclaimed after jamming his right middle finger on the wheel. The throbbing pain took him out of his rage. Overwhelmed with emotion, he laughed maniacally for several minutes. Once he finally regained his composure, he took a deep breath and stepped out of the car, leaving his phone and computer inside.

As he walked into the house and took off his shoes, he thought to himself, *It's too quiet. Something feels off here.*

He paused and scanned the darkened living room. He then noticed Alyssa waiting on the couch, silent with her electric blue eyes burning right through him. Bella and Danny sat next to her, extreme upset written on their faces.

Alyssa spoke in a measured tone. "Isabella, Daniel, go to your rooms. I need to speak with your father alone."

The children stood up and climbed upstairs.

Paul started to speak, "Hun, what's going on..."

Alyssa put her hand up in front of her. "Now!" she yelled up the staircase. A moment later, doors could be heard closing.

She turned her attention to her husband. "Paul, where were you today?"

"Honey, you know I was at work."

"I'm going to ask you one more time. Where were you?"

"Like I said," he replied sternly, "I was *at work*."

"Okay." She handed him an envelope.

"Wait, why do you have the mail? I told you I would get it when I got home."

"Doesn't matter. Open it."

Paul opened the envelope and read the heading at the top of the enclosed letter:

NOTICE OF FORECLOSURE
15 Everglades Cres
Neptune Beach, FL 32266

He shook, dropping the letter and envelope onto the hardwood floor.

"How did this even happen, Paul?"

He tried to gather his words. "I, I..."

"No, Paul – what the hell is going on? I want a straight answer."

He took a very deep breath. "Alyssa...okay, hear me out. Please don't get upset."

"It's too late for that. Just answer me."

He inhaled deeply, then exhaled. "I lost my jo—"

"You *what?*" She stood up, furious.

"Stop cutting me off! Listen to me, dammit!" His voice rose. "Yes, I lost my job, I kept up with the bills as long as I could while I was looking for another one, until I couldn't!"

She inhaled and then said calmly, "Paul...how long have you not been working?"

He sucked his lips in. "Three months."

She cocked her head to the side and looked at him with a burning anger. "You *pretended* to go to work for *three months?* The hell were you doing with all that time? You lied to me."

"I'm sorry, hu—"

"Don't 'hun' me! You lied to me. And if you only stopped working three months ago, why the hell are we getting a foreclosure notice *already?* What about that six-month cushion you saved up just in case?"

"About that..." Paul confessed quietly, "that was spent a long time ago."

"What could you have possibly spent that on? Whores?"

"The fuck? No, Alyssa. I didn't spend it on whores. No, it went to sports betting. I had a few bad streaks, and I meant to replace that money but then I got laid off."

She sat back down and buried her head in her hands, speechless.

He perched himself in the cerulean loveseat opposite her, and recited in a measured, yet trembling voice, "I'm so sorry. I'm sorry

it even came to this. I thought I could fix it before you found out. I
didn't want to worry you. I just need more time..."

Alyssa looked up, white-hot tears streaming down her face. "I
have stood by you through everything. I stood by you when you
were working your way up in your career and you stayed late nights
at the office. I stood by you when you were too busy with work and
God knows what else to show up at the hospital when I was having
Isabella and Daniel, and when I had that ectopic pregnancy. I stood
by you while you were having affairs throughout our marriage."

He looked at her in sheer confusion. "What?"

"Yes, Paul, you don't think I knew about Bianca for years before
you bothered to tell me she existed?"

"You knew..." he uttered in bewilderment.

"Yes. You're not that clever. And you don't think I know about
the other women you cheated on me with pretty much the entire
time we've been married?"

"Goddammit..." he mouthed, shaking his head.

"Even at *church*. Can't even keep your dick in your pants in God's
house. The other ladies there, I know they're laughing at me behind
my back. You humiliated me time and time again. You lied to me
time and time again. I have stood by you through all of it. I have
been a faithful wife. I have honored you to the best of my ability and
I have continued to stay a hundred percent committed. You know
why?"

"No," he whispered.

"Because I take my vows seriously. I take my commitment to you
seriously, when I said, 'I do,' and I said that before God and our
family and friends, I meant it. You might not've cared, but I sure
did, I still do."

"I *do* care."

"You have a funny way of showing it. I've been by your side through all of your shit. Even when I found out about Gracie, I not only stood by you, I welcomed her into our family just like our own babies, because for fuck's sake she didn't ask to have a cheating bastard for a father."

Paul winced but remained silent.

"All I wanted was for you to tell me the truth. To trust me with the truth. One of the things I loved about you when we first got together was your honesty. Sometimes you were too honest, but I loved that about you. *What happened to you?*"

He shrugged dejectedly.

"I prayed for you to once again be a man worthy of my trust. I have been on my knees for years, crying out to the Lord for you to just be the man you were on our wedding day. And for that, we're about to be *homeless?* No. That's too much. I can't do this anymore."

"What do you mean?"

"I said what I said. I can't do this anymore. When I saw the foreclosure notice, you know what I did?"

"What?" he asked, defeated.

"I called my parents and let them know the situation, and they told me to come home. I'm going back to Michigan, and the kids are coming with me. They already know."

Paul bawled. "No, no, Alyssa...don't do this, please don't do this."

Alyssa rose from the sofa and began her climb upstairs. "Answer the door for the process server, Paul. You have no reason to hide anymore."

———◆◇◆———

"Could you please bring over the check?" Paul asked the server.

"Sure thing! One check or two?"

"One's fine."

"I'll be right back." The server walked away to print out the bill for the meal at Uno.

Paul turned to his friend. "So, that's what happened. I know it's a hell of a lot worse than confessing to masturbation at CK large group."

Luke chuckled and shook his head. "Holy hell, Paulie. I saw on Facebook, like, three or four years ago that you and Alyssa had split up. It had been too long, so I didn't reach out. I'm sorry, bro."

"No worries. I get it."

"But oof, that shit is crazy. So, are you okay now?"

"Yeah, pretty much. We did lose the house in foreclosure, which sucks. The divorce was fairly amicable though, thank God. And not long after she filed, I got a job as chief engineer for the city."

"That's good – you landed on your feet."

"For sure. I've been there ever since. You know, it didn't save our marriage; it was too late by that point, but things are a lot better now, at least financially. I've recovered monetarily and things are going a lot better. Mentally, too. I've got a therapist I've been seeing since the divorce, and I've been making a lot of headway working through my issues. No more gambling. And I still go out on dates with women, but I'm not so reckless."

"How well do you and Alyssa get along now that y'all are divorced?"

"Alyssa and I are okay. We're friendly. I still talk to her every once in a while, mainly about the kids and things. She's back in Niles, her hometown, she's got her own house, and she seems to be doing okay. I know she runs into Morgan Haas from time to time, you remember Morgan from CK?"

"Yeah, of course...Morgan...how can I forget? How's she doing?"

"She got married, she's Morgan Banks now."

"Oh..."

"Her husband's a military guy, I think Marines. They have I believe four kids? Yeah, and they're living in Saint Louis."

"Saint Louis?"

"Yeah, but she goes up to Niles from time to time to see her family, that's when Alyssa sees her. I think she said her mom's dealing with dementia."

"Ooh, that sucks. I'm sorry to hear that."

"Yeah. But other than that, she seems to be pretty happy."

"That's good...um...good to hear. She deserves a good life." Luke then switched gears. "So yeah, I know you said the kids aren't talking to you. That really sucks."

"Yeah, it does, but that's on me, man."

"I'm sure that doesn't make you feel any better, though. Do you still see the baby?"

"About that...well, around the time Alyssa and I were divorcing, Bianca met another guy, and they got married. Her new husband wanted to raise Gracie as his, and they asked me to sign away my parental rights. Something about 'not wanting her to grow up confused about who her dad is,' something like that."

"Oh."

"At the time, I was still broke and I was trying to rebuild my life, and I mean, I hadn't been the best father to the kids I did raise, so I signed my rights over. I still don't know if I made the right decision. Part of me really regrets it, but at the time it made sense."

"I hear you. No judgment, man."

LIKE OLD TIMES
June 26-28, 2023

After the meal at Uno, the men headed to Luke's apartment in the working class Losanti neighborhood of Marydale.

"Kia Rio, huh?" Paul commented on Luke's silver economy sedan.

"Yeah. It gets me where I need to go, which is usually not far," Luke reasoned.

"That's perfect, then. I'm sure it's got decent fuel economy, too."

"Yeah, it's a stick shift."

"Nice. Don't see a lot of those anymore."

"True."

"So, what happened to the old Saab?"

"Eh, it got old and too expensive to keep going. It's been gone for at least a good five years."

"Well, at least you got really good use out of it. I remember that being your steed back in college. Station wagon, lots of room. We'd all ride in that thing up and down the highway from Michigan to Tennessee for those spring retreats."

"Yeah, the CK Infinity retreats."

"Uh-huh. You'd floor it at ninety miles an hour up and down I-75 and somehow never get stopped by traffic cops. That was the most reliable car ever!" Paul recalled fondly.

Luke laughed. "For sure. It was great – so many memories in that car. It was tough junking it, but my ex convinced me it was a money pit, so now it's in one of those lots being sold for parts."

They walked down the interior hallway to his first floor unit. He unlocked the door and let his friend inside.

"This is my place. It's not much, but it's mine. Come on in, make yourself at home."

"Thanks, man." Paul removed his shoes and walked around the apartment. "Where's your bathroom?"

"Just past the kitchen. Make a right and it's the door at the end."

"Cool, thanks!"

While waiting, Luke sat on the futon and leaned back. He felt more at peace than he had in quite some time. *Paulie's here.*

After a few minutes, Paul returned from the bathroom, two full pill bottles in hand. "Talk to me, man. What's this?"

"It's my meds."

"Yeah, I know. You aren't taking them, are you?"

"How do you know?"

"Brother, did you forget we roomed together in college? I could tell as soon as I walked in here. Everything is spotless and perfect. Not just clean — it's on another level. It's like I stepped into a fucking Ikea before it opens up in the morning. You're not taking your meds, man. Why?"

Luke shook his head. "Shit, Paulie. I don't know."

Paul sighed. "Alright. First of all, start taking your meds." He threw the bottles into Luke's lap, then continued. "Are you talking to a therapist?"

"I *was*..."

"But?"

"But I cancelled the last couple of appointments."

"Why?"

"Ugh, I overslept."

"Stop that shit and get back in to see your therapist."

"Alright, Dad," Luke snarked with a chuckle.

Paul sat down on the other end of the futon and faced his friend with a stern expression on his face. "I don't think I told you why I'm here, did I?"

"No, not really, but I was wondering about that. I mean, your parents are down in Florida with you. I was guessing you came up here maybe to see relatives or something?"

"They think I shamed the family. I'm not seeing them, man."

"So, why are you here? To eat Riverview coney dogs?"

"Don't get me wrong, those coneys *are* good – but nah. So, Luke, I'll be honest with you, and I know you're gonna think I've lost my mind. See, I had this weird sense I needed to come up here and see you."

"Really?"

"Yes. Back in the day, I'd think to myself that sense came from God, maybe the Holy Spirit. Now God and I, we're not exactly close right now. But I can't *not* listen to that sense. I had a ton of PTO to burn anyway, and things were a bit slow at work, so why not just come up here?"

"You know what? I'm glad you came."

"I'm glad too." After a short pause, he continued. "So, what *has* been happening with you? I mean, there was vet school, and there was Rachel...what happened with all of that?"

"That's a whole ass story, man."

"Alright, cool. You can tell me all about it in the truck. Pack up, brother."

"Huh?"

"You heard me."

"Um, what?"

"Okay, so you remember how back at UGL, every April, we would pack up and go to Infinity?"

"Yeah, but we're not in college anymore. We're in our *forties*. We have responsibilities. Besides, to be honest, I'm not exactly flush with cash right now, especially for a trip. Look around, you see how I live."

"Look, Luke...I can look at you and tell you need this. We both need this. And you don't need to worry about the money, I'll take care of it."

"No, I can't let you do that."

"Let me do this. I just want my best friend with me. It'll be like old times, except we're grown men, and we're not bound by CK rules and religion. And no, we're not actually going to Tennessee. We're not 'finding God in the mountains.' We're going west."

"But work..."

"Call your job, tell 'em you need to take some mental health days or something. A lot of places encourage that now. What are you doing these days, anyway?"

"I don't even wanna talk about it."

"If it's really that bad, just tell 'em to get fucked."

Luke snickered.

Paul continued. "Now let me ask you this. I remember how you wanted to be a vet to spite your brother, the GPS guy?"

"Yeah. You know he's the dean of the school now?"

"You serious, Luke?"

"As a heart attack, Paulie. I guess inventing something that nowadays nobody can live without makes you a big shot."

"Big man on campus, huh?"

"Yeah, pretty much."

"But look, man, if you weren't worried about spiting your brother, what would you be doing for a living?"

"Uh, I'd be a filmmaker, like a documentarian or something."

"Alright. And what is, like, one thing about that kind of job that excites you the most?"

"To be completely honest, the travel. I absolutely love the open road, the scenery, new people, new places. All of that."

"Then you know what you gotta do. Get your shit in order, and we're gonna get the hell out of Losanti."

———◆○◆———

"You're calling me instead of me calling you? That's a first," Libby noted while on the phone with her younger son.

"I know. I should call you more."

"Dear, you sound very happy. You're still not taking your medication, are you?" she asked, worried.

Luke sighed. "I started back taking it yesterday."

"I hope that's true. If it is, I'm glad to hear it."

"It is, I swear."

Libby admonished him. "You know that taking an oath is a sin."

"I know, Mom. 'Let our yes be yes and our no be no.' I'm sorry."

"It's alright...just don't do it again."

"Okay. So, you know Paul's in town."

"Paul?"

"You remember Paul...Paul Chu, my best friend from Great Lakes. We roomed together my first three years up there. He's from here too; he came over quite a bit on breaks back then."

"Oh, yes...I remember him. He was that really sweet Oriental kid you used to hang out with all the time, right? He talked *so much*."

"It's 'Asian' nowadays, Mom. 'Oriental' is just for things, like rugs. 'Asian' is for people."

"Ope, I always forget these politically correct words. I dunno. I'll get it right one day, I suppose. Anyway, you two were always connected at the hip. I always wondered what happened to him. How's he doing?"

"He's good, he's visiting from Florida."

"Oh, that's very nice. What's he doing down there?"

"He's an engineer, he works for the city of Jacksonville."

"Oh, that sounds like an excellent job."

Of course she would say that.

"If Paul's staying long enough, you should bring him over for Sunday supper. He would've just missed your brother, though. They all flew out this morning back to California. But your father and I would love to see him."

Luke exhaled. "Um, well, about that...I'm actually going out of town for a while. The two of us are going on a trip."

"Oh...you didn't tell me you were leaving town. Where are you going?"

"We're just gonna do a road trip, I'm going with him to Chicago or something."

"Oh, okay. That's a long car ride, at least for me. I couldn't do it, but you're still young. When are you leaving?"

"Tomorrow."

"And when will you be back?" Libby asked.

"Uh...I don't know yet."

"Luke, are you okay? That's a bit impulsive."

"Mom, I'm fine. Trust me. Paul wants me to go with him because he thinks time away will help me clear my head. Since we'll be together, everything will be okay. You know things have gone terribly for me here. It's getting to the point that I'm in a dead-end job and you're paying my rent, and y'know, I'm so grateful for that. But deep down, I know I need to do better, and maybe some time away will help me get myself together."

"Alright, dear. I hope this helps you. And then, when you get back, you'll consider trying to get back into veterinary school or even look into medical school?"

"Mom..."

"These days, the news is always talking about how there's a shortage of doctors. You know you're not getting any younger, and your father and I won't be around forever."

Luke rolled his eyes. "Okay."

"Since you're traveling, I'll add some spending money to your bank account. I would hate for you to get stranded and not be able to get back should something happen."

"You don't have to worry about that. I got paid from the Dairy Union last Friday."

"I'm your mother. I want to make sure you're okay. Think of it as souvenir money."

"Alright – thanks, Mom."

"You're welcome, dear. Don't forget to bring your medications with you and call me when you make it to where you're going."

"Okay."

"Be safe, Luke."

"I will."

—◆◇◆—

"How the hell did you go from a Tesla to a Jeep?" Luke inquired as he slid his suitcase and backpack in his friend's Wrangler Sahara 4xe painted "bikini pearl" green.

"You want the truth?" Paul asked, moving over his guitar case and closing up the back of the truck.

"Sure."

"I got the Tesla to impress women."

"Really?"

"Yeah. Women are really into that conservation and clean energy shit."

"Not to be a dick, but Teslas kind of suck. Try driving them around up here right after the snow and ice hit, your suspension would be shot."

"Yeah, I know. Never dared to drive it anywhere with a real winter. Now after the divorce, I traded it in for this." Paul pat his truck like it was a prize baby elephant. "This is something *I* actually like, and it's a hybrid, so it's still decent for the environment."

"I will say, this is very nice."

"Thanks, man."

The men got into the truck and buckled in.

"You cleaned up nicely," Paul noted.

Luke smiled. "It's nothing. I shaved up and then decided to get a haircut. Couldn't be on a trip with Mr. City Engineer looking like a bum."

"It's more like Mr. Florida Man, just saying."

Paul pulled out of the parking area of Luke's apartment building. After a few turns, he entered the interstate heading west. As they were on the road, Luke rummaged through his small gym bag on the floor in front of him and took out a black camera with a selfie stick attached.

"Hope you don't mind, Paulie, but I wanna play with this a little bit. Y'know, I took what you said to heart, so last night I went out to the electronics store and got this. Maybe I should try out filming things, y'know, like a vlog of our trip."

"Man, now you're talking!"

Luke explored the settings on the GoPro and started filming.

"Hey, I'm Luke, and this is my best friend, Paulie." He panned over to show the driver.

"'Sup?" Paul waved at the camera while still facing the road.

Luke then brought the camera back to himself. "We're from Losanti, Ohio, and we're on a road trip to...uh..."

"Brother, you'll find out when we get there."

Luke shook his head, surprised. "What? I thought we were going somewhere!"

"We are. I know exactly where we're going. We're going west. How west? You'll find out soon enough."

Luke shook his head and snickered. "Christ – I thought I was the impulsive one."

Paul laughed. "It's gonna seem impulsive, but it's really not. You'll see."

The men hit the open road. As the densely-packed neighborhoods and rolling hills of Losanti gave way to lush farmland and open fields, Luke mused, "I've never noticed how beautiful this area really is."

"Of course not. You don't see it until you have to leave it." Then, Paul changed the subject. "So, what's been going on with you? What happened?"

Luke looked over at him, confused. "What do you mean, 'what happened?'"

"You would say that shit. What's been happening in your life? Your marriage? Your career?"

"Like I told you before, it's a long story."

"Brother..." Paul motioned to the windshield, pointing out the cornfields and pastures of eastern Indiana passing by on either side of them, "We've got nothing but time."

September 2005

One Saturday evening, Luke spoke with his mother over the phone.

"You're going to church with us tomorrow. It's been too long," Libby instructed her younger son over the phone.

"I can't, Mom. I need to study for an exam on Tuesday."

"We always make time for Jesus, Luke. Besides, you need to trust God. If you devote time to Him, there is nothing for you to worry about."

"I know, but..."

"And your father expects to see you there."

He sighed. "Okay, I'll be there."

The next morning, Luke arrived at Third Baptist Church of Losanti in his midnight blue Saab station wagon, located a mile away from his parents' home in Denbytown. He stepped out of the car wearing a white dress shirt, brown tie, belted khakis, and loafers, worn black King James Bible in hand. He saw his parents in the asphalt parking lot and walked over to them.

"I'm glad you decided to come to church, son. We always make time for the Lord."

"Yessir," Luke responded to his father.

"Dear," Libby said, smiling, "I'm glad you came early. I have someone you should meet."

"Mom, if you want me to talk to the outreach pastor about recommitting to Christ, or you have yet another girl lined up for me, I'm not interested."

"Luke, don't sass your mother," Cam snarled.

"Yessir."

The three walked up to the front of the pearly white church building, where a crowd of congregants was milling about. Libby pulled Luke through the crowd until she came up to another family.

"Marianne and Rob, this is my son Luke. Luke, these are the Richters."

"Hi, Luke," greeted the couple.

"Hello, ma'am. Hello, sir. Great to meet you both." Luke shook Rob's hand and Marianne gave him a friendly hug.

"A pleasure to meet you too," Marianne said. "This is our daughter, Rachel."

The young adults waved at each other. Rachel was a few inches shorter than Luke's six-foot frame, with a thin, straight build. He studied her plain, unremarkable face, and noted her shoulder-length blonde bobbed hair.

She's alright. Definitely the type of girl my parents would pick out for me.

"After service, I think we're going to head over to Riverview Coneys on the corner. Luke, you're more than welcome to come," Marianne said.

Before he could open his mouth to decline, Libby gave him a death stare. He cleared his throat. "Yes, I'll be happy to."

After Sunday service, the Phillips and Richter families strolled to the diner, and after a few minutes, the party was seated.

Marianne said, "Luke, your mother said you have a bachelor's in chemistry from University of the Great Lakes up in Michigan, and you're now in veterinary school at Ohio Valley Tech here in Losanti."

"Yes."

"That's great. Great Lakes is an excellent sciences and tech school. My brother went there and he's an engineering professor. How far along are you in vet school?"

"I'm in year two, ma'am."

Rob chimed in and asked, "So, Luke, is vet school like medical school where you finish and then you go through a residency period?"

"Yessir, something like that."

"Okay. That sounds impressive. Looks like you have a nice future in front of you."

Luke nodded.

"And we need soldiers for Christ in these science-heavy environments. Shining a light in the darkness."

"For sure." *Ugh. I get it, but everything doesn't have to be a holy war.*

"So, Rachel is a teacher," Rob said of his daughter. "She works at Maple Hills Elementary School here in the neighborhood."

"Okay, great...shaping young minds." He turned to the young lady his parents matched him with. "So, Rachel, what grade do you teach?"

"Oh, um...second grade," she answered in a soft, mousy voice.

"How do you like it?"

"Oh, I love it. My kids are wonderful. It truly is a great school."

After their meals, while the parents were engaged in conversation, Rachel pulled Luke aside.

"Uh...Luke, right?"

"Yes."

"My parents are always trying to set me up with men, sons of their friends, so I'm sure that's why this happened. Don't feel obligated to go out with me or anything."

"I get it, Rachel. Mine are the same way, 'man isn't meant to be alone,' y'know. But I would like your phone number, so I can call you and get to know you better. We can go out again by ourselves, maybe for coffee or something."

She smiled. "That's very nice. I can text you and then you'll have it in your phone." He gave her the number to text, and she sent a "hello" text. "You got it?"

"Yes, I do. I'll call you tonight."

"Looking forward to it."

She's not my type, but she's not terrible-looking. Besides, when do I have time to find someone? Might as well give this a shot. At least that will get Mom and Dad off my back.

After Luke arrived home from Sunday supper that evening, he called Rachel.

"Uh, hi, Rachel."

"Hi...who is this?"

"This is Luke. I'm the guy you met earlier, from church?"

"Yes, hi, Luke. I'm sorry, I have one of those old Nokia phones from a few years ago that just displays the number and no caller ID."

"Oh, okay. I was just calling 'cause I would like to go out on a date with you, y'know, just us."

"Sure, that'll be great."

There's a cool coffee house I know that's kinda close to the church."

"Oh, okay, what coffeehouse?"

"Norman's. It's on the corner of Broadway and Schott."

"Okay, I think I have an idea of where that is."

"Great. How about Wednesday at five o'clock?"

"Uh, I usually have to stay for a bit after school lets out. I should be done by then, but I might be running late. How does five-thirty sound?"

"Sounds great. See you then!"

A few days later, Luke showed up to Norman's Coffeehouse early for his casual date with Rachel. He wore a polo shirt, light jacket with a Green Sox logo on the left chest, relaxed fit jeans, and Converse shoes. *Might as well be comfortable for the first and last date with this girl.* He sat down at a small wooden table and waited for Rachel.

At half past five, Rachel strolled in with a full face of makeup, wearing a blue and white diagonal striped boatneck shirt, fitted bootcut jeans, and brown heeled boots, holding a blue sweatshirt and brown tote purse in her right arm. She sat down with Luke.

She's pretty cute all dressed up.

"Hi, Rachel," he greeted her.

"Hi, Luke. This wasn't hard to find. Nice place."

"It is. Norman's is great. It's not like your typical Starbucks. By the way, you look very nice."

She blushed a bit and smiled. "Thank you."

"Of course. I'm gonna head up to the counter and order. What would you like?"

"I'll have a small Americano with four packs of Equal if they have it."

"I'm sure they'll have that. I'll be right back."

After a few minutes, Luke brought back two cups. He gave Rachel her drink, then sat down with his.

She took a sip. "This is perfect. Thank you, Luke."

"No problem."

"What did you get?"

"I got a German chocolate mocha with an extra shot of coconut. It's their monthly special."

"How is it?"

"It's delicious. Wanna try it?" He moved the cup in her direction.

She took a sip, winced, and then gave it back to him. "Ooh, that's a lot of sugar. That makes my teeth hurt."

"Yeah, I probably should've figured since you got a coffee with Equal."

"Yeah, I'm pretty used to sugar-free drinks. So, Luke, tell me more about yourself. I just know you're twenty-five, so we're the same age, you're in vet school, that's pretty much all I know. I assume you're from here in Losanti?"

"Yeah."

"What high school did you go to?"

"Denbytown High School. I grew up not far from the church."

"Oh, that's nice. Middle class, pretty houses."

Luke nodded. "What about you? Where did you grow up? What high school?"

"I grew up on the east side, Brotherton Township, but I went to Our Lady of the Angels for high school."

"Oh, all-girls, Catholic, huh?"

"Yeah. We're not a Catholic family, obviously, but my parents sent me there so I wouldn't be around boys."

Luke smiled. "I've heard that's why a lot of parents send their kids to the Catholic schools. Knew someone in college who went to a single-sex high school for much the same reason. How did you and your family end up at Third Baptist?"

"I grew up going to Fourth Baptist, which is also on the east side. But, five years ago, our pastor retired, and we got a new pastor. He came in from My parents really didn't like him."

"What was wrong with him?"

"Too relativist, too worldly."

"In what way?"

"Well...he joined the Losanti Interfaith Network. So, he was working with pastors of other denominations, Catholic priests, Jewish rabbis...my parents really didn't like that."

"What do *you* think?"

"I...I believe the Bible is the infallible word of God. I trust my parents' judgment, my dad especially. He's one of the most upstanding believers I know."

She's giving me a lot to live up to.

Rachel continued. "Anyway, since Third Baptist is more faithful to scripture, they felt it was worth the drive. I decided to buy a small house in Mount Paradise, which is near the school where I teach, and it's maybe fifteen minutes away from the church. My parents helped me with the down payment."

"Your parents sound very supportive."

"They really are. I'm blessed to have them in my corner. How about you? Where do you live right now?"

"So, I'm living in an apartment near OVTU, but I do plan on buying a house once I finish my residency."

"That's understandable."

"So, after you went to Angels for high school, I assume you went to college, since you teach?"

She nodded. "Yeah, I did. I went to Tech for both undergrad and my master's in education."

"Oh, that's nice. So, I assume you just started teaching?"

"Uh-huh, this is my first year. It's really exciting. Haven't gotten burned out yet," she remarked with a small laugh. "So, what made you decide to become a veterinarian?"

"Good question. In college, I was a chemistry major and journalism minor, and I learned a lot about chemical compounds, and how so much of nature consists of chemicals. I love animals, so I thought it would be a logical next step." *I'm not telling this girl that I'm in vet school to one-up my brother.*

"Interesting. So, how is it being a Christian in the hard sciences?"

"What do you mean?"

"Well, I'm sure you had to learn evolution, and I bet you work with a lot of atheists."

"You'll be surprised at how many Christians are in the hard sciences. Programs like chemistry are not some godless cabal they make it out to be in church."

Rachel sipped her sugar-free coffee. "That's a relief. So, do you have any pets?"

"No, my schedule right now doesn't mix well with pets."

"Well, I hope it'll mix well with a woman."

"I'm sure I can make time," Luke said with a grin.

"You're funny," Rachel mused. "So, you went to college up in Michigan?"

"Yeah, University of the Great Lakes."

"I caught that from when we first met. What made you decide to go there?"

"It had an excellent chemistry program, which I figured would be conducive to my career goals." *Nope, I'm not telling this girl I decided to go to school there because of some other girl.*

"Did you like it?"

"Yeah, it was so fun. I made good friends, and I was in a campus ministry there, Christian Kingdom. Have you heard of it?"

"Yes, yes I have. They had a chapter at Tech. But I wasn't a part of that one. I did Seafarers, you know, the campus ministry that's connected to the Southern Baptists. But yeah, I could see Christian Kingdom being a fun time, if it was anything like Seafarers."

"Yeah, it was great. It was interdenominational, so it wasn't as strict on doctrinal minutiae as Seafarers, but they were super serious about evangelism, being Bible-based, salvation – the important stuff."

"Glad to hear it."

"So, when we met, you said your parents had been trying to set you up. Why? I'm sure any man would feel lucky to be going out with you."

She blushed. "Thanks, Luke. Do you remember the 'Relationships in Christ' sermon series Pastor Al did over the summer?"

"Uh, not really."

"I don't know how you could've missed it. It was every Sunday morning in July and August. It was a whole thing. It was about relationships between men and women, and how God wants our relationships to be structured from beginning to end."

"Oh, okay. I admit, with school, I probably wasn't there for it. But y'know, I've been trying to go back to church more often these days."

"Any man I'm with needs to be in church."

"Oh, for sure. Jesus is important and all. So, about that series, what kind of stuff were they talking about?"

"They were discussing courtship, and sexual purity, and marriage between one man and one woman, and our obligations to each other, and how men and women complement each other in marriage, you know, we have different roles, a bunch of things."

"That's a lot." *Glad I missed it. Pastor Al's obsession with what people do behind closed doors is getting old.*

"Yeah, I'm guessing it's because of all the state amendments they passed last year defining marriage as between a man and a woman, including here in Ohio."

"Oh, I guess I missed that too." *Really? There are people starving in the world, and locking gay people out of marriage is what these churches spend their time on. Something about that just doesn't seem right.*

"Oh wow, it was a big deal on the news, as well as in church. Everybody was talking about it at the time."

"I guess I've been too focused on school."

"I understand. So, um...anyway, one of the things Pastor Al covered was that as Christians, parents should be very involved in selecting and approving of a mate for their children. So, ever since then, my parents have been trying to get involved in my dating life."

"Oof, that reminds me a lot of this book we read back in college about courtship versus dating."

"Dating Is Wack?"

"Oh, you too?"

"Yeah," Rachel sighed. "We really got that book pushed on us in Seafarers. I'm thinking it's because the man who wrote it is an SBC pastor."

"Oh, I see. Forgot about that part. I just remember him being kind of young when he wrote it."

"It was pretty ridiculous. Personally, I don't have a problem dating. Just know my parents can be a bit much."

Luke nodded. "Mine too. I'm thinking they took those sermons to heart, just like yours."

⚫

While on Interstate 74 going west toward Indianapolis, Luke watched the cornfields while Paul focused on the road.

"You know how, in some cultures, couples get matched up by their parents?" Luke asked.

"Yeah – arranged marriage, pretty much."

"Uh-huh, and the idea is that as the couple get to know each other and get married, they'll mesh together and grow to love each other?"

"Sure."

"That's courtship, and that shit doesn't work."

Paul corrected him. "It didn't work for *you*."

CONFLICTED
June 28, 2023

As the Jeep approached Indianapolis, Indiana, the friends continued their conversation.

"Are you implying I didn't do courtship right?" Luke asked, a bit perturbed.

"I'm not implying anything," Paul answered. "You know as well as I do that courtship is part of purity culture, and it's all part of a rotten tree. It probably wasn't going to work anyway, at least not in a way that would make you both happily married. But that's not why it wasn't gonna work for *you*."

"What? Why do you say that?"

"Let's be serious. When it came to your marriage to Rachel, you were conflicted on day one."

⬥

June 2006

The vast expanse of the Pacific Ocean felt dark and foreboding, as the waves slipped against the sand. The night sky disappeared slowly in front of twenty-six-year-old Luke, who sat with legs crossed along the shimmering beach of Coronado Island, as the sun crawled behind his back. A new dawn beckoned. The simplicity of his white tee and khaki-colored linen shorts stood in stark contrast to the event set to occur in just a few hours.

"Brother, I figured you'd be out here," a voice called out in the distance.

He leaned his head to the side to suss out who beckoned. "Paulie! It's incredible out here. I'm surprised you're up."

"Why are you surprised, man? I've got a toddler and a baby. Sleep is a thing of the past. My internal clock is all screwed up."

"Makes sense."

Paul sat gged on the beach next to the groom. "You're nervous about the wedding, aren't you?"

"How'd you know?"

"I've been there. Remember? You were right there next to me, pushing me right along to my doom."

Luke chortled. "You're always good for a laugh."

"That's what I'm here for, bro."

"I appreciate it. I really do. Y'know, believe it or not, it's not the wedding I'm worried about. Maybe I should be. A lot went into it, it's stupidly expensive. Rachel was dying to have this destination wedding way out here in California, and I mean, she's the bride – she gets what she wants," he complained, rolling his eyes.

"Oh yeah, that's how it is, man."

"Thank God her parents paid for it, but Jesus, a lot goes into a wedding. And she's all wound up. Oh my God, she's a lot right now...but that's not even what's got me worried."

"What are you worried about, then?"

"I'm worried about being married."

"Why?"

Luke took a deep breath. "I'm still a virgin. And so is she. I don't know what the hell I'm doing."

Paul laughed. "I'll tell you what – you'll figure it out. When Alyssa and I first had sex, it wasn't complicated...you know, the mechanics. The only weird thing was the mentals."

"Hmm?"

"Yeah. We get told all our lives 'sex is a sin,' 'don't do it,' 'a moment in the sheets isn't worth an eternity in hell,' 'your purity is a gift to your future wife,' 'If you sleep together before marriage, you're living in sin.' I still feel guilty, and we've been married for four years now."

"It's in the past. God forgives."

"I know. But the weird thing is – you have a party and you get a ring on your finger and all of a sudden you're allowed to have all the sex you want, sin-free. It's a real mindfuck."

Luke nodded in agreement. "I've spent my life holding back for the Lord, and in just a few hours, I won't have to anymore. What if I can't?"

"What do you mean?"

"What if I've been keeping it in all this time, and then when it's time, I can't rise to the occasion?"

"Brother, you'll be good. I promise you...when you and Rachel do the do, the floodgates will open and you won't be able to hold it back."

"Eh, I hope you're right. I dunno, my therapist calls it 'catastro-phizing.' I worry about my dick not working, I worry about if I'll suck at being a good husband to Rachel – if I'll fail her. Shit gets into a loop in my head and it won't stop. It doesn't matter what I do, it won't go away. Y'know, there are times when I think to myself, y'know, if things had been different...if I had done things differently back in college."

Paul's face contorted. "Luke, you're still thinking about Morgan? You broke up with her seven years ago. I'm sure she's moved on and she's living her best life. You've got to let that girl go."

"No, not Morgan. She's beautiful and I've always hated how our relationship ended, but y'know, I'm over her."

"Then who...what are you even talking about?"

"I-I can't believe I'm saying this..."

"Spit it out, man. It's just me."

Luke's eyes panned down, then stared straight at his best friend. "You're not gonna believe this. There are times when I wonder to myself what would've happened if I had gotten with AC."

"Wait a minute...AC? Ann Corbin?"

"Yeah."

"Ann Corbin...like from UGL? *Ann Corbin?* The hell?"

"Yeah...I know."

"Bro...*you* told me you didn't wanna be with her, *you* weren't into her like that."

"I did."

"*You* said she called you too much. *You* said she couldn't get over you, *you* had *me* tell her to back off because you didn't have it in you to tell her yourself."

"I lied, Paulie! *I lied!*"

"Are you serious, Luke? Are you for real right now?"

Calming down a tad, he responded, "Yeah, for real. The truth is, I would call her all the time...she hardly called me. She didn't have a chance to. Truth is, I loved hanging out with her. She made me feel alive. I *did* want to be with her. I *loved* her."

"Damn. All this time, I thought she was lying! She told me you would call her first, and I thought she was delusional and just coping." Paul got up and started pacing. "Can't believe I'm hearing this."

"I was wrong to involve you. I should've been man enough to pull the trigger. I dunno. I guess it was my ego or something. I wanted to impress everybody. Something about AC drew me to her. Sure, she wasn't some kind of model, but she looked beautiful in her own way, and she was just an all-around amazing girl. But I knew everybody would have something to say if we had gotten together."

"Why would anybody care? What are you talking about?"

"Everybody would care. Y'know, what would my parents say? My dad didn't even want me with Morgan...he would kill me if I got with AC. What would my friends say? I didn't want to be laughed at for being with her...I don't wanna be the butt of their jokes."

"Why would anybody laugh at you?"

"You have no idea."

"We are grown ass men. Literally nobody cares. Besides, why the hell do you worry so much about what other people think about your life or what you do or who you're with?"

"You don't understand..."

"There's nothing to understand. You've always been like this. As long as I've known you, all throughout college and even now, you've been like this. It doesn't make sense. If Ann makes you happy, if she's the one you love, fuck what your parents think, fuck what your friends think, fuck what *I* think, shit."

"I dunno. AC would say the same thing...I worried too much about what other people thought about the decisions I made." Luke looked down at the sparkling grains of sand as the sun continued to rise. "Eh, it doesn't matter anyway. It's too late. Y'know, she stopped talking to me almost three years ago."

"Ope..."

"Yeah, I know."

"Ugh...I can't believe you lied to me, and I'm your best friend."

"I'm really sorry, Paulie."

"So, now that we're doing the whole 'honesty' thing, let me ask you this. Why the *fuck* are you marrying Rachel?"

"She's nice, she's God-fearing, she comes from a very good family, my parents and her parents are friends from church..."

"Is this your list or your parents' list?"

Luke was silent.

The best man crept down to face the forlorn groom. "Luke, I'm gonna level with you. In two hours, you're scheduled to marry Rachel. And then that's it, you're officially married, death do you part, and you'll have to make it work at that point. But right now..." Paul looked around and sighed, "right now, it's not too late. You can turn back now."

"Paulie, I—"

"Hey, asshole!" Luke and Paul turned around to see Trey, wearing a dress shirt, pressed khaki pants, and Birkenstocks, trudging along the beach towards them like a man on a mission. "C'mon, let's go little brother, you got a girl to marry."

———◆———

"Luke," Paul recalled, "I'll be honest. I lost a bit of respect for you that day."

"Ouch."

"Sorry, not trying to be a dick, but I did. It kind of hurt that you didn't trust me enough to tell me you wanted Ann."

"It's not that I didn't trust you. Of course I trust you, and I did then. It's just...I knew admitting my feelings aloud would make them more real, and I wasn't ready to deal with that."

"I could see that. The other thing I couldn't understand is that...you know...I couldn't believe you actually went through with it. You had all those doubts, dreaming about Ann, saying you loved *her*. You didn't even like the woman you were getting married to, and yet you did it anyway because mommy and daddy said so."

"It's not that I didn't like Rachel...just wasn't in love with her. But I thought I'd learn to fall in love with her over time. Thinking back, it's not my proudest moment."

"You know, one thing about the church is that it's great at producing hypocrites. Not too long after you and Rachel got married, I started placing bets, and next thing you know, I was cheating on Alyssa, and I was lying about all of it. I was living a double life. I couldn't live that way and look you in the face."

Luke nodded in understanding.

"So, the weird thing is, back in college, a part of me had a feeling there might've been something between you and Ann, but you were so adamant there was nothing there, that I took you at your word. The thing is, I never quite got how you fell for her in the first place."

"Yeah. So, we got assigned a project. We all needed to be in groups of two or three, and we had to come up with some kind of sketch and present it for a joint grade. Terah happened to be in the same section, so we decided to pair up. So, while we were trying to plan it out, she decided to bring along AC."

"Oh, okay."

"They were best friends from Detroit, and they were roommates at school. We needed a third person to act out the sketch, and she was gonna help out with it. So, she came in, and we gave her a part to play. At first, I thought she looked alright, but what really got my attention was that she was funny."

"Sometimes it's like that," Paul agreed. "Personality matters, too."

"Y'know, the funny thing is, I call her 'AC' because the character she played in our sketch was named 'Anna Claire.'"

"Seriously? All this time, I thought you called her that because her name's Ann Corbin."

Luke smiled. "It's a happy accident."

"That it is. But yeah, that's some real butterfly effect shit."

"For sure."

"Now, you've got me wondering, man. How did you end up falling for Ann? Did she grow on you or something?"

"Eh, to a degree. I liked her more as we spent more time together, but there was always this tension because I didn't think I could go there...y'know, reasons. But Paulie, there was one moment, it was fall semester of our second year at UGL, where I truly saw *her*."

October 1999

On a grassy knoll at the University of the Great Lakes, Luke removed a roll of 35-millimeter film from his Canon EOS Rebel G camera and slipped in a new cartridge. He then readied it to take photos. The gentle wind whipped his straight brown hair into his face as he snapped photos of the Quad, a verdant mall on campus with crisscrossing paths to each of the buildings that bordered the expanse.

Students enjoyed the Quad on this mild day, studying on the grass, chatting with friends, and playing hacky sack to pass the time. The weather cooperated; the sky was bright with light clouds shading the sun. Luke photographed the active campus and took in the vibrant energy.

He then set his sights on the Main Library at the opposite end of the mall. He peered through the viewfinder and began snapping photos of the majestic Art Deco building.

As he continued running through the roll of film, he found himself focused on a young lady, wearing a long-sleeved navy blouse, khaki capris, and sandals, on a platform bookending the grand stairs winding to the entrance. Her gaze rested upon a thick book atop her soft thighs, which extended out from her ample body. She took brief respites to lift her head and absorb the blend of nature and architecture surrounding her.

I need to get closer.

Luke came down from the mound and moved intently across the lawn. Once near the ornate building, he positioned himself in the grass mere yards from the library stairs. He crouched down, partially obscured by the opposite pillar, and gazed upon the woman. As the calm wind whipped through her coily locks of bright brunette and auburn, he caught the moment on film. He was mesmerized by her regal, Nubian profile, juxtaposed with skin the shade of sand, and irises the hue of flint. Her skin shimmered like silk, and her curves were supple yet strong.

I must have her...

Enchanted, he stood up to approach.

"Oof!"

He tripped over a loose shoelace dangling from his Nike high-top sneaker and fell flat on his face. His camera fell from his grasp and landed on the ground.

"What the..."

The woman slid her book into her messenger bag. She descended from the platform and down the stairs to find the source of the commotion.

Luke dusted himself off and rose to his feet. "Uh...hey, AC, what's up?"

Ann picked up his camera and handed it back to him. "Uh, Luke...what were you doing?"

He was relieved to see his camera was undamaged, and the film had not been exposed to the elements. "I'm out taking pictures for a project. It's for my photography class."

"Oh, cool. You weren't taking pictures of *me*, were you?"

"Uh...yeah, maybe a couple. I'm capturing nature, including people doing the things they naturally do."

"Ah, okay. Hope you don't get an 'F' on account of me."

"Why would you say that?"

"Welp, I'll put it this way. Photogenic, I am not."

Luke rolled his eyes. "Give yourself at least a little more credit. Besides, it's a black and white photo project, so these pictures won't be like normal color ones."

"Huh, that's interesting."

"You know what the other cool thing is?"

"Um...what?" Ann asked.

"I'll be developing the film myself. Since I'm taking this class, I have access to a darkroom."

"Oh, that's pretty cool. I'm sure your pictures will come out awesome, mine notwithstanding."

"Yours will be great, AC," he assured her. "Anyway, what were you studying?"

"Chemistry – I've got a midterm coming up at the end of next week for organic chemistry."

"O-chem – awesome. That's in my wheelhouse. Let me know if you want me to help you study."

She smiled. "You know what, Luke? I think I'm gonna take you up on that."

"I owe you one since you helped me with my project."

"Without asking, might I add," she quipped.

He flashed a cheeky smile. "Yes, since you 'helped' me, helping you study is the least I can do. How about tonight at six? We'll meet right here by the library stairs."

"It's a 'date.'"

Paul said, "Sometimes, it's like that."

"For sure," Luke agreed.

"So, why didn't you pull the trigger?"

"Part of it is that my parents would've never been okay with it."

"Should've known. I have no idea why I even asked. She was Christian, though, and from what I remember, her family went to a non-denominational church that was formerly Baptist. Close enough, right?"

"I dunno. See, my parents had an image in their minds of who I should marry, and I was pretty sure AC wasn't it, just like Morgan. They were very picky, but when it came to her specifically, they weren't the only problem."

February 2000

The snow fell softly on a cold winter evening on the campus of the University of the Great Lakes. Christian Kingdom's Tuesday night Bible study had just concluded in the third-floor study lounge of Farrell Hall. Paul stood up from an upholstered chair and grabbed his hardcover Bible. "I'm gonna head back to my room. Gotta get up for an exam, starts at seven-thirty, sharp." "Oh, wow, that's an early test," Mei Chen noted.

"I'll be quiet when I get back," Luke reassured him, "so I don't wake you up."

"I'm pretty tired, man. Doubt you'll wake me."

After Paul left, the other Bible study attendees remained in the room, engaging in conversation. Steve Lopez, who was sitting on a couch forming part of a circle, spoke up. "We just read the scripture in the Old Testament, in Genesis, about Jacob being married to two sisters, and how he loved one, but didn't love the other. It's got me thinking – do any of you believe in soulmates?"

"Yes...yes I do," Greg Harris opined. "But purely in a God-ordained sense, nothing mystical. God orders our steps, he stirs something within us, and in that way, he unites us with our helpmeet." "Is it really that deep?" Megan asked. "I think we can choose for ourselves. We all have free will. Just as long as we include Jesus, I think it's fine."

"What do you think, Luke?"

He was entranced by the flurries outside the study room window. "Uh, Greg...it's complicated. Look at how in the scripture, Jacob loved one sister more than the other, but the less attractive, unloved sister, Leah, gave birth to the line that ultimately led to Jesus. So really, who was Jacob's true soulmate?"

Megan laughed. He turned to see her smug expression.

"What's so funny?"

"That *would* be your answer. 'It's complicated.'"

"Huh?"

"Think about it. You and Morgan broke up, like, a year ago, and you've been single since. Then, you've been hanging out an awful lot with that Black girl that just started coming to large group with Terah...what's her name?"

"Ann. So?"

"We're not stupid. Morgan, then Ann?"

"Jungle Fever, dude," Greg jumped in. "Patterns."

"What are you talking about?" Luke shot back. "Ann and Morgan are very different people. Just because they're both Black doesn't mean they're exactly the same."

"I know," Megan said. "We can see that. But it's like, Morgan was, you know, more of a match. Ann...well..."

"Y'know, Ann and I are just friends. She's helping out on a class project with me and Terah. Besides, even if I *were* into her like that, as long as we're not doing anything sinful, what's the problem?"

"Nothing's wrong with it," Steve explained, "but it's as if you're replacing a Mercedes with a moped."

"And you know what they say about mopeds," Greg added. "They're fun to ride, but you don't want anyone seeing you on it."

Everyone laughed, including Luke. As chuckles and guffaws filled the room, the door abruptly opened.

"Uh...hi, guys!" Ann leaned in the doorway, backpack in hand. "Sounds like you're having fun."

Oh, no...

"We just finished wrapping up Bible study," Steve said. "We're hanging out. Wanna join us?"

"Yeah, sure." She joined them in the circle as they quickly changed the subject.

Luke returned to viewing the gentle snowflakes blanketing the ground. Face flushed and feeling a vague sense of shame, he could barely look at his friend.

———◆◇◆———

"I don't get it," Paul mused. "Greg, Steve and Mei were morons. I never told Alyssa, but I never cared too much for Megan either. Why did you care what any of them had to say?"

"Probably because I was nineteen."

"Touché."

"I guess more to the point, Greg and Steve reminded me a lot of my brother. They were popular and cool, and I wanted to be accepted. I felt like shit for laughing with them and then having to look AC in the eye. But with the way they reacted, I realized there was no way she and I could be together out in the open. And I've never been the kind of guy who wants a secret relationship, so it would never work at all."

"But you kept Morgan a secret from your parents."

"I did, and it sucked the whole time, but at least I didn't have to keep her a secret from my friends, too."

"Did you think that if you and Ann ended up in a relationship, our friend group would've reacted the way our Bible study did?"

"Thinking back, probably not, but I didn't want to chance it."

"Ugh. I get it, but I wish you could've trusted us to be better people."

"I truly wish I had done things differently back then, but there's nothing I can do about that now."

"Bro, it's never too late to make a different decision."

Luke looked at his friend in confusion. "What?"

As the truck coasted along the Indianapolis Loop, Paul started searching through the windshield. "Where the hell is I-70?"

"Uh, we passed it a few minutes ago."

"Shit!"

"Sorry, should've been looking. Alright. Look," Luke pointed to the dashboard screen with an interactive map, "GPS is turning us around. Just take this next exit."

"Alright. Let's go."

"In two miles, use the right lane to exit onto Rockville Road," announced the AI voice.

"Okay, it looks like we just gotta drive across the bridge and enter back onto the highway," Luke directed Paul.

"Great. Sounds easy enough."

Once returning to the freeway, Luke eyed the airport to their right and panned the camera over to the runway as they passed by. "Y'know Paulie, we could've flown to wherever we're going."

"Yeah, we could," Paul mused, "but what's the fun in that?"

After a couple of minutes, the signs for Interstate 70 appeared.

"Bro, there's I-70 West."

"Way over there?" Paul peered over to the right-hand lanes sending loop traffic to I-70. Unfortunately, the Wrangler was all the way over to the left, as he had tried to speed through traffic to get back on track and miscalculated how long it would take to get to the exit. "Let's do this!"

"Shit!"

Paul gunned the truck over several lanes of traffic to make it to I-70, but he made it. "Like a boss."

"Don't do that again! I swear to God!"

"We're alive, right?"

"Yeah, sure," Luke uttered, exasperated.

"So shut the fuck up."

LUNA PIER
June 29, 2023

Luke slowly opened his eyes to the bright morning sunlight beaming through the open window. He took in the silhouette of Paul standing in front of it, toned arms outstretched enjoying full freedom, completely nude from head to toe. He then rolled to a sitting position and scanned the dated room decorated in more shades of brown than he knew existed, with two full-size beds including the one he was on, and a bubble-screen television from the nineties.

It took mere minutes for the scene to register in his mind.

"The fuck?" Luke called out.

"Had to get some sun, brother."

"Man, that's what the pool deck is for."

Paul turned around to face his travel partner and asked, "Have you seen the pool area here? I wouldn't touch that fucking thing with a ten-foot pole."

"I mean…"

"Yeah. It's gross, bro. Anyway, hit the shower, we gotta get going."

"Yeah, I'm about to. Go put on some clothes, man." Luke stood up and threw a towel at his friend. He then glanced at the old plastic alarm clock on the bedside table. It was a quarter before eight. "Where are we going today?"

"West, and you're driving this leg." Paul threw his keys onto Luke's bed. "I programmed it all in the GPS, so you should be fine."

"When'd you do that?"

Paul smiled but said nothing.

Less than an hour later, they checked out of the neglected roadside motel and packed their suitcases in the back of the Wrangler. Paul then moved his guitar case to the back seat and then entered the front passenger seat.

Luke stepped up into the driver's seat and adjusted the seat and mirrors accordingly. He then instructed Paul to grab the GoPro from his bag on the floor in front of him and showed him how to use it.

"It's stupid easy."

"Yeah, I'm sure. These are pretty snazzy."

After they were buckled in and ready to go, Luke started the truck, and the men got back on the road. Paul started rolling tape.

"So, why'd you move your guitar? It's not like we have a ton of stuff in the back."

Paul said, "Uh, just moving stuff around and I figured Katie needs to be where she is now."

"Katie?"

"Welcome to Illinois," announced the female voice coming from the dashboard map.

Paul explained. "Yeah, Katie. My guitar. She's a Taylor 614ce Special Edition. She's beautiful. Plays wonderfully. You'll see her before too long."

"Why 'Katie?'" Luke inquired.

"So yeah, back when I was in high school, you know, Bishop Callahan, there was this really hot girl named Katie Kim. Long jet black hair, sultry brown eyes, super-hot body."

"Nice."

"There weren't a lot of other Asians at BC, and I mean, she was Korean too, so she stuck out. Her family moved to the area from, I think Vancouver? Yeah, she had the cutest Canadian accent."

"Huh, Katie. You never told me about her. What happened to her?"

"I mean, it was, like, homecoming junior year. I asked her out, she said, and I remember this like it was yesterday, 'You're very nice, Paul, but I want to focus on my grades right now. My goal is to be accepted into Harvard.' I was kind of sad, you know, but I understood. At least I did until she turned up at homecoming with somebody else."

"Oh, damn."

Paul huffed. "Yeah, man. Zach Schultheiss. Motherfucker was on the football team. Built, popular, pretty much everything I wasn't back then."

"White?"

"Yeah, didn't wanna say it, but yeah. Blond and blue, you know. No offense man."

"None taken," Luke reassured him. "But damn, bro. I'm sorry."

"Eh, it was a long time ago. But yeah, never forgot about her."

A couple of hours later, the GPS recommended the truck make several turns.

"Where you got this taking us, Paulie?"

"Well, we got a stop in Springfield."

"Springfield? I think we should've taken 74, not 70."

"Ope – well, at least this is a hybrid...not gonna lose much in gas."

"True. So, yeah, what's in Springfield?"

"Kyle," Paul responded.

"Kyle?"

"Kyle Tracey. You know, he was on CK's worship team back at UGL."

"Oh! Yeah yeah, I remember him. God, it's been at least a good twenty years since I've seen him."

"I know. He knows we're coming, and he's looking forward to seeing you. When we get close, I'm gonna give him a call, we'll hang out."

"Yeah, sounds good."

"So, totally off the subject – I know yesterday we were talking about Rachel and everything. But how did you end up not finishing vet school? When you got in, you seemed pretty stoked about it."

"Oh, Paulie, that's a hell of a story."

"I'm all ears, man."

<hr />

September 2006

Luke sat in a navy chair against the wall of a light-blue painted waiting room. His head rested on the wall, and his eyes were closed.

Did I wash the dishes?

Did I wash the dishes?

Did I wash the dishes?

I wish these thoughts would go away.

I'm behind on my labs.

I need to stop oversleeping when I have class in the morning.

Dr. Simmons is gonna fail me, I'm sure of it.

I wish Rachel would clean up behind herself.

Did I wash the dishes?

Did I wash the dishes?

Did I wash the dishes?

I could use a drink.

But when I drink, I sleep late.

"Luke?"

He opened his eyes and focused in the direction of the voice. He followed the curly-haired woman who called him into a room at the end of a long hallway. The room was painted white with large, floor-to-ceiling windows on two sides covered by blinds. He sat on a soft beige seat. She closed the door and sat opposite him.

"Hi, Luke," she said.

"Hi, Stacy."

Stacy looked down at her notes. "It looks like the last time we met was two months ago."

"Yes...got busy."

"I understand. How have you been feeling since our last session?"

He sighed. "Just...off."

"Okay. When you say you feel 'off,' what does that mean to you?"

"I can't stop my thoughts from racing."

The counselor continued. "Okay. So, before we get into the specific thoughts, let's talk about what has been going on in your life right now. Do you feel that you're under a lot of stress?"

"Eh, sort of, but not more than usual."

"Could you share a bit more about the stress you're currently encountering?"

"Y'know, my wife and I have been married for just a few months, it's the 'honeymoon period,' so everything should be perfect. Vet school...the work's not hard, at least not in theory, but I'm having so much trouble waking up to go to class. I don't get it. Things are good, but something's wrong with me. I mean, Rachel and I went on vacation with friends just a couple of weeks ago. Something's wrong. Why can't I just be happy?"

"It's understandable to have a level of stress and anxiety when you're going through a major change in your life. A new marriage is often exciting, but it is a change, and when you're living with mental health challenges such as bipolar disorder II, coupled with obsessive compulsive disorder, changes in your life, even positive ones, can upset your routine and lead to worsening symptoms."

"I guess that makes sense."

"So, let's talk about your thoughts. What thoughts are you dealing with?" Stacy asked.

"Sometimes, it's small stuff that keeps tugging on me. Sometimes, it's larger problems."

"What are some examples?"

"Uh, right now, I keep having these thoughts about the dishes. That they're not washed, that I didn't wash them. I get that a bit. Usually, it's either that or locking my car door. Other times, it's big stuff, like being worried about failing out of class, or making a mistake getting married in the first place. It's awful, it's crazy-making."

"I would imagine that is very distressing for you. For the routine thoughts, such as washing dishes, it's helpful to explore those, and reassure yourself that even if you didn't do these things, it's okay."

Luke nodded his head while rubbing his slightly sweaty hands on his thighs.

"So, Luke, let's take washing dishes. What do you fear will happen if you didn't wash them?"

He paused for a moment to think. "If I don't wash them...then they'll pile up, and the pile will attract bugs."

"Has that happened?" the therapist inquired.

"No."

"Why do you believe it will?"

"I dunno. My mom would always say that to me when I was a kid. If I missed a spot, I got it when my dad got home."

"When you say you 'got it,' what do you mean by that?"

He looked away. "Y'know...I don't think I wanna talk about it."

Stacy's face softened. "That's fine, Luke. When you're ready to explore it, we can."

He sat with his arms folded, outlining his therapist's slightly curved visage with his eyes.

"But as of right now, you'll want to work on redirecting your thinking a bit. You're no longer the child who has to fear your parents. You're an adult who is now married and has his own home. It's important to keep reminding yourself of that."

"Alright."

"If the dishes are unwashed now, you can wash them later. The chance of bugs being attracted to them is unlikely. And as unlikely as it is, if it does happen, then you and your wife will find a way to have the bugs exterminated. There is always a solution. You will be okay. Remind yourself that no matter the outcome, you, Luke, will be okay."

"Yes, Stacy, that makes sense."

"As we continue these sessions, we'll discuss the possibility of exposure therapy, which is the most effective treatment for obsessive compulsive disorder. For many patients, it can be scary and tough at first, but in the long run, it should lessen your obsessive thoughts and compulsions."

He continued to listen.

"Now, there are the other issues you brought up. You mentioned school."

"Yes."

"What about school is challenging for you right now?"

"Every morning, when I get up and drive to campus, I have knots in my stomach. I dread going."

"Do you find the classwork overwhelming?"

"Yes and no. Y'know, when I was a kid, my parents tested my IQ. I scored a 138, just two points below genius."

"Impressive."

Luke explained, "See, the work itself isn't all that hard, at least on paper. It's just...there's a mental block or something. My thoughts just take over and I can't concentrate."

"I know you also work with a psychiatrist and have been prescribed medication. Have you been taking your prescribed medication regularly?"

He sighed and touched his temple. "Honestly, no, but I know I should."

"What stops you from taking your medication?" she asked.

"I guess part of it is that I start taking them, they get in my system, and then I'm fine, so I think to myself that don't need them anymore."

Stacy nodded. "That's a pretty common sentiment. I see that in a lot of my clients. It's tempting to think this, but part of continuing to feel better is taking your medication as prescribed on a consistent basis. What's the other reason you're not taking your medication?"

"Y'know, my wife and my mom want me on the pills, and they tell me to take them. But my dad has always been opposed to them. He thinks the pills are a crutch, and real men suck it up and tough it out. He always says I'm 'soft.' Intellectually, I know the pills help me function, but a part of me wants to prove it to myself and to my dad that I can get along well enough on my own."

"Luke, think of it this way. If a type one diabetic requires insulin to regulate their blood sugar, would it make sense for them not to take it, so they can prove they can live without it?"

"No, not at all."

"Why?" she asked.

He explained, "They need it to live. Otherwise, they'll get sick and die."

"Right. You see, mental illnesses are like physical illnesses. They require treatment, or there are negative consequences. It's okay to need help. Medication is not a crutch. It's necessary for you to have a good quality of life."

———◆———

November 2006

Luke rubbed his brow in exhaustion as he sat at the home office computer typing, a glass of merlot next to the mouse.

This is too much. There's no way I'm gonna get through these labs.

Just then, he felt a gentle embrace from behind. "Honey bunny..."

"Hey Rach." He gave her a peck on the cheek.

"What are you doing?" she asked softly.

"Ugh...just studying. I've gotta pass my courses this term."

"Bun-bun, you're not only handsome and smart, but you're humble, too. I have no doubt you'll do just fine."

"Thanks for the vote of confidence."

"Of course. On another note, do you know what I want for Christmas?" she cooed softly.

"Hmm, I dunno...a Woven Memories Longaberger basket...in bold blue?"

She chuckled. "You're funny. You must've overheard me on the phone. Close, but I'm thinking something else."

"Well then, do tell."

"What I'd love for Christmas is for you to give me a baby."

He cleared his throat and his body stiffened. "No way, Rach. Not right now. Let's wait at least until I'm out of school."

She stood up and paced behind him. "Look, I get it...I really do. School takes up so much of your time. But I'm not getting any younger."

His irritation grew as he stared at the monitor. "For fuck's sake, you're only twenty-seven. You're not even thirty yet."

"Stop swearing at me, Luke."

He turned around to look at her. "Okay, okay hun, I'm sorry. This is just a lot."

She took a deep breath. "I know, and I want to do my best to support you, but I want us to live life. It's hard watching my friends having babies and seeing them hit their milestones, and we're not even discussing it."

"Well, we're discussing it now, and the answer is no, not yet."

"If not now, when? You say twenty-seven isn't old, but time goes by so fast. Women have biological clocks; I won't be able to have them forever. And besides, do we want to be old trying to chase around little kids?"

"I don't need this right now. Seriously, I don't." He took a sip from his tumbler. "I have labs tomorrow. I only have a few left before the end of the term."

She homed in on the glass. "Luke – how much wine have you had?"

He rolled his eyes. "Not that much."

"What's 'not that much?'"

"Just what I said. Not that much." He took another sip.

Rachel left the room, and after less than a minute, returned holding an empty bottle of 2003 grocery store Merlot and another three-quarters empty. "What is this?"

"They're bottles of wine."

She got increasingly upset. "You wiped this one out all by yourself, and this other one I just got yesterday. I was supposed to take this to the teacher in-service over the weekend."

"I'm sorry," he responded sarcastically. "As if I was supposed to know. Not like you told me."

"Well, now you know. Maybe you should've asked. Wine doesn't just magically appear on the counter."

He buried his head in his hands and exhaled. "Okay, Rachel."

She got into his face. "Call the counseling center at Third Baptist tomorrow."

"I already have a therapist. Besides, the ones at the counseling center aren't real therapists. Why would I talk to them?"

"You don't even talk to a 'real' therapist anymore, Luke. When was the last time you showed up for an appointment? It's been months."

"It's only been two months."

She stepped back and held up her hands in frustration. "Honestly, all this science is making you forget to rely on the Lord for your strength."

"I've told you that's not how it works."

"Well – it doesn't matter. You need Jesus. Stop with the excuses. Call the church tomorrow. And you're sleeping on the couch tonight."

"I can't – I need a real night's sleep. I got labs!"

Rachel slammed the door behind her.

The next morning, an exhausted Luke, clad in a tee shirt and grey boxer briefs, opened his eyes and slowly sat up on the living room sofa. He checked his phone.

"Oh shit." *It's after ten in the morning. Labs started at eight. This is the fourth time I've missed. Shit, I'm gonna fail another class.*

He stood up and walked around the empty house. He arrived in the stark white kitchen with granite countertops and found the partially empty Merlot bottle placed next to the stove. He reached into one of the top cabinets to find a glass tumbler.

Ugh, they're all in the dishwasher. I wish Rachel would put things away.

These dishes need washed...

These dishes need washed...

These dishes need washed...

Shit, Stacy said to remember nothing's gonna happen. But dammit...

He sighed, then tipped up the glass bottle and poured the remaining contents down his throat. He rinsed it in the stainless steel sink and placed it carefully in the green recycle bin. Afterwards, he returned to the couch and added to his hours of sleep.

December 2006

On a Wednesday morning during school break three weeks later, Luke was home alone while Rachel was at work. As he did each day, he opened his laptop. This time, an official-looking email in his school inbox caught his eye. He opened it with trepidation. It stated:

OHIO VALLEY TECHNICAL UNIVERSITY
SCHOOL OF VETERINARY MEDICINE
December 15, 2006
Dear Mr. Phillips:
We regret to inform you that you are being terminated from the Doctor of Veterinary Medicine (DVM) program effective immediately. Reasons set forth by the program include failure of four courses, including two in the Fall 2006 term alone. In our view, you have demonstrated poor fit for the rigors of the DVM program, and in our view, it is best you do not continue. We wish you well in your future endeavors.
Sincerely,
Timothy Taylor, PhD

Dean of Academic Affairs
Ohio Valley Technical University

Fuck.

Upon reading the letter, Luke calmly slipped his feet into his grey and red Nike Air Max gym shoes and tied them. He then swiped his wallet and keys and left the home he shared with Rachel. He jumped into his station wagon in the driveway and sped off.

Four hours later, he noticed the giant blue and white sign on the side of the highway:

> **Pure Michigan**

A few minutes later, he turned off at the "Luna Pier" exit – mile marker six.

He made a right-hand turn, and after passing a gas station right by the interstate, he found himself cruising the main road of the sleepy town, dotted with restaurants, shops, a church, a fire station, a post office, and a motel.

At the end of the short street was a picnic shelter with a desolate beachfront. He parked his car in the designated lot. As he made his way past the spartan structure and playground to the beach, he noticed the calm, flowing waves of Lake Erie, and took in the crisp, fresh air with a hint of the winter shortly to come.

He slipped off his shoes and socks, and sat on the chilly, damp sand. He pulled up his knees and held them tight with his hands. The reality of the situation dawning on him, warm tears flowed down his face.

Oh my God, I'm a failure. How am I gonna tell Rachel?
How am I gonna tell Mom and Dad? I can't face them.

Mom is gonna tell me how much of a disappointment I am.

Dad was right about me after all...I am a failure and a loser.

And Trey. Oh my God, Trey is gonna gloat...I won't hear the end of this.

'I told you so'

'I told you so'

'I told you so'

I can't do this. I can't go home. I'm a failure.

The time continued to tick by as Luke contemplated his situation and his future. After several hours, the freezing lakeside temperatures numbed his feet. He stood up to regain the feeling in his toes, returned to the Saab, and cruised through the dark, quiet locale, finding a small, dilapidated roadside motel. He booked a place to stay for the night, and when he entered the room, he slipped into bed and fell fast asleep.

The next day, around ten o'clock in the morning, Luke woke up and walked to the motel lobby to speak with the clerk.

"Good morning!" the middle-aged woman behind the counter greeted him.

"G'morning. I'm in room 104. I'd like to stay another night."

"Alright, that's fine. It'll be another $47.99 plus tax and fees."

"That works. Uh...ma'am?"

"Uh-huh?"

"Where's a good place to eat around here?"

", there's a diner down the road, it's called Luna Pier Diner. You just turn out here..." she pointed to the street next to the motel, "and you go one and a half blocks. It don't look like nothin' from the outside, but it's real good."

"Okay, thanks!"

"You're welcome."

Luke left the lobby, entered his car, and followed the directions given by the clerk. He came upon a nondescript beige brick building. A sign hung from it with "Luna Pier Diner" in painted black script. He parked on the street and stepped into the restaurant.

The server, a woman who appeared to be in her thirties wearing a white dress and matching apron, said, "Go on ahead, have a seat anywhere." Luke sat at a small booth. As he sat, he stared outside at the street on the other side of the window.

"Hi, welcome to Luna Pier Diner, my name's Heather," the waitress said to him as she walked up to the table. "Would you like anything to drink? We got coffee, decaf, orange juice, milk, pop, and water."

"Hmm, coffee's fine. Could I get cream and sugar please?"

"Yeah, sure. I'll bring that over to you. Take a look at the menu, it's right over there." She motioned to the menus clipped on the side of the table closest to the window. "I'll take your order once I'm back with your coffee."

"Thank you."

Luke scanned the diner. He took note of a few other patrons, mainly couples and adults with children. He then peered outside and noticed a few pedestrians walking along the street, passing by the restaurant on their way to parts unknown.

These people look so content, so happy. They're just going about their lives in this little lakeside town. Why can't I just be happy?

The server came back to Luke's booth.

"Are you ready to order?"

"Yeah, sure. I'd like a stack of four pancakes with butter and syrup, two eggs, and two pieces of bacon, well done."

"How would you like your eggs?"

"Sunny side up."

"Alright, I'll put this in for you. Shouldn't take too long."

"Thanks."

I wonder how easy it would be for me to find a job up here. Maybe even work at a place like this, and rent a small apartment or something? Or maybe even a room out of somebody's house...but I dunno about that, I might drive them crazy since I need everything in its place.

Rachel gets so annoyed at me when I clean up. She says she can't ever find anything. That's because everything's in its place.

But anyway, I could literally start over again right here in Luna Pier...where nobody knows me and nobody would ever find me.

"Here you go!" Heather came back with breakfast, sitting it on the table in front of him.

"Thank you."

"You're welcome. Here's the check, too. Take your time, you'll pay up there at the register. Did you need anything else?"

"More coffee, that's it."

"Alright, I'll be right back."

As the server left to retrieve more coffee, Luke began to prepare his pancakes to eat by smearing butter onto the flapjacks and covering the stack with thick maple syrup. He then dug into the stack with a fork and took a large bite.

This is delicious. This diner reminds me of a restaurant up by UGL, Dave's Mooncakes, I think it was. I used to go there with AC all the time. They had awesome pancakes, and it was right by the Grand River. I miss those days.

"Here you go," the server said while providing Luke with a refill.

"Thanks."

"You bet."

"Heather, can I ask you something?"

She nodded, her netted brunette ponytail bouncing with her movements.

"How is it living up here?"

"Up here near the Ohio border?"

"Yeah."

"It's not bad. I mean, we used to have factory jobs either in Toledo or up in Detroit, but a lot of that's gone away now, so it's not easy for a lot of folks. But we make it work. It's quiet here in town; nobody really bothers you. Not a lot of crime like what you get in the cities. And we've got the lake. I wouldn't drink out of it if I were you, but it's nice to look at."

"I see. That's not bad."

"I like it. I guess I'm partial, though. I'm from here, born and raised. We all kind of know each other around here. You're not from the area, I figure."

"No, I'm from southern Ohio, uh…Losanti, but I did go to college up at Great Lakes."

"Oh, alright. My niece goes to Great Lakes. Nice school. She really likes it."

"Yeah, I graduated from there a few years ago. It was fun, I loved it."

"That's good. But yeah, around here near the border, it's not winning a 'best place to live' award, but I like it. It's home."

"Cool. Thanks!"

"You're welcome! Have a great day!"

"You too."

After a few minutes, Luke got up, paid for his meal at the register, and then returned to the lake to sit with his thoughts for a little while longer. This day was slightly warmer than the day before, but it was still fairly cold.

At dusk, he returned to the motel. When he entered his freshened room, he reclined on the neatly made bed and turned on the television. *Jeopardy!* was being broadcast on the old CRT screen. He watched, immersing himself in the various prompts on different topics and answers in the form of questions.

During the first commercial break, he found himself immersed in the ads.

Ha...'so easy a caveman can do it.' If only life were as easy as insurance.

Just then, reality set in and he grew panicked.

Oh shit, I don't have my cell phone! I forgot to bring it with me yesterday!

I hope I didn't worry Rachel...oh my God!

Well...I could just stay unreachable for a little while longer...

No, I can't do that. Waiting is gonna make it worse.

It's just delaying the inevitable.

He reached over to the solid beige telephone on the small polished wooden nightstand, picked up the receiver, and dialed a number. A woman's voice answered.

"Hello?"

"Rachel?"

"Luke? Where are you? What's going on? Where have you been?"

"Don't freak out Rach. I'm in Michigan right now, just inside the border."

"Michigan?!" Rachel screamed. He overheard muffled voices and movement in the background.

"Rachel...Rachel, calm down."

"Don't tell me to calm down! You just disappeared yesterday and you didn't come home last night and I've been worried sick and now you're telling me you're in Michigan and you want *me* to calm down? Are you serious right now?"

"I hear noise in the background. Where are you?"

"I'm at home, where *you* should be, Luke. I have you on speakerphone. I'm with my parents and your parents, and Lori and Sarah are here too. We're all stationed at the house."

"What? Your friends are there?"

"Of course they are. And Bible study has been praying around the clock for you to be found safe. Why are you in Michigan?"

Luke sighed. "Rachel, I don't wanna talk about it, especially with an audience. They don't need to know our business. And your Bible study? They *sure* don't need to know our business."

"I don't care what you don't want to talk about! You need to tell me what's going on!"

"I will tell you when I get home."

"No! You're going to tell me right now, Luke. I've been waiting for you long enough."

"I really don't wanna get into it. Don't make me talk about this. Not with my parents and everybody else being there."

"Luke! Out with it!"

He got choked up. "Rachel...I got a letter yesterday, it was from the school. They're expelling me."

She went dead silent. He could hear multiple gasps in the background.

"Hello?"

After a few more seconds, she found her voice. "I'm here. Get home. Now."

<hr />

"Damn, bro, that's rough," Paul commented.

Luke stared out the window. "It was a pretty low point in my life, I had never felt so embarrassed and ashamed in my life. I didn't know it at the time, but the worst was yet to come."

SPRINGFIELD
June 29-30, 2023

After another hour on the road, the men noticed they crossed into the city of Springfield, Illinois.

"Welcome to Springfield! Haha!" Paul exclaimed.

"Hell yeah!" Luke shouted. "Y'know, haven't seen Kyle in some time. Can't wait to see him."

"Me too. He's great. I still talk to him every so often. I'll give him a call and let him know we made it."

Paul clicked his way through the touchscreen on the dashboard, found Kyle's number, and initiated the call. The phone rang through the speakers, and after a few seconds, a deep masculine voice answered.

"Paulie!"

"Hey, Kyle! What's up?"

"Not a lot, dude. You're still coming?"

"Yeah, I'm here in town now. By the way, I'm on speaker in my car, and guess who's here with me?"

"You got Luke?"

"I sure do!"

"Awesome! Hey, Luke!"

"Hi, Kyle!"

"Yeah dude, it's been too long. Can't wait to see you guys."

"Same," Luke responded.

"Oh, by the way, you'll be just in time, boys. We're having a party this evening with some friends from the neighborhood and our church. We get together on the last Thursday of each month, and tonight, we're celebrating the beginning of summer. We're gonna be jamming all night. Paulie – you got your guitar, right?"

"Of course, man. I came prepared," Paul confirmed.

Luke interjected. "Bro, do you want us to run to the store and grab something for the party?"

A response came through the speakers. "Nah dude, you're good. You've come all this way; your presence is all that's needed."

"We'll be over there in another...let's see," Paul said while checking the map, "about twenty minutes it looks like."

"Yeah, that's great, dude. When you get here, park in the driveway behind my car."

"Sounds good, be there shortly."

"'Kay. See ya soon."

After twenty minutes, Luke and Paul found themselves in an older neighborhood filled with small late nineteenth and early twentieth-century homes. They slowed down in front of a two-story white Dutch colonial revival with dark green trim and large floor planters on the porch. Luke parked in the driveway behind a red Ford Focus, and the men got out of the truck. Paul pulled Katie out of the back seat.

The door opened, and a husky man emerged. He jogged down the green-painted porch stairs and gave the visitors a giant hug.

"Hey guys, good to see you!"

"Hi, Kyle!" Paul and Luke responded to their friend.

"Glad you came out here. You look great! Come on in!" He directed his arm towards the painted green and white door.

They walked into the home and were led into the living room to the right of the staircase. The living room was covered in fluffy beige wall-to-wall carpet and furnished with a light green sectional, matching lounge chair, and polished wood coffee table. A simple dark brown box sat atop the coffee table with a cross engraved in it. Two gold floor lamps with off-white lampshades sat in the room. On the walls, there hung a giant windcatcher and several framed photos.

"Have a seat, guys!" Kyle said. The men sat down, and he offered, "Do you want anything? I got juice, root beer, Heineken, Corona and water."

"Heineken for me," said Paul.

"Me, too," Luke responded.

"Two beers, coming right up!" said Kyle. "Oh, and by the way, in a couple hours, we're gonna have a few more friends over from the neighborhood, and we'll have food out back. Myron's been smoking some ribs since early this morning, and we're gonna have hot dogs, burgers, veggie patties, and probably some other stuff. Does that sound good?"

"Yeah, that's perfect, thanks so much!" Paul said.

"Thanks, man, sounds great," Luke said.

Kyle then disappeared to grab drinks. He then returned with three beers and a bowl of chips, gave one bottle to each of the guys, kept one, and placed the yellow plastic bowl on the table.

"So how was your trip?" Kyle asked while getting comfortable in his recliner.

"Smooth, not bad at all," Luke answered.

"Yeah Kyle, it's been good. I drove up to Losanti from Jacksonville, got Luke, and then we've been heading west...on a road trip, 'cause why not. And, we figured we couldn't do that without swinging by here and seeing you, man," Paul responded.

"I hear you, brother. Glad you did. So, Luke, last I heard you were in vet school and got married. How's everything these days?"

"It's been alright. Vet school didn't work out, neither did the marriage."

Kyle's face frowned in sympathy. "Oh, I'm sorry about that."

"It's alright. I've been okay; I've been surviving. Life happens."

"It does, I understand. Plans change."

"So true."

"I get it. Back when we were at Great Lakes, I was bound and determined to go into music ministry. Things took a turn along the way, and now I'm a nurse tech at Springfield General Hospital."

"That's gotta be a hard job, brother," Luke said, taking a swig of beer.

"It is, but you know what? I love it. It gives me a way to help people when they're at their most vulnerable."

"That's admirable, but it's a huge shift. Why did you decide to make that kind of change?"

Kyle looked over to Paul and narrowed his eyes. "Paulie, I'm surprised you didn't tell him."

"Nah, brother. Not my story to tell, but Luke's good people."

"Luke, I'm gay," Kyle revealed.

Luke took a second, much closer look at the photos on the wall. The largest one was a studio photo of Kyle embracing a lean, deep russet-toned man with a shiny bald head and black oval spectacles, both in white suits with an airbrushed outdoor background.

"Wow, okay, cool." Luke affirmed.

"Myron is my husband. We've been married for six years now. He's the best thing that ever happened to me."

"I tell you, Kyle, you seem truly happy. I don't remember you being this chill when we were in college."

"I truly am. I'm a lot more at peace with my life, but it took work to get there. And a crisis of faith, too."

Paul chimed in. "It's funny you mention faith. I mean, Kyle...you were one of the hardest-core Christians in CK, especially when it came to relationships. Like pro-literalism, pro-purity culture, all of that."

"And that's the thing, dude – I still love Jesus, but I had to figure out what that looked like as a gay man. You guys know, coming from that conservative Christian background, they tell you being gay is a sin, and they trot out the same six Bible verses to prove it."

"Yeah, man," Luke responded.

"And to be honest with you, I pretty much always knew I was attracted to men, but I was a big tryhard. I didn't want to face my truth because it would mean I would lose everything and everybody. And when I came out, that's kind of what happened."

"Ooh, that's awful. I'm sorry, man."

"Luke, don't be. It was hard to come out with the reality of who I was, who I am, but it needed to happen. At one point, I was engaged to a woman my head pastor at the time set me up with. She was a lovely person, but I got to the point where I felt like I was lying to myself and wasting her life, and I couldn't even look at myself in the mirror. So, I had to end that relationship and then come out."

"Wow, that's heavy."

"For sure. I got kicked off the worship team, then they excommunicated me. I lost friends. I don't talk to most of the people I knew in CK anymore, including Greg Travis and Brother Craig."

"Seriously?"

"Yeah. You knew how they were. It shouldn't be a shock."

"You're right. They were so hardcore in their beliefs. No room for any thoughts or interpretation outside of what they thought was right. Greg would always say, 'It's in the book!'"

The friends all laughed.

"God, he would always say that!" Paul added.

"Yeah, that was so 'Greg.' His way of looking at things was the only way...his way or the highway. But I can't say too much about that. I was the same way. It was how I protected myself," Kyle explained.

"For sure...that makes total sense. So, how did your family take you coming out?" Luke asked.

"Oh boy...some of my relatives stopped speaking to me. My older brother still doesn't talk to me, and it's been over a decade since I've been out. My parents had a hard time with it at first. They've come around now though. They love Myron. But coming out was so tough at first, and then having my crisis of faith was the toughest. I wasn't sure if I could be Christian and gay, or if it was worth the effort."

"Wow. Losing your faith is so hard, especially it being such a huge part of your life. I get at least that part of it. After my divorce, maybe even before that, it just wasn't working out, y'know, being a Christian. Still trying to figure that part out."

"I hear you, Luke, but I promise you, it's worth the effort, at least it was for me. I channeled my zeal for being a 'good Christian man' into figuring out if there was a way God would still accept somebody like me. Was there a place in the faith for me?"

Luke and Paul nodded.

"Through that, I really dug into those Bible verses that had been used against people like me, and you know what? Come to find out, a lot of those verses have been used out of context, but more than that, I discovered that I can still be a Christian, I can still love Jesus, and at the same time not have to deny the reality of who I am."

"Wow, that's awesome Kyle," Luke responded.

"Yeah, I'm so thankful that Jesus didn't let go of me when I thought I would have to let go of him. I ended up at the church I'm at now, it's an open and affirming church, Bounty United Church of Christ. That's where I met Myron, and the rest is history. Dude, if I could do it all over again, I would in a heartbeat," Kyle shared, radiating with happiness.

"You know, Kyle, I remember when we reconnected, and you told me everything. It made me think a lot about my son, Danny. He hasn't officially come out to me...he stopped speaking to me for other reasons...you know, the divorce, but I've known for a long time that he's gay. It's part of what makes him 'him,' and I accept that. It doesn't change anything for me."

"Your son having an accepting parent is a good thing, man. Even if he doesn't know it now, I believe it will make all the difference one day."

"I hope so. You know, I wish for him to be in the kind of environment that will accept him and not judge him. That's one of the things that worries me about church these days...I would hate to turn back to the church and then end up in a place that wouldn't accept my son. I don't want him to go through the same things you did."

"Dude, that's understandable. If you do ever decide to go that route, give me a call, and I can help you find a church down in Florida that's open and affirming."

"I may take you up on that one of these days, man. But right now, I'll be honest. I can't say I'm where you're at when it comes to faith. At this point, I'm probably more spiritual than anything else," Paul mused, sipping on his lager. "Man, I still got a lot of mess to sort through. I wish I could be at peace like you, but I hope to get there at some point."

"Yeah brother, it's not easy, but it's truly worth doing...working through everything, and finding your way to what you truly believe at your core...what will make you whole. Nothing is hopeless until we're six feet underground."

After nearly an hour of additional conversation, Myron came inside.

"Sunshine!" Myron called from the kitchen. "Ribs are resting. Bobby and 'em will be over in a little bit."

"Sounds great, thanks Ronny! Come here, I want you to meet my friends from college."

Into the living room came a slim man wearing an orange apron with "mmm-mmm grits!" printed on the front, covering his summer clothing.

"Paul, Luke, this is Myron. Ronny – these are my friends from Great Lakes I was telling you about."

"Hey!" he came up to them and shook their hands. "It's great to finally meet y'all. Kyle told me a lot about you."

"Good things, I hope," Paul quipped.

"Of course, bruh!" Myron laughed, flashing his pearly whites.

There was a knock at the door. Kyle got up to answer it, and several people entered the home, some bringing dishes. The married couple greeted them warmly.

All were ushered into the backyard, where two long picnic tables were waiting, along with a side table designated for the food. Kyle and Myron brought out dinner and refreshments. Myron announced, "It's time to say grace."

Everyone, including Luke and Paul, stood in a circle around the tables. Myron projected, "Dear Lord, bless the food we have prepared, we pray it nourishes our bodies, and that the fellowship we have here tonight nourishes our souls. In Jesus' name. Amen."

The crowd said "Amen."

The partygoers took paper plates and plasticware, helped themselves to the meal, and milled about. Kyle introduced his old friends to his new ones. Paul gravitated towards the musicians, while Luke found himself chatting for much of the night with Myron, who, like Luke, was a huge fan of travel and nature. The food was delicious, and the night festive, with rounds of horseshoes and shuffleboard. Then, the hosts invited the party to the basement.

"Paulie," Kyle said, "Grab your guitar."

The open floor basement was finished with bean bags and large pillow cushions. In one corner was a slightly raised platform with a drum set, keyboard, and small sound system. The scent of crisp patchouli wafted past Luke's nostrils. The party took seats at the bar and along the floor. A woman named came up to play bass, and another friend of Kyle and Myron's named Julian also came forward to play keyboard. Kyle would be the drummer.

Kyle went up to Paul, who was sitting on a barstool next to Luke, and said, "Brother, I want you to come play with us."

Paul smiled, "I would love to. What are you all playing?"

"We don't have a setlist. We just like to jam out – folk rock, reggae – that kind of vibe. Think of it like what we used to do sometimes before large group back at Great Lakes."

Paul then sat down his guitar case and took out Katie, a maple and spruce acoustic grand auditorium guitar stained in the color "Pacific Blue," and strapped it on his body.

Julian approached him and studied his guitar.

"Ooh, that's a beaut, brother."

"Thanks, man."

He then pulled his neat, ebony locs in a bunch along his slender back, and looked straight at him. "Let me hear you play it...wanna get an idea of what we're working with."

"Oh, for sure," Paul happily complied.

Luke assured Julian. "Believe me – you're in for a treat."

Paul then played the song 'Drifting' by Andy McKee. The melodic tune led Thalia to approach the men. Her deep brown eyes sparkled, and her mouth curled upwards as she listened to the song and bobbed her head.

After he was finished, she cooed, "Sounds beautiful."

He smiled. "Thanks, Thalia."

"Damn, that's good," Julian asserted. "With you joining us, our jam sesh will be kicked up a notch."

The band started playing. The sound was pure synergy, and the diverse crowd bobbed, cheered, and danced to the melodies they heard. Luke, feeling very much at home, captured the magic on film.

While sound asleep, Luke felt a tap on his shoulder.

"Lukie baby," a sing-song voice softly spoke into his left ear.

He slowly opened his eyes. A tiny bit of sunlight was shining through a basement window. Seeing Paul kneeling over him, he chuckled quietly.

"Let's get ready man," Paul switched back to his normal but toned-down voice. "We should be going."

"But I wanna stay here," Luke mumbled. "This was so cool."

"It was amazing, wasn't it? Aren't you glad you went on this trip with me?"

"Paulie, you were right."

"I know," he responded with a smile. "And we're not done. We're still going west, brother."

"But this *is* west."

"No, I mean *west* west. This was just one stop. Now go get ready. There's a full bath upstairs on the first floor. No one's in there yet so you'll wanna jump in there before everybody else wakes up."

Luke sat up and scanned the room to take note of several of Kyle and Myron's other guests fast asleep on large plush cushions. He then rose to his feet and quietly took his toiletries into the bathroom to use the toilet, clean up, shower, and shave.

An hour later, Luke and Paul were leaving. Kyle was awake and dressed to see them off.

"It was so wonderful seeing you both. So happy you came to visit!" He hugged Luke, then he gave Paul a giant hug. "It was so awesome being able to jam out with you one more time."

"Yeah, that was sweet, brother. Amazing. It was like old times, but better. We've gotta come back sometime."

"Door's always open."

"Thanks, man."

"So, Paulie, you guys are now heading down to visit Morgan, right?"

Paul silently shook his head, gestured with his hand, and mouthed, "Shut up!"

"What?!" Luke exclaimed. "Paulie, you didn't say we were going to see Morgan."

"Dude, my bad." He turned to Paul "I'm sure I heard you wrong. We did party hard last night."

"You're so full of it man," Luke looked at Kyle and laughed.

"I got this, Kyle. Don't worry about it. It's all good," Paul reassured him.

"Alright. It was truly fun, guys. Take care and safe travels."

After the friends packed up the truck, Paul took the wheel. Kyle waved from the front porch as they pulled away.

"The fuck? The actual fuck, Paul? Are you shitting me? Morgan?" Luke exclaimed.

"No, I'm for real. Chill bro. It's all good."

"No, it's not 'all good.' That's gonna be weird as fuck."

"No bro, it's all good, trust me. Morgan knows we're coming. She wanted to see you. She's happily married, nothing's gonna happen. Her husband knows we're coming and he's fine with it."

"Sure about that?"

"Yeah. A hundred percent."

MORGAN
June 30, 2023

"Okay, good news," Paul said as he returned to the Wrangler, where Luke was sitting in the passenger seat wiping down his camera. "They're gonna let us check in early. Good thing, 'cause I talked to Morgan, and she and her husband invited us to a dinner cruise on the Mississippi. The steamboat takes off at five o'clock, so we need to get cleaned up and wear something nice."

"Oh wow, that's fancy."

"Hell yeah," Paul said. "I got the keycards, let's go, room 313."

The two unloaded and hauled their luggage inside the clean three-star hotel off the highway just outside the city of Saint Louis. They took the elevator to their floor and entered the suite, which included two queen beds, a flat-screen television, a yellow synthetic leather sofa, and a small kitchenette.

"Ah, this is nice," Luke marveled.

"Sure is. Figured we could use more comfortable sleep."

The men spread out on their respective beds.

Paul muttered, "I'm so tired, guess I'm getting old, but I'm looking forward to some nice sleep later."

"I hear you. We have been doing a lot of traveling."

Paul rolled over to face Luke. "So yeah…why are you so freaked out about seeing Morgan again? I mean, it was twenty years ago, you dumped her, she moved on to somebody else. It seems mutual enough."

"See that's the thing, Paulie. It wasn't. My parents made me break up with her."

Paul snickered. "Really? Shit, Luke. At this point, I shouldn't be surprised. Your parents literally run your life."

"Damn, bro. Ouch."

"It's true, man. Sorry, but it's the truth."

"Yeah, I guess you're not wrong."

"So, I just got the tail end of things when it came to you and her, but I don't think I ever asked you how you got together in the first place?"

Luke turned to his side to look at Paul. "So, you know she and I went to Denbytown High together, right?"

———◆◇◆———

September 1997

The sun hung high in the sky on a bright Friday afternoon, as seventeen-year-old Luke walked down the street from his home to meet up with his friends, Caleb and Tony.

He walked up the path towards the porch to Caleb's home, where he and Tony were waiting. "You ready to go to the mall?"

"Yeah, bruh. Of course. I just got my paycheck from the Swirl Shack, so I'm gonna get Bone's *Art of War* CD," Tony said.

"Bone is good shit," Caleb opined.

"Uh...yeah, that Bone guy, he's good," Luke muttered.

"Luke...you don't know who we're talking about, do you?" Tony sussed out.

"I do...some singer guy, right?"

"What's your favorite Bone song?"

"Um...all of them?"

"Dude," Caleb explained, "Let me help you out. It's not one guy. They're a group, you know, Bone Thugs-n-Harmony. They're hip hop."

"You know the song 'Look Into My Eyes' from the *Batman & Robin* movie?" Tony asked.

"Yeah, it's everywhere," Luke said.

"That's Bone."

"Oh, okay. I've heard them. I guess I didn't know whose song it was. My parents don't let me listen to rap."

"Mine don't either."

"Neither do mine," Caleb added, "but we're seniors now. It's not like they can stop us."

Luke reminded his friends, "You know how my dad is. He's crazy as he—"

"Dudes!" Tony interrupted with his index finger extended. "Look over there!"

The boys had their attention drawn to a moving truck in front of a colonial across the street and three doors down from Caleb's bungalow. "Oh, looks like a new family's moving into the old Schoenburger house."

While burly men brought boxes and furniture into the home, a teen girl tended to a small group of running children.

"Ah, that girl's fine..." Tony noticed.

"Oh, yes," Caleb agreed in a low voice.

"How do you know?" Luke asked. "She looks alright, but for all we know, she could be their mom."

"Come on, guy," Caleb looked at him. "She's gotta be the babysitter. She's Black, and the kids look like they can melt in the sun. Totally the babysitter, maybe the nanny."

"Eh, okay. Anyway, what are we waiting for? Let's get to the mall."

On Monday, Denbytown High School was in session for the first week of the 1997-1998 school year. Several teenagers filed into room 128 for second period advanced placement English class. A woman in a navy pencil skirt and sky blue sweater sat atop the metal teacher's desk welcoming in her students, pointing them to the pile of books next to her. "Take one before you sit down," she repeated.

Luke sat in the row closest to the windows, halfway between the chalkboard and the back of the room. Caleb sat behind him and Tony sat next to him.

"Ah, *Lord of the Flies...*" Luke quipped as he noticed the cover of the book he picked up. "That's bleak."

Then, Luke felt a tap on his shoulder. He looked behind him to see Caleb nodding to his right.

"What?"

"Look, dude – it's the girl we saw on Friday."

A teen girl wearing a pink top and matching pink-hued jeans was approaching their general direction. She stopped short of reaching the boys, plopped her beige backpack on the floor and slid in the desk in front of Luke. She adjusted her long, jet black hair with her smooth sienna-shaded hands.

"She's even hotter close up," Caleb whispered.

The girl turned around and asked in a silky, self-assured voice, "Hey...do you happen to have a pen I can borrow? I forgot my pens in my locker and it's too late for me to run and get one."

"Ye-yeah, sure." Luke quickly found one in his black backpack and handed it to her.

"Thanks so much...uh..."

"Luke."

"Luke...thank you. I'll give it back after class."

"No problem, don't worry about it."

Tony looked over at his friends, then at the girl. "She's fine, dawg."

Luke rolled his eyes at his ogling friends. "Calm down, guys."

"You're just saying that because you'd never ask her out," Caleb snarked.

The woman then stood up and pulled her long red hair into a quick bun before speaking up. "Class – I'm Miss Meyer and I'll be your AP English Literature teacher. If you haven't already picked up a copy of *Lord of the Flies*, raise your hand and I'll give you one."

A few students raised their hands, and Miss Meyer provided each with a copy.

"I'll need to take roll right quick, and then we'll get started."

The teacher took attendance. After calling out and marking several students present or absent, she called, "Anthony Greene?"

Tony raised his hand.

"Morgan Haas?"

The girl in front of Luke raised her hand.

After several more names, she called, "Luke Phillips?"

Luke was busy staring out the window, thinking of the girl who borrowed his pen.

"Luke?"

"Oh...yes!" he exclaimed, raising his hand. His friends chuckled.

Once class was over, the bell rang, and the students flooded out of the room to rush to their next class.

"Hey – here you go," Morgan turned to him, pen in hand.

"Oh, thanks."

"Thank *you*." She turned and left the room with the others.

After school was dismissed, Luke left with his friends and headed for home.

"Sixth period anatomy is gonna kick my ass," Caleb commented.

"I'm sure Luke can help you out," Tony offered.

"What are you volunteering *me* for?" Luke spoke up.

"You're on track to be valedictorian. Of course you can help him out."

Luke then noticed the new girl walking ahead of them by herself.

"I think I'm gonna go ahead and see if Morgan wants somebody to walk her home."

"You know you're just gonna get friendzoned that way, right?" Caleb warned.

"Just like you always do," Tony added. "I love you, man, but you're such a lame."

"You're what they call a 'nice guy.' Hot girls like her say they want a nice guy, but they don't. You wanna play it cool. If you walk her home, you're just gonna be *nice*."

"She's way out of your league. She's gonna be hooking up with the captain of the football team next week, bruh. I promise."

Luke shrugged. "Who said I wanted to get with her?"

With that, he sped ahead and caught up with her.

"Hi, Morgan!"

"Oh – you're the guy from AP English. Luke, right?"

"Yeah. Y'know, I happened to see you walking by yourself, and I just wanted to see if you'd like some company."

She flashed a bright, warm smile. "Eh, sure, why not?"

Luke grinned. "And that was pretty much all she wrote."

"Valedictorian, huh?" Paul noted.

"Ugh...I almost got there, but I ended up being salutatorian instead."

"Still an accomplishment. You never told me that."

"Eh, it wasn't a big deal. I got an 'A-minus' in Spanish instead of an 'A,' so I missed it by a sliver. Since Trey was valedictorian of his class, my parents saw it as yet another way I failed, and they blamed Morgan for it. Said she was a 'worldly distraction.'"

"Jesus." Paul shook his head.

"That's how they were, though. Still are. If I give a hundred percent, they ask me why I didn't give a hundred and ten."

"So, changing the subject – when you first saw Morgan move in back in high school, who were the kids she was watching?"

"Oh, those were her nieces and nephews. Her older brothers and sisters were in town helping out with the move, so they brought their kids. Since Morgan was the youngest, she was the designated babysitter."

"That makes sense. And I guess you guys didn't know at the time she was adopted."

"Yeah. It all makes sense now – hindsight is twenty-twenty."

"So, you said your parents made you dump her. How'd that happen?"

"See, they were weird about who I dated, and they didn't like the idea of me dating her. She and I were in different churches, and they didn't care for her church. And y'know, they had other reasons."

"Other reasons?"

"Yeah – I'm gonna get to that. Anyway, her parents...well, they didn't want her dating at all. Neither of us went to prom, but we snuck out and went over to the park. We laid on the grass and watched the stars – that was back before Denbytown installed streetlights. Shocked neither of us got found out."

"That's nice, man. High school love and shit."

"Yeah, something like that. So, we decided we were gonna both go to UGL and figured we could be free to be together that way. It was out of state, they had programs we were both interested in. Neither of our families had any idea. I went there because of her, she went there because of me. But we didn't tell our parents."

"Yeah, of course not."

"We went to UGL, decided to do CK together since it was an interdenominational campus ministry, so it didn't matter that I was Baptist and she was Christian Reformed."

"I get it, man."

"But a couple of things happened to where everything fell apart."

"Oh, really?"

"Yeah. So, first of all, her parents were planning a move up to Niles. You know that's where they're originally from, and she didn't know they were moving up there until we were already at Great Lakes."

"Oof."

"Yeah, I know. Now Paulie, that might not've been the end of the world. But see, my dumb ass got careless."

December 1998

The navy Saab station wagon pulled into the rounded driveway of the Phillips' abode in Denbytown. Luke parked, stepped out of the car, and retrieved his jet-black duffel bag and matching backpack from the hatch. He used his key to enter the front door of the house.

"Anybody home?" he called out while standing in the foyer. There was no answer. He looked around, breathed in the smell of cinnamon from his mother's candles and pine cleaner from the spotless hardwood floors, and made his way upstairs to his bedroom to drop off his things.

Luke's bedroom appeared the exact same way he had left it when leaving for college mere months previously. The beige walls included a framed poster of the Arizona desert, another one of sports cars, and a calendar still dated August 1998 hanging above his cleared slick oak desk. He changed it over to December, then sat on his bed.

He leaned over to the front pocket of his backpack and removed a pack of color photos he had developed. Flipping through them, he smiled as he perused the glossy snapshots of his first semester at the University of the Great Lakes. These included photos of his new college friends Paul and Alyssa, as well as another friend, Terah Sanders, and their fun activities and antics. He also thought fondly of the times he enjoyed with Morgan, immortalized in print. He missed her and could not wait to be back on campus.

Eh, Mom and Dad must be out. Why not just give Morgan a quick call? I don't think she left for break yet.

Luke sat his head on his freshly laundered pillow and leaned over to the cordless telephone sitting on the oak nightstand next to the twin bed. He picked up the phone and began to dial the numbers to make the long-distance call. After a few rings, a young female voice answered.

"Hello?"

"Morgs, it's me, Luke. I made it back to Losanti."

"Oh...hi, sweetie. I'm glad you made it home. Why are you calling me?"

"Because..." he paused, and then continued, "I miss you."

"I miss you too, but we agreed not to call each other, we were gonna wait until we're both back at campus. It's not worth chancing it."

"My parents aren't home. So, I figured, what's the harm?"

She audibly sighed. "Okay, I suppose. So anyway, what do you want for Christmas?"

"I can't think of anything, honestly. Surprise me."

"I'll try, but I don't get it. I hate surprises."

Click.

"What's that?" Morgan asked.

"What?"

"The noise."

"Eh, I dunno, Morgan, probably wasn't anything."

Click.

"Maybe it's crackling on the line. Lemme call you back."

"Sure."

"Love you," he said quickly.

"Love you too," Morgan responded softly.

Luke rushed to hang up the phone. *Hopefully, it was crackling on the line. Mom and Dad can't be home. I didn't even hear the door.*

A moment later, his bedroom door opened. "Dear, you're home. Why didn't you let me know once you made it?"

"Uh, you could've knocked."

"Don't get smart, Luke."

"Sorry, Mom."

Libby sighed. "You could've let me know you were home."

"I did, I walked in the house and called out to you, but you didn't say anything."

"That's because I was in the cellar with your father working on preparing the flowers to plant for spring. You didn't check the garage?"

Shit.

"Anyway, who was that you were talking to on the phone?"

"Uh, um, it was my friend Paul from school."

She gave him an annoyed look. "No, it sounded like a girl, and you said 'Morgan.' I heard everything you said. Don't tell me it's that girl you got all entangled with while you were in high school."

Luke hung his head.

"It *is* that girl. You're in college, there are plenty of other girls there. I know your school is secular, but there must be Christians there. You joined a Christian student ministry, aren't there some nice girls up there who love the Lord?"

"Morgan *is* a Christian, Mom."

Libby shook her head. "We've been over this. When it's time for the rapture, you want to be ready for Jesus to take you up to heaven, so you don't have to deal with the horrors of the end of the world. Morgan's family doesn't believe in the rapture. You would be unequally yoked."

"I think the Reformed Church does believe in the end times."

"Sure, they might, but not in the rapture, I know that. Pastor Al preached on it when he did the Holy Heretic series at church. You heard him preach about it last year. If you're left behind, you'll have to live through the tribulation before God ends the world, and you don't want that...but it's up to you."

"It'll be fine."

"No, it won't. You'll be unequally yoked with her, and when that happens, she will drag you down and take you away from Christ and his truth." Libby's voice began to crack. "That's not what your father and I want for you." She then left her son's room and closed the door.

A few hours later, the Phillips family, including Luke, his mother, and his father, sat down for their evening meal. Tilapia was served, along with long-grain wild rice and chopped broccoli. Cam was on his third can of Guinness while the others had Coke.

"Son, your mother told me you were talking to *that girl* Morgan."

Luke sighed. "Yessir."

"What did your mother say?" Cam asked while eating a forkful of rice.

"Mom said I shouldn't be with her. We're unequally yoked."

"She's right. Y'know, it's not a good fit."

Here we go. Another lecture on religion.

"We're Christians. We love everybody. We don't make a difference based on color or anything. We don't care if somebody's white, black, yellow, or purple, you treat people with respect. Your mother and I have taught you that."

Luke silently nodded.

Cam took a long sip of beer. "But culture is different."

What is Dad talking about?

"Your mother and I know Morgan was raised in a red-blooded American family. The Haases, they're very nice people. They're great neighbors, they keep their house and yard neat, they're very friendly. It's a real act of Christian love that Jim and his wife have opened their home to orphaned children. But that girl was born the way she is. No matter what, you can't take the culture out of her. It's innate to them."

Luke squirmed in his seat.

"You can be friendly with her. Say 'hi' to her. But dating her? *Marrying* her? No. Not happening. That's over."

"What?"

"You heard me. That's over. And if it gets back to me that you're still with her, we're no longer paying for your college, you can no longer live here, you're cut off completely. We love you, but we're not supporting you living as a degenerate." This was Cam's final word on the matter. The rest of the meal was eaten in silence.

After dinner was over, Luke quietly cleaned up his spot at the table and began to walk upstairs.

"Come back here," Cam called out to his son.

Luke trudged back downstairs.

"Call her now and tell her it's over."

"Yessir." He turned toward the staircase.

"No, you'll do it right here." Cam pointed to the living room.

To Luke, the few steps to the living room sofa felt like the longest mile of his life. He sat down, and Libby handed him a large cordless telephone. He dialed the phone number, and Morgan answered.

"Hello?"

"Hi, Morgan, it's Luke."

"Hi, sweetie! I'm getting ready to leave for home, but when we get back to cam—"

"Morgan?"

"Yes...what's up?"

"We need to talk."

"Huh? About what?"

Luke was quiet for a moment.

"Luke?"

Cam and Libby stared daggers into their youngest son.

Luke exhaled hard. "Morgan, this isn't going to work out."

"What? What do you mean?"

"It's not gonna work out. We're too different. I can't..."

"Are you...are you breaking up with me?"

"Yes, Morgan. We can be friends, but we...we're over."

Luke could hear Morgan breathing, and then the dial tone blaring in his ear.

"That's wild, man."

Luke nodded. "Yeah, I know."

"You know what the funny part is?" Paul mused.

"What?"

"Your mom felt so strongly about dispensationalism, you know, Jesus coming back to earth, the rapture and all that. But you know Southern Baptists aren't supposed to drink?"

"They would always push what the pastor said, even now they do that shit. And I know for sure he's preached about alcohol being sinful. He's even said the wine Jesus drank was grape juice."

The men both laughed.

"But half the damn fridge at the house is full of beer and they got cabinets full of wine and the hard shit."

"For real, brother?"

"Yeah man, for real. Been like that for as long as I can remember. I knew it was hypocritical, but my parents always said there were some things we kept in the family. They would say these things weren't other people's business, even the church folks."

Paul turned to stretch out on his bed. "I'm curious, Luke. How much of your parents' problem with Morgan was her family's church, and how much of it was the color of her skin?"

"Ooh, that's a good question. I think Mom cared more about the religion. Dad – well, he made it clear what he thought. The weird thing is, though, he never talked like that before, and hasn't since. So, it was a shock to me. I don't know if it was the beer talking, or how he really felt."

"Alcohol is a truth serum."

"True. Now, lemme ask you this. When you think back to all the women you've been with..."

"Shit, man – you make me sound like a manwhore."

"Well, Paulie..."

"Yeah, you're right, I was a bit of a manwhore in my day," Paul admitted, snickering.

"'In my day?' C'mon, man! I saw how you were undressing Thalia with your eyes last night."

"I mean, sure – but she was hot, and she can play a mean bass. Besides, she was checking me out too."

"Yeah, I noticed that. Did you get her number?"

"Nah."

"Why not? You're single."

"Sure, but she's Kyle's friend, I don't want things to get strange."

Luke nodded. "I get it. So anyway, when you've gotten into relationships, did you ever have any problems with their parents?"

"Uh..." Paul started to think back. "Occasionally, but not due to being Asian, at least as far as I know, if that's what you're getting at."

"Yeah, that's what I mean, since, y'know, Morgan's half Korean."

"She is, but I would imagine if I were also half Black like her, I might have a different answer."

"Ooh, I see what you're saying. Anyway, the whole point of me deciding to go to UGL to begin with was to be with her, and then I had to let her go. By the time I could do what I wanted, she had already moved on."

"Man, you could always do what you wanted. It wouldn't have been easy, but you had choices."

"True, but I was young, and it was hard to see it back then. Maybe that's why I still think of her sometimes, even though we've been broken up since 1998. God, I can't believe it's been that long."

"A quarter century."

"Shit. I think to myself, what if I chose to be with her anyway? Sure, I would lose my parents' support, but would I be happier? I don't know."

"Yeah, brother, who's to say?"

"But then again, I'm glad I stayed at UGL after the breakup. You and I became best friends, and I met a lot of other great people there. Y'know, I wouldn't have met AC at all if my relationship with Morgan continued past the first semester."

"Ann started coming to CK that first year, though."

"No...I mean, yeah she did, but it wasn't until later in the school year."

"Oh, I forgot about that."

"Yeah. Terah started coming to CK first. She came in around the same time we did, and that's how we met."

Paul nodded.

"Then, the semester after I broke up with Morgan, I took the English prereq with Terah. Originally, I was signed up for a different course during that time slot, but after Morgan and I broke up, I swapped out the course so I didn't have to see her, and I could try to get over her."

"Oh, I see. That makes sense. Funny how life works."

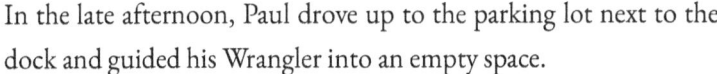

In the late afternoon, Paul drove up to the parking lot next to the dock and guided his Wrangler into an empty space.

"You ever see those douchebags who double-park their trucks?"

"Yeah, man."

"I'll be honest, I've thought about it. I mean, I love this thing," Paul said, softly rubbing on the waxed dashboard with his hand. "But there's levels to douchebaggery. I'm not quite on that level."

The men left the truck, ready for the evening's festivities. Before heading for the dock, they stood around and observed their surroundings. Luke had prime scenery to film, and he took full advantage.

"The Saint Louis Arch — the gateway to the West, brother," Paul remarked.

"For sure," Luke nodded while filming the arch and the exterior of the riverboat.

They walked to the dock, provided the cruise attendants with their tickets on their cell phones to be scanned, and then stepped aboard. The guys headed to the bar next to the entrance to the boat and sat down, ordering stiff drinks and waiting for Morgan and her husband to arrive.

Luke recited while nursing a glass of Evan Williams bourbon mixed with Coke, "Liquor before beer, never fear."

"Beer before liquor, never sicker." Paul then giggled, sipping his Old Fashioned.

Ten minutes later, they heard a woman's voice carrying along the starboard side of the boat. "Luke! Paulie!" The men turned around to see a slight, toned woman with deep golden skin, burnished brown eyes, and dark hair in a pixie cut with sweeping bangs.

The men stood up and hugged Morgan. She then brought forward a towering, stocky man with smooth chestnut skin.

"Guys, I want you to meet my husband, Thomas. Sweetie, this is Luke and Paul."

"Nice to meet you," Thomas greeted them with a deep Midwestern voice and a solid handshake.

After the friends paid for their cocktails, the four began their walk to the dining area. Luke held Paul back, outside earshot of the married couple.

"Paulie," Luke asked in a hushed tone, "I thought Morgan was with some professor guy from Russia?"

"Nah, man. I dunno what happened to him. I guess plans changed. You know how it is."

"That's for sure."

The group sat down together at a white linen-lined table with a lit candle in the middle, Thomas holding out a silver Chiavari chair for his wife to sit in before taking his seat.

"So, I hear Morgan knows y'all from college?"

She corrected him. "Sweetie, Paulie and I met in college, but I've known Luke since high school."

"Yeah, that's right bae, my bad," Thomas replied.

"So, how's your trip so far?" Morgan asked.

"It's been great," Paul responded. "Came up from Florida to get Luke in Losanti, and we stopped in Illinois to see Kyle Tracey."

"Oh, cool! How's he doing?"

"He's really good."

"I'm happy to hear it. Last I heard, he got married and he and his husband are part of a progressive ministry up there."

"Yeah. We got a chance to meet the hubby and some of their friends. We had a wonderful time. So how have things been here?"

"Good, really good. Thomas and I have been married for fifteen years now. We have four kids — they're thirteen, twelve, ten, and seven."

"All boys," Thomas chimed in, smiling.

"Yes – I'm a boy mom!" Morgan took out her cell phone and flipped it to proudly show her friends pictures of her sons.

"I have two kids, a girl and a boy, they're grown though, nineteen and eighteen. Raising them was hard enough, but four boys? How is it?" Paul asked.

"Yeah, it's not easy. They're good, well-behaved kids, but they are boys, so they're very active. And of course, I always want to protect them. They're my pride and joy."

"They're our pride and joy. We're raising up solid young men," Thomas added.

"And Thomas is such an involved dad. He takes them to their practices and games, he helps them with their homework, guides them as they grow into manhood. I'm lucky," she gushed, holding her spouse's left arm.

"Morgan's the best – she's an excellent wife and such a great mom to the boys. We make a perfect team, don't we, bae?"

"We do. Thanks, sweetie. It's nice to get a night free, though. The kids are with Thomas' parents while we're out here."

"That's very nice," Paul said. "So, Thomas, I heard you're a former Marine?"

"Yeah, did two tours in Afghanistan. Honorably discharged as an E-4 Corporal."

"Thank you for your service," Luke said to Thomas.

Thomas nodded. "So, after the Marines, I moved to New York, it sounded cool at the time, went to City College for a minute, studied business."

"Is that how you met Morgan?" Paul asked.

"Yeah. It was just random. I was living in Prospect Heights, and I was waiting on a train headed for work, I was working down at the College at the time while I was in school, I remember it clear as day, it was a Saturday. And I saw this girl, she looked real, real good, and I guess as I was checking her out, she kinda noticed..."

"I sure did!" Morgan interjected, laughing. "You made it way too obvious!"

"Yeah, I was trying not to, but I wasn't as good at checking her out on the sly as I thought I was. She saw me, and she gave me a smile back. So, I stepped to her and started chatting her up, and that was a wrap. We started seeing each other, but then I wanted to move back to Saint Louis, you know, this is where I'm from. So, she came with me."

"I did." Then Morgan added, "But I told him I wasn't moving down here with him until he put a ring on it."

"Yeah, that makes sense," Paul said. "Alyssa was the same way. I got a job in Florida, and I wanted her to come with me, but she wouldn't unless we got married. I get it."

"Yeah, we do what we gotta do for the ladies we love," Thomas said.

"Yeah..."

"So, got married, we came down here together, I'm in real estate and we have investments on the side, it allows us to live comfortably, and Morgan gets to be home with the kids. We volunteer, we give back to the community. It's good – we have a good, fulfilling life."

The server, dressed in a black button-down dress top and black pants, approached the table.

"Hello, Lady and Gentlemen, the first course will be brought to you shortly. What would you like to drink?"

Morgan spoke first. "I would like a Moscato, please."

"For you sir?" the server said, gesturing toward Thomas.

"I'll have a Pinot Noir."

The server then went to Luke.

"Uh, I'll have a Merlot."

"And for you sir?"

Paul responded, "Hmm, I'll have a Cabernet."

After the server left the table, Morgan smiled and asked Paul and Luke, "So what have you guys been up to these days?"

"Ooh," Paul said, "So what happened wa—"

"Cliff's notes version, Paulie," Morgan stopped him. "Cliff's notes. I know you!"

Paul laughed. "Okay, okay!" He continued. "Yeah, I'm living in Jacksonville, I'm working for the city as the chief engineer. Divorced, but you knew that."

"Any new prospects?"

"No, not really. I'm focused on me these days. Trying to work on myself. I wanna do better by my kids."

"Smart. You wanna get your mind right. I don't blame you," Morgan assured him. "So how about you Luke? You're such a mystery!"

"Yes, Luke Phillips, international man of mystery," he quipped with a laugh. "So yeah, I guess there's not a lot to report. I was married for a few years, that ended. Went to school for a while, that ended. Started a career as a researcher, that ended. And I've been, y'know, getting back on my feet."

"Alright...I'm sure you'll figure it out. Any kids?"

"Oh, no. Got two nephews though, they're pretty cool. They're fourteen and seven."

"Yeah, that's how you do it," Thomas said. "You can go spend time with them, bond with them, have fun, then give them back to their parents when you're done."

"True, man." Luke smiled.

The server came back. "Here are your drinks," he announced, placing a glass by each in the party. "Appetizers will be served shortly."

The group enjoyed their four-course meal as the boat set sail on its leisurely journey on the Mississippi River.

"This filet mignon is perfect!" Paul mused.

"Yeah, medium rare, not too heavily seasoned. The best way to eat steak," Thomas noted. "It's one of the nice things about the Mizzou Riverboat, the chef here is on point. That's why I told Morgan this would be the perfect place for us all to meet up."

"This was a great idea — thanks, man," Luke commented.

After the dinner, light music and entertainment were featured on deck. Paul and Thomas were engrossed in a conversation about house flips. Meanwhile, Luke and Morgan went to take in the scenery on the port side edge of the deck. The sun was meeting the horizon to the west, and the sight of the water was serene.

"Morgan, the last conversation we ever had until now, you told me you were with a professor you met up north."

"I remember that, Luke. You and I were getting ready to graduate from college, and we saw each other at the Christian Kingdom retreat in Tennessee."

"Uh-huh. So, what happened to that guy?"

She took a breath. "Buckle up, buddy."

"Alright, Morgs. I'm all ears."

"So, to make a long story short...you broke up with me, then later on my parents shipped me to Grace College. They wanted me to be a devoted Christian woman – pure, virginal, you know the drill."

He nodded. "Yeah, I remember."

"But, when it came to their vision for my life, I couldn't get there. I began questioning so much of what I was taught about my faith, the teachings I had always taken at face value. I wanted to hold onto it, but I just couldn't square what I was taught in church about

God with what I read in the Bible. I guess they call it 'evangelical deconstruction' nowadays."

"I know what you mean...I went through something similar."

"I was adopted into a faith I was passionate about but didn't truly accept me, and then, you dumped me over something I couldn't control. My parents shipped me to a Christian Reformed college against my will. I was angry. So, I pushed back the best way I knew how."

"So, that's how you started dating the professor guy?"

"Yeah, Nadei...the man I told you about at the Infinity retreat – he was from Russia and he taught international relations. It was a government course and fit a requirement I didn't bring over from Great Lakes."

"I see...makes sense."

She continued. "He was married but in the middle of a divorce when we got together. The school was getting ready to let him go anyway for violation of Grace's faculty morality policy. The administration knew about us, but him sleeping with one of his students didn't matter, at least when it came to him – just the divorce and how it looked having a divorced man working for the college."

"Eh, par for the course at places like that."

"Yeah. I got in some trouble for it, though. I was shunned by Grace's CK chapter, not that I cared. Those people were real weirdos. Then, the school put me on probation for violating the student morality policy, but luckily, they still let me walk."

"Well, that's good at least. Hate to do all that work for nothing."

"Totally. So, not long after I graduated from Grace, Nadei took a nice position with the United Nations and moved to New York. He wanted me to join him out there, so I did. My parents were so pissed.

They were disappointed I was moving in with a man without being married. My dad even told me that I broke his heart."

"Must've been hard to hear."

"Oh, for sure...and that's with them not knowing how he and I got together to begin with. I'll carry that to the grave. Anyway, my parents felt the way they did, but at that point, they couldn't do anything about it. I was no longer under their control."

He nodded.

"So, I went out there with him, but...it didn't work out, he...he wasn't a good guy, shocking," she disclosed with a hint of sarcasm.

"I'm sorry, Morgs."

"Things happen, Luke. That's life. To be real, the way everything turned out just made me more mad at God." She stopped, her face softening as she looked into his eyes. "I asked God why it didn't work out with us – you and I – and why I ended up in the situation I got into with Nadei. Sometimes there isn't an answer, or at least not a good one."

"I understand."

"There isn't that certainty, that 'peace that passes all understanding' they try to sell us on in Sunday service or chapel or campus ministry or whatever, and I had to learn how to be okay with it. I learned how to live with uncertainty, not just when it comes to us or Nadei, but with life in general. So, that's where I'm at. I still don't know."

"About God?"

"Yes. I say I'm agnostic, and I'm good with that."

"I hear you there."

"Not long after I left Nadei, I met Thomas. He's absolutely amazing."

"Y'know, I'm truly happy for you, Morgan," Luke said. "He seems like a nice, stand-up guy, and you look so happy with him."

"Thanks. That means a lot to me – it really does. The best thing about him is that he makes me feel safe, he makes me feel at home."

"At home?"

"Yep. You know how I grew up an Army brat, and it was like as soon as I started making friends somewhere, getting a little comfortable, then it was like 'Nope, we're leaving.' That kind of life made it hard for me to feel rooted, to feel the concept of home. But Thomas is that to me. No matter my highs and lows, no matter what, he's home to me."

"You deserve to be happy. Y'know, I'll be honest with you, Morgan. I was nervous about how this night was gonna go."

Morgan smiled and laughed. "Why? I mean, we've been done and over with for more than twenty years."

"Yeah, it has been that long, hasn't it?" He laughed, holding his hand against the back of his neck. "But honestly, I guess I didn't know what to expect. We ended on weird terms, and I've always been ashamed of how we ended things. I sometimes ask myself if things would be better in my life if I handled things differently back then." He was entranced by the flowing water and the moving shoreline.

She nodded, breathing in the cool marine air.

"But at some point, we would've broken up anyway. We were probably better as friends."

"Yeah, I definitely agree. Let's be honest – we stayed together to piss our parents off."

He chuckled. "Yeah, probably. It was my one moment of rebellion, I suppose. I just...I've got this pattern of making choices for other people and not myself. I've done that a lot, even after you were out of the picture."

She smirked as she looked up at him. "Ann, huh?"

"How did you know? I told nobody about that back then, not even Paulie."

"Come on, Luke. Back when we were in college, once she started coming to CK meetings, you changed. I could never put it into words, but things changed, for sure. You seemed...conflicted."

"Ugh...I suppose that's the best way to put it. I *was* conflicted. I still had feelings for you at the time, but I liked her a lot...I dare say I loved her."

"I know you did. Part of the reason I decided to move on was because I knew your heart had already moved on from me. If you were going to move on, there wasn't a point of me holding onto the idea of us."

"I get it, Morgs."

"But I take it you and her never made a go of it, you know, romantically."

"Nah, we didn't. AC got tired of waiting years ago, and she broke off the friendship."

"When you said you got married and it didn't work out, I just knew Ann wasn't the woman you married. If you loved her, why didn't you go for it?"

Luke took a deep breath. "I thought so much about being judged, and I'm not just talking about my parents."

"What do you mean?"

"God...I suck so bad for even saying this. In high school, the guys would always say, 'No fatties.' In college, the guys in CK were the same way, but worse. They would talk about wanting 'pure' hot, virginal girls Jesus promised them if they stayed devoted to him, and their definition of 'hot' included the same few girls. They talked about AC behind her back, and it wasn't great."

"Eww...so gross, but I'm not surprised. She defriended just about everybody from CK on social media and pretty much went dark. I didn't get it at the time, but since you told me that, it all makes perfect sense. People know when they're being shut out...when they're not wanted."

"Y'know, in the real world, people usually get with who they like regardless, but the things I heard stuck with me longer than it should've. Despite my feelings for her, I just knew I would catch hell for being with her. She moved down to Losanti after graduation for work, and we stayed friends for another year or so, but then it all ended....and I've spent the last twenty years regretting it."

"Regret is hard to live with, Luke. At some point, you've got to let it go."

"You're right. See, I got inside my own head, focused too much on 'woulda,' 'coulda,' 'shoulda.' Then I kept doing the same thing that made me miserable in the first place – letting others make decisions for me. I went to vet school to try to impress my parents. Then, I got married to somebody my parents set me up with."

"Really?"

"Yeah. I'm not proud of that. And, because I didn't stand up for myself, my marriage didn't work out, school didn't work out, my career didn't work out, and I ended up a bum living off my parents."

She gave him a look of pity. "You're trying to find your own way, and that's okay. We all make mistakes, we do dumb shit we end up regretting. But we learn from it, at least we would hope so, then we keep going, keep moving forward."

Luke looked at her. "Morgan, I'm sorry I broke up with you the way I did."

She looked down and sighed, then faced him once more. "It's okay – it really is. If you hadn't, I wouldn't have met Thomas. I wouldn't have had my babies. I wouldn't have found my home."

"True."

She gently touched his chest with her index finger. "Luke, find your home."

BABY
June 30, 2023

"How was it connecting with Morgan?" Paul asked, facing Luke in the hotel hot tub.

Luke smiled a bit. "You know what, Paulie? It was good."

"Told you, bro."

"Honestly, I was worried that I would see her, and this would just be weird, and all the feelings I had years ago would start flooding back, but that's not what happened. I'm glad we met up, and I'm glad she found happiness with Thomas."

"Yeah, he's pretty cool. Nice guy, lots of charisma. Thank God his line of work kind of meshes with mine. Otherwise, I would've had such a problem keeping him occupied."

Luke shook his head. "You were really playing wingman so I could talk to a married woman. Ah, Paulie..."

"Yeah, I know. I told you – deep down, I'm still a manwhore. But seriously, I knew nothing was gonna happen."

"Of course not, you can tell she's in love with that guy."

"No no no. I mean, sure, she's in love with Thomas, but I don't think you were really in love with her. You were in love with the idea of her."

"It's funny...when she and I were talking earlier, that's what we both figured, more or less. It's like I had everything built up in my head that things might be awkward, and feelings might even stir up again. But then, as soon as she was there, in the flesh, I dunno, it just wasn't there. There was nostalgia, I guess, and she's still gorgeous, but there's no spark."

"Sometimes it's like that, man. I mean, it has been twenty years since you've seen her."

"Yeah, it has."

"And I even remember back in the day, I'll be honest with you, I just didn't see it. Let me ask you something."

"Sure, Paulie."

"Do you think you were so drawn to Morgan because of her as a person, or because of what she represented to you?"

"I mean, the only thing tying us together was that our parents didn't want us together. That and she was hot. That was it, really," Luke explained. "Morgan and I pretty much admitted as such on the riverboat earlier."

"I figured."

"Y'know, I needed this. I can finally put that time in my life behind me."

"Yeah, you did need this. That's why I promised Morgan we'd stop by. Maybe in a way, she needed it too."

"Sure, I think so."

"So completely off subject..."

Luke laughed. "Wow, not a segue or anything, huh bro?"

"You know how I am," Paul remarked, smiling. "Of course not. I say what I gotta say."

"You sure do."

"So, Luke, I gotta know, 'cause this has been on my mind ever since the boat cruise, we were all talking and you got really vague when it came to what you've been doing the past few years."

"To be fair, you were too."

"Only because Morgan's heard about it already. I mean, some of it."

"You left out the fucking around, didn't you?"

"I'm a gentleman, brother."

"Bullshit."

"But anyway, you started telling me about it when we began the trip, but you never finished the story. What happened between you and your ex-wife?"

"Paulie, you know how it is...the end isn't *how* it ends."

April 2007

Luke lay awake in the dim bedroom, but with his eyes closed, alone in the plush queen-sized bed he shared with Rachel. The tumbler on the nightstand was empty but retained a faint odor of Malbec. The creak of the front door alerted him.

Shit, she's home.

A few minutes later, the bedroom door opened.

"Honey bunny?" the voice called quietly. "Are you up?"

"Does it look like I'm up?" Luke responded, low and irritated.

"You don't have to speak to me like that, Luke," Rachel reacted in kind. She flipped on the lights.

"What'd you do that for?" He squinted in a vain attempt to adjust to the brightness of the room.

"Why are you asleep right now anyway? You're going to be exhausted when you start work."

"I'm always tired, Rach. I'm not gonna be able to sleep."

"You should try."

He sighed loudly. "So anyway, how was Bible study?"

"It was so uplifting. We focused on Luke 1, when the angel is talking to Mary about giving birth to Jesus. 'Nothing is impossible with God.'"

"Ah, that's nice," he mumbled, feigning interest poorly.

"You know, our Bible study has been praying very hard for you to find work for the past year and a half. The request has been part of the Third Baptist prayer chain and everything. So, they were so excited and thankful to God you got hired at Ohio Valley Ranch."

Ohio Valley Ranch was both a nationally distributed food staple made in Losanti and one of the largest employers in the area. Losanti was considered the "home" of ranch salad dressing. Ohio Valley Ranch dressing in particular was the most popular brand in the United States. What made their dressing stand out was its mild, smooth taste – so mild and smooth, it was almost as if it was not ranch at all.

"Rach," he responded flatly, "why did you have to tell them I was unemployed? Everybody doesn't need to know our business."

"It's Bible study, it's fine. That's what they're there for, to pray for us."

"No. No, it's not fine. It's embarrassing. No wonder the old church ladies look at me with pity in their eyes. Should've fucking known."

"Luke, I hate when you swear at me."

"I'm not swearing at you."

"You know what I mean. Use your words."

Luke exploded. "Stop that shit! I'm not one of your fucking students!"

Rachel went silent, then walked out of the bedroom and loudly shut the door.

———◇———

May 2011

Luke excelled in his new position as Researcher I at Ohio Valley Ranch. Despite his periodic insomnia, this role was mentally stimulating. In addition, he appreciated not being required to take his work home with him.

His days consisted of aiding with experiments on rodents in a laboratory. While none of the substances fed to the lab rats were considered toxic to animals, the ethics felt a bit questionable, at least to him. Nevertheless, it was a job, and because of it, he was the official breadwinner of the household.

Over the next four years, Luke and Rachel were stable, at least financially, and he moved up to Researcher II. This role increased his responsibilities, including running low-level experiments himself and assisting with top-level experiments. It also meant a modest pay increase.

"What are you doing bun?" Rachel asked Luke one night after arriving home from work.

"Ah, just watching TV, hun."

She sat down next to him and rubbed his thigh. "You know what? I think it's time."

"Time for what?"

She vocalized softly while gazing into his eyes, "You know. It's time we finally start trying for a baby."

Damn...I can't talk her out of this.

He sighed. "Yeah, I suppose so."

Rachel's voice took a disappointed turn. "You don't sound thrilled about the idea."

"Hun, I am. Trust me. Let's go."

The couple went into the bedroom and reclined on the bed. They began to kiss, disrobe, and lightly touch each other in intimate places. But as their silent foreplay session continued, Luke found he could not progress past this stage.

Fuck...I can't. He simply gave up and stopped.

"I'm sorry, Rach. I don't know why this keeps happening. I dunno, maybe it's my lack of sleep," he apologized as he sat back up.

"It's okay, bun, I suppose that happens," she tried to reassure him, while sliding her undergarments back onto her body. "Have you considered going to a doctor about this?"

"Eh, I don't need to do that."

"Yes, you do. This has been happening a lot. And it's kind of hard for us to have a baby when you can't even get it up."

"I know hun. I'm sorry," Luke responded remorsefully.

Rachel sighed. "Have you thought about getting back into counseling? I don't know, maybe there's some things you need to work out. Heck, maybe we should do couple's counseling."

"No, we're not doing couples counseling. It's not your problem, it's mine."

"But it's affecting the both of us." She then exhaled. "I just wish you would do something. *Anything*."

"I'll figure it out, Rach. I promise." He rolled out of bed and retrieved his blue boxers. After pulling them on, he slowly left the bedroom and made a stop in the kitchen. He found himself, almost robotically, pouring himself a full glass of red wine, and taking it down in one shot.

<hr />

March 2013

One night, Luke and Rachel invited her parents, Marianne and Rob, to their home for dinner.

"Rach, this meatloaf is great!" Luke complimented his wife.

"Thanks, bun," Rachel responded. "I was taught by the best."

Luke turned to her mother and schmoozed. "So, it was you that showed her how to cook so wonderfully? I shouldn't be surprised."

"Ah, I do okay," Marianne replied.

"You know your cooking's not just 'okay.' How do you think I got so fat?" Rob quipped, laughing heartily.

"Could you please pass me the broccoli?" Rachel asked.

"Sure." Luke handed his wife the serving tray of broccoli from across the dining room table.

Marianne commented, "So you two have been married for quite some time now..."

"We have. It'll be seven years in June," Rachel noted.

"Oh wow, time does fly, doesn't it?"

Luke and Rachel nodded.

"So anyway, like I was saying, have you started focusing on creating a family of your own?"

"Sure, just need to figure out the right time," her daughter explained.

"Of course. But Rachel, you're about to be thirty-three. Pregnancy gets so much harder after thirty-five, and that'll be here before you know it. You and Luke both have good jobs, you own your own home, there's no better time than the present."

"Your mother has a point," Rob added. "If you're worried about the 'right time,' there's never a 'right time' to be parents. When you have a baby, it'll come naturally to you."

Luke continued eating his meal in silence, watching the conversation from an emotional distance. *Please, God, don't get her started.*

"I suppose," Rachel responded softly.

"I don't want to pressure you, sweetie. It's between you and Luke and it'll happen on your time, but I know you've always wanted to be a mom, ever since you were little and you were playing with your dolls."

"Mom..."

"Oh Rachel, you're such a nurturing person, that's why you became a grade school teacher. I just don't want you to miss your opportunity to have children of your own."

Rachel nodded somberly and continued eating.

After her parents left their home, she quietly placed the dishes in the sink, entered the bedroom, and closed the door behind her. Luke waited for a few moments, then walked past the door and slowly opened it. He observed his wife curled up, bawling into her favorite pink pillow. He closed the door just as softly and returned to the kitchen.

After pouring himself a full wine glass of Malbec, he trudged into the study and shut the door. He sat at his desk and downed the wine, hoping in vain to quiet his distressing thoughts.

My in-laws must hate me.

I'm such a bad husband.

Rachel is crying and it's all my fault.

Why can't I get it up when I'm with her? The doctor says it's not physical. It's not my meds either, so he says.

I can't fix this.

Should we even have kids? What if I end up being a bad father too?

Do I even want kids? What if my kid ends up just as fucked up in the head as I am?

Why am I such a failure? Dad called it. He was right all along.

Why do I keep having these dreams about AC? I'm sure she's moved on. What would I do if I ran into her?

Losanti's like a small town. I'm surprised that in all these years, I've never run into her anywhere. Does she still live here? If only I had a second chance.

God, I suck.

Luke quietly left the study, wine bottle and glass in hand, for the kitchen, still cluttered from entertaining his in-laws.

Damn it Rachel, why didn't you bother to clean up?

For the next hour, he washed the dishes by hand and wiped down the countertops and tile floor until all was immaculate. Then, he turned up the open wine bottle, which was half full, and drank the rest of the Malbec. Once the kitchen was to his liking, he returned to the study to continue contending with his running thoughts for the rest of the night.

The next morning, Luke slowly sat up from the daybed in the study, having not enjoyed even an ounce of restful, consistent sleep. He showered and shaved, and once in the bedroom, tiptoed to avoid waking Rachel, whose alarm would not sound for another half hour. He slowly put on his boxers, socks, khakis, and casual blue top, and slipped on his safety shoes.

He could barely keep his eyes open as he drove to downtown Losanti, but he arrived safely by six o'clock in the morning. After parking in a permit lot, he dragged himself to the animal laboratory in the basement of the imposing Ohio Valley Ranch Building and swiped his keycard for authorization to enter.

Inside were clear animal enclosures full of rats, mice, and hamsters, along with vials of several chemicals. He was tasked with carefully testing these chemicals on live rodents and logging the results on the computer. The collection of substances was intended for use in proposed varieties of the company's Ranch Blend products.

He logged onto the computer to check the day's schedule in order to find out when his supervisor and coworkers would be arriving. *Nice – they won't be here until ten. Might as well listen to some good music while I prep for the day.*

He reached into his pocket and took out his MP3 music player. He plugged the device into the computer, which was equipped with auxiliary speakers. He flipped through the music collection on his device and found his guilty pleasure, Fleetwood Mac. He then started the playlist and got to work, speeding up as he began to catch a second wind. He started placing the various vials on the stainless steel work table for testing.

Luke belted out the lyrics to "As Long As You Follow" as he cleaned the rodent cages.

As he wiped down the third cage, he heard faint noises behind him, barely rising above his beloved soft rock tunes. Enjoying his music, however, he tuned out the squeaks.

Eek eek! Eek eek!

Eek eek!

The rodent noises broke Luke's concentration.

What's that? He peered to his right, and the situation became crystal clear.

"Oh...shit." Luke turned around to scan the lab. The cages had not been secured as he was cleaning them. On the table, several vials Luke set out had been knocked over, and the loose mice frantically licked up the contents.

"Oh no...oh no..."

Just then, the lab door opened.

"What in the hell is this?!" the voice shrieked.

"Uh, Dr. Lawrence...you're here early. I...I don't know what happened."

The supervisor took a deep breath. "It should be okay, Luke. It happens. Let's get these mice put away."

As the researchers chased and retrieved the excited mice, Dr. Lawrence stopped and noticed a particular slot in the temperature-controlled chemical cabinet was empty – a slot where a vial should be.

"Luke, what happened to the SilverStar vial?"

"It should still be in the cabinet."

"It's not. Are you sure you didn't take it out?"

Luke, continuing to gather up wiggly mice, answered, "I'm sure, Dr. Lawrence."

The head of research and development began to scour the chaotic laboratory in search of the important vial. A couple of minutes later, she found it.

"You said you didn't remove the SilverStar vial."

"I didn't."

"So why is it here?" She held up a labeled vial in her gloved hand, cleared of its contents.

He looked up, took note of the tube, and went white as a ghost.

"This is a problem, Luke. The SilverStar extract is being held here temporarily as the factory's cooler was being repaired. It is scheduled to be picked up by courier later today. It's intended to be used for our high-end ranch product, to be placed in Michelin Star chef kitchens worldwide. There are preorders we'll have to find a way to fill!"

"Uh, I don't know what...to say," Luke stammered. "I'm so sorry...I guess I can fill out an emergency request to reorder?"

Dr. Lawrence rejected his idea out of hand. "No. That won't do. This extract is incredibly difficult to source. It comes from the wilds of Southeast Asia, and it's sourced from the same civets that process kopi luwak."

"Uh, the coffee that comes from cat excrement?"

"Yes, Asian palm civet excrement, to be exact...but there is a subset of rare, specially-bred civets that produce SilverStar extract, and it is only excreted in a one-week period out of the entire year. It fetches ten thousand dollars per 0.05 milliliter drop. So, an entire vial? That's a huge cost to the company. How do we account for this loss?"

Luke was speechless.

"Pack up and leave. You're done here."

The words of Dr. Lawrence did not register immediately in Luke's mind. "Do you need help with the mice?"

"No." She sighed. "Just leave. Do not come back."

———◆◆◆———

"That's wild, man," Paul marveled as he and Luke were leaving the hot tub.

"It was," Luke agreed. "Honestly, I'm surprised they didn't sue the shit out of me."

"Yeah, you were lucky, but it does suck that you were going through all that and you lost your job. Were you just tired, or..."

"Yeah, I was tired," he recalled as he toweled himself dry. "I hadn't slept, plus that whole conversation with Rachel's parents gave me these obsessive thoughts. Y'know, at that point, I just...I couldn't drown out the thoughts. I tried so hard to get those thoughts to stop, but it just wasn't happening."

"Were you on your medications at that point?"

"Eh, I don't think I was by then. My job was going well, we were doing good...I mean, other than the baby thing. We were fine, or at least I thought we were. So, I guess I thought to myself 'I'm good now' and stopped taking them."

"Ope, hubris."

"Exactly, Paulie."

"Yeah, I was a lot like that when Alyssa and I were married and it seemed like I had a string of good luck. Were things perfect? No. But I thought it would last forever. So, I made stupid decisions."

Later that night, after the men showered and changed into sleep clothes, Paul chose to go out onto the hotel balcony connected to their room.

Luke peeked his head out of the balcony door. "It's not bad out here."

"Yeah," Paul responded, looking out over the railing. "It's pretty nice."

Luke stepped on the balcony and noticed the freeway in the near distance with traffic flying by.

"It's oddly peaceful, y'know."

"For sure. So, what happened after you lost your job at Ohio Valley Ranch?"

"Uh, I bounced around from job to job, with strings of unemployment in between. Eventually, I ended up working as a vet tech in an animal hospital, and I did that for a long time. Of course, my parents were disappointed in my career trajectory and basically called me a failure. Rachel was surprisingly good about it, but deep down, I think she saw me as a failure, too. Then there was the men's retreat."

"Men's retreat?"

"Uh-huh. I was going on a retreat down to Falmouth, Kentucky with the men of the church. That's a hell of a story there. I'll tell you about that at some point. So anyway, what's the next thing on our agenda?"

"Good question. My Auntie Rina called me about an hour ago. I had left her a message before I left Jacksonville saying I was traveling and she just got back to me. She wants me to come visit."

"Oh, nice. Where is she?"

"She's in Oklahoma. Tulsa."

"Okay cool. I'm sure I can dick around somewhere in town while you do that."

"Oh, no. You're coming with me. She wants to meet you."

"Alright. You sure?"

"Yeah. She's great – she's probably the only family I have that doesn't see me as a big disappointment. It's probably because she's a lot younger than my dad – her brother, and she's very Western. She grew up in Losanti."

"That's cool. Oh, Paulie...didn't you say your son's in a commune out there?"

"Yeah, I probably mentioned that."

"Have you thought about seeing him?"

Paul paused for a moment. "Of course. I worry about him all the time. I would love to see him, but I doubt he'd wanna see me."

"I hear you, but it's worth trying. I mean, you're still his father."

THE MEN'S RETREAT
July 1, 2023

Slam!

Luke was jolted awake to see Paul in a white A-shirt and grey sweats, taking off his shoes and casting his towel on the sofa in the suite.

"What the...Paulie, I was asleep!"

"Sorry, man," Paul apologized. "I was working out in the downstairs gym. Didn't mean to close the door so hard."

"It's alright," Luke said calmly. "How was it?"

"It's not too bad," Paul said while stripping off his sweaty gym clothes. "It's got what I needed. You know, treadmill, elliptical, some free weights."

"That's good."

"I'm gonna jump in the shower, you can get in after I'm done, maybe pack up while you're waiting. We're gonna check out and head out here soon."

"It's kind of early."

"It's like, what, five in the morning? But we're talking an almost six hour drive, and I wanna spend a good part of the day with my favorite aunt."

After the men got ready, they packed up the Jeep.

"You get this leg brother," Paul said, handing Luke the keys. "It's a straight shot on 44 West. I'll roll tape. It'll keep my mind occupied."

"Makes sense, man."

Just as they climbed into the Wrangler, Luke noticed a bright yellow object on the hood. "What...is...that?" he whispered.

"What's what?"

Luke jumped out of the car to identify the object. He reached over and grabbed it. *A rubber duck?* He picked up the duck and returned. As he got in, he showed it to Paul.

"Check this out. This was on the hood."

Paul laughed. "Looks like we got ducked!"

"Ducked?"

"Yeah, it's a Jeep thing. Jeep people sometimes put ducks on other people's Jeeps. It's a camaraderie thing."

"That's different." Luke then placed the duck on the dashboard.

After the friends filled the truck with gas and rode along the highway for a while, Paul started talking.

"I tried calling Danny when we were at the gas station, but he didn't pick up."

"Maybe you can try again when we're inside Oklahoma."

"Yeah, I suppose I can do that."

"When you called him earlier, did you leave a message?" Luke asked.

"No, I didn't. Didn't know what to say."

"It's simple, Paulie. Tell him Dad's coming to town and you wanna see him."

"Yeah, I could say that. But there's so much more I want to say though. I'm sorry I broke up the family, I'm sorry I haven't been there for him..."

"You know, you can say whatever else you wanna say, but if you're struggling with what to say, straight to the point might be the best idea, especially on a voicemail."

"Yeah, sure man."

The men sat in silence while the cornfields of middle America whooshed past them.

"So, Luke," Paul began, "you said you were gonna tell me the church men's retreat story. What was that?"

Luke laughed heartily. "Oh, boy..."

October 2017

"Bun, my dad wants you to come with him to the annual Third Baptist men's retreat the last weekend of the month," Rachel informed Luke as she entered the marital home after attending Sunday service. "It's an overnight camping trip down in Falmouth."

While his eyes were trained on his cell phone screen, he muttered, "I can't, Rach. I'm working that weekend."

"Get that weekend off," she demanded as she shut the front door.

Tuning out his wife's apparent screeching, he mumbled to himself while furiously tapping his iPhone 8, "Declawing a cat is torture, dipshit..."

She stood in front of the couch, ripped the phone from his clutches, and tossed it on the recliner, no longer within arm's reach of her dear husband.

"Hey! I was in the middle of a tweet!"

"Tweet fights can wait. I'm talking. The least you could do is look at me."

His attention secured, he rolled his eyes.

"You've got three weeks. I'm sure you can tell Barky Paws you need that weekend off."

"It's a vet hospital...it's not guaranteed."

"I don't believe that. You're a vet tech, not one of the vets."

Luke's eyes narrowed. "Why'd you have to go there?"

She urged, "Get that time off."

"Whatever happened to me directing my own life?"

"*What life*, Luke? You go to work, come home, and that's it. You're not doing anything."

"What are you talking about? Work *is* doing something."

"You don't see your friends anymore, you don't even talk to them. We hardly ever go to your parents' Sunday suppers because you always find some excuse to back out. My parents barely know you. You snap at me half the time. We don't even make love anymore, you don't even try."

Luke took a deep breath. "Ugh, I'm sorry, Rach. I'll get myself together. I promise."

"You have said the same exact thing for the entire eleven years we've been married. 'I promise.' 'I promise.' 'I promise.' It won't happen if you're just sitting there on your phone watching porn, arguing online, and chugging your stupid wine!"

"Oh my God...not this again! I told you I would get my shit together. Is that not enough for you?"

"I want action, Luke!" Rachel took a slow, deep breath and calmed herself down. "You're going camping with Dad. Make it happen." She then stormed to the bedroom and slammed the door shut.

A few Fridays later, Luke sat on his front porch waiting for his father-in-law to arrive, black camping backpack and blue sleeping bag in tow. After a few minutes, a polished yellow beauty with sleek double black stripes over the hood came into view. It stopped along the curb in front of the house.

"Hop on in, Luke!"

Luke opened the door, placed his gear in the back, and sat in the ribbed leather passenger seat.

"Hi, Rob! Nice car!"

"Thanks! It's a 1970 Plymouth Barracuda. Took me years to restore it. It's my baby. I rarely take it out, but I thought this might be a great occasion."

"I didn't know you restored cars."

"Yeah, I'm surprised Rachel hasn't mentioned it to you. Anyway, it's fun to do. I've got this one, and a '69 El Camino. Come out to my garage sometime."

"Sounds cool...I think I will. Anyway, thanks for inviting me out."

"Anytime, son. We're gonna have a great time! We're gonna make a couple of stops, and then we'll be down in Falmouth."

The men stopped at an ATM, and Rob withdrew some money. He then advised Luke, "You might want to get yourself some cash for where we're going. Some ones."

"What ATM gives you ones?"

"This one. LME Bank's ATMs mostly do that."

Why do we need ones, anyway? Maybe to put in for my share of camping costs...that would make sense. Luke used his debit card to withdraw thirty dollars in one-dollar bills.

After the quick errand, Rob drove nearly twenty more minutes, crossing the Ohio River into the bright Kentucky outpost of Marbro. The enclave had once been a company town that manufactured Marlboro cigarettes. However, over time, the town name morphed into "Marbro," in speech, in print, and in the public consciousness. While the factory had long since closed, a slight odor of cigarette smoke lingered in the town to that very day.

Once across the rickety bridge connecting the two cities, the neon lights and billboards came into view, advertising booze, cannabis, and all other manner of vice.

"You ever come down here, Luke?" asked Rob.

"N...no, never."

Rob inhaled deeply and deliberately, taking in the musky scent of burnt tobacco. "If you do, it's fine. I love this place. Sometimes, as a man, you need to let loose every once in a while," he said with a slight belly laugh. "We don't need to tell the wives. You just gotta know where to draw the line."

Luke nodded.

"We'll stop and relax awhile, and then we're gonna head down to Falmouth and meet some of the other men of the church to camp overnight."

"Sounds fun."

After a few minutes, they pulled into a dirt parking area in front of a grey concrete box building without windows. The pink neon sign read in all caps, "NOTIONS." Rob parked the muscle car and the men exited the vehicle.

Luke followed his father-in-law into the dimly lit establishment. Scattered around the room were several basic black matte tables surrounding a raised platform. The platform was glossy with two chrome poles bolted in the floor that stretched to the ceiling. Three other men were sitting at tables by themselves. Rob and Luke found an empty table with a black plush-covered menu propped on top and sat down.

Luke perused the menu. It included both a specialty drink list and a basic food selection. Also listed was a full bar. After a few minutes, he gave it to Rob.

A long-haired, orange-skinned brunette strolled up to the table where the men were sitting.

"Hi, gentlemen! Welcome to Notions – my name is Emma, would you like anything to drink?" asked the server.

Rob ordered first. "I'll have a whiskey sour."

She turned to Luke. "And for you sir?"

"Uh..." He found his attention drawn to the server's strappy shoes, shiny leather pants, and white cropped tee that barely covered her oversized, ample bosom. "I'd like a bourbon and Coke."

"Which bourbon?"

"Um, Evan please."

"Nice choice. I'll be right back."

Luke was taking in the surroundings. "Y'know Rob, this is one strange men's retreat."

Rob guffawed. "We're men from the church, and we're out at the gentlemen's club together, retreating from the world."

Luke nodded uncomfortably.

"This is just a stop to loosen ourselves up a bit before we meet the guys down in Falmouth. We'll be there by sundown...nothing happens till then anyways. That's when we build the bonfire and smoke some hot dogs and smores. It'll be great."

Just then, the server came back with drinks. "Would you like to open up a tab?"

"Sure!" Rob reached into his shorts and removed his thick brown wallet. He then removed a plastic card from it and handed it to the server.

"Thanks gentlemen!" The server responded as she left with the card. "I'll be back to take food orders."

The men took a sip of their drinks.

"Ope, this is strong."

"This is why I like this place," Rob shared. "That and the food. ..and the ladies."

Luke leaned in towards the older man. "So, what made you decide to bring me out here? Rachel's gonna kill me!"

"She doesn't have to know, son. You know, as men, we have testosterone flowing through our veins, so we of course have our appetites. We have to get that release so we can be good husbands to our wives. And it's better to do it this way than go too far, you know what I mean?"

"Uh, sure."

"And too, you don't come out to church with Rachel anymore, and she's always over our house by herself. She never really brings you by. So, I wanted to spend some time with my son-in-law, have a nice night with just us."

The younger man took a gulp of his Evan and Coke. "Makes sense. Thanks for bringing me out here."

"No problem, for sure."

The server returned, "Show's starting here soon, gentlemen. Would you like to put in for some food?"

"Sure. I'll have a full rack of ribs."

"That's a great choice, sir! And for you?"

Luke scanned their very basic menu. "I'll get the chicken tenders and fries."

To that, Rob raised an eyebrow.

"Good," the server responded. "I'll put in the order, and I'll be back in the meantime if you need more drinks." She then walked away to submit their food order.

"They have steak and ribs on the menu, Luke. Why didn't you get that?"

"Uh, I mean, I didn't wanna go crazy getting something like steak. Besides, chicken tenders are pretty good."

"Son, trust me, if you're out with the guys and you want to be able to keep your wits about you, go for steak or ribs. Something nice and heavy."

Upbeat dance music began to play, signaling the beginning of the show. The server came by and took a second drink order for Luke, as he had finished his first Evan and Coke.

As the second drink came, two dancers pranced on stage, stepping up from the left. The first one was voluptuous and sand-skinned and was wearing a leopard-print bikini and a black sheer coverup, while the second was buxom with sienna-toned, weathered skin, modeling a purple two-piece lingerie set.

Within a few minutes, the food arrived at the table. Rob tore into the baby back ribs, while Luke took a tiny fry from his own plate and munched. He downed his second mixed drink, then when the server came by, requested another.

"These ribs are Marbro's secret. Some of the best in the Metro Losanti area," Rob told Luke between vigorous chews. "Oh, and by the way, you might wanna slow down on those drinks, son."

Luke could barely hear Rob enjoying his meal over the music and his desires, as he keyed in on the sensual gyrations of the full-figured dancer in purple as she twirled around the solid pole. His pole became solid as well.

"Sure, Rob," he responded quietly, as his attention was prioritized elsewhere.

The third Evan and Coke was dropped off as Luke slowly finished a dry tender. As he sucked down the third drink and asked for a fourth, the dancer sensually untied the straps that kept her lingerie set together. Rob's smacking and concerns faded into the background. Completely mesmerized by the sight, Luke found himself lifting his thin black wallet from his pocket. He rained crisp one-dollar bills onto the stage.

"Oh yeah, come to Daddy, girl!" he called out with a sly grin.

The dancer in purple seemingly floated off stage, and her lush brunette hair whipped about, along with the lavender streamers in her hair, as she sashayed his way. Overwhelming power and ecstasy coursed through his body.

In the blink of an eye, a lightning bolt ripped from the base of his neck to the top of his skull.

"Luke! What the hell is wrong with you?!"

Luke could barely open his eyes.

What the fuck happened?

He touched the front of his tan corduroy pants and laid his hands on a rather large damp, slimy area.

Ugh...I gotta get cleaned up...

"Dad told me about your 'outing.' Can't trust anybody these days, not even my own father." Rachel sighed in disgust.

"What, Rach? What are you...what are you talking about?" Luke was now in the marital bed, sitting on his side, head in his hands. He murmured audibly to himself. "Oh God, I feel like shit. My head is pounding."

"Your 'outing.' Dad was supposed to take you to an outing with the other men from church, some nice male bonding with a group of believers. But instead, he took you to a strip club? And then on top of that, you got wasted and you tried to cheat on me? I'm sure my dad didn't make you do that!"

"Oh God, Rachel, stop yelling at me. My head hurts."

"You were in some back room, some stupid 'VIP room' with a naked stripper, and next thing you know, you pull your penis out. And you want me to stop yelling at you, are you serious right now?"

"I...I did what?"

"Yeah. I made Dad tell me everything. You drank too much, because of course you did, then you tried to have sex with a stripper. A stripper! You could get all hard and ready for her. You came for her. But nope, not for me, though! And I'm your wife!"

"Ugh, Rachel," he moaned in agony and sheer embarrassment. "I...I'm sorry..."

"Yeah, be sorry. Like you always are. And the only reason why you didn't do it is because your pathetic ass got kicked out of the strip club. Dad told me he had to talk the police out of arresting you."

"The police? Oh no..."

"Yes. The police. You know, Luke, maybe he should've let them take you to jail." With that, Rachel left the room and slammed the door behind her.

———◆◇◆———

"Well, at least she got the action she wanted," Paul commented.

Luke laughed sardonically. "Yeah, that's for sure, man."

"Seriously, though, that's some real shit."

"It was. It really wasn't the best time in my life."

"I hear you." He then cleared his throat and continued. "I imagine you didn't get along well with her parents after that."

"Pretty much. I mean, they never told me to my face that they didn't like me. But I got the feeling they didn't once I lost the job at Ohio Valley Ranch. It was like they were kinda looking down at me or something. But it was clear as day after the strip club thing happened. They would only say 'hello' when they happened to see me, and that was about it."

"Mmm, that's not a good feeling."

"Yeah. And y'know, they distanced themselves from my parents, too, which was awkward 'cause they still had to see them every Sunday. One time, my mom even called me and asked me if my in-laws had a problem with them. Of course, I said no, but I'm sure they stopped associating with them because of me."

"Oh man, that's rough. But what I don't get is that your father-in-law was the one that took you to a strip club even though he was deep into the church. Yet he and his wife were judging you?"

"Yeah, he was. Isn't that crazy? Though to be fair, I was married to his daughter at the time, and she was a real daddy's girl. And my behavior surely hurt their relationship."

Paul felt a twinge of sadness. "I get it. You know Luke, my Bella was my ace, she was a real daddy's girl, at least until my marriage to her mom blew apart. You know, fathers and daughters – that's a real bond there. I'm sure that your father-in-law had to feel some kind of guilt."

"Eh Paulie, maybe, yeah." Luke considered some more. "Probably. But I didn't think about it at the time. I didn't think about much of anything, to be honest."

"Man, it is hard sometimes to get outside ourselves when we're the ones screwing up."

"True."

"So...that had to be the end of your marriage, right?" Paul asked.

Luke shrugged. "You know how it is, it's not just one thing most of the time. It's a whole bunch of things. Our finances and my career going down the shitter, our sex life, which also affected our ability to start a family, ugh, and my drinking, too. So. Many. Things."

"I get it."

"Yeah, I mean...and then I was questioning things, y'know, stuff about the church, and the nature of God, a lot of shit I heard my entire life about what it means to be a Christian. Is this shit even real, you know?"

"Been there."

"And at the same time, Rachel was getting deeper into Jesus and the whole church thing. Not just church every Sunday, but then going to Bible studies, and volunteering there too, on top of teaching. I was disconnected and off by myself, and she wasn't where I was, y'know. Not at all. She needed connection, and I couldn't give it to her."

"Sounds like maybe you weren't compatible, and you two just drifted apart."

Luke nodded. "Sure, thinking back on it, we really were two different people. But I'm convinced the break in our bond happened that night, Paulie. Things weren't 'good' before then, but after that? I swear, it truly was the end of our marriage, but neither of us knew it yet."

BROKEN ARROW
July 1, 2023

After a gas and restroom break just off the interstate, Paul explained the day's itinerary.

"So, Luke, I talked to my Auntie Rina, and she said she's going to be doing some volunteer work in downtown Tulsa today, and then afterwards, we can head to her house for dinner."

"That sounds great. When should we go by there?"

"We're heading there now. She wants us to come along and help out where she volunteers at. Said they could use some extra hands. I said yes, didn't think you would mind."

"Oh, of course. I'm down for that. Where are we going? What are we gonna be doing?"

"We'll be volunteering at a warehouse run by this charity, Oklahoma Storm Relief."

"Oh, that's cool. Just out of curiosity, is this a faith-based charity?"

"Oh God no. It's a secular non-profit. They help everybody, and from what I understand, they don't have any hangups about who is and isn't deserving. That's one of the things that was important to my aunt."

"Yeah, I get it. I take it she's a bit more liberal than the rest of your family?"

"Oh, yeah, totally. She's pretty progressive, she's the activist of the Chus. She's different, she's super aware, really into helping others and not judging them, and she's awesome for it."

"That's cool, man."

Another hour and an exit later, the men noticed a sign on the side of the road:

Welcome to Broken Arrow: Where Opportunity Lives

"Okay, we're pretty close now," Paul noted.

"Yeah," Luke added. "GPS says just a couple more minutes."

Less than five minutes later, the men stopped at a small, tan brick ranch-style home with a wind chime on the tiny porch next to the door, and a multi-colored windmill garden decoration in the yard.

"I'll be right back." Paul got out of the car, approached the dark brown front door covered by a metal screen, and was let in. A couple of minutes later, he emerged from the building with a short, thin woman who looked to be in her thirties, with porcelain skin and dark brown shoulder-length hair with blonde streaks. Paul let the woman into the back seat of the car.

"*Gomo*, are you sure you don't want to sit in the front seat?" Paul asked. "You might find it more comfortable."

"Oh, I like the back more, *joka*, I'm kinda short," she replied, with a slight Southern twang.

After closing the back passenger-side door, Paul let himself back into the front seat. "Luke, this is my Auntie Rina. *Gomo*, this is my best friend, Luke."

"Hi, Luke. I've heard a lot about you from Paul, I'm happy to finally meet you."

"Oh, it's great to meet you too, uh..."

"You can call me Auntie. Anyone who's family to Paul is family to me."

"Oh, thank you, Auntie."

"Of course." She then turned to her nephew. "Paul, do you know where you're going?"

"I've plugged it in the GPS right here."

"That's perfect. Now, when we get closer, I can give you better directions if you need them. Sometimes, traffic is crazy over there."

"Sounds great, Auntie," Luke responded.

The truck began its twenty-minute jaunt to the Storm Relief warehouse.

"*Gomo*, you were telling me about the warehouse we're going to."

"Yes...so, it's a charity in downtown Tulsa that focuses on storm relief throughout the state, sometimes beyond if needed. As you know, Oklahoma is pretty much ground zero for Tornado Alley. We get a lot of them every year."

"Yeah, I've seen it on the news. I can't imagine how you deal with that."

"Well...we do what we can. Now, honestly, most tornadoes don't really do a lot of damage. The funnel might not even hit the ground, or if it does, it's in more rural areas with less to hit, and it might not last long, but that's not always the case. Oklahoma Storm Relief helps out quite a bit – with food and water, toiletries, furniture, building supplies, even temporary housing."

Luke was complimentary. "That's such a great cause."

"Yes, it's good for the community, and what's even better, we don't put any expectations on those we help. It's not religious – it's not like we're out to convert them or anything. And I love going every Saturday. It's kind of like my church. It's refreshing, and we have a great group of people."

"How did you get involved in that?" Paul asked.

"Luke might not know this, but you know, I moved out to Oklahoma right after I turned eighteen. I wanted something different than living in Ohio. I suppose a lot of romanticizing of Native cultures, nowadays it's called appropriation. Now, of course, you learn better, you do better."

"Sure."

"So, you know, I've been out here for well over thirty years..."

When she said this, Luke shifted his eyes at his friend, confused, and mouthed, "No, she can't be that old."

Paul cocked his head to the side disapprovingly.

Rina continued, "I got married to Adam, I'm sure you remember him, *joka*."

"I remember Uncle Adam. I was kind of young, though."

"He was a wonderful man – very peace-loving, such a caring and gentle spirit. We were together for five years and married for two. Then, one night, he was on his way home from work and stopped by a gas station for a pack of Camels. Wrong place, wrong time. Never found the guy who did it."

"I'm very sorry to hear that," Luke said.

"Thank you. So, with losing my husband, especially in such a violent way, I went to a very dark place. And at a certain point, I realized I needed to find my people – folks who got me and could hold space for me, so I could find myself through the anger and the sadness and the grief."

"That makes a lot of sense."

Rina nodded. "One thing I realized is that healing comes through gratitude, and in turn, being active in my community, helping people, being of service to people. Through being involved in my community, I learned about the Storm Relief charity, and I've been working with them ever since. It keeps me sane, and it keeps Adam's memory alive."

The trio arrived at the Oklahoma Storm Relief warehouse, which sat on the corner. Luke parked on the street, and he, Paul, and Rina got out of the car. The warehouse was two stories high, brick and painted dark grey with "STORM RELIEF" etched in black on the front side of the building.

"Here we are!" Rina announced. "Come with me."

The guys followed her through a nondescript side entrance. They then walked through the open steel door and down a narrow corridor. Luke and Paul hung back a little bit to chat amongst themselves.

"You're eyeing my auntie, aren't you?"

"Uh...no, no." Luke's eyes averted to the side.

"You're full of shit."

"Bro, don't kill me – but I gotta say, she *is* quite nice-looking. Is she seriously around fifty? She doesn't look anything north of thirty."

"Asian don't raisin, brother," Paul quipped.

The three then turned left into a large space covered by rows of long wooden folding tables with steel legs. In the rows were piles of items, such as canned goods, water, and other supplies. Several volunteers, mostly younger people, were milling about, working on loading, unloading, and transferring items within the space.

Rina took a moment to chat with a slightly plump person with bronze skin and closely-faded dark coily hair shaped like a mohawk. After a couple of minutes, Rina brought them over to Paul and Luke.

"Taylor, this is my nephew Paul and his bestie Luke," Rina introduced them. "Guys, this is Taylor, they're the volunteer coordinator, and they'll show you what you'll be doing this afternoon."

Taylor pointed to a large wrapped pallet on one end of the floor. "Hi, Paul and Luke! Glad you're here, and thanks for lending us a hand this afternoon. We have this pallet of bottled water that just arrived here not too long ago that was donated to us. Can you lift up to fifty pounds at a time?"

Paul nodded, "Yeah, I can definitely do that. How about you, bro?"

Luke thought back to the times he passed out large care bags to impoverished people during urban missions trips in college. "Sure, Taylor. I'm fine with those."

"Excellent. So, we're wanting this unloaded, and placed at the end of that second row," they explained, pointing to an empty table at the end of the second row from the pallet. "You'll wanna break open the packs, and line the water bottles up on the table. Ainsley over there can help guide you."

An energetic young man waved them over and showed them their assignment. Once trained, the two got to work.

As Luke lined up individual water bottles on the table an hour in, he noticed a slightly pudgy man standing to the side staring at Paul.

Luke tapped his friend.

"Paulie," he said quietly, "Look over there to your left."

Paul peered to his left as directed to see the dark-haired, blond-tipped man standing against the wall. Their eyes met, and the volunteer slowly approached him.

"Dad?"

Paul's eyes began to well up. "Danny..." He held out his arms.

Danny hesitated at first, but then ran to him, and gave him a big embrace.

Rina walked over to Luke, who by this time had stopped to take in the reunion. He leaned over and quietly said, "Auntie, you knew Paulie's kid was gonna be down here, didn't you?"

Rina smiled. "He comes down here every Saturday. This is home for him. He had friends here from Florida, and I was here too, so he made his way here to Tulsa."

"Oh wow, he was very lucky."

"He was, but it was hard for him at first. He struggled mentally. I mean, imagine believing in something so much, so deeply, that you give up everything and everybody for it. You put your whole self into it. And come to find out, it's all one big lie? And the leadership acts as if they don't even believe what they preach?"

Luke shook his head. "Yeah, that's a lot, especially at his age."

"For sure, but thank God he had support so close by. His friends really helped him get through that time. They all love volunteering here, and he's so close to them, probably more so than most of our family. Really, he's a big reason why I'm here. He's family, I support *him*."

In the green Wrangler returning to Broken Arrow were Luke, who was driving, Paul in the front passenger seat, and Rina and Danny in the back.

"Danny – how did you make your way here to Tulsa?"

"So yeah, Dad – I was just drifting around with Maddie, Chase, and Jordan – you remember them from back home, right?"

"Of course. You and Maddie have been best friends since kindergarten, and Chase and Jordan...weren't they from band?"

"Yeah, we met in middle school, but we got close when we were in band."

"Okay...I'm pretty sure I remember them."

"So anyway, we were just kinda traveling across the country. I didn't know what I wanted to do with my life, none of us really did. I'm still figuring that out long-term, I guess. Anyway, we heard about this commune here in Oklahoma through some friends down in Jacksonville, friends of friends. It's called Acts of Abba, it's in the grasslands, western part of the state. Chase and Jordan didn't love the idea, but me and Maddie thought it sounded great. One with nature, all of that. So, we get there, and it starts out nice. We share and share alike, like in Acts 4, we meditate and smoke lots of Js...uh, Dad, I'm sorry. I'm sure you're disappointed in me doing drugs."

"Don't worry about it, son."

The young man breathed a sigh of relief. "So yeah, Acts of Abba was great, my kind of people, my kind of place, at least at first. Then it got weird all of a sudden."

"What happened?"

Danny sighed somberly.

"You don't have to get into it if you don't want to," Paul reassured him.

"It's alright. I can talk a little bit about it. So, the guy leading our commune, Abba Amos...he started getting kind of paranoid. He got this huge stash of weapons – lots of guns, bullets, the works. Totally knew where this was going. Watched enough true crime shows with Mom," he explained with a sarcastic chuckle.

"Yeah, she's always been into that."

"For sure. Then some of the people in the commune started disappearing, and Abba Amos would come up with reasons why, but after a while, it got suspish. So, Maddie and I made a plan to get out, and when we had our chance, we took it."

"Glad you were able to get out. How did you make that happen?"

"It's a long story, Dad, and I don't wanna get too deep into it, but I knew Auntie Rina lived here, so I called her. She picked us up, and she saved us. We stayed with her at first and we got in touch with Chase and Jordan. I was shocked they hadn't gone back to Jacksonville, but anyway, the four of us got a place together around the corner from the warehouse."

"That's a dangerous situation – I wish I knew about it so I could've helped you, but I'm so thankful you and your friend got out of that safely and Auntie was there to help you."

"Heck yeah. I'm glad to be free."

"Are you doing okay now?"

"Yeah. I'm working two jobs right now. I'm working in the kitchen at a steakhouse, and I pick up shifts at Hot Topic. Life keeps me busy."

"Danny, I hope you know that if you need anything, you can call me too. I'm still your father and I'm here for you."

"I know. So, Dad, who's your friend?"

"I'm Luke, I'm an old friend of your dad's."

Paul reminded his son, "Yeah, I've shown you the pictures from when your mom and I got married."

The young man nodded. "Okay."

"So, Luke was the guy next to me, he was my best man. We've been friends since college, and we met back up recently."

A few minutes later, the truck arrived back at Rina's house. She welcomed everyone inside.

The short foyer was painted deep taupe, and led to the living room area of a slightly pinkish hue of the same color, with two paintings on the wall framing the tan brick fireplace. In the corner of the area was a small flat-screen television on a stand. A dusted pink plush sofa sat in front of it with a carved coffee table in between. A matching ottoman sat perpendicular to the couch. The dining area was next to the kitchen, and it included a glass table and four black metal chairs with felt cushioned beige seats.

Everyone took off their shoes at the entrance, and Paul and Danny sat on the couch.

Rina gently pulled Luke aside. "Luke, would you like to keep me company while I make dinner?"

Luke nodded and headed into the kitchen with Rina. It was fairly small, with a turquoise refrigerator and matching stove in a retro line, Formica countertops and checkered linoleum floors.

"Auntie, what can I do to help?"

"Just sit there, Luke, and keep me company. You don't need to do anything, I've got this." She pointed to a barstool set up in a corner. He sat as directed.

Rina bent down and took a bag of rice out from the bottom cabinet. She opened it and washed the rice in the sink.

"Y'know, Paulie's raved about you," Luke said. "I take it you two are pretty close."

"Yes, I would agree. I'm his father's sister, but I'm the baby of the family. The 'surprise,'" she quipped. "I'm closer to Paul's age than to my brother, Sang-Ook, so my relationship with Paul is more like an older sister and younger brother than auntie and nephew."

"That makes sense."

"So, Luke, where are you from? Tell me about your family."

"I'm from Losanti, like Paul, but we grew up in different parts of town, so we didn't meet until college."

"So, you and Paul met up in Michigan?"

"Yeah."

"I take it you also know his ex-wife?"

"I did. We all hung out in college, but I haven't seen her in several years."

"Yeah. I've talked to her, but I didn't know her well. And I wasn't there for his wedding. When they got married, I had been struggling...you know, depression. I didn't want to distract from his day, so I stayed home."

Luke nodded in sympathy. "I get it."

"It's something I really regret, not being there on the biggest day of my nephew's life. But it was the push I needed to start seeing someone, you know, a therapist, and work through my sadness."

"I hear you. I've done that too, on and off. It's just not easy to face."

"Ooh, don't I know! It's work, digging in and facing things I kept locked away for years. It hurts, so I tried to run away from it. I wanted to find ways not to deal with the pain but at a certain point that doesn't work. So, I got the help I needed. I still do."

Luke nodded. "I need therapy myself...something I need to go back to."

As Rina prepared the banchan for the meal and made sauce for the main course, bulgogi, she continued. "If you feel you need to, it's worth doing. It was important for me to find myself and my sense of purpose. I stay active in my community, I surround myself with positive people, I give back as much as I can. What I found is that self-pity is a selfish act. I can't be my best self if I'm focused only on myself."

Luke nodded.

"Now, tell me about your family. Are you married?"

"Oh no, not anymore. Got divorced, like, three years ago."

"I'm sorry to hear that, or I'm happy for you? Take your pick!" Rina said, chuckling.

Luke laughed along. "I guess a little of column A and a little of column B."

"Yeah, marriage is complicated. Do you have any kids?"

"No, no kids."

"Any other family?"

"Yeah, my family's kinda small, there's my parents, they're in Losanti, and I've got an older brother, we're like six years apart. He's married with two kids, and they live out in San Francisco."

"Oh, that's nice. Do you ever go out there to visit your brother?"

"Eh no, we're just, y'know, very...different people."

Once dinner was ready, Rina brought the meal to the table to be shared, family-style, along with plates and silverware atop orange placemats.

"What would you like to drink? I have Coke, Sprite, and Diet Sprite."

"I'll have a Coke, *gomo*," Paul responded.

"Yes Auntie, I'll have the same thing," said Danny.

"Sprite sounds great, thank you," Luke requested.

Rina then brought soft drinks for her guests and herself and then took a seat at the table. They passed around dishes, served each other, and enjoyed the lovingly prepared meal.

Luke said, "Oh man, this is so great, Auntie."

"Thanks Luke. I might be a bit rusty in my cooking. My dinners are normally just...make some rice and whip up something from the freezer."

Paul interjected. "Don't be so modest, your cooking has always been excellent. And God, it's been so long since I've had a meal like this – I dunno, maybe since I was a kid?"

"It's great, isn't it Dad? It reminds me of how *halmeoni* would cook."

"Yeah, for sure, kiddo. It does remind me of your grandma."

After a scrumptious dinner, and another couple of hours catching up, it was time to head out. Paul and Luke agreed to take Danny home.

Rina hugged Luke and Danny, then hugged Paul for a while. "*Joka*, don't be a stranger," she implored him. "I mean it. Your baby needs his father."

"Yes, *gomo*. Thanks for everything. And thank you for saving my boy and taking such good care of him."

"Of course. We're family."

They left Rina's house and headed over to Danny's apartment in downtown Tulsa. It was dark out when they arrived at a three-story brick building with a renovated glass door main entrance. Danny got out of the truck, and Paul got out to see him off.

"Danny, you're free to come along with us on our trip if you want, and you can come live with me back in Florida. I have plenty of room for you, I've got you."

"I appreciate it, but I'm good. I'm happy here. My friends are here. Auntie is here. It's not an easy life, but it makes me happy. This is my home."

Paul took a deep breath. "I get it. You're living life in your own way, on your own terms. And you know what? I'm so fucking proud of you and the man you've become." He gave his son a giant hug.

"Thanks."

"I love you, son."

"I love you, too…Dad."

Paul saw his son disappear into the red front door of a beige Four Square house. He then slowly opened the passenger door to the Jeep, got in, closed the door, and wept.

DESERT
July 3, 2023

"Alright, Paulie – they had Ricola, so here you go," Luke reported back while handing him a bag of cough drops. "And I got us some chips, a couple of Cokes, and like, four waters."

"Thanks, man," Paul responded. He opened the bag and removed a lozenge. "We hit these desert states, and you know, the air gets pretty dry. Help yourself if you start feeling it too."

"I'm fine, but if that changes, I'll take one. Thanks."

They had stopped in Amarillo, Texas after spending the day with Paul's family in Oklahoma, then the next day they stayed overnight near Albuquerque, New Mexico. Once fueled up, the friends continued their trip west.

After a moment of quiet, he said, "Danny finally came out to me."

"He did?"

"Yeah. When we were at my aunt's house the other day, and we were by ourselves talking, he told me."

"Wow. How are you taking it, man?"

"Well, like I've said, I already knew, but it's another thing for him to tell me. It's like...he trusts me."

"That's a big step, Paulie."

"Oh, for sure. It means a lot to me that he felt like he could reveal to me that he's gay. I'm a bit surprised, though, that he came out to me after years of barely speaking to me."

"My guess is that you making the effort to show up in Oklahoma was exactly what he needed."

"Maybe so, Luke."

"So, at this point, I take it we are indeed heading to California."

Paul chuckled. "Sure."

"Why? What's in California, anyway? It's really nice, y'know. But what's even there? 'The Happiest Place on Earth?'"

"This has been a hell of a trip so far, right, brother?"

"Hell yeah."

"So, trust your boy."

Luke nodded and relaxed. "Alright, man."

"Now we do have one more stop before we get to Cali. This one's for me. It's a bucket list thing, might as well do it while we're out here."

"Oh, really?"

"Yeah. It's something an old friend from grade school first told me about, and Bianca would sometimes rave about it too. She loved the Southwest."

"Yeah, the Southwest is great. When Rachel and I got married, we booked a room at an on-site resort and honeymooned at the Grand Canyon. It's an absolutely breathtaking and beautiful area. The rock formations, the colors, just the expanse of it. Pictures don't do it justice."

"So I've heard. Now I do want to see the Canyon one day, but that's not what I'm talking about."

"Hmm. What are you thinking?"

"So, I have a buddy I went to high school with. His name's Co nor...Conor Hayes. There was a group of us who used to hang out back then. Do you remember him?"

"Yeah, he came up to UGL to hang out with us a couple of times and he was in your wedding party," Luke recalled.

"Yeah, I thought so. So anyway, Conor and I were part of a group of normies in high school. We were really into music, and one time we formed a grunge band. He was the lead singer, and he played bass guitar. I played acoustic guitar, sometimes electric, and our other friend Dakota played drums. We practiced a few times, and we weren't horrible, but we sucked at staying committed to anything, so it never went anywhere. We didn't even come up with a band name," Paul recalled, laughing.

"Sounds like fun times, man."

"They were. Damn, I gotta piss like a racehorse."

As he said this, they passed a road sign stating:

REST AREA 45 MILES

Paul shook his head. "Forty-five miles from here? Too far – fuck that."

He pulled the truck over to the shoulder of the desolate freeway and got out. He then walked to the other side of the truck and further away from the desert highway to shield himself. Luke got out to stretch his legs and follow his friend.

"So anyway, after high school," Paul continued while stepping into the bright New Mexico desert a little bit more so he would not expose himself to the interstate, "Conor left town and he ended up in Arizona. Got crunchy, you know, like a hippie, got into transcen-

dental meditation, altered states of consciousness, astral projection, time travel, a lot of mystical shit. He's a shaman or something like that."

"Oh, that's interesting," Luke responded, following behind.

"It is pretty fascinating. So, since he's been out there and into
his mysticism, he's been wanting me to come over his way, take
part in a ceremony where we drink some special tea and go on a
guided 'experience.'"

"Special tea?"

"Yeah, it's a tea with this psychedelic brewed in it. It's called
ayahuasca."

Luke was a bit stunned. "Eh, sounds kinda weird, man."

Paul looked to reassure his friend while readying himself to
urinate in the desert. "I know. I said 'no' to it a bunch when
we were younger. Thought the idea of altered consciousness was
demonic."

"Not surprised. Y'know, back then, you were more anti-drug
than DARE."

Paul chuckled.

"Oh, and I'm sure the leaders at CK would've loved that shit,"
Luke joked while turning around for privacy.

"I know, right?" Paul responded as he began to relieve himself.
"Not to mention my hometown pastor. No way. I'd probably be
made to confess my sin in front of the entire congregation, but
I see things differently now and I'm not beholden to the church
anymore."

"True, same here."

"I've heard these ceremonies are eye-opening and life-changing,
especially with a proper guide. So, that's where we're going next."

"Y'know, Paulie, this is strange coming from you. You've changed a lot since we last saw each other."

"Well, I have, but I haven't. I mean, even when I was married, I was never a drug guy...not even alcohol, other than a social drink here and there. But the way I see things now, life is too short."

"Fuckin' A."

"Yeah. The way I look at it, it'll be amazing to try once, at least to say I've done it, and what better place to experience this than the great outdoors – in the American Southwest, no less?"

Luke shrugged. "Yeah, that would be cool in a way."

"Besides, ego death is just what I need."

"What's ego death?"

"It's separating the self from your consciousness. It's when the things that you think make you 'you' are stripped away, and you're primed for a new perspective on life and existence. Some people who drink ayahuasca experience it."

"Sounds like a lot of woo." He then took a breath and added in a facetious tone, "Anyway, glad I'll be there to support you and your decision to live on the edge."

Paul finished with his potty break and zipped up his pants. "You're doing it with me."

Luke blinked with shock. "The fuck I a—"

"No, you *are*, motherfucker."

"There's no way I'm gonna drink some tea out in the middle of nowhere, what the actual fu—"

Paul cut him off. "N-now Luke, hear me out. You have spent half your life groveling for your parents' approval and the other half wanting more but being too much of a pussy to grab the brass ring."

Luke seethed. "Why are you calling me a pussy? Don't call me a fucking pussy! My dad says that sh—"

"Shut up, Luke. I'm not done! See, here's the difference between me and your dad. Your dad doesn't expect anything of you other than to chase after the approval he'll never give you in life no matter what you do. He tells you you're a pussy because he's a small, miserable man who lives to make you feel the exact same way."

Burning with intense anger, Luke was speechless.

"I tell you you're a pussy because I know you can do better, you can be better, and you deserve a hell of a lot better than the kind of life you've been living since Great Lakes," Paul explained loudly. "But you gotta choose it, man. Sometimes it means trying something that's scary. Sometimes it means falling on your face, then getting your ass right back up. Sometimes it's facing tough ass shit, even your own fuck-ups, and making things right the best you can. And sometimes – yes – sometimes, it means living on the edge every once in a while."

His irritated friend was calming down.

"I'm not saying you gotta be like me," Paul clarified, softening his tone. "Years ago, I overdid it. I was an adrenaline junkie and a scumbag, and it fucked my life. I lost too much. Honestly, I'm still an adrenaline junkie, but I had to chill out a bit so I would stop hurting the people I love the most. What I'm talking about here is balance."

Luke nodded slowly.

"You said 'yes' to this trip, you've taken a step. The ceremony in Arizona is another one, and you know what? There's at least one more step. You're gonna know soon enough what that is, and I think deep inside," he said as he poked Luke's chest, "you already know what that is."

"Paulie, when you're right, you're right."

"Now come here brother, let's hug it out."

The best friends embraced, then hiked back to the truck to continue their adventure.

———◆◯◆———

"You okay, bro?"

Paul began a coughing fit shortly after pulling back onto the highway. "Yeah, I'm okay. I think it's from being out there in the middle of the desert, got some sand in my throat or something. Could you hand me a Ricola and some...water?"

Luke reached into the plastic bag in front of him and retrieved a cough drop and a bottle of water. He unwrapped the drop and handed it to his friend, then screwed off the top of the bottle and handed it over as well. Paul popped the drop into his parched mouth, then drank the entire bottle.

"Okay, that did the trick."

"That's good."

"So yeah, I think we were saying earlier that you started drifting away from the Christianity you grew up with, while your ex-wife got closer to it."

"Yeah," Luke confirmed, drinking from a bottle of water retrieved from the bag. "I guess she at least stayed the same, probably did get closer."

"You know, me and Alyssa were kind of like that too. I mean, we met at CK, everything was carefully guided by Brother Craig as well as her pastor in Niles. My parents and hers were heavily involved too. Very much a courtship situation. We had our screwup, and then we got married and we moved to Florida. I was away from their influence and it had me thinking differently."

"Huh…"

"But it took a long, long time. I mean, I was still deep into my faith while I was cheating on her and bleeding us dry financially. But after many years, we weren't on the same page when it came to where we were in our faith journeys, and my actions didn't help."

"I get it. Sometimes I wonder if things would've been different if at least I had been able to talk through it with Rachel," Luke reflected. "But we weren't friends. We were together, we were married, but you know how people always say they married their 'best friend?' She wasn't that. The only girl I was ever able to have those conversations with in a real way was AC."

"Hmm."

"We were able to talk about everything, and it was amazing."

June 2002

It was graduation day at the University of the Great Lakes, and Luke walked down the third-floor hallway of one of the campus dormitories. Once arriving at an open door near the end of the hallway, he knocked hard on the painted door frame.

"Come in," he heard from the other side of the frame.

He entered the dorm room. "Hey, AC!"

Ann turned around in her sturdy school-issue chair. He could tell from glancing at her monitor that she was in the middle of a music download on her computer. "Uh, hey Luke, 'sup?"

"Y'know, not a whole lot. Just getting ready for graduation on Saturday. My family's coming up tomorrow."

"Oh, that's cool. Looking forward to it?"

"Graduation, for sure. Family...well..." Luke cringed. "Anyway, what d'you got going on today?"

"Uh, can't really think of anything. Finals are done, and my mom and my sister won't be here until Saturday morning. It's a shorter drive for them. I think they're coming with my aunts, uncles, and cousins. But today, uh, no."

"I'm gonna go for a drive. You wanna come with?"

"Uh...sure. Gimme one second, I'm gonna get ready right quick."

Once ready, the two left campus.

"Um...are you excited about starting vet school?" Ann asked.

"Yeah...or at least I should be."

"You know you'll be good at it. I mean, just two points below genius, am I right?" she remarked with a chuckle.

"Oh God," Luke smiled. "I did say that shit, didn't I?"

"You sure did! How could I forget?"

"You make me sound like a braggart!"

"Welp...just a little bit...but for real, though. It's not that bad. My point is that I know you can do great, but will your heart be in it?"

"I dunno, but guess I don't have a choice."

Ann, sitting in the passenger seat, looked over at Luke. "Why do you say that?"

"'Cause, there's a lot of expectations on me."

"You know, if you keep trying to live up to other people's expectations, you'll never be happy."

He shrugged. "I guess so, but what is happiness, anyway? Can we ever truly expect to be happy? Is that even the goal of this life? Doesn't God want us to live for him?"

She was quiet for a moment, then spoke. "Do you think you're living for God?"

Luke looked straight ahead as he drove, but was also deep in thought.

"I mean, you talk about expectations, but you and I both know where those expectations come from. And it's not from God."

He sighed but otherwise remained silent.

"Anyway though, I believe we're given certain talents, certain drives, uh, desires, for a reason."

"Kinda how you love telling stories and researching random shit?"

"Yeah, something like that, though it's not random in my head," Ann explained. "I see how it all connects. There's context, everything has a story. It's just stream of consciousness, you know?"

"Yeah."

"You love to travel around and see things. You like to showcase the beauty of both the glorious and the mundane through sight, like pictures. That's probably why you wanna film documentaries."

"You remember that, huh?"

"Of course I do." Then she put him on notice. "Oh, uh, by the way, we're just outside Detroit now, folks drive fast around here. You'll need to keep up."

"But I gotta be careful, I don't wanna miss my turn. Oh shit...AC, could you grab the directions from the glove box? I made sure I printed them out."

Ann removed the directions from the glove box and studied them. "Dude, these directions suck."

"Do they?"

"Yeah, they do. Since we're going to Metro Beach, I'll tell you how to get there from here. Keep heading up this way, then take I-696 east. That way you'll bypass the city and you'll get there faster."

"Thanks. I'll try that. It's great to have somebody with me who knows Detroit."

"When I was a kid, I would always tag along with my dad on his errands around town. That's how I got to know my city so well. I could drive this whole thing in my sleep. Of course, I wouldn't," Ann chuckled, "but you know what I'm saying."

A half an hour later, they arrived at Metro Beach, a lakefront park located on the edge of Detroit's northeastern suburbs. The beach faced Lake Saint Clair, a large expanse of water connected to the much larger Great Lakes by way of the Detroit River. Luke parked and the two stepped out of the car. He then walked to the hatch to retrieve a maroon blanket. They stretched their legs before continuing to the sparsely populated beach.

"It's decently cool out here," he noted.

"Um, yeah, it's pretty windy. Glad we're wearing jackets," she thought aloud.

The two strolled towards the edge of the vast lake.

"Have you been here before?" Ann asked.

"Nah, but I love the water. It's got this calming effect."

"Yeah, it does. That's one of the things I love about home. The lakes – they're really pretty and it's easy to take them for granted until you move away. I can't imagine not settling down somewhere where there isn't water nearby."

"What's that on the other side?" Luke asked, pointing to a land mass that could be seen in the distance on the other side of the lake.

"Oh, that's Tecumseh, in Canada."

"Woah! Canada's that close?"

"Yeah, of course. Never noticed it on maps?"

"I mean, yeah, but I guess I never thought about it."

"Eh, that makes sense. I suppose it was always there when I was growing up. I can see not knowing that if you're not from here."

"Yeah. It is cool though. Wish we had gone at some point while we were at UGL."

"Uh...yeah, I think you'd like it." Then Ann added, "So, like, Windsor, which is on the other side of the tunnel and the bridge, it's kind of like Detroit, but cleaner. There's a very pretty park there, can't remember the name of it, but it's got a bunch of flowers and landscaped greenery. It's so beautiful. Lots of things to take pictures of."

Luke unfurled the blanket, and the friends sat and watched the waves from the shore.

"So, AC, have you thought about what you're gonna do after graduation?"

"I dunno. Um...in the short term, I'm gonna go home, spend some time with my mom and my sister. She's been having a hell of a time after my dad died. Not so much financially, but unexpectedly having to do so much by herself, and raising my sister as a single mom."

"Damn, that's gotta be tough."

"Yeah, it is. Figure I can try and help out at least a little bit. Now in the long term, I've put in for jobs in different places across the country. We'll see what happens."

The two sat in silence for a while, taking in the sights of the outside.

"Luke, do you ever wonder if what we get taught about faith in Christian Kingdom, or even at church, if it makes sense in real life?"

"Hmm, what do you mean?"

"You know, we get taught about having faith 'like a child,' 'delight yourself in the Lord and he'll give you the desires of your heart,' 'God answers believing prayer,' and other simple things, like, if we believe the right things, and if we do the right things, we're gonna have a good life."

"Uh huh."

"But it's not always like that. My dad was a good person, he did so much for so many people. He was generous with his time and impacted so many lives. He was like a mentor, a best friend to me. He had a good heart, and he showed that. But he got sick."

"That had to be hard to witness, AC."

"I remember one time I came home on a break, this was like maybe freshman year...no, um, I'm pretty sure it was second year at Great Lakes. And when my parents were there waiting for me at the bus station in downtown Detroit, my dad...as a kid I always pictured him, like invincible, like he could do anything...but in that moment, he looked weak. I mean, he ended up dying of a major stroke, so I guess it was technically sudden, but I had a feeling for quite some time that he didn't have long to live."

"Oh, damn."

Ann sighed. "I never shared this with anybody at the time because I didn't want to put that out in the air and have something happen to him. You know, 'blessing and cursing' and all that. I prayed he'd be okay, that he would get better, but at the end of the day, it didn't make a difference, did it?"

Luke shook his head sympathetically.

"You know, it's wild how good people die young and evil lives forever."

"Yeah, AC. I wonder about that too. 'The problem with evil' and all that shit."

"Oh yeah, there is that, but there's more to it, at least in my mind. God allows free will, so humans can make good choices and bad choices, and unfortunately that can affect ourselves or other people."

"Yeah, true, though there's a lot of people who deal with evil and have nothing to do with it, like when innocent people, like kids, get blown up in Afghanistan or Iraq."

"True. The problem of evil isn't the easiest thing to contend with, but I guess I'm thinking more simply. What if this life isn't as 'paint-by-numbers' as Brother Craig or Sister Rhonda teach, or what they say at church? Maybe we're just supposed to do the best we can with the cards we're dealt."

"Yeah, enjoy the joy with the pain, the good with the bad, and the beauty with the ordinary."

Ann nodded. "Exactly. I guess I'm finding a simple faith isn't making sense to me anymore. It's more complicated, it's messy, because life is complicated and messy. We just do our best with what we have."

"Makes sense, AC. Y'know, this makes me think of when we were talking about happiness earlier. It's hard. Is it okay to pursue happiness? I'll be honest, I struggle with that a lot. There's what would make me happy, but then there's what would make my parents happy, y'know, 'honor thy father and mother' and that. Then there's what pleases God, and how do we even know?"

"Um...I don't know if we really can know. Obviously, we don't want to do things that have a real negative effect on other people. But beyond that, I mean, we only have one life, and none of us know how long it'll be. Why not live that life in a way that brings us joy?"

"AC...she was awesome...just amazing to be around," Luke reminisced. "Y'know, in our fourteen years of marriage, Rachel and I never had that. I really did underestimate how important it is to be with somebody who could get me to think, who can stimulate my mind."

Paul cleared his throat, then responded while directing his eyes at the road, "I hear you, brother."

"But y'know, I pushed her away. It wasn't that she didn't look good, at least to me, but I was scared of what my family thought, the guys too, like I needed to impress them, y'know, make everybody jealous of me 'cause I had a hot girl, or at least a girl everybody else wanted."

"Ego, man. But I never got that. People like what they like, it's not always gonna be the same. As long as you're happy, who cares?"

"Yeah, Paulie, I know that now. It was stupid as fuck. Just couldn't get out of my own way."

"Sometimes it's like that. So, what actually caused your divorce? How did you end up in an Ikea-fied bachelor pad at 40-something? Y'know, not that I can judge, but just curious."

"It was anticlimactic, really. At some point, I think it might've been after the strip club thing, she stopped pushing me about sex, about having a baby, about any of it. Things seemed alright, we weren't arguing as much. We weren't really sleeping together either, but I guess I didn't think about it. Then, in 2016, I lost my job at the vet clinic…downsizing or whatever. You know how it is."

"Oh yeah, man."

"Bounced around, ended up at the Dairy Union, working nights."

"Oof, that's brutal."

"It was tough going…Rachel worked days, I worked third shift, we were two ships passing in the night. She took on the bulk of the bills, but she never complained. I felt horrible because I knew I wasn't pulling my own weight, y'know, the whole 'man being the breadwinner' thing that got drilled into my head. And what made it worse…my parents had a lot to say about it, especially my dad. Gave me a lot of shit for that."

"Damn brother. Sometimes, life happens."

"I know. And the job sucked too. Real mind-numbing. Thought to myself, 'I make so little, so why not look into things I'd actually wanna do,' but then, that voice in my head would constantly tell me that would make my parents disappointed. But they were already disappointed, and I couldn't see myself doing anything that would make them proud of me. I wasn't taking my meds, I wasn't seeing anybody for my problems. In my mind, I was stuck, and I just didn't see a way out."

February 2020

Luke returned home exhausted after his overnight shift at the Dairy Union. The work night had been mundane. A few customers appeared here and there, mostly regulars, including a couple who had too much to drink, but Luke understood their plight and felt no need to judge. None who came into the store were particularly remarkable. He thought to himself, *I didn't get held up, nobody pulled a gun on me, so it was a good night.*

He arrived at the small bungalow he and his wife shared, clicked open the garage door, and pulled into his space. He then quietly walked inside the warm house and shut the door behind him.

Everything was dark, as expected. Rachel could generally be found in the bathroom getting ready for work, but standing in the boxy foyer, he sensed something was amiss.

I don't hear the shower running. Hope Rachel didn't oversleep...but she never oversleeps. Weird.

He then crept into the living room. His eye caught a figure on the far edge of the Davenport in the shadows. He could only see the whites of a pair of eyes.

Startled, he screamed, "Shit!" He got his wits about him and took a second look.

"Rach, why are you out here? Shouldn't you be getting ready?"

"I called off," Rachel voiced in a tone devoid of clear emotion. "Luke, sit down."

He sat on the couch on the opposite end facing his spouse. The bright moonlight shone in the window. Her tear-streaked face now came into view, but her expression was made of stone.

"Rachel, what's going on?"

"Luke, this isn't working."

"What isn't working?"

"Us. This marriage. It isn't working."

Luke was stunned. "What do you mean? What are you talking about?"

"I can't do this anymore."

"Look, Rach, I know it sucks, y'know, me working nights and not pulling in much of a paycheck, but I'll try harder to bring in more mo—"

"It's not the job, Luke. It's not the money. I couldn't care less about what kind of work you do as long as it's an honest living."

"So, what's the problem?"

Rachel sighed. "Your heart is not in this marriage. Your heart is not with me."

"Oh, that's not tr—"

"No, Luke. It is true. You knew who I was when we got married. My faith is important to me, and I thought you felt the same way."

"Really? Nothing h—"

"Yes, Luke, *really*. And you knew I wanted children so badly." Her voice cracked. "I went into teaching because I love kids, I wanted to sow into their lives. And I wanted children of my own. And I prayed to God that I would become a mom. You knew my heart, and you never took me seriously."

"No, that's not true. I did take you seriously. I *do* take you seriously."

"You don't act like it. Our intimacy has always been pretty much nonexistent. You have trouble but you don't bother to do anything about it. You don't prioritize it, you treat it like a chore. It's as if you're not attracted to me at all."

"Rachel, no, that's not it at all."

"Then what is it? I've been waiting nearly fourteen years for an answer."

He was silent.

"I thought so. I stopped saying anything, because me telling you how I felt and what I wanted wasn't working. I hoped that maybe if I let it go, you would find you wanted the things I wanted – that you wanted *me* – and you would do what you needed to do to make us work. But that never happened."

Luke laid his head back on the ottoman and closed his eyes briefly. "Christ," he muttered. Then he sat his head back up and looked at Rachel.

"Do you remember me telling you I had an appointment with my gynecologist after work yesterday?"

"Yeah. Was I supposed to go with you or something?"

"No, you weren't. I went there straight from the school. That's not the issue. The doctor says I may be entering early menopause. I turn forty this year, and my prime childbearing years are behind me. I have already lost too much."

Luke exhaled. "Oh, I'm so sorry, hu—"

"Save it."

His head weighed a ton, and he was out of words.

She continued. "Tonight, I was in our room, and I decided to open the box sitting on your nightstand that you never open around me."

He looked up as his neck grew hot. "You *what?*"

"Yeah, I did. It has been sitting there forever, you've never shown it to me, and you're always guarded about it. It's like you were hiding it from me in plain sight. Now, I understand why. All those old pictures, and so many of them with some fat Black woman, maybe she's mixed, I don't know, it doesn't matter. Point is, you have a lot of pictures with that same woman."

"It's nothing, Rach. Those were just pictures from college. She's an old friend from campus ministry, her name's Ann. We were never together, and we haven't talked in a very long time, since before you and I met. You have nothing to worry about."

"No, Luke. You don't understand. It's not that you kept the pictures. I didn't see anything untoward in there. It's just that you looked truly *happy*. I have never seen you so happy in the fifteen years we've been together."

"Hun, that's not tr—"

She cut him off. "When I realized it, I had to face the fact that there was nothing left between us worth fighting for."

Luke sighed, feeling pained. "I'm sorry, Rachel. Please give me another chance, I can make it work..."

"The house is in my name since I brought it into the marriage, but I'm not interested in fighting. We can split everything down the middle if you want, you've lived here long enough. We can sell the house and split the proceeds; you can keep whatever furniture you want. I don't care. I'm done, Luke."

"No, Rachel, the house is yours."

"Okay. Let me know when you plan on moving out. I know it'll take you some time." She then stood up and went inside the bedroom, softly closing the door behind her.

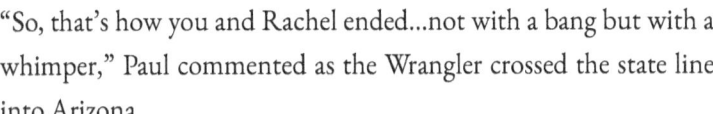

"So, that's how you and Rachel ended...not with a bang but with a whimper," Paul commented as the Wrangler crossed the state line into Arizona.

Luke nodded. "Yeah, pretty much. She was over it. I mean, I could tell in her voice she made her decision long before I walked through the door that morning."

"Sounds like she had been sitting on that for a while."

"I dunno. I guess I had to learn that people don't just magically stop caring about the things they tell you they care about. The way I looked at the situation at the time, I figured when she stopped talking about sex and babies, it was just less noise in my head, so everything was fine."

"What it sounds like is, she did tell you what she wanted from you, but you did nothing. You stuck around, but you didn't make the changes that would make her happy, probably figuring she wouldn't go anywhere."

"Paulie, you're probably not wrong."

"I hate to say it, 'cause God knows I'm no better, but Luke, that's worse than nothing."

Luke sighed. "The way I saw it, I was already a failure in school and my career. I was a failure at being the breadwinner and even in pulling my weight financially. I was a failure as a son and as a son-in-law. I didn't wanna fail as a husband, too."

"I know, but just like me, you failed at being a husband before you even got the divorce papers."

"Shit, I suppose so."

Paul nodded. "Curious, man – why didn't you ever show her the box? I assume it's one of those wooden boxes we made at one of the CK Infinity retreats?"

"Yeah...exactly. How'd you know?"

"Well, I remember after you made yours, it sat on your desk in our dorm room, and every time you would get pictures developed – you were always taking pictures and having other people take them – you'd get 'em developed and the ones you liked most would go right in that box."

"Yeah, that's it. I still have it in my apartment."

"Not surprised, you're kinda predictable." Paul cleared his throat. "But anyway, why'd you never show her? You guys were together for quite a while."

"You know what? I...I don't know."

THE RESORT
July 3, 2023

"Ooh, I'm drained," Paul uttered while focused on the road.

"Paulie, you want me to take over?" Luke asked, concerned.

"Nah, I'm fine. We're just about there. This'll be a relaxing stop, we'll be here for, like, three days. We'll sleep, we'll meditate, get entranced, and recharge. Then it's on to Cali."

"Sounds good. Honestly, I could use the rest too."

A few minutes later, while on the dusty Arizona desert road, a large attraction came into view from the distance.

"I think that's it, Luke!"

"That's massive!"

They approached an expansive, modern desert resort decorated with palm trees, small cacti, and water spouts. The exhausted friends entered the white-painted iron gates of the facility and parked.

"We're here!" Paul announced.

"Oh wow, this is nice!" Luke concurred. "But I do wonder how wasteful it is to run all that water out here in the middle of the desert."

"I know, but let's not think about it too much. Just focus on slowing down and laying out for a couple of days. Now, let's get checked in."

The friends exited the truck and walked through the clear glass doors. As soon as they entered, Luke breathed in the scent of fresh linens and wildflowers. The men approached the front desk. A petite woman clad in a light grey suit and purple scarf stood behind the polished maple wood front desk to greet the exhausted men.

"Good afternoon and welcome to Mystic Oasis Resort and Spa! My name is Milena, how may I assist you today?"

After checking in, they proceeded to their room. Inside were two plush queen beds with stark white sheets, white comforters, giant pillows, and tall, quilted fuchsia headboards. White towels, matching bathrobes and slippers were laid neatly on the beds. A simple pine desk sat against the wall, as well as a microfridge and a mounted television. Several decorative floor plants rested on the hardwood floor. A large window faced the beds, and beyond the sheer curtains, a patio complete with high-end deck chairs and hot tub awaited the two.

"This is...whoa," Luke said while wondering at the room.

"Told you this will be great."

"This is great...but 'shrooms though..."

"Not 'shrooms. It's ayahuasca. Anyway, it'll be fine. We'll be tripping together. It'll be great. Besides, as long as you're in a good place in your mind with good people, people you're comfortable with, you're more likely to have a good trip."

Luke took a deep breath. "Alright. I guess we'll do this."

"Awesome. glad you're on board with the program. Conor's gonna come and get us tomorrow night. Ope – I should say 'Casper.'"

"Casper?"

"Yeah, Casper's his shaman name. But yeah, he'll come by tomorrow around eight."

"Oh, sounds good. So, what do we wanna do now?"

"We got plenty of time to relax and enjoy the resort. Nothing will be more relaxing than a sauna," Paul suggested.

"So, a bunch of guys in a hot box with their junk hanging out?"

"I mean, when you put it that way..."

Luke narrowed his eyes. "Bro, I don't get what's supposed to be relaxing about a hot wooden box, especially out here in the desert."

"It's counterintuitive, but it actually helps you get acclimated to the heat of the desert, and sweating out all those toxins is healthy in its own right."

"Eh, I guess it's worth trying. I'm already gonna do something I've never done before, so what's one more thing?"

"Luke...you're telling me that in your forty-plus years of life, you've never used a sauna?"

"Swear to God."

"Well, damn. Let's do it!"

The friends changed into their resort-issued bathrobes and slippers and strolled around the facility. The two noted three restaurants serving a variety of cuisines and a lounge area. They also walked past a gigantic outdoor water area with a curved-edge infinity pool, wave pool, artificial waterfall, and three hot tubs. Young, scantily-clad guests occupied the lounge chairs, and the area was serviced by a tiki bar.

"Bro, look over there! See those hotties by the pool?"

"Sure, I guess."

"I might have to take a detour."

Luke looked at his lusty comrade disapprovingly. "Paulie – those girls don't look north of twenty. I'm sure they're your daughter's age."

"Ugh, now I feel like a dirty old perv. Thanks, bro," Paul responded sarcastically.

"That's what I'm here for."

The friends then passed by an outdoor game area picturing a giant chess board, shuffleboard, and cornhole setup with Ohio State and Michigan boards and matching bean bags.

"I bet you Conor suggested the cornhole."

Luke was not so sure. "Eh, a lot of people like cornhole."

"But that's the special 'The Game' edition," Paul pointed out. "Conor was always kind of a sports guy. Big Buckeyes fan."

"I see. But those are popular schools with national followings, so I dunno."

"I'll try to remember to ask him later."

A short time later, they arrived at a barrel sauna on the edge of the resort grounds. They each hung up their robes, removed their footwear, took clean white towels to sit on, and entered the empty sauna. The men rested across from each other, leaning their heads against the cedar wall, taking in the heat without a word.

After several minutes basking in the warmth, Luke admitted, "This is great, bro."

Paul smiled. "Told you."

"So, I've been thinking about some things. I wonder to myself what happens once our road trip is over. I want us to keep in touch, talk more regularly."

"Yeah, we will. Not gonna speak for you, but for me, a part of me was so ashamed of the life I was living down in Florida, especially back when I was still married. For the longest time, I didn't want you to see that I wasn't the same Paulie you knew at Great Lakes."

"I get it. To be fair, I didn't do my part to keep in contact either. I pushed everybody away. Ended up with nobody – no wife, no friends, and family judging the fuck out of me. Nobody in my corner. But when you called me that night, I knew I had to answer. You saved my life."

"Nah..."

"No, seriously. Paulie, you saved my life. I haven't told anybody this, but when you called, I was getting ready to end it."

"Like, *end it*, end it?"

"Yes."

"Fuck, man. Nothing's worth taking yourself out the game."

"It was stupid, I know that now. Now that I have a second chance, I still have no idea what to do with it."

"You know, you can do what you wanna do. It might mean your parents won't be onboard, but you've got to start living your own life. You have nothing tying you down anywhere. You can go where you wanna go and do what you wanna do. You are *free*, brother."

Luke sighed. "I suppose so, but sometimes it's overwhelming thinking about how much I lost. I made decades of dumb decisions."

"Sure, that part's not easy. Thing is, you've gotta make peace with your past and keep moving forward."

Luke was silent for a moment, then he had a realization. "Pauli e...I just thought about this...it's like, so much of this trip is about making peace with my past life, so I can move forward now."

"Exactly man – you got it. Sometimes we're so stuck in the thick of things, we can't see a way forward. We're swimming in our past lives, and it's heavy. It drags us down to the bottom if we let it. We just need to confront the muck we're swimming in and then get out of the fucking pool."

"True. But, y'know, there's one thing though. I haven't seen AC in like, twenty years, and we stopped speaking on kinda bad terms. She basically said she couldn't get over me if I was still in her life. Then, that was it."

⸺◈⸺

August 2003

The heavy, intense fog fell after a warm summer rain over the outskirts of Marbro, Kentucky. On a hillside road lined with small, Southern-style bungalows with tin roofs, Luke, with Ann in tow, parked his station wagon.

"So, I heard this place is popular. It's a country bar, but they have music and dancing. From what my vet school friends say, it's gonna be a great time," Luke said.

They both got out and began to walk uphill. Ann had on a pair of heeled black boots and flared black pants, with a matching sleeveless top over her bountiful torso. Luke wore a green button-up dress shirt, relaxed-fit dark blue jeans, and gym shoes.

"C'mon, it's starting to get chilly out here. Let's go," he called out to her. He began the trek uphill toward their destination.

After several minutes, he made it to the top of the hill. In view was a bustling roadside bar with country tunes clearly audible from the outdoors.

"Okay, Loose Lily's — this is definitely it," he said as he turned around. However, he did not see his companion. *Oh shit, didn't realize I left her behind, thought she was keeping up. I'll wait for her at the bar. She'll know where to find me.*

Luke entered the dim, smoky tavern, where a cover band was playing "Stop Draggin' My Heart Around." Several tables were taken but the bar had plenty of seats available. He grabbed a stool at the end of the bar counter and sat down, straightening up his side part haircut with his fingers.

Behind the bar, a man with a shiny bald head and long, grey beard came over to him.

"Hey man, what ya drinkin'?"

"Hey – I'll have a Pabst Blue Ribbon."

"Alright, sounds good, be right back." The heavy-set man carefully poured a draft beer and returned, placing the beer on the counter. "Here you go, three bucks."

Luke gave him four dollars in cash. "Here you go, keep the change."

He began nursing his beer when Ann trudged in, out of breath. She sat next to him and ordered a Stella Artois.

She was furious. "What the hell, Luke?!"

He took a swig of his PBR and looked at her. "What?"

"Dude, you left me behind. I don't know this area. I was losing my breath trying to keep up with you."

"My bad. Thought you were with me."

She nursed her Stella. "When did you even notice I wasn't with you? I could've been kidnapped out here."

"Nah, you'd have been fine."

She shook her head, still angry. "You don't know that, not like you could've seen it since you left me behind."

"C'mon, AC, nobody's gonna carry you away or anything."

"Really, Luke? Are you for real right now?"

He stopped and thought for a brief moment. "Shit – no, I didn't mean it like that."

"How *did* you mean it?"

"Not like that, it was stupid to say, I'm sorry."

She took another sip of her beer. "It's okay, don't worry about it."

He changed the subject. "So, how's work been?"

"Work is work. I'm the lead on a huge market research project for a major client. It's the first time they've given me a lead assignment of this caliber."

"That's great – congrats!"

"Thanks...it's a bit nerve wracking. I hope I can exceed their expectations."

"I'm sure you will. You're excellent at what you do."

Ann finished her beer and ordered another. "Thanks, Luke. Oh, by the way, you know how I told you about that guy Trevor I went out with once, who ghosted me, and then he started working at my job?"

"Yeah."

"So, Trevor was on the news; he was robbing a gas station with a company-issue shirt on."

"Wow, what a dumbass."

"Yeah, he's a moron. Anyway, how's class?"

"My classes are, y'know, what they are," Luke shared, still sipping on his initial drink.

"Have you gone out with anybody since that girl Shannon from school?"

"Nah. My parents have been trying to match me up with girls from church, though. A lot of them are pretty decent-looking, conventionally attractive, but they're kind of stupid and narrow-minded."

"Don't you hate that?" Ann commented as polished off her second drink and sent for a third.

"Yeah. I need a smart woman...gotta match me, y'know. But yeah, anyway, school sucks so bad right now."

"Uh...you're so smart. How is that even possible?"

"I dunno. I'm capable of doing the work, but I just can't get into it."

"Luke...are you sure vet school's for you?"

"Eh, I dunno, it has to be. I mean, if I had my choice, I would get away from all of this shit, travel, make documentaries, be fucking happy." Luke then finished his first PBR and ordered another.

"So, why don't you?"

"You know why."

Ann rolled her eyes. "Don't tell me the problem's your pare nts...again."

"Why'd you have to say it like that?" Luke responded incredulously.

"Look...I'm saying this in the nicest way I can, but you're twenty-three years old. Aren't you too old to be worried about what your parents think? Aren't you tired of living for them? Aren't you ready to go live your own life?"

"No, you don't get it, my parents won't let me hear the end of it. There is no 'living my own life,' AC. Y'know, 'honor your father and mother?'"

"Uh, yeah. But I thought you stopped believing in God."

"I mean, yeah...sure, I guess, I dunno. Still trying to figure it out. You know how that is."

She sipped on her beer. "Uh...sure. I get that completely. But I guess to your point, there's a difference between honoring your parents and letting them run your life so you don't get to make your own decisions as a grown man. For every 'honor your parents' verse in the Bible, there's another that says 'when I became a man, I put away childish things.'"

Luke paused and shook his head. "It's complicated."

"Is it though? Either do what you wanna do, or don't."

"No, seriously. It's complicated. You don't get it. You don't have to worry about your parents and their expectations, I mean, your dad died, and you don't even know your mom. It's a bit of a different thing than what I've got going on."

Ann stared down into her emptying third glass and started to tear up. "Be happy your parents are still here and you know them. I do have a mom that I know. She's not my birth mother, but she's still my mom. But yes, my dad is dead, and I would kill to have him back. And I've had to live with the feeling of knowing that for almost my entire childhood, I lived in the same city as my birth mother, and she never reached out to me, not even once. No visits, no letters, no birthday cards, not even a phone call. I live with the expectations of ghosts. I still wish I could make them proud of me, I'd love them to tell me, 'Ann, I'm proud of you,' but I'll never hear those words from their lips."

"Didn't mean to go there, AC."

"I promise you I wasn't trying to be mean. It's just that I care about you, and I wanna see you live a good life. I just want for you to be happy. You know, we only get one life, and we don't get to choose how long that life will be."

After speaking these words, she sat in silence for a few moments staring off into space. She then quickly finished her beer, which she had already paid for, hopped off the bar stool, and slipped outside.

After a few moments, Luke finished his beer and followed Ann out front. He made it just in time to see her folding up her clamshell cell phone.

"It's cold, why'd you come out here?" he asked.

She moved the long, damp strands of hair from her face. "I just called a cab. I'm heading home."

He shook his head and looked at the ground. "Why? Look, I'm sorry I said all that stupid shit back there, alright?"

"Um, let's see," she said pointedly while staring into his eyes. "You left me behind, you didn't notice, and when I said something about it, you thought it was a joke. And then the whole thing about my parents...I'm sorry I made you mad, but that was a low blow."

"Again, I'm really sorry."

"You know, back there, when I said to you that we only get one life, it dawned on me in that moment that I should've been saying this to myself all along. I've been in love with you from the very beginning, from when we first met in Terah's English class back at Great Lakes. And there have been times in our friendship that it seemed like you felt the same way, but for whatever reason you couldn't pull the trigger."

Luke, stunned, looked up at Ann's tear-soaked face.

She continued. "But at some point – it was when you had Paul reach out to me to say I was calling you too much and being clingy..."

"I fucked up there, I shouldn't have let him do that."

"It is what it is. Guess I needed to hear that. Point is, even though we both know that's bullshit, I'm not stupid. I've always felt that even if nothing would ever happen between us romantically, I wanted you to stay in my life, even if it was as a friend."

"AC, I've wanted that too."

"But back there in the bar, I realized I'm being chained by my own decisions. Even if you don't think I'm thin enough or pretty enough to be wanted or to be seen with, there's probably a man out there who thinks differently, who sees me and can truly accept me for who I am. But as long as you still have my heart, I'll never find out for sure. As long as you're still in my life, there's no way I'll be able to get over you. And just like you, I only have one life to live."

A yellow Ford Crown Victoria pulled up to the front of the roadside tavern.

Ann turned to him, her sparkling slate eyes met his, and simply said, "Goodbye, Luke."

She stepped into the taxi, and it drove off, leaving Luke in front of the bar in the fog of the night.

Paul laughed. "The thing is, the way you two ended your friendship, that was more intense than the end of your fucking marriage!"

Luke shook his head while viewing the desert sunset through the half-moon window of the sauna. "Shit, you're telling me. It's wild thinking about it."

"It's been twenty years, and you haven't gotten over a girl you never dated and you could've had, but you chose not to."

"Bro…you put it that way, it is pretty insane, isn't it?"

"It kinda is. Luke, I'll be honest with you. I think Ann did the right thing. She was crazy about you, and she needed to do what you couldn't."

"It sucks, but how do I deal with it now? After she stopped talking to me, she unfollowed me on the little social media that was around back then. Haven't heard from her since."

"I guess she meant what she said."

"Sometimes, I find myself looking her up online, y'know, on Facebook and other sites, but she's not an easy girl to find. She could have met somebody else and got married and might've changed her name for all I know. I don't know if she's still in Losanti, or if she moved, or even if she's still alive. Seems like you kept up with a lot of the old gang. Are you still in touch with her?"

Paul was quiet, then gave a small smile. "Yeah."

"Why didn't you say something? What's she up to? Wh-where is she? Is she married? Is she with somebody else? Don't hold out on me, Paulie! Tell me!"

"Nah, brother. Not gonna do that."

Luke calmed down. "Okay, will you at least tell me this? When y'all talk, does she mention me?"

"No, she doesn't. We get into our current lives, the here and now, not so much the past. She really did wanna move forward with her life. I mean, if you think about it, that stretch wasn't easy for her."

"True, I guess it wasn't. Her dad died right before we graduated from UGL and she moved down to Losanti. I remember talking to her about that, and y'know, they were really close. And she was just starting to learn some things about her mother...her bio mom that she didn't know, not her mother who helped raise her. Then, y'know, she moved down to Losanti, and I was the only one she knew there."

"Yeah, can't imagine being an outsider in fucking Losanti."

"Same, bro, same. Losanti's so parochial, my God. I was the only one she knew there, and, y'know, I took her for granted."

"Wow, I knew about her dad, but that's a lot. That's heavy."

"It is, and I made it so much worse. Started to neg her a bit and was kind of pushing her away. I dunno, I was in denial about what I wanted. If I'm honest with myself, I can't blame her for figuring she was gonna start over."

"Eh, I don't know if that's all on you, brother. See, I have a different take."

"I'm all ears."

"Why do you think she moved to Losanti in the first place?"

"Uh, from what I remember, she got the job at a marketing agency in town, so she ended up there."

Paul stared at his friend. "C'mon, Luke. No one, absolutely no one, just shows up in *Losanti* without having a damn good reason. Think about it. She's like a data scientist, a numbers chick, and she was at the beginning of her career at the time. She could've gone anywhere. I could even see her moving back to Detroit, where she's from. But she chose to move to Losanti of all places."

"Yeah?"

"I'm gonna ask you again. Why do you think she moved to Losanti?"

Luke expression changed to one of wonder. "Damn it! Did she tell you that?"

"No, but Stevie Wonder could've told you."

"Fuck...I don't know why I didn't get it then, but it's probably a good thing I didn't. That would've scared the shit out of mid-twenties me, but me now? I don't know how that's supposed to make it any better."

"I'm not saying it should, but what I am saying is, she made a choice, she took a chance, she took a leap of faith. It didn't work out. Sometimes it's like that. That's not your fault. It's not like you owed her anything."

"I suppose that's true."

"And when she realized it wasn't working, she did what you were not willing to do. Though, what you should've asked yourself is this: Why didn't you cut her off when it was clear that what she wanted, you weren't willing to give her?"

"True," Luke conceded.

Paul shook his head. "Of course. See, that's why I was so pissed at you when you came clean about your feelings for Ann when you first got married. No one cares how she looks. Literally nobody. You like what you like, not my business. But she was a nice girl, still is. You were selfish and full of pride. You lied about her, and you got me tangled up in your bullshit."

"Yeah, that was pretty bad."

"Oh, I know. And when you were telling me what happened to your marriage to Rachel, it reminded me of Ann. All these years, and it was as if you learned nothing. You weren't really in love with your ex, but you stayed in a marriage that wasn't working for over a decade. For what? To please mommy and daddy? And then in the end, she had to make the decision you weren't willing to make."

"Really? We're rehashing this?"

"We are, Luke. What I'm about to say is gonna sound mean, but it is what it is. Friends tell each other the truth."

Luke quietly scowled at his preachy friend.

"If you didn't want to be with Ann, the best thing you could've done was to end the friendship. But you didn't want to because deep down, you wanted the relationship, but you just didn't wanna deal with any potential shit you might get from your parents and the boys 'cause she's not a fucking ten."

He continued listening to what Paul had to say.

"So, here's what needs to happen. You have a decision to make, but it's up to you. After we relax here and trip, it's your call. Either way, you're moving forward with your life, but you can only do that if you take action."

"Action? Wait a second, Paul – the decision was already made for me twenty years ago."

Paul stood up and wrapped a towel around his waist. "Just because she made a decision back then – or really, a series of decisions – doesn't mean you don't have one to make in the here and now."

"Did you forget? I don't even know where she lives!"

The sauna door opened. As he left, he reiterated, "I said what I said, brother. You need to make a decision."

THE EXPERIENCE
July 4-5, 2023

The next night, Luke and Paul lounged in their luxury hotel room after enjoying dinner at a Navajo-themed restaurant on the resort grounds.

"That fry bread was so delicious!" Luke raved.

"For sure, it was incredible! And the hominy stew was scrumptious too!"

"Oh yeah, man."

"Ugh, I don't know why I still feel so tired," Paul noted while lying down on his bed.

"I dunno," Luke responded while sitting on the side of his bed facing his friend. "Food coma?"

"Nah. I'm more tired than what I would get with a food coma."

"Could it have been the sauna from yesterday?"

Paul shook his head. "Nah, after sitting in the sauna, I normally feel refreshed, not drained. Maybe I'm getting old."

"You're not getting old, but I hear you. It has been a long drive. Do you think you'll be fine for the trip later?"

"Oh yeah, totally. Maybe a short cat nap will do."

An hour later, the guys woke up from their alarm and jumped into comfortable clothes. Luke donned a light blue polo shirt, khaki shorts, and Birkenstock sandals. Paul decided to wear a white tee, grey track pants, and black flip-flops.

"Paulie, how'd you sleep?"

"Alright, I'd say. I'm still a bit beat, but the nap helped. Are you ready to trip, brother?"

"Uh, I guess I'm as ready as I'm gonna be. You sure you're good?"

"Yeah, wouldn't miss this for the world."

A firm fist knocked on the door. Paul rolled out of bed to answer it. A tall, thin, tanned man with aviator-style glasses was let into the room.

"Paulie!" the man exclaimed, holding out his arms inviting a hug.

"Hey Conor, my man!" Paul hugged the visitor.

"It's been too long, dude. Been wanting you to come out here since forever, glad you finally made it."

"You know how it is, but being out here you know I had to see you, man."

"So excited!" the man replied. "Glad you're here. You got skinny, dude!"

"Ah, just been working out," Paul replied.

"Nice," the visitor responded. He then turned to Luke, who had stood up as well. "I take it this is your friend you were telling me about?"

"Yeah," Paul said, turning to include Luke. "Conor...I mean Casper, right?"

"Yeah," Casper responded.

"Sorry, man. That'll take me a bit to get used to. Casper, this is Luke. Luke, Casper."

Luke waved at Casper, who motioned with his hand to join him. Luke obliged.

"Any friend of Paulie's is a friend of mine. Are you a hugger?"

Luke nodded, so he and Casper embraced as well.

"It's great to finally meet you, Casper. Paulie had a lot of great things to say about you," Luke told him.

"Likewise, dude, likewise. So, are y'all ready to start our journey?"

"Hell yeah!" Paul excitedly responded.

"Sure!" Luke replied, a tiny bit less excited.

"Alright brosephs, let's go! Oh, and by the way, bring jackets if you got 'em. It does get a bit chilly in the desert, even in the summertime."

Luke and Paul retrieved hoodies, and the men left the hotel room. They walked out to the front entrance and looked up at the darkening sky.

"I'm surprised we haven't seen fireworks since it's the Fourth of July," Luke noted.

"It's hot and dry out here," Casper reminded him. "Fireworks pose a bit of a fire risk."

Luke glanced at Paul with a face of slight anxiety, to which he shrugged. They then followed Casper out to the parking lot, where a dark blue Ford F-150 Raptor was parked.

"This is my steed, boys! We got cases of water and supplies, so you'll be just fine. Hop on in and be sure to buckle up!"

Paul got in the front seat with his old high school friend, while Luke sat in the back seat. Once everyone was in their seats and ready, Casper tied his salt-and-pepper locks into a ponytail, started the large pickup truck, and zoomed out of the lot. The sun was slowly falling downward in the great desert expanse as they headed southwest from the resort.

"This sunset is breathtaking," Paul remarked.

"It truly is. I've been living out here for decades and it never gets old. I'm glad you were able to come out here, Paulie. I wondered if that would ever happen, especially when you were talking all that religion," Casper recalled.

"Yeah, I was in deep back in the day. Figured I knew all there is to know about God and Jesus and the spiritual world, and the right way and the wrong way to do things."

"My guy, I take it you got humbled."

Paul sighed. "Yeah, yeah man, I did. In a big way."

"Not surprised. That happens to a lot of people. I mean, the folks who use their religion as a sword and shield are usually the least secure about it."

"Hmm, how so?" Luke asked.

"Well, Luke, think about it." Casper explained, "If you're confident in what you believe in, you don't need to fight other points of view, and you don't have to run away from the experiences that might be a bit outside of those beliefs, right?"

"Yeah, I suppose so."

"I mean, if you're truly all in with Christianity, for example, you might get super involved in practicing it because it's what you love, like going to church on Sunday, praying, reading the Bible, stuff like that. But you're not gonna need all the extra rules to be faithful, or try to control how other people live, and you'll probably be more open to the unknown and the unexplained, know what I mean?"

"Yeah, I think I understand."

"What a lot of people don't get about what I do out here is this – the idea isn't to take away from what you already have faith in. It's more about getting in touch with your inner self and seeing your life more clearly."

"I hear you. That's awesome."

"So, Casper, what kinds of people do you get taking you up on the excursions you offer?" Paul asked.

Casper laughed. "Oh, it's a lot of folks, Paulie. You'll be surprised. On weekends, I might get groups of ten or fifteen people at a time, fifteen's my limit. All different walks of life, different ages, colors, religions, all of that. The main thing is that most are looking for something a little different than what they get in their normal, every-day lives."

"How do you take all of those people out to where we're going? You're not taking this truck for that, are you?"

"Oh, no way, dude!" Casper gave a wheezing laugh. "I use my party bus. But since it's just y'all and we're friends, I figured we'd take my pride and joy. This is what I drive when I go out into the Sonoran by myself."

"This is quite nice," Paul said. "Feels very comfortable."

"Thanks, dude. That's the idea."

"So," Luke started, "Paulie and I noticed back at the resort that they have cornhole, of all things. Was that your idea?"

Casper snickered. "Yeah, it was."

Paul looked back at Luke and mouthed, "Told ya!"

"Here they call it 'beanbag toss,' but, you know, where we're from, we know it as 'cornhole.' And I'm sure you noticed what set it was."

"Of course. That's how I knew it was your doing."

"Yeah, I still love *The* Ohio State. And I suggested The Big Game set to the folks running the resort since they get a lot of visitors from the Midwest. Figured it would give them something familiar."

"Makes sense. So, how involved are you with the resort?"

"I'm a vendor partnered with them, so we have a nice profit-sharing agreement. It's a great deal, and it allows me to live my dream and not have to struggle financially. Can't complain."

Paul smiled. "That's beautiful shit, man."

Luke piped up. "That is pretty cool. But I gotta ask, what about the legality of it?"

Casper smirked. "You're not a narc, are you?"

"God, no."

"Nah, man," Paul interjected. "Luke's good people."

The shaman laughed. "I'm just fuckin' with ya. Anyway, Luke, that's a really good question. On paper, my excursions are called 'Native ceremonial experiences.' That's how we can offer the tea legally-ish. I don't advertise – folks in the know are aware of what I do and seek me out. And the cops around here, they don't care. They're more worried about border jumpers than some old white hippie from Ohio."

A half-hour later, the men were traveling in the middle of the dark, increasingly cool desert, with seemingly nothing and no one as far as the eye could see. Then Casper spoke up. "Alright dudes, we're about to turn off onto a dirt road. Then it'll just be a few more minutes, and we'll be at our destination."

The pickup swerved to the left and sped onto a road of sand and dirt. Only the shaman knew where they were going.

"Wow, we really are in the middle of nowhere," Luke quipped.

"Yeah, this is gonna be amazing!" Paul noted in anticipation.

Less than five minutes later, the truck stopped. "Wait here," Casper told his passengers. He then picked up a flashlight in his center console, shut off the ignition, and stepped out of the truck. Luke and Paul could see absolutely nothing in the pitch darkness.

"I don't know about this, Paulie," Luke spoke quietly.

Paul looked back at him. "It'll be fine. Don't get worked up, man."

They could hear the tailgate come down and items being moved. Several minutes later, a bright orange flame came into view to the right of where the two were sitting. The fire illuminated what appeared to be a small outdoor camping area.

"Oh okay, that looks pretty cool," Luke commented.

Paul laughed. "I told you, brother."

Shortly after this, Casper came to get his friends.

"Alright dudes, the ceremonial circle is ready," he announced.

The men exited the F-150 and took a look around. A dark cast iron kettle was suspended atop a small bonfire, and fold-up lawn chairs, buckets, and blankets were placed on the dusty ground around the contained flames. To the side sat a wheeled rectangular blue cooler and a case of bottled drinking water.

"Make sure you start drinking water," the shaman advised. "It's pretty chilly out here, but remember, we are in the desert. And the desert can dehydrate you fast."

"No shit," Luke spat out, his lips feeling desiccated.

The excursionists grabbed a bottle of water and sat in two of the three available lawn chairs, which included cup holders they could use for their bottles. Meanwhile, Casper walked over to the edge of the encampment and began urinating in a circle around their designated area, facing away from his guests.

Luke whispered, "What's he doing?"

Paul shrugged and responded in a low voice. "I dunno...I guess he really had to take a piss."

After the shaman was finished, he sat in the unoccupied lawn chair. "The desert has all kinds of wild animals. Male urine repels many of them. For the others, including the most dangerous of all, I have this." He raised his blue graphic tee slightly to show the wood grain handle of a pistol holstered at his side.

"What's the most dangerous animal out here?" Paul asked.

"Probably humans," Luke mused.

Casper smiled, "You're right, Luke. Humans are more likely to be a danger to us than anything else out there. We've got constitutional carry here, so I stay armed, as is our second amendment right."

"I thought you were a hippie," Paul commented.

"I *am* a hippie, but I'm not stupid."

Luke looked over at Paul. "Man's got a point."

"So, before we start, I wanna give you an overview of how this night's gonna go," Casper announced. "We're gonna spend some time in quiet, guided meditation. This is to help improve your likelihood of having a positive spiritual experience. Then, after our minds and bodies are fully prepared for the experience, I'll give you a small cup of hot tea, and you will drink it. You'll let go of your worries and anything holding you back, and let the ayahuasca, the active ingredient in the tea, take over. The experience can last up to eight hours."

"Eight hours?" Luke whispered to himself.

"Yes. Likely it won't be that long, but it can be. I will be here with you both, so you are not alone. Also, buckets are available in case you purge – in other words, throw up. If that happens, do not be alarmed. It's the negative energy, feelings and toxins leaving your body. Any questions?"

"Where's the bathroom?"

Casper pointed away from the group into the dark expanse. "Out there. This isn't civilization, this is the desert. Any other questions?"

The ceremony participants shook their heads.

"Oh, this is something I need to make sure I say before we continue. This was in the packet where you signed up, but to reiterate – I will do everything I can so you have a positive spiritual experience, but unfortunately I cannot guarantee it. Negative spiritual experiences, or 'bad trips,' can happen, and neither myself nor Mystic Desert Resort and Spa are responsible for negative experiences, animal attacks, hypothermia, medical events, or any other harm that could befall you during the ceremony. Do you consent to continuing with the experience?"

"Yes," Paul said.

Luke hesitated, then said, "Yes."

"Alright, this will be incredible guys! Now let's get started."

Casper directed the men to two quilted blankets laid atop the sandy ground. "You'll want to take a space and lie on your back facing up. As you know, I'm Casper, and I am your shaman, your guide for tonight's ceremony. I will lead you through a meditative exercise, so you'll be prepared for the spiritual experience."

"So, this is kind of like foreplay?" Paul quipped.

The guide shook his head and laughed. "You could say that."

The participants took space and reclined on their respective blankets. The men used small, plush pillows to rest their heads.

Casper, while pacing, began to guide them through the meditation.

"Get comfortable, and hold your hands to your stomach," Casper began. "Breathe in, one...two...three...four...five...hold . Then breathe out, five...four...three...two...one. And again..."

Luke felt his body relax as he followed the shaman's lead. The stars in the sky sparkled, and the sounds of the outdoors were clear and pronounced.

"Now begin to feel the ground beneath you. Sink your body into the ground. Your legs...breathe in...one...two..."

The ground became one with his body as all his worries fell away.

"Your arms...breathe in...one...two..."

Luke slowly shut his eyes and felt the soft breeze flow over his face.

"Focus on your breathing...breathe in...one...two...three..."

Luke began to visualize himself standing on a vast oceanside beach, the wind flowing through his strands of hair and atop his head. He could feel warm, grainy sand between his toes, and the tide flowing calmly onto shore and back out again.

"The sun is shining down, warming your skin..."

Luke could hear the whistling of the seagulls in the sky, as the tepid ocean water began to wash over his feet. He could smell the freshness of the air as it traveled up his nostrils. Peacefulness and calm overtook him. He felt at home.

"Breathe in...one...two...three...four...five, hold. Breathe out...five...four...three...two...one. Now open your eyes."

He opened his eyes, and he felt incredibly serene. He peered over to Paul, who had a relaxed smile on his face.

"Are you ready for the next step?" Casper asked the men.

"Definitely," Paul replied, smiling. He then glanced at Luke.

Luke then replied. "For sure."

Casper began to speak. "You'll want to sit up, but get nice and comfortable." As Luke and Paul sat up, the shaman coached their inhalation and exhalation. "Breathe in...one...two...three...four...five. Hold. Breathe out...five...four...three...two...one."

As Luke and Paul sat on their blankets in a calm state, Casper recommended, "While I prepare the tea, make sure you drink plenty of water."

The men each drank water and continued sitting serenely. Casper produced two glazed mugs in burnt orange, as well as a long, silver ladle, from his black backpack at the edge of the circle. He used the ladle to stir the open kettle, then scooped up the contents to pour into the two mugs, which were then placed on the ground. After a minute to cool, he gave a mug to each of them.

Luke peered inside the mug and noticed the average-sized vessel was filled halfway. *This stuff smells really strong. Must be concentrated or something.*

"In your mug is a brewed tea made from a plant-based compound called ayahuasca. Ayahuasca has been consumed as part of religious rituals and for therapeutic purposes in indigenous communities for generations. Ayahuasca helps us bridge the gap between this world and the spiritual realm, brings us closer to nature, and can often help us see reality in a completely new way. Think of what you are about to experience as a journey of possibilities."

Then, Casper came Luke's way.

"Drink." The earthy, odd taste was novel. It sloshed around his mouth for a short period, then he swallowed. *Oh boy, here we go.* He sat the mug on the blanket next to him, took a swig of his water bottle, and then continued to sit and wait.

Casper then instructed Paul. "Drink."

Paul drank from his mug as Luke had done and waited silently.

"Breathe in...one...two..."

Casper's voice deepened and the counts slowed. "Five...four..."

Incredible...

The bonfire turned purple and swirled around them. *The warmth.* The fire turned into a soft, warm hand cupping Luke like a precious pearl. He was lifted up higher and higher. He could see himself sitting in lotus position next to Paul, near the desert fire, and Casper walking around the fire.

The periwinkle hand of flame elevated him upward and away from the camp. He felt one with the burning fire. He was taken higher and higher, beyond the Sonoran Desert. He was wowed by the incredible beauty of the Grand Canyon as he glided by. The expansive Rocky Mountain Range impressed him, as did the thin air at high altitude. As he continued to fly by the earth below, the stars sparkled and danced. Then, the majesty of the Northern Lights astounded him. Tears streamed down his face as he was overwhelmed by the stunning beauty of the world he was seeing.

The palm of fire then brought him to the heavens. The sky became brighter until it was the whitest white he had ever seen. And then, a short time later, the flame placed Luke at rest. He was sitting cross-legged, embers in violet encircling him. A man in a lilac robe bisected by a broad gold sash, whose skin was like burnished bronze, with a full head of brilliant, woolen hair, appeared sitting facing Luke.

"Hi, Luke," said the man.

"You know my name?"

"Of course I do."

"Who the hell are you?"

The man chuckled and replied in a soft-spoken tenor voice. "I am Spirit."

"Spirit? Like...God?"

The man flashed his brilliant, perfect white teeth.

"Shit. How did I get here? I'm not dead, am I?"

"Oh no! You're more alive than you've ever been," Spirit remarked. "You drank some tea that shaman dude gave you, remember?"

"Uh...yeah. Shit was weird." Luke looked around the illuminated space in wonder. He realized his innermost thoughts were audible in this celestial realm.

"Now this doesn't happen a lot, and it doesn't happen to most folks," Spirit explained. "Most of 'em don't get all the way up to me. But it looks like your soul was open to the experience. So here I am."

"Oh man, that's...I don't know, uh, Spirit. I got nothing right now."

"No worries," Spirit laughed. "A lot of folks have that reaction."

"Um...if I told my parents, they would be really, really surprised, but then again, they'd never believe me. They'll think I've lost my damn mind."

"A lot of folks have that reaction, too. I'm not quite like Charlton Heston."

"More like Morgan Freeman?"

"Nah, I'm pretty cool, but not that cool."

Luke laughed.

"Just so you know," Spirit continued, "I'm always with you. I've been with you the entire time you've been alive."

"Oh, wow. So does this mean my parents have been right about you the whole time?"

"What, that I exist?" The robed man then held out his hands and shrugged. "Yes – and no. A lot of folks try the best they can with what they know and what they've been taught. Your mama and your pops? They're like that. The folks at your church? They're like that. Your ex-wife is like that, too. I get it."

Luke nodded.

"But this," Spirit continued, raising his hands up wide, "The spirit world, life after death and what it all looks like – it's not as cut and dry as they make it out to be. Most folks say they want freedom, they love it, but in their day-to-day lives, they feel more comfortable with a lot of rules and regulations, 'specially on other folks. It gives 'em the feeling of certainty and control."

"Understandable..."

"If they believe the right stuff and do all the right things, and stay away from the wrong things, they know where they're going after they die. And if they don't, they get grace and mercy, but everybody else gets judgment. Real easy. Truth is, nobody knows what happens after death." Spirit leaned in, his face just inches from his visitor's. "*Nobody*. If they say they know, they're lying to themselves. Death is the biggest unknown."

"So, um...Spirit, what does freedom really look like?"

The deity leaned back. "Freedom – true freedom – means letting go of the idea of certainty. There are no guarantees, nobody really knows. It's all made up anyway. Be okay with what you don't know, and use this life to do good for other folks and for yourself. You only get one life. As for death, you don't know until you're at the crossroads. And that hasn't happened yet."

"Oh, okay. So, uh, since I'm here, what should I do with my future? My parents say I should do what they want me to do, y'know, 'Honor thy father and mother.'"

Spirit sighed. "Of course, you honor your folks, but honor's not the same as acting like a child, depending on them to dictate what your life's gonna look like, choosing to pass on making decisions for yourself, and ducking and dodging accountability. Honor is doing right by them when they need you. See, that's love, that's honor."

"I see."

"But, Luke, this life is still yours to live. You're not living for your folks, and they don't get a do-over through you."

"Oh wow, never thought about it like that."

"C'mon. I'm sure I'm not the first to tell you."

Luke looked down. "Yeah, my best friend Paul has said it. And then, Ann...AC, my old friend. She would say it a lot, and I remember it made me so angry. I lashed out at her, and then she stopped speaking to me."

"Welp, sometimes the truth hurts."

"You're right, but pushing her away – it's the biggest mistake of my life."

"Seems to me you've got some amends to make."

Luke shook his head. "I know, but it's not like I know where she is. Paulie knows but he won't tell me...and even if I did know, she said she needed me out of her life. What if she still feels that way?"

"Hmm," Spirit responded. "Welp, at the time, she said what she felt she needed to say – and she might still feel that way."

"Could you at least tell me for sure? Paulie thinks I should see her. But he won't tell me anything else."

"I'm not gonna tell you either. Paul's a great friend to you both, and he was a real one for saving your life. Just so you know – there will come a time when he'll need you as much as you needed him. Make sure you're as good a friend to him as he is to you."

Luke took a deep breath. "I will."

"Lemme ask you this. If you were to see Ann again, how would you like things to turn out?"

"Oh wow...you want me to be honest?"

"Nah. I want you to lie to me," Spirit quipped sarcastically. "What do you think?"

"Yeah, that was a stupid question."

The celestial being pressed his head in his hand and slowly shook it.

"So yeah, honestly, I would want AC to forgive me. I want us to be friends again and I don't wanna lose her. I love her and I truly wanna be with her. She's uniquely beautiful, one of a kind. Back when we were friends, I enjoyed her presence and she was fun. She was safe, and at the same time, she pushed me to be a better version of myself. Not a day goes by without me thinking about her and wondering to myself what might've been if I had acted on my true feelings instead of being so prideful and cowardly at the same time."

"Okay. That's fine. Two things."

"What?"

Spirit reiterated. "Two things. There's a chance she could say 'no.' There's a chance she could say 'yes.' It's up to her. You can't be certain, and you don't get to control the outcome. But that's okay."

"Is it, though?"

"It is. If she says no, at least you have closure and you can move on with your life. And it's better to know than to wonder 'What if?' That's what life's about – taking leaps of faith, trying something new, doing things differently."

"Kinda like what she did when she moved to Losanti?"

"Exactly. Some of the chances you take work out. Some of them don't. But you haven't truly lived if you never try."

"Yes, Spirit. I'm pretty sure I understand."

"And the other thing."

"What's that?"

"How did you make Ann's life better when you were in it?"

Luke was silent.

"Dig deep, Luke. If you're real with yourself, do you think you would be good for Ann right now? Would you elevate her, or would you bring her down?"

"Ope, I dunno. Hadn't thought about it."

"You should. While your wants and needs matter, not everything is about *you*."

Luke took a deep breath and averted his eyes. "Ugh, that's true. I mean, what could she do with a broke divorced loser who works third shift at the Dairy Union?"

"Nah, Luke, that's not the point. Nobody cares about your job but your folks. Everybody's gotta eat."

"So, what's your point?"

Spirit clarified. "Alright, here's what I'm talking about. All this time, you thought about how much you miss her. On your wedding day, you missed her. Throughout your marriage, you missed her. It's been twenty years, and even now, you miss her. You missed her presence, you missed being around her and the positive impact she made in your life."

"Yeah...true."

"But she stopped talking to you because of the impact you were making in hers."

Luke felt a twinge of embarrassment deep in his soul.

"To even have a chance of being with her," Spirit added, "it can't just be about you. It has to be about her, too. Be the kind of man she can say 'yes' to."

"I'll do my best. Thanks Spirit!" The reddish-blue flame whipped back up and cupped him to carry him away.

"No problem Luke, anytime," Spirit called out. "Oh, and by the way – all that drinking and carrying on – if you don't quit that mess! Don't be like your pops!"

Within seconds, the traveler was transported by the warm bluish flame back the way he came and returned to his body.

◄◆►

Luke awakened to the gorgeous rising sun, still sitting yoga style. The bonfire was out, the kettle was packed, and most of the campsite was cleaned up except Luke's blanket and bottled water. Casper and Paul were standing over him with grimacing faces.

"Hey Luke," Casper called to him. "Your experience lasted for quite a while, man. I was starting to get worried."

"Yeah, brother," Paul added. "I came back some time ago, it's been at least a few hours. Are you okay?"

"Uh, yeah. I feel great...amazing." Luke stood up. He shook out his legs, as they were a bit weak from his cross-legged sitting position. "What time is it?"

"Dude, it's like five in the morning," Casper told him.

"What?" Luke was shocked. "It didn't seem like it was anywhere near that. Maybe an hour, if that. But it was fucking amazing."

"C'mon, we're gonna go ahead and head back now," Casper said, as he finished cleaning up the last of the campsite. "We'll talk about it in the truck."

Once the men and the rest of the supplies were loaded up in the truck, Casper got in, started it, and turned it around in the dry desert sand to head back to the resort.

"Paulie, what was your experience like?" Luke asked.

"It was good. I saw some really neat visuals, lots of cool colors. I realized I'm holding onto so much guilt, and I was able to purge it. Now, I'm at pea—" Paul began coughing hard.

Luke handed him a bottle of water from the back seat. "You okay, man?"

After a few minutes and a giant sip of water, he responded. "Yeah, I'm good. Just got a little sand in my lungs from the desert."

"I know how that is. Can't feel good," Casper sympathized.

"Yeah, it sucks, but I'll be okay," Paul reassured him.

Casper turned to Luke. "How was your experience?"

"Oh my God, it was amazing. I was carried above the campsite by a giant flaming hand, imagine the hand of King Kong holding the girl but made of fire and holding me. I was floating up and I saw us all there at the site. And I saw mountains, the Grand Canyon, the Northern Lights, talked to God..."

"What?" Casper was a bit taken aback.

"Yeah, I talked to God, we had, like, a conversation."

Casper was quiet.

Luke noticed the silence and narrowed his eyes. "Should I be worried?"

Casper responded. "No, not really, dude. I mean, you came back to your body, so you're fine. It's just that what happened to you was very unusual, especially for a first-timer."

"God said pretty much the same thing."

"So, Casper, what happened to Luke?" Paul asked, sounding a little scratchy.

"From what it sounds like, he did what's called astral projection. It's an out-of-body experience while you're awake. When it happens, you leave your body, and you see the real world around you, and you can go into other realms and realities. Some travelers don't go far, some go super far, like around the world. Travelers talk to gurus, wise men and women, people who have passed on, deities, whoever. It's an amazing thing."

"Have you ever done it, Casper?" Paul asked.

"Yes, but my out-of-body experiences haven't been quite as spectacular as his. Can't say I ever talked to God. Now here's the thing. It's ridiculously hard to do, especially for a first-timer, that I didn't think to warn you of the dangers."

"Dangers?"

"Yeah. Occasionally, travelers who astral project run into negative energy, bad spirits, stuff like that. They won't kill you or possess you or anything like that, but it can affect your experience negatively. Then — I haven't seen this firsthand, but at least from what I've read, there's the very small chance you don't make it back into your body."

"What?!" Luke exclaimed. "What happens if you don't make it back?"

Casper waved his hand next to his neck and made a clicking sound with his mouth. "Then, that's all she wrote, dude."

ADMITTED
July 6, 2023

Two days later, the traveling companions left the resort to continue on the next leg of their trip.

"Hey man," Paul said to Luke as they wheeled their bags to the Jeep. "I'm kind of under the weather right now. Are you okay to drive today? It's a bit of a long one."

"Yeah, sure. I figured I was gonna do that anyway." Luke noticed that his friend appeared a bit pekid. "Are you alright, Paulie? You're not looking too good."

"Yeah, I'm alright. Maybe I just need to finish getting the tea out of my system."

"That was two nights ago."

"It was our first time doing it. I guess I'm not used to it."

"I'm not either, but I'm fine."

"We're all different, kind of like how your experience was longer than mine even though we had the same brew."

"Look, man." Luke stopped and touched Paul's shoulder to get his attention. "If you get any worse, we're gonna find you an urgent care and get you checked out."

"Nah bro, I don't really do doctors," Paul protested.

"When's the last time you've gotten a checkup?"

"It's been years, the last time was probably while I was still married."

"Bro..." Luke sighed. "You pushed me to get back on my meds, and yet you haven't been to a doctor in at least five years?"

"I dunno. It's easier to tell the people I care about what they need to do than to do those things myself."

"Fair. But anyway, if you get any worse, I'm taking you to a doctor. I'm dead serious."

"Alright, but I really don't wanna hold us up. We have a destination to get to."

"Fuck that. Your health is more important. We can figure out our schedule and any arrangements later if we have to."

"Sure. But trust me, Luke, I'm okay, I just need to sleep it off and I'm sure I'll feel better."

The men loaded up the Wrangler. Paul reclined the passenger's seat a bit to get comfortable, while Luke got into the driver's seat and started the truck.

"By the way, where are we going?" Luke asked.

"We're going to California. The GPS will guide the way. It's fine."

"You don't think I should have an idea of where we're driving to?"

"You'll see when we get there. Trust me, man. Have I steered you wrong yet?"

Luke sighed. "No."

"So yeah, trust me and trust the GPS."

The travelers drove onto Interstate 10 West. Paul fell asleep quickly as music played in the otherwise quiet interior. The men traveled uneventfully through the desolate, peaceful desert. Taking the wheel, Luke breathed in the scenery, unencumbered by the constant companions of his needling thoughts. Ever since the desert experience, he felt more peace than he had in his entire life.

An hour later, they crossed the Colorado River Bridge and passed by the blue "Welcome to California" sign with brilliant yellow flowers on it.

We made it to California! Now, what's next?

✦

Luke had driven for two and a half hours while Paul remained asleep. After making their way through hours of sparsely populated desert, a bit more civilization came into view. Suddenly, the tranquility was broken by a rough, strangled bark.

"Oh shit! Paulie, are you okay?"

Paul was unable to speak. He woke up from sleep with a choking, uncontrollable cough. Luke pulled over on the side of the road.

"Here's some water."

Paul barely noticed the water and appeared to be in distress. After a couple of minutes, he finally regained his breath and drank.

"Oh man, that sucked," Paul said. He then coughed a bit more.

"Alright," Luke responded, trying to remain calm. "I'm gonna look for an urgent care now."

"No, Luke!" Paul coughed some more. "I...I'll be fine!"

"No, you're sick. You need to be looked at. We're going." Luke conducted a new search on the dashboard GPS, this time for "urgent care near me." It pointed to a facility in Indio, a city about five minutes away. "Alright brother, let's go."

A few minutes later, which felt like an eternity, they arrived at the urgent care center. Paul trudged to the reception desk to be checked in. Luke went with him for support.

"Hi, welcome to CareAlpha Urgent Care," recited a masked middle-aged woman with glasses behind a computer. "What is your name and date of birth?"

"Paul Chu, C-H-U. Twelve...ten...seventy-nine."

"Okay, do you have any insurance?"

"Yeah, it's out of state, though, so I don't know if you take it or not. Here's my card." Paul pulled out his wallet and gave them his insurance card.

"We'll also need your driver's license or state ID."

Paul slid over his Florida driver's license.

"Okay Mr. Chu, so it does look like we take your insurance. So, what are you being seen for?"

Paul explained, "Um...bad cough, shortness of breath, extreme tiredness, fatigue, thirst, uh...headache."

Luke shot a look at him, irritated that his friend was worse off than he had previously disclosed.

"How long have you had these symptoms?" asked the receptionist.

"Uh, I don't know," Paul said, appearing confused.

Luke interjected. "He's been coughing for the past few days, I wanna say it started, like, around July 3rd. But it got really bad this morning."

The receptionist typed in the details. "Okay, so we charge fifty dollars upfront for the copay. We take cash or credit. If it ends up being more, we will bill you for the balance."

"That's fine," Paul consented.

"Okay, Mr. Chu, have a seat over there please." The recep-tionist pointed to a section of empty chairs in the waiting area. "There are a few other patients in front of you, but we'll get you back there as soon as we can."

The two took a pair of plush plum-colored seats in the waiting room. On the wall-mounted televisions played a home improve-ment reality show. Luke picked up a sports magazine and began to flip through it.

"So, I see the Rays are having a pretty good season."

"Yeah, they are. If I was still out here betting, I'd probably be making a killing. But..." Paul coughed a little. "The Green Sox, hopefully the owner will finally decide to field a good team."

"You and I both know that's not gonna happen."

"Yeah, don't I know it? But a man can dream."

After several minutes, a woman wearing light blue scrubs and a medical mask opened a side door. "Paul?"

Paul began to get up, as did two other men in the waiting room.

"Which one?!" a man yelled out.

The nurse's eyes floated down to her clipboard. "Oh, um, sorry. Paul C."

Paul got up from his chair and said to Luke. "Hopefully it won't take too long. They'll give me some good shit and send me on my way." He met the nurse and slowly dragged himself through the solid white door, which closed loudly behind him.

Nearly an hour later, the nurse returned to the waiting room. "Luke?"

Luke looked around, then he went up to the nurse. "I'm Luke."

She said, "Paul called for you."

He followed the nurse through the sterile, nondescript hallway to a room on the left. Once he entered, he noticed Paul sitting in a slouched posture on the examination table with a yellow gown in place of his tee shirt, which was sitting on the chair next to the table. He sat in a chair across from his ill friend.

"Paulie, what did the doctor say?"

Paul responded quietly. "Luke, they're saying I need to go to the ER."

"What? Why? What's going on?"

He cleared his throat. "So...I'm negative for COVID. But my pulse ox is 81 percent."

"What does that mean?"

"I have lower than normal oxygen in my blood. They think I have some kind of lung infection. They don't know why."

"Damn."

"They also told me my blood pressure is sky high, 220/118."

"Jesus..."

Paul coughed hard, then sputtered out, "I'm...sorry..."

"Don't apologize. Shit happens man. We're gonna go to the hospital, they'll do what they need to do to get you better, and we'll get you home. And when you're healed up, I'll get down to Florida to hang out, or we can finish the trip, or whatever you're up for."

"Thanks, man."

The doctor knocked, then walked into the room. She pulled her long black and auburn microbraids into a quick bun and then washed her hands.

"Hi, I'm Dr. Reynolds. You must be Paul's partner, Luke."

Paul cracked a small smile. "Uh, yeah."

"Paul, do I have your permission to discuss your diagnosis and treatment with Luke?"

"Yes, Doctor."

"Okay. So, Luke, Paul has tested negative for COVID-19, and we don't believe he has the flu. But he does seem to have a lung infection of some sort, perhaps pneumonia. The level of oxygen saturation in his blood is very low. We like to see that number at ninety-five percent or higher. Below ninety-two percent is concerning. Paul's blood oxygen is at eighty-four percent, which means he needs to be in the emergency room."

Luke reacted, "Oh boy..."

"His blood pressure is also extremely high, which puts him at great risk for heart attack or stroke, and the hospital should hopefully be able to get that down. Unfortunately, we don't have the resources to take care of him here at urgent care. I recommend LA County General Hospital, here are directions to get there." The doctor handed Luke a printed piece of paper with directions. "We can call an ambulance, but you're better off driving there yourself."

He looked at his friend. "Are you sure you don't want an ambulance? I can ride with them if they let me, or I can meet you at the hospital."

"It's like a thousand dollar ride. I'm good for it, but that's money that could go towards pretty much anything else. You got this, partner."

The nurse then came in with discharge papers and handed them to Paul. "Here you go, Mr. Chu."

The doctor then said, "You're free to go, the hospital is about twenty minutes away. The address is in the discharge papers. I have called ahead so they can expect you. I hope your day improves, sirs."

"Thank you," Luke said.

After the doctor and nurse left the room, Luke stood up, grabbed Paul's shirt, and helped him off the table.

"Let's go, partner."

⬥

"'Partner?' Really?" Luke commented incredulously, while driving with haste to the county hospital.

Paul shrugged. "Yeah. Why not? They asked me, I said yes. I want them to be willing to share my details with you. Honestly, I feel like shit, and if you're listening in when the doctor's talking, you can catch things I'm not able to."

"Fair enough."

The men arrived at Los Angeles County General Hospital several minutes later. It was a very large white and grey building, bigger than any medical facility either had ever seen previously. Luke dropped Paul off in front of the emergency room entrance, found parking in the visitor section, then walked over to meet him at the door.

Entering the medical center, they went over to the reception area to get checked in. Paul provided his identification and personal details to the ER receptionist, as he had at the urgent care facility. The receptionist was then able to access his information from the CareAlpha visit.

"Oh, okay, it looks like uh, Dr. Shonda Reynolds has notified us of your arrival, with all the details," he noted. "Please have a seat, and we'll call you back shortly."

Paul and Luke took seats to wait to be called back. A couple of minutes later, a man wearing grey scrubs came through the swinging double doors with a wheelchair. "Paul Chu?"

They went to get up, but the nurse brought over a wheelchair.

"I don't think I need that," he squeezed out before another coughing fit ensued.

"Paulie, you do. Sit down," Luke told him sternly, pointing to the wheelchair. The nurse wheeled the patient back with his companion following closely behind. They were brought to a designated area covered by curtains.

Over the course of a few hours, Paul was on an examination table, hooked up to an intravenous line for fluids and medications. He was physically examined, and blood tests and scans were administered to determine a more definitive diagnosis. Luke stayed by his side on a cushioned beige chair.

A little after seven o'clock in the evening, a masked, middle-aged man in blue scrubs entered the area where Paul was being seen. He logged onto the computer and pulled up his information and test results.

"Hi, Paul, I'm Dr. Hernandez, and I'm the ER doctor tonight. How are you feeling?"

"Not great, I'm getting a little bit better, though," Paul said, tiredly.

"That sounds good. Since we've started you on blood pressure medication and steroids, you should be feeling a little better." He paused to peruse the medical chart on the computer next to him.

"When was the last time you had a routine check-up?"

"Uh...honestly, it's been a long time. At least since before my divorce, so like, at least five years ago?"

Dr. Hernandez faced Paul, sighed, and took off his glasses. "Well, Paul, you're really lucky to be alive right now. Radiology has taken a look at the scans, and we've examined the results, and you have advanced coronary artery disease. Quite a lot for a man your age."

Paul shook his head. "Fuck...but how? I work out all the time, and I don't think I eat like shit, or at least too much like shit."

"Well, that's a hard question to answer. It could be genetics, or it could be other underlying issues we're not aware of yet."

"So, is that why I have this horrible cough too?"

"Possibly it's part of it, but you also have pneumonia." The doctor looked back at the chart. "The sputum test results tell us you have fungal pneumonia, which is pretty rare. We usually see this in people who are immunocompromised."

"What?" Paul responded, shocked. "I hardly ever get sick. The last time I got really sick was almost ten years ago."

"Have you been around birds or farm animals recently?"

"No, not that I can think of. I mean, we've been traveling cross country for about a week or so, but no farmland or big groups of birds that I can think of."

Luke shook his head. "Yeah, I'm pretty sure we weren't around anything like that."

The doctor's tone turned solemn. "I have some additional questions to ask you, Paul. They're of an intimate nature. We can have your friend sit in the waiting room until we're done."

"No, Luke can stay," Paul responded. "It's fine."

"Are you sure? We typically advise patients to answer these questions without family or friends present. I want to make sure you feel free to answer these questions openly and honestly."

"I'm sure. I have nothing to hide. He stays," he insisted.

"Okay." The doctor returned to the computer screen and typed in some notes, then clicked on another tab. "Paul, right now I will ask you a series of questions about your sexual history. Please answer to the best of your ability. We ask these of everyone, and it is simply to assist in your diagnosis and treatment."

"Okay," Paul responded softly.

Dr. Hernandez began. "Are you currently sexually active, meaning engaging in oral, vaginal, or anal sex?"

"Uh, what do you mean by current?"

The doctor took a moment to reformulate the question. "Do you have a current partner, or engaged in a sexual relationship with anyone currently?"

"No."

"Have you ever been sexually active?"

"Yes."

"In the past twelve months, how many sexual partners have you had?"

Paul paused for a moment. "Uh, two."

"Prior to the past twelve months, how many sexual partners have you had?"

"Oh God, I have no idea."

"An estimate is fine."

"Um...I dunno, at least 25, maybe 30 or so."

Luke blinked.

"Were these encounters part of a monogamous relationship, or casual?" the physician inquired.

"Uh, both."

"What are the genders of your sexual partners?"

"Women, just women."

The doctor continued to ask additional questions. "Do you and your partners discuss STI prevention?"

"STIs?" Paul asked.

"Yes, sexually transmitted infections. You may have heard them referred to as sexually transmitted diseases — STDs — or venereal disease — VD."

"Oh. Um, no, not really."

"If you use tools to prevent STIs, what tools do you use? These may include male or female condoms, and dental dams, among others," Dr. Hernandez explained.

"Uh, yeah. I use condoms...uh, male condoms."

"How often do you use condoms?"

"All the time now."

"Was there a point when being sexually active that you did not use condoms or other forms of STI protection?"

Paul explained, "Ooh...there was a long time, I think it was up until my divorce, like five years ago, that I wasn't using protection at all."

"Were you monogamous prior to five years ago?"

"Oh, no. I was having a lot more sex with many, many more girls than I am now."

The doctor spent a few moments typing something up on the computer.

"Have you ever been diagnosed with STIs or HIV in the past?"

"Uh, no."

"Would you like to be tested?"

"Um, I guess. I'm sure I'm fine. But if you think it'll help, I'll do it."

"We want to make sure we have your express consent before you're tested."

"Yes, I consent."

"Okay. Thank you, Paul, for your responses. This will help assist in your diagnosis and treatment. A nurse will be by shortly to administer your STI and HIV tests. After that, you'll be admitted, and we'll get you into a room. And, the cardiologist and pulmonologist will be by to advise on your specific conditions."

"How long do you think I'll have to stay in the hospital?" Paul asked.

"At this time, I can't say," the doctor explained. "We're looking to eradicate the pneumonia and get your blood pressure stable. The goal is to get you well enough to go home. The cardiologist and pulmonologist will be able to advise further."

"Thanks, Doc."

Once the physician left to attend to other patients, Paul turned to Luke.

"Shit, man. I can't believe any of this," he groaned. "Never felt anything, healthy as a horse, then it's like my body's breaking down all of a sudden and I don't know why."

"I...I don't know what to say, Paulie. I'm sorry man. But, y'know, you're a strong guy, you'll find a way to get through it. I'm sure of it."

"I don't know, Luke. I just don't know."

EAST LA
July 7-8, 2023

Luke opened his eyes to a dim space. Alone in a queen-sized bed with white linens and a floral comforter, and surrounded by spartan, clean walls and surfaces, he struggled to find his bearings.

Where am I? That's right, I'm at the Bargain Inn. Yesterday was a long day.

He rolled to his side so the digital alarm clock was in view.

It's eleven...I really needed sleep. I hope Paul's doing alright. I wonder if they figured out what's wrong with him.

He grabbed his cell phone and unlocked it, expecting to have received a call or text from his best friend, but nothing had come through.

That's weird.

Luke entered the bathroom to shower and clean up, then put on some fresh clothes, including loose jeans, a blue polo shirt, and canvas shoes. He then left the motel, jumped into the Jeep he was given permission to drive, and headed to the hospital.

Once he arrived, he took the elevator to the fifth floor, where Paul's private room was located, and walked past the nurses' station.

"Hey! Hey!" a nurse called out.

Luke turned around. "Please?"

The nurse looked confused.

"Oh, uh, I'm sorry, pardon me?"

"Who are you here to see?"

"I'm here to see my friend."

"Who's your friend?"

"Paul Chu – he's in Room 513."

"The patient is not accepting visitors."

Luke sighed. "No, tell him Luke Phillips is here."

"I'm sorry sir, he has specifically instructed us not to allow any visitors. He didn't provide any exceptions."

"Okay. Could you please at least let him know I was here and to call me when he's up for it? He has my number."

"Yes, we'll pass along the message."

He left the medical center feeling confused and rejected. He got into the Wrangler and pulled at his hair.

What did I do wrong?

I tried to be a good friend to Paul, I tried to be there for him, and then he just doesn't wanna see me?

Did I offend him in some way? Did I say something wrong? Piss him off?

I'm stuck out here in LA — I don't know shit about this place — what am I gonna do now? Should I just drop off the keys at the hospital and find my way home?

Everybody gets sick of me.

Everybody leaves me.

I'm a failure and a loser. Even Paul sees it.

Luke drove in the direction of the motel, but before arriving at his destination, he spotted a grey, run-down cinder block building adorned with dirty glass double doors covered with cigarette advertisement decals. Metal security doors were rolled outward from the doors. A neon "OPEN" sign hung in its only window, which was streaked with dust and rain residue.

He carefully turned into the adjacent parking lot, which was full of potholes and bumps.

Entering the small convenience store, he slowly explored the snack aisle and decided on a bag of nacho-flavored tortilla chips. Then, he walked towards the back of the derelict store and found what he truly sought.

Bingo.

In front of him sat a cooler of inexpensive wine bottles.

I've tamed my drinking this whole trip, just one or two drinks a day. Enough to soothe the itch. But that's not gonna work for me right now.

He picked up two of the cheapest bottles of Merlot he could find. He then grabbed a bag of bright red disposable cups on his way to the front of the store to pay for his goods. The cashier was a ruddy-skinned, gruff man who appeared to be in his thirties, but a very rough thirties. He slowly scanned each of the items.

The cashier mumbled, "It's $20.84."

Luke dug into his wallet and handed him a credit card.

"No, we just take cash. ATM's over there." The cashier lazily pointed to a nondescript ATM machine on the other side of the entrance.

Luke walked over to the ATM, inserted his bank card, and checked his balance. *Hmm, it looks like Mom put quite a bit of money in here. Thank God for that. Shit, I need to call her.* He requested one hundred dollars from the machine. On the screen, it read:

A $10.99 banking fee is assessed for each transaction. Would you like to continue?

"Fuck," Luke mumbled under his breath, but he clicked 'yes' to continue. The money dispensed, and Luke returned to the counter to pay for his items.

Dear God, I feel like shit.

Luke's head ached terribly, and the room was spinning. The screeching cell phone did not help.

Oh, that's Mom. I can't deal with her right now.

After a few minutes to find stability, he peered over at the clock.

"What the..." he grumbled. It was three o'clock in the afternoon the next day. He sat up and scanned the darkened motel room. The shades were drawn, and a rancid, disgusting smell filled his nostrils. He then stood up and ambled toward the bathroom.

"Whoa!" Luke's right foot caught a pile of dark-colored, liquefied vomit, and he almost crashed on the wood-paneled floor. Fortunately, he remained upright and found a used towel to clean up the mess. He turned on the lights and slowly made his way to the shower to wash off.

Once clean, he looked through his cell phone. He realized he had called Paul a few times over the course of the previous day and evening but with no response. He had called the hospital as well, but could not reach his friend.

The second bottle of Merlot was three-quarters empty. He poured the last of it into one of the plastic cups he bought and turned it up. *This should take the edge off the hangover.*

He threw on a pair of khaki shorts and a black tee, along with his sandals. Then, he bundled up the used towels to take to the motel office to exchange for clean ones.

After completing the exchange, he passed by an attractive young woman with long, straight brunette hair. Their eyes met briefly as he left the building, but he continued on his way.

Luke returned to the convenience store for two more bottles of Merlot. He came back to the Bargain Inn and pulled in a parking space in front of his motel room. The woman from the lobby was now leaning against the exterior wall next to his front door.

"Hey baby, wanna date?" the woman asked.

Luke sighed as he fumbled through his pockets for his keycard. "Uh, how much?" *I guess that's how it's supposed to work.*

"Twenty an hour."

"Eh, how about two hours?"

"Okay."

"Come in."

Luke opened his room door and let in the woman, who was wearing a white and yellow striped crop partially exposing a muffin top, blue jean shorts, and dirty white flip-flops. He got a whiff of her perfume, which had the pleasant smell of fruit candy. Once inside, he shut the door behind him.

"We can do anything you want but pay upfront."

"A-anything?"

"Yeah."

He fished his wallet from his shorts and pulled out two twenty-dollar bills. He gave them to the woman, who took a seat on the cushy brown chair in the corner of the room and crossed her legs.

"I just got this," he said, pointing to the bottles of unopened Merlot he sat on the table. "I haven't opened it yet, but I'm gonna have some. Uh...would you like some?"

"Yeah, sure."

Luke poured a serving into a clean cup and handed it to her. Then, he poured himself a full cup and sat on the bed facing her, taking a big swig.

"What's your name?" the woman asked.

"Luke. What's yours?"

"Destiny," she cooed, flipping her hair.

"Uh, you're cute."

"Thanks. You look nice, too. So, like, what do you wanna do?"

He was hesitant, but the Merlot did the talking for him. "Uh...come here. Do what you normally do, I guess."

Destiny came over and stood in front of the bed. He reclined to watch, his head placed against the headboard, and his legs out in front of him. As she pulled off her shirt, he got aroused seeing her full, natural breasts and pointy, dark nipples. She then slipped off her shorts and panties, and climbed onto the bed, crawling toward him in a suggestive manner. Then, she straddled his legs and began to rub the zipper area of his bottoms. His shorts became full.

Oh yes...

Destiny slowly pulled down his zipper, and his fully erect member appeared, shielded only by the material of his briefs. She then uncovered it and stroked it rhythmically. She bent down and placed it in her warm, inviting mouth. Her head bobbed up and down vigorously, her shiny hair bouncing and flowing through his hand.

Luke was moaning in ecstasy, fully engaged in the experience.

"Mmm...keep going..."

This feels so good...

She gently yet firmly sucked, her long locks covering his hips. Enjoying the feeling, he knew he was getting closer.

"You're doing good...I'm almost there..."

What the fuck are you doing, Luke?!

The thought shot through his brain like a .22 round.

Luke sat up and gently moved Destiny away from him.

"What's wrong?"

"Nothing...uh...you're great, you're very attractive, you're good at what you do, but I can't do this."

She got off the bed and hastily put her clothes back on. "Must be your first time, huh?"

He fastened his pants and sat up. "Uh, no, but yeah. Not my first time having sex, but the first time doing, uh...this."

"Yeah, I get it. It happens. You still got me for a little less than two hours."

"Uh...we can talk. I hope that's fine."

"Yeah, of course."

"You can sit on the bed if you want."

She then returned to the bed facing him. "So, Luke, are you a local? Or are you visiting?"

"Um, I'm visiting."

"Where are you from?"

"Ohio."

"Ohio's cool, I went to Cedar Point with my family a long, long time ago. It was fun, I really liked the roller coasters. Couldn't live there though. It's too cold in the winter and the food's too bland."

"I get it. I take it you're from here?"

"Yeah. East LA, born and raised."

"Do you like it here?"

She nodded. "It's alright. It's home. So, like, you were saying you were visiting. What are you looking to check out here?"

"Well, um, my visit wasn't exactly planned. My friend and I were passing through while on a road trip, and then he got sick and ended up admitted to the hospital."

"Oh wow, that's awful. You don't have to tell me if you don't want to, but what's wrong with him?"

"He's got pneumonia and some heart problems. The hospital around the corner decided to keep him."

"Ooh, I'm sorry that happened. County Gen's a good place, though. I mean, if you get sick, that's where you wanna be."

"It's good to know. I had no idea. The urgent care I first took him to in Indio said that's where he should go, so it's pretty much how he ended up there. Anyway, last I saw my friend was about two or three days ago. He's still there but he decided he doesn't wanna see me. I don't know if he's pissed at me or what."

"Have you tried to call or text him?"

"Yeah, a bunch of times, but nothing."

"Maybe he's dealing with some things. Sometimes people don't deal with being sick, or any kind of bad news, in a good way. A few years ago, when I was fourteen, my mom died of cancer."

"My condolences."

"Ah, it's been, like, five years, but when she was first diagnosed, I was, like, twelve. She shut herself in her room for like a week. She didn't wanna talk to nobody. I could just hear her crying. Me and my brothers and sisters, we were on our own. I'm the oldest, so I fed everybody ramen noodles and Spam for days. Still can't eat that now 'cause of that...I'm sorry, I'm, like, talking too much."

"Oh no, it's totally fine."

"Okay. I guess I brought that up just to say that maybe your friend is going through some things. Hopefully not cancer like my mom, but whatever it is, like, he might need time. Being sick is hard on some people. But I'm sure he'll come around when he's ready."

Luke had a realization – he had consumed nothing but Merlot and chips for the past two days. "Hmm, I'm starving, wanna go somewhere?"

"Sure."

"Is there anywhere within walking distance you recommend?"

Destiny began thinking. "Uh, there's a diner down the street. It's retro, it's got burgers and shakes. It's great. If you're into that kind of thing, you'll like it. I really like it."

"Perfect." Luke checked his watch. "Let's go. It's on me."

⊷◆⊷

Luke and Destiny walked a quarter mile up the road from the hotel to the diner she recommended. The 1950s-inspired building was encased in chrome, and a "Sockhop Holly's" sign was affixed to a pole in front. They entered the doors and once seated, the hostess provided menus.

A woman wearing a pink dress with a white smock and cap walked up to the table, pad and paper in hand.

"Hello, welcome to Sockhop Holly's. What would you like to drink?"

"Coke, *por favor*," Destiny responded.

"Uh, decaf coffee please?" Luke requested.

"Okay, I'll be right back. I can take your food order then."

Once the server left the table, Luke asked, "What would you recommend from the menu?"

"Hmm...if you like burgers, the Hollyburger is the best. And it's filling, too."

Luke looked down at the menu and read the description of the Hollyburger. It consisted of two quarter-pound ground beef patties, cheddar cheese slices, lettuce, tomato, mayonnaise, and special sauce between two toasted and buttered pieces of bun bread. A platter came with an order of french fries.

"That sounds delicious. I guess I'll try that. How are their shakes?"

"They're the best around," Destiny raved. "All of them are good. My favorite is banana."

"How about the chocolate malt? How's that one?"

"It's super good. It's rich and creamy."

The server came back to the table with their drinks. "What would you like to eat?"

Destiny responded, "*Uh, ensalada de pollo frito.*"

"*¿Qué aderezo?*"

"*Ranch, por favor...y una malteada de plátano.*"

"*Gracias.*" The server then turned to Luke. "And for you, sir?"

"I'll have the Hollyburger platter. Could I get cheese on the fries?"

"Yes."

"And I'll have a chocolate malt, please. That's all."

"Okay. Thank you. I will be back shortly with your food." The server headed to the kitchen to give them the order.

Luke looked to Destiny. "So, you're bilingual, huh?"

"Yeah, a lot of us are around here," she explained. "I grew up speaking Spanish at home and English in school. My family's from Mexico, but I was born here."

"I see. So, at this point, do you still live with family, or are you on your own?"

"I live with my aunt, it's me and my baby, his name's Mateo. He'll be two in November."

"Oh wow, Destiny, I wouldn't have guessed you had a baby."

"Most people say that. Like, I've been on my own since I was sixteen. After my mom died, my father took me in with my brothers and sisters. He had remarried so it was him and my stepmother. I would, like, sneak out a lot and do whatever I wanted to do. Like, I missed my mom, my father wasn't really around until she died, and this other lady was trying to take my mom's place. So, I skipped school and I partied, that's how I dealt with it. But when I got pregnant, they kicked me out. I was working fast food, but that doesn't pay the bills, especially with a baby on the way. Mateo's dad got locked up, so it was just me. So, that's how I started in the life."

"I see."

"My aunt ended up taking me in once I had Mateo. She didn't want me to be on the streets with a baby, and she didn't want me to have to give him up. But she doesn't have a lot of money either. She cleans houses. So, like, I do what I can to pull my weight and take care of my son."

"That's understandable. Have you thought about what you wanna do long-term?"

"Good question. Like, I don't wanna be doing this forever, and I wanna give my son the best. I got my GED a couple of months ago, and I'm starting classes at the community college. I wanna go into nursing, I like to take care of people."

"Hmm, it's a noble goal."

"Sure. So, Luke, what do you do?"

As he got ready to answer, the server returned with their order and the check.

"*Gracias*," Destiny responded.

"Thank you," Luke said.

"Let me know if you need anything else," the server told them.

When she left the table, Luke took a bite of his burger. "That's very good. Thanks for recommending this!"

"Of course! It's quite tasty."

Luke looked over at Destiny's meal. "Oh, you got a fried chicken salad. Y'know, I was wondering what you ordered."

"Yes. It's very good. I'm trying to slim down, but I really like fried chicken."

"Not trying to be weird, but you look pretty the way you are," he complimented her.

Destiny smiled. "Thank you." She then opened a packet of ranch dressing provided with the meal and squirted the contents onto her greens.

"So, you see that packet of ranch there?"

"Yeah."

"The company that makes it – Ohio Valley Ranch – I used to work for them a long time ago."

"Oh wow, that's so cool! How was it working there?"

"It was okay, not bad. I was a researcher there, worked there for a few years."

"That's very nice. What do you do now?"

"Uh, I work at a store called the Ohio Dairy Union."

"Oh, from dressing to dairy. Seems to be a theme."

He ate a small handful of fries. "Uh, never thought about it before, but yeah, sure."

"So...like, where were you and your friend going before he got sick?"

Luke laughed. "The funny thing is, I don't really know for sure, just somewhere here in California."

"Uh...really?"

"Uh-huh. My friend, his name's Paul, he drove up from Florida and picked me up in Ohio, then we went for a road trip out here. He knows where we're headed but I don't."

"That's...strange."

"Yeah, but you don't know Paulie...he's like that. He's into adventure, and he's a bit impulsive. And I came along for the ride, he and I have that in common. I had been going through a hard time recently and I needed to get away. He did too. We're both divorced and in our forties, and I guess we're trying to figure things out."

"Oh, like a mid-life crisis?" she suggested, sipping her banana milkshake.

He chuckled. "Yeah, I guess you could put it that way. We came out this way to clear our heads, get ourselves together. It's a shame things went left like this."

Destiny finished her shake. "Luke...I hope you find what you're looking for."

YES
July 9-10, 2023

Beep!

Luke slowly woke up to the alarm going off on his cell phone.

Too loud! God, I still feel like ass.

It was eight o'clock in the morning.

Spirit said, "Be the kind of man she can say 'yes' to..."

He rose from his bed, showered, cleaned up, and dressed in a white polo, clean khaki shorts, and sandals. He then sat on the bed and made a phone call.

"Associated Counselors, how may I help you?"

Luke spoke. "Uh, hi, I would like to make an appointment with Stacy Dieter."

"Are you a current client?"

"Uh, current-ish. I've been a client of hers, but it's been some time since I've made an appointment."

"Okay. What is your name and date of birth?"

"Uh...Luke Phillips, date of birth one...eleven...nineteen-eighty."

The receptionist placed him on hold for a moment, and Luke could hear light typing in the background. "Okay. How soon would you like to get in with Stacy? She's taking both virtual and in-person appointments."

"As soon as possible, and I'm out of town right now so if it's in the near future it'll need to be virtual."

"Okay, great. We had a late cancellation, so there's an opening today at one o'clock."

"Okay, um, one o'clock eastern, so a little less than two hours, right?"

"Uh...yes, it's 11:15am, so it'll be in less than two hours."

"I'll take it."

"Okay, we'll go ahead and send you the virtual invite at the email address you have on file with us. You'll want to try to log on five minutes before the appointment to make sure the connection is successful. Please call our office if you have trouble connecting or you need to cancel."

After the call, he went outside to the truck to pull out his electronics bag. He brought it in the motel room and took out a laptop computer, plugging it in and setting it up for the upcoming counseling session. In the meantime, he connected the GoPro to the laptop and began uploading recordings of the trip to YouTube to back them up.

A little bit before ten o'clock local time, Luke clicked on the link provided in his email for his counseling appointment and jumped on. When it was time to begin, a curly-haired woman with glasses popped onto the screen.

"It's been a bit since we last spoke. How are you feeling?"

"Uh...honestly, not great," Luke confessed.

"Oh, I see. What's happening in your life right now?"

"I'm in California...LA. I was just on a two-day bender, drank a lot of wine. Almost slept with a prostitute, kinda did but not really...long story. And I guess I don't like where my life is going."

"Okay. So, what I'm hearing is, you're in Los Angeles, you have been consuming an abundance of alcohol, you had a sexual encounter of some kind with a sex worker, and you have some frustration with the direction of your life at this time. Is that correct?"

"Yes, pretty much. We did get started, but I stopped before it became, y'know, full-on sex."

"Okay Luke, I understand. So, are you there on vacation? Are you traveling alone or are you with anyone else?"

"I'm kind of on vacation but not really, and I'm alone right now, but I didn't travel by myself."

"Can you elaborate on that, as much as you're comfortable with?"

"Yeah. Um...I'm on a road trip with my friend Paul, and we were supposed to just be passing through, but he got really sick, and he's been in the hospital since Thursday."

"I'm sorry to hear that, Luke."

"Thank you. Y'know, since he's been admitted there, he won't speak to me, and I don't know why. I don't know if I did something wrong, or what. So, I'm staying at a motel around the corner. I've been trying to get ahold of him. I've tried to call him, he won't answer, and he won't get back to me. I've gone up to the hospital, but they tell me he doesn't want any visitors, me included."

"Luke, it sounds like you're in an unfamiliar place dealing with an incredibly stressful situation alone."

"Yeah, that's, y'know, exactly what it is. I dunno...when I was told at the hospital he didn't wanna see me, I went to the corner store and got bottles of wine. And I just...started drinking, and I couldn't stop. Then yesterday some girl just showed up at my door, and y'know, I let her in, I paid her, and we were starting to get intimate, and then I just couldn't do it."

"Luke, what stopped you?"

"I started having thoughts that sobered me up, and y'know, it just killed the mood."

"What kinds of thoughts?"

"Just second thoughts, like, 'What are you doing?' and things like that. I've never paid anybody for sex in my life. It's the first time I did that," he explained.

"From what I'm hearing you say," Stacy noted, "it sounds like you recognized you were in a pretty low place, engaging in activity out of character for you."

"Yeah, I would say so. When everything was happening, I realized I need to be a better person, but y'know, not for my parents this time."

"That's good. That's progress. It's good to recognize that." Stacy then switched gears. "So today, I think we want to focus on your short-term situation, and we'll discuss some ways to address that. Then, over the next few sessions, we can focus more on your long-term mental and emotional health. Does that sound like a plan you would like to move forward with, Luke?"

"Oh, yes," Luke responded.

"You said your friend is in the hospital and is very ill, and he doesn't want to speak to you."

"Yeah."

"Well, he may be dealing with a reality that is very upsetting to him. It may not necessarily be something you've done. But either way, you cannot control your friend's feelings or actions. Have you considered returning home? Is that something you have the resources to do currently?"

"Yeah. I'm able to get home. But I would feel so horrible leaving Paul, y'know, my friend, behind by himself. And then I have his truck too."

"You can always drop your friend's truck off at the hospital. If being in Los Angeles is leading you to struggle mentally, going home is always an option."

"Yeah, but home isn't any better for me stress-wise. Besides, I don't know if I can live with just leaving Paul behind like that. I mean, he brought me out of a really dark place just a couple of weeks ago."

"Okay Luke, tell me a bit more about what happened a couple of weeks ago."

"So, Stacy, it was kind of the same thing, but worse, I guess? I felt like a total failure, worthless. My family thinks I'm a disappointment, my friends don't come around anymore – I pushed them away, I was just by myself, in my apartment, with my wine. I was off my meds...I thought about suicide, and I even got ready to do it."

Stacy interrupted. "Right now, Luke, are you having any thoughts of harming yourself or ending your life?"

"No, not right now."

"Have you had thoughts of harming yourself or ending your life within the last seventy-two hours?"

"No. I haven't felt that way since that time two weeks ago. Even with this whole hellscape I'm living in right now, weirdly enough, I still wanna live."

"Okay."

"Just as I was about to, you know, end it, Paul called me. Te was in town, and then we just kinda decided to go on this trip, so I could get out of Losanti and clear my head, y'know?"

"It sounds like Paul was there when you needed him the most, and you want to do the same for him, but at this time, he's not allowing that."

"Yeah."

"If he doesn't want you to be there, you'll have to honor that. Sometimes, being a supportive friend means allowing them space to process their reality. He is in the hospital, so he's in a safe place. If you need to go home, you don't need to feel guilty about that. But if you want to express to Paul that you want to simply be a friend to him, and be there for him, then one thing you could do is to write a letter expressing how you feel."

"What? What would that look like?" Luke asked.

The therapist advised, "My suggestion would be that when you write him, you focus more on your feelings about the friendship and his well-being than about the current situation or his behavior. Then, if you want to give the letter to him, drop it off at the hospital. He may choose to read it, or not – that's up to him – but this will allow you an opportunity to express your intention and desire to be present for your friend."

"Alright, I think I'm gonna do that, and I'm gonna try to give him another few days, and if he doesn't come around, I'll just drop off the car keys at the hospital and head home."

"That's a sound plan. Just make sure you stick to it and give yourself a solid deadline. One other thing I want to address in this appointment, and this is something we'll continue to work on, is your alcohol use."

"Yeah, I know it's a bit of a problem."

"It seems from this and previous sessions, alcohol has affected your relationships and factored into your involvement in risky and even dangerous behavior. Is that accurate?"

"Sure. I mean, if I'm honest, it was part of why my marriage ended. It was easier to drink and pass out than talk to my ex-wife. It's why my career went down the shitter. And then there's this situation – I mean, I was this close to sleeping with a random girl from off the street...she was barely legal, at least from what she said. No condoms, could've caught something, could've gotten arrested. That was stupid as hell."

"Okay. We'll work through your alcohol use during the next several sessions. But in the short term, we do offer a program through this practice focusing on alcoholism recovery. We may be able to partner with a practice where you are. If you would like to learn more about that, I can send you additional information, and you can reach out to our billing office to discuss insurance coverage and pricing."

"Okay."

"There are also free twelve-step programs such as Alcoholics Anonymous which could provide you with some support and accountability starting today. I'm sure there are meetings held in Los Angeles you could visit, and they may have online meetings too. AA has a website that will point you in the right direction, so that's something you could look into."

———◆○◆———

"Don't be like your pops!"

Spirit's words continued to loop through Luke's mind at various times throughout the next day, as he edited and uploaded more videos from the trip, washed clothes for himself and Paul at the laundromat across the street, and bought a medium pepperoni pizza from the Italian pizzeria next door. He even stepped foot inside the small gym just off the motel lobby. He ran on the treadmill, managing fifteen minutes. *Gotta start somewhere.*

After returning to the motel room, Luke logged onto his laptop and searched for twelve-step meetings for alcoholism recovery near him.

Oh, there's one starting at 3:30 PM at the hospital.

He got ready and then headed around the corner to the medical center. He stopped by Paul's floor and went over to the nurse's station. As soon as the nurse on duty saw him, she shook her head.

"I'm sorry, Room 513 is still declining visitors."

"Okay, Nora. I just wanted to check and see," Luke said, a little disappointed, but at this point, becoming used to it. "Thanks anyway."

"Thanks for coming by," the nurse said sympathetically. "Hopefully he'll come around."

Luke returned to the first floor, where the Alcoholics Anonymous meeting would be held. He walked into the room, where fellows were talking amongst themselves and enjoying refreshments ahead of the meeting. He grabbed a coffee and bagel and found a seat in the circle.

Once the meeting commenced, the participants recited the Serenity Prayer. Individual members shared the twelve steps and other tenets of the program. Then, the chairman asked, "Are there any newcomers? Please share your first name so we can welcome you."

He spoke up solemnly. "Hi, I'm Luke, and uh...I am an alcoholic."

"Hi, Luke," welcomed the group.

He listened as the meeting continued. Partway through the meeting, a fellow read a short passage from the Big Book of Alcoholics Anonymous, and several other fellows gave short shares on the reading. One in particular stuck out to him.

"Hi, I'm Sean, and I'm an alcoholic."

"Hi, Sean," the fellows responded.

The pudgy middle-aged man continued. "This passage spoke to me. I told myself for a long time I didn't have a drinking problem. It wasn't like I was out on the streets or getting DUIs or anything like that. Started out good. I went to Stanford, did pre-med, graduated with a degree in chemistry. I went on to medical school at UCLA, went up to Fresno and did my residency in internal medicine."

Some in the circle mumbled, "Mmm-hmm."

"Boom, I'm a doctor. A physician, an MD. I drank the whole way through, attended conferences and program events, went out on dates, had a drink, or a few, wherever I went. But it didn't register that my drinking was a problem. Figured it was all good. I was a doctor, and I could finally make my parents happy because I never could. I mean, most parents would love having a doctor for a son."

Others in the group nodded.

"But nah, not really. It's not that they disapproved. They just didn't care. It wasn't the reaction I was working so hard for. I coped by drinking, it was what I knew, it's what got me all the way through school. And it slowly made my mind foggy. I started to make mistakes, which in my line of work is...not good. Affected my bedside manner. I didn't catch things I really should've. My actions were hurting my patients – could've killed them in some cases. And I didn't know how I could live with that. Pushed friends, family, and women away, isolated myself to this disease of alcoholism. My rock bottom wasn't Skid Row, but at least for me, it might as well have been."

I know that feeling.

Sean continued. "So that's how I made it through the doors of AA. And it's helped me see so much of my life differently, not just the drinking. Sure, I have my daddy issues and mommy issues, and it might not be my fault, but it is my responsibility. Been sober for eight months, the fog's lifted, and I'm living in the solution. Thanks for letting me share."

"Thanks, Sean," the group replied in unison.

After the meeting, Luke returned to the motel and sat on the bed watching online videos. He then grabbed the branded pen and notepad from the nightstand and wrote:

Dear Paulie,

You have been my closest friend since we met at orientation in our first year at UGL. We were almost inseparable back then. Staying up late discussing our faith, philosophy, sports, whatever we wanted to chat about, the road trips for missions and Infinity, visiting each other's families in Losanti, it was wonderful. You were the passionate zealot, I was the grounded one. In that way, we're not so different than how we were 20 years ago, even though life has continued to throw curveballs. You're not just a best friend, you're my brother from another mother.

When you called me two weeks ago, you truly saved my life. I'm not exaggerating, I'm so serious. The hard road you're undoubtedly facing now, I want to be by your side, as your best friend and as your brother. It's not a burden, it would be my pleasure and an honor. You're an awesome person, a beautiful soul, and you don't have to go it alone.

Your brother,

— Luke

Luke reread the letter to make sure he expressed what he wanted to say, folded it up, and headed right back to the hospital. When he arrived on the fifth floor, he approached the same nurse he encountered earlier.

"Hi, Nora. I know the answer will be the same, but could you please give this to him?" He handed her the letter.

"Sure, I will."

As he boarded the elevator, he told her, "Thanks."

"You bet. He's lucky to have you as a friend."

PROMISE
July 14-21, 2023

Luke pressed the silver button on the elevator at Los Angeles County General Hospital to make one more trip to the fifth floor. While in the elevator, he looked down at the car key in his hand. *Well — if he still wants to be left alone, that's it I suppose. Can't stay out here forever.*

A few moments later, the now-familiar automated voice announced, "Fifth Floor," and the door slid open to the nurse's station. As he had done each day for the past several days, Luke approached the desk to speak with the nurse on-call, Nora. The woman, sporting a blonde bob, had a different expression on her slightly lined face.

"Good morning and happy Friday, Luke!"

"Hi, Nora! How are you?"

"Living the dream. Today's your lucky day. The patient in Room 513 now wants to see you. He requested you by name."

"Oh wow, great to hear. I was going to head home tomorrow, but I wanted to try one more time. So glad I did. Thanks!"

"You're welcome. Have a great day!"

"You, too!"

Luke entered Room 513.

Paul lay on the hospital bed, appearing incredibly tired, and had since become slightly thinner. He was hooked up to wires and an intravenous line, but he was otherwise awake and alert.

"Hi, Luke. Sorry, man."

Luke sat in a chair next to the bed. "Paulie – don't worry about it. I'm sure it's hard being laid up here. I know I kept trying to reach you, I hope I didn't upset you more by doing that."

"It's fine. I would've done the same thing. I appreciate that you cared enough not to leave me behind. I wouldn't have blamed you if you'd gone home. Can I tell you something?"

"Sure, you can tell me anything."

"So, uh...they gave me good news and some really bad news. The good news is that at least for right now, the cough meds and the antifungals are helping a bit."

"That's good."

"Um...I'm not contagious either, just so you know."

"Hadn't thought about it. So, what's the bad news?"

Paul took a deep breath. "Uh...come to find out, my health is a lot worse than they thought when I first got here. They, uh, figured out the kind of pneumonia I have. It's called pneumocystis pneumonia, or PCP. It's rare and healthy people usually don't get it. People who get it have weak immune systems."

"Oh, wow. That's crazy, bro. So, do they know how you would've come down with something like that?"

He paused for a moment, then teared up. "Luke, I have AIDS."

Luke sat back in the chair, stunned. "Uh...Paulie...are they sure?"

"Yeah. The test came back the day after they admitted me. And they retested me to confirm."

Both sat quietly together, Luke leaning over and placing his hand on Paul's shoulder.

"Ugh, that sucks. That really does."

"Yeah," Paul responded quietly.

"Y'know, once they put you on the AIDS pills, won't things be better, like Magic Johnson? He's got it and he's been doing fine for decades."

"No, probably not at this point. If it was just HIV, I would have to take meds for life, but the virus could be brought down to virtually undetectable levels, and I could otherwise live a pretty normal life. Problem is, it wasn't caught early enough. My T-cells, you know, the white blood cells that fight infections, they're just about non-existent now. Taking into account my health issues and my T-cell count, they think I've had the virus for at least seven or eight years."

"Fuck."

"I said the same thing when they told me. It's not just HIV at this point, it's AIDS, and the type of pneumonia I have is more common in people with AIDS than the general population. My heart and my arteries? AIDS. The pneumonia? AIDS."

"Damn." Luke paused for a bit, then continued. "Paulie, how long do they think you have?"

"Not long."

"Like maybe a few more years or so?"

"Nah, I wish. More like...maybe a week or two. The medicine's helping, but my body doesn't have the ability to fight this off. The doctors say there's a slim chance my T-cells could rebound, but at this stage it's unlikely."

Paulie just came back into my life. He was so vibrant, and just that quick, he's dying.

Like, now. AIDS.

What the fuck is this? How could this be?

"'Unlikely' doesn't mean you're automatically gonna die. You've got to fight. You've got to give yourself a shot."

"I hear you, and I'm doing my best, but at this point, I have to face that dying is a distinct possibility, and even a probability. Believe it or not, man, dying is not the worst thing. You know what the worst thing about this is?"

"What?"

"The crazy thing is, it's not being sick like this or even the idea of dying. At this point, I can live with that, it is what it is. The worst thing is…I had to call Alyssa." Paul began to cry.

"Whoa."

"I had to call Alyssa, and I had to tell her that I exposed her to AIDS. She never deserved that. She was loyal, she was a wonderful wife, and as a husband, I was supposed to protect my wife. I'm the one who fucked up, I'm the one who cheated on her and I didn't protect her."

Luke continued to listen, holding his hand.

"That's why I didn't want you to see me. When they gave me those results, they also told me about something called the 'partner notification program,' where they tell the previous people you slept with your diagnosis instead of you having to do it yourself. They told me I didn't have to sign up, but I said yes. It's the right thing to do, you know?"

"Yeah," Luke replied softly.

"I had to write out a shit-ton of names, go through my phone and my emails. Ended up being something like twenty-five names over the past ten years. But I had to make two calls myself. I didn't want some anonymous entity calling Alyssa, and I needed to call Bianca because of Gracie. I owed them that much to hear it straight from me."

"Ugh, that's rough."

"It was, but I had to be a man and do it." Paul, with glazed eyes, stared out the window, then glanced back at Luke. "It was too much to do that, and then see you afterwards and have to tell you this...I just...I didn't have it in me."

"I get it. Don't worry about it. Just know that at this point, I'm not going anywhere. I'm gonna be up here every single day until they let you out of here."

"I appreciate it, Luke, but you really don't have to do that. You've got a life to live, I don't wanna take you away from that."

"You're my best friend, you're my brother. I'll figure it all out. Don't worry about me. Worry about you getting better." Luke gently squeezed his friend's hand.

"You know, it's crazy. I don't know about you; you went to public schools. But going to Christian schools, I didn't learn much in the way of sex and avoiding HIV and STDs. It was just 'don't have sex before marriage' and 'don't be gay.' Oh, and 'don't shoot up drugs.'"

Luke looked at him. "Really?"

"Yeah, that was it," he said with a small laugh.

"It's funny you say that. If it had been up to my parents, I wouldn't have learned anything either. My parents never had 'the talk' with me. They just let the church do it, youth group, and you know how that goes."

"Oh yeah, for sure."

Luke continued, "But I remember when we had sex ed in high school, our parents had to sign a permission slip to opt in. So, I just waited until my dad was really toasted on Guinness and bourbon, fucked up, nice nice, and I gave him the permission slip, just said it was for a school field trip or something, and he signed it. Didn't bother to read shit."

"Huh...I'm surprised you did that. I could never picture Luke Phillips deceiving his parents."

"Bro, I hid Morgan too, remember? I just sucked at it."

"True. But anyway, that's how you do it, man." Paul smiled. "Since I went to Catholic high school, we got the 'abstinence is best' talk. But you know, they pushed the whole 'don't have an abortion' thing too."

"Yeah, that's a big thing for them, isn't it?"

"Oh, for sure. The school had us going on field trips to DC every year to protest abortion being legal at the time. Most of us didn't give a shit, we were going out of town for a few days, and you know, girls, so it was whatever. Parents didn't care 'cause the alumni were paying for it...and that's while in class they were teaching about abstinence and how premarital sex was a mortal sin, like a one-way ticket to hell."

"In other words, they were like, 'Sex before marriage and you're going to hell, and if you get pregnant, you must have this baby or you're going to hell, but you're going to hell anyway, so...'" Luke noted sardonically.

"Guess if you have an abortion, super hell awaits."

"With extra hot lava."

"And a side of sprinkles."

The guys laughed.

"Y'know," Luke pointed out, "CK was kinda like that too."

"I don't know about that," Paul countered. "I don't remember them talking about HIV. Do you?"

"No, I'm pretty sure they didn't."

"Okay, that's what I thought."

"Right, but they did talk about how premarital sex was like giving your pearls to pigs, and girls who did it were like used tissue."

"They did say that...and they said we had urges we couldn't control so we weren't supposed to be alone with girls."

"The crazy thing was, AC and I were by ourselves quite a bit and I don't remember anybody saying anything about it."

"This is gonna sound so shitty, but a lot of them didn't see her as the type of girl that could tempt you to sin."

Luke shook his head. "I know, but they were wrong."

"To be honest, even before you told me, I had a feeling something was there between you and her, and it wasn't just one way. Remember back during September 11th, and we were all cooped up together at Brother Craig's?"

"How could I forget? We thought the world was gonna end."

"We sure did. Scary times for sure. That night, though, you and Ann went off somewhere for a while, can't remember where, and Alyssa and I tried to go with you guys, but you put the kibosh on that."

"Yeah, I think we were going to get food for the group, but we had a stupid long wait, like several hours, so we drove out to the edge of town and hung out at the lake. I don't think I ever told you this, but I was this close to making my move."

"Really?"

"Uh-huh, but I was too scared of going there. Same shit. God, I was so stupid."

"I didn't pay much attention to it then, but thinking back, she was excluded a lot when it came to CK. It was cliquish and she wasn't one of the 'cool kids.'"

"Y'know, Morgan said she thinks that's why AC left social media."

"Yeah, she's right. Ann defriended a lot of CK people on Facebook over the years. By 2016, it was just me, Alyssa, and Terah who made the cut, and Terah barely counts because they went to high school together."

"Huh...2016? What happened?"

"C'mon, man. The election?"

Luke then nodded. "Oh...that's right. Guess I'm not surprised. She told me something one time that I still remember, don't know why. Back when we were at UGL, one time, a bunch of other CK people were chatting after large group, I wasn't there, I think I left right after for some reason. Anyway, somebody, I don't remember who it was, said they don't date Black people 'cause they could never bring them home to their parents, and pretty much everybody else in that group agreed with them."

"Oh, I don't think I was there for that specifically either, but I'm sure it happened. It sounds on-brand for CK."

"Yeah, I believe it too. Y'know, that really got to her. I remember her saying she never forgot that. She felt the prejudice, but I guess she stayed in the group 'cause God wanted her to forgive."

"That sucks. In college, a lot of times you're joining these student groups hoping to date and get into relationships."

"Sure...makes sense, you have the same interests, the same worldview."

"Yeah, but imagine picking a group because you believe the same things, especially something as important as faith, and then finding out nobody there would ever give you a second look because of the color of your skin and the way you look, and most of them barely even want to be your friend. And especially a group that claims to be about loving everybody because Christ did. It's so fucked, if you really think about it."

"Yeah, Paulie, it is. Y'know, I think deep down, everybody just wants to be accepted. CK didn't deserve her. It's one of the reasons why I don't do organized religion anymore. God's cool, Jesus, I can get behind. But the people...eh..."

"I hear that. God is one thing, but his representatives can get fucked. Though with all this," Paul said, pointing to the equipment he was attached to, "God and I, we're not exactly on the best of terms either."

<hr />

Luke woke up in bed at an extended-stay hotel, which he switched to after Paul began allowing him to visit in the hospital. He cleaned up, showered, got dressed, ate a small breakfast of bacon and eggs he made in the kitchenette, then headed over to see his friend, as he had done each day.

He walked into the room, and Paul was still there, stable and awake, though increasingly weak.

"How are you feeling, Paulie?" Luke asked as he sat in the chair beside him.

"I'm doing alright. The meds are great. They're giving me the good shit now."

Luke chuckled a bit. "Well, that's good. At least you're comfortable."

"Oh, I meant to tell you this, but thanks for bringing over my clean undies the other day. I was starting to get kinda gross that week I was up here by myself."

"No problem."

"Um, Danny and Auntie Rina are in town to see me today, and they're stopping by soon. Could you do me a favor?" Paul asked.

"Yeah, sure."

"There's a big black folder-like thing in the glove box of my truck. You'll know it when you see it. Could you grab that and bring it back up?"

Luke returned to the Wrangler and located a large plastic envelope fastened by a zipper in the glove compartment. He retrieved it and reentered the medical center.

Once back in the room, he gave him the envelope. "Thanks, man. You got a pen?" Paul asked.

"No, but I can get one."

"Oh, and could you see if the hospital has a notary?"

"Yeah, sure. Whatever you need."

Luke left the room and sought out a pen and a notary public. Sometime later, he returned with both. When they entered the room, Danny and Rina were sitting there with Paul.

"Hi, Luke – we're very glad you're here."

"Of course, Auntie Rina." He then turned to Paul. "Alright, this is the notary."

"Hi, I'm Gabriela Beltran, and I'm a notary public. I'm not an employee of Los Angeles County General Hospital, but I am a vendor contracted by the hospital. What am I here to notarize?"

After Paul introduced himself, he explained, "I have two documents I want to get notarized. One is this." He pulled a document from the envelope and gave it to her.

"Ah, okay. 'Last Will and Testament.'"

"Yeah, I wrote it out while on the trip, but I hadn't had a chance to sign it or anything. I was gonna type it up when I got back to Florida, but you know, shit happens."

The notary thoroughly reviewed the basic will. The Jacksonville condominium and its contents, as well as his boat, would be inherited by his two older children. Life insurance money, stocks, and bonds would be split three ways – Bella and Danny would receive one third each, and Gracie's third would be placed in a trust. Half of the cash he possessed in bank accounts would go to Alyssa, with the remainder going to his children.

"Are you sure you want to give that much to your ex-wife?" Rina asked.

"I'm sure. No matter what, I still love her. I owe her at least that much."

Paul signed the will in the presence of the notary. Rina and Luke signed as witnesses, and the notary sealed and signed it.

He folded the will and handed it to his son. "I haven't been able to get ahold of Bella, but please make sure she gets this."

Danny took the will and nodded.

Paul then produced another document and gave it to the notary.

"Ah...this is a car title," Gabriela stated.

"Yeah. Luke, I want you to have my Jeep. I paid for it cash, so this will be yours outright."

Upon hearing this, Luke's eyes widened. "I...I can't take it. That's too much, bro. I don't deserve it. Wouldn't one of y'all want it?" he asked, looking at Danny and Rina.

"Nah, Luke," Danny said. "I'm good."

Rina shook her head. "Luke, I don't need it. We are fine. And I'm sure Bella wouldn't want it. She's well taken care of in Michigan. Besides, Paul wants you to have it. What *joka* wants, *joka* gets."

"I'm so serious, Luke. I really want you to have it. You have a trip to finish making. Don't forget, I've seen your car. It's not happening in that."

"But Paulie...I can't do it without you."

"No brother, you need this, and you'll finish the trip, even though I can't go with you. I'll be with you in spirit, you know, some shit like that." Paul laughed a bit. "I know I didn't tell you where we were going. But you're a smart motherfucker. Just two points below genius. Might as well have given you those two points. I believe in you. You'll figure it out."

"Alright, but if you beat this, and you will beat this, you're getting your Jeep back."

"Nah, sorry Luke. It's not gonna happen, but I appreciate the optimism," Paul grinned.

He signed the title over to his closest friend.

"Promise me, Luke. Finish the trip."

Luke grasped his hand. "I will, Paulie. I promise."

LATE
July 24, 2023

"Man, Luke, we had a lot of fun together."

"We sure did, Paulie. And we can again."

"Yeah, maybe in the next go-round. But I want you here on earth for a while longer, kicking life's ass, before I see you again."

"I hear you."

Luke could not help but notice that over the past few days, Paul had grown weaker and was losing weight. He could no longer ignore the state of his closest friend and deny the reality of the situation.

"I remember one of the last times we hung out right after you got married, before we lost touch. Remember the couples trip we took to the Outer Banks?"

"Oh, I remember that," Luke recalled. "Oh, that was a fun vacation. Wasn't it, like, the summer of 2006? I think it was a couple of months after my wedding."

"It was a nice time for me and Alyssa to get to know Rachel – or, I should say, for Alyssa to get to know Rachel."

"Yeah, they fucked off and did girl shit together, and you and I got a chance to just relax on the beach and hang out."

August 2006

Paul and Luke reclined on the deck of Frisco Tavern and Cigar Station along the island coast, enjoying the vast ocean view.

"Oh man, these cigars are strong!" Paul remarked while puffing on one and feeling the burn.

"Paulie, these *are* cigars," Luke snarked as he placed his cigar in the ashtray on the patio table.

"Brother, this is the life. Nice ocean breeze...we can see clear out to the Atlantic. Amazing shit. We need to enjoy such beauty more often. Life's too short, you know what I mean?"

"For sure."

Paul thought aloud. "Do you ever worry about things getting so crazy that we're gonna lose touch?"

"What are you talking about?"

"I mean, I'm early in my career, and married with kids now. Soon enough, you'll be a veterinarian, and now that you're married, it's just a matter of time before you start having a family, too."

"I'll be honest. The idea scares me," Luke said while sipping on a lager.

"Of us losing touch, or you having kids?"

"Well, I don't think we'll stop being friends. It's funny. Even when we haven't talked in a while, when we do, it's like old times and nothing's changed. But having kids? That's scary to think about."

"Why? Kids are great. Sure, it's scary. It's like parts of me are out there in this world, and there's only so much I can do to keep them happy and safe. One day, they'll be out on their own, and there'll be nothing I can do to protect them."

Luke nodded.

"But, at the same time, kids are such a blessing. Seeing these little beings Alyssa and I created live and grow has been life-changing. They're so curious about the world, and they have their own little personalities. Isabella's always talking, babbling about something, and Daniel's so relaxed and just takes things in. I absolutely love being a dad."

"I'm really happy for you, but I don't think it's for me."

"Why not?"

"If Rachel and I had kids, I would be responsible for little humans. I'd be somebody's father, and I don't wanna end up like my own parents. What if I fail at parenting them? What if they end up with my mental problems, and they end up just as screwed up as me?"

"We all have our baggage, man. We just do the best we can. In all things, we're supposed to die to self, to trust God, and to live by Jesus' example."

"I know, Paulie. 'For me to live is Christ, and to die is gain.'"

"Yeah, Philippians 1:21, there's a reason why it's my favorite Bible verse. Live in service to others, live as Christ lived here on earth, and die to our own desires, our own wants, our own worries and fears. That's what I try to remember about marriage and parenting especially. It's not about me. It's about them."

"I guess that makes sense."

"Does she know how you're feeling about the idea of being a dad?"

"No. She's dying to have kids. I can't tell her how I feel. It would kill her."

Paul took a swig of stout. "Bro, it's a bad idea to keep something like that from her. I mean, she's gonna figure it out sooner or later."

"I dunno. I'd hate to crush her dreams."

"Or she might leave you over it," Paul opined, shrugging.

"Eh, I don't think she'd do that. She doesn't believe in divorce."

"Do you?"

"Uh...no...I don't, but growing up, there were times when I wished my mom had divorced my dad. She's always tolerated way too much from him, his drinking, his selfishness, his anger problems. She spends a lot of time worried about me because of him, since he took a lot of his anger out on me, but she's still with him. She still lets him be the way he is. She could've done things differently. She still could."

"Your mom's doing what she believes is right by the Lord."

"I'm well aware."

"Are you expecting Rachel to be like your mom?"

"No, I mean, I...I don't know. We literally just got married. I do love her, and I want this to work. I guess part of me is thinking she'll just let it go."

Paul took a deep breath. "C'mon, man. You and I have both known girls like Rachel in high school youth group and in CK. They've been taught all their lives that this is what they're supposed to live for, you know, being a mother. She's not gonna let that go."

"We'll see."

"Luke, you're either gonna have to tell her, or suck it up and get used to the idea of becoming a dad."

The men continued to spend time together over the course of the evening, drinking and smoking.

"Paulie, can I ask you something? I know it's a bit weird."

"Yeah, sure."

"Do you ever worry that while we've spent so much of our lives going to church, reading the Bible, praying, evangelizing, trying not to sin, that's it's all a waste of time?"

Paul arched his eyebrow. "What do you mean, man?"

"Like I said, what if all this we're doing, following Jesus, doing what the Bible tells us to – what if at the end of it, after we die, what we see isn't what we expect? Or worse yet, there's nothing at all?"

Paul took a moment to think. "Obviously, what we believe and what we know are two different things. We can't know what's gonna happen after we die. People pretend to know, but saying we're certain just makes us feel better, I suppose. The truth is, none of us die, like, for real, and then come back."

"True."

"But we can hope, and we can live by the hope we have. Regardless of what the afterlife looks like, what we can do is make this life as good as it can be, not just for ourselves, but for others."

"Heaven on earth. Cheers to that!"

━━◆◇◆━━

"That was a hell of a time," Luke said in a subdued voice.

"It was," Paul whispered.

"Glad you brought it up. It makes me think of the serenity prayer."

"The serenity prayer?"

"Yeah. I learned it in AA. 'God, grant me the serenity to accept the things I cannot change, the courage to change the things I can, and the wisdom to know the difference.'"

"Okay...I think I've heard it somewhere. It's simple, and it's true."

"How are you feeling, Paulie?"

"I'm good. I...I think I'm gonna be okay."

Luke nodded and grasped his friend's hand.

"I love you, Luke. You're my brother, thank you for being with me through this. You didn't have to, but you're here. And that..." Paul took in a small bit of air, "means the world to me."

"Of course. I love you too. There's nowhere else I'd rather be right now than by your side."

"And please...tell Bella, 'Daddy loves you so much, Bella Donna.'"

Luke took a deep breath. "I will."

"You remember how at Infinity, we would sing praise and worship songs around the campfire?"

"Yeah, I remember."

"No matter how I was feeling about my life, and about God, and my relationship with him, hearing those songs always brought me comfort. Do you remember 'Be Thou My Vision?'"

Luke responded quietly, "Yeah. I do."

"Can you sing it?" Paul requested, almost in a whisper.

"It's been forever, and my singing's a bit rusty. But I'll do my best."

"Thank you, brother."

He then sang softly, holding his friend's hand.

"Be thou my vision, oh Lord of my heart; Naught be all else to me save that thou art."

Paul closed his eyes.

"Thou my best thought by day and by night; Waking or sleeping, thy presence my light."

As Luke continued, Paul's breathing became increasingly shallow.

"High King of Heaven, my victory won; May I reach Heaven's joys, O bright Heav'ns Sun!"

A tear rolled down Luke's face as his friend's grip loosened.

"Heart of my heart, whatever befall, still be my vision, O Ruler of all."

As the final note escaped Luke's lips, Paul's breathing ceased.

The doctor arrived to officially pronounce Paul Chu dead on July 24, 2023, at 2:15 PM. As the hospital staff carefully removed the tubes and wires from his lifeless body, Luke wept harder than he had in his entire life.

At 2:22 PM, a voice called from the doorway of Room 513.

"Daddy?" A bespectacled young woman appeared. "Is he..."

Luke nodded and said gently, "Yes, he's gone."

The woman became weak on her feet, her slender visage sliding down the door frame. A loud, pained cry was heard from a small body.

"Daddy!"

Luke rushed over to catch her, and he guided her to a seat in the hallway, where she calmed down after several minutes.

After an hour, she finally spoke. "I can't believe I missed him."

"You must be Bella."

"Yes," she said through a sniffle. "How did you know?"

"I'm a friend of your father's. My name's Luke...Luke Phillips. Last time I saw you, you were just a toddler."

"I remember my parents talking about you. You're my dad's best friend."

"Yeah, your dad had quite a bit to say about you, too. He was very proud of you. He told me to tell you, 'Daddy loves you so much, Bella Donna.'"

Bella broke down again and wept. Broken as well, Luke held her as she leaned into him, unleashing her immense grief.

PHOTOGRAPH
August 7-9, 2023

Luke sat on an upholstered chair in a hotel just outside Tallahassee, Florida, on a warm Monday morning. He was waiting for Bella to arrive in the lobby as they were checking out and resuming their trip from Los Angeles to Jacksonville. After helping her settle affairs in California as the executrix of Paul's estate, he volunteered to drive her to her father's home so she would not need to make the trip alone.

The elegant woman walked off the elevator with her straight hair in a bun and whisps of brunette strands framing her smooth, oval face.

"Ready, Bella?"

"Yeah."

The two left the hotel and started on the last leg of their journey.

"It took me way too long to fly out to visit my dad. I'm always gonna regret that," Bella disclosed.

"It's not your fault," Luke reassured her. "There's no way you could've known how long your dad had to live. None of us really knew."

"But see, that's the thing. I stayed angry at him for years. I can almost say I hated his guts. You two were best friends, but as much as he'd fake it in church, my dad was no saint."

"I know. He'd say so himself."

"You know, the way he treated my mom, it was awful. He never hit her, he never laid a hand on her. I never heard him put her down or say anything mean. But I saw how the things he did affected her."

He glanced over at her, then focused again on the road, still listening.

She continued. "When I was a kid, you know, I had no idea. He was just my daddy and he was the best. He was always great to me. But I saw Mom was always tired, always sad. She would take care of me and Danny, make sure we were fed, and we had clean clothes. She drove us to and from school and took us to practice for all our sports and clubs. But...she always seemed like she was in another world. If she wasn't doing things for us, she would just be in her room, asleep, and back then, I thought it was my fault, because no matter what, I couldn't make her happy."

"I hope you know it wasn't about you at all. It wasn't your fault," Luke reassured her while his eyes were trained on the highway.

"Thanks. I know that now, but I didn't get it back then. I didn't know just how bad things were between my parents."

"That makes sense. There's a lot we don't know about our parents when we're kids."

"True, but I'd overhear things, see little things. One time, when I was, like, eight, my mom went up to Michigan because my grandma had surgery. While she was out of town, my dad brought over some lady, a "friend." I wasn't allowed to tell my mom about it, because they were 'moving furniture around' in their bedroom and he wanted it to be a surprise for her."

"Oof. Some things we see as kids, we don't realize what was really happening until we're adults, and we can put things into context. Like, my mom wearing sunglasses in the nighttime..."

"Yeah. I didn't realize that my dad was having affairs until I was in high school, and I could put two and two together. Then, we found out about Gracie and the whole truth came out. My mom dealt with it...dealt with my dad and who he was, until she couldn't. Then, we all moved up to Niles and Dad got left behind."

Luke shook his head.

"You know, to this day, my mom never says anything bad about my dad. And to be fair, he never said anything bad about her either, at least not to us."

"For what it's worth, when I caught up with your dad, he had nothing but good things to say about your mom, and you as well. He told me a bunch of times he knew his actions were his own fault."

"Yeah, I think he's told my mom that, too, but there are some things you just can't fix."

"Understandable."

"See, I had started to warm up to the idea of maybe letting Dad back in after I heard he came to Oklahoma to see Danny and Auntie Rina. But then, when he was in the hospital, he called to tell Mom he may have given her HIV, and she needed to get tested. You know, she stayed with him for a long time. Too long. She was faithful and he wasn't. She doesn't deserve this."

Luke nodded. "I'm sorry, I can't imagine."

"But at some point, I had to realize that yeah, he's done some horrible things, but he's still my father. My parents' relationship was theirs, and it didn't mean I couldn't have my own with my dad. I just hate that I didn't realize that until it was too late."

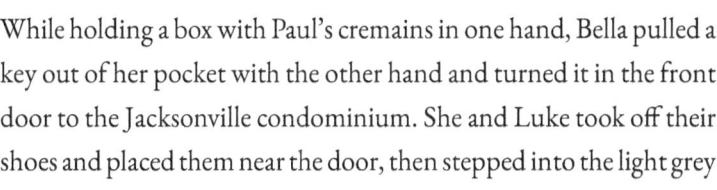

While holding a box with Paul's cremains in one hand, Bella pulled a key out of her pocket with the other hand and turned it in the front door to the Jacksonville condominium. She and Luke took off their shoes and placed them near the door, then stepped into the light grey painted, open-concept first floor.

"Daddy, you're home," Bella murmured, placing the cremains on a shelf in the living room.

"Have you ever been here?" Luke asked.

"No. He bought this within the last couple of years, I think, but I was basically no contact with him at that point."

Luke looked around the front room as Bella wandered through the rest of the unit. Besides the wall shelving where the urn sat, the living room area was furnished with a grey leather couch and recliner, a glass coffee table and large flat-screen television on a stand matching the table. On the table were Christian and secular humanist philosophy books neatly organized, and Korean knot art on the wall behind the couch. The living room floor was carpeted in grey.

The kitchen was adorned with granite countertops, stainless steel appliances, a matching island, and marble-patterned floors. The exposed wall in the kitchen area was adorned by a large framed poster of toast. In addition, there was a small area between the kitchen and the living room area furnished with a glass table and four steel dining chairs with grey leather seats.

"And you said my apartment looked like a fucking Ikea. I might as well be in their showroom. Damn it, Paulie," Luke vocalized to himself.

He climbed the stairs to the second floor. At the top of the stairs was a door to a bedroom in front of him. Two other bedrooms, as well as a bathroom, were to his left around the corner and down a short hallway. He turned and went down to the furthest bedroom, where he found Bella.

The room was painted lavender and furnished with a twin bed, a white dresser, and a matching desk and chair. The bed was neatly made with white pillows and lavender sheets. She was perched on the side of the bed, tearing up. "My dad always had a room ready for me. I...I had no idea."

Luke took a deep breath. "Bella, I'm sure your dad knows you love him. I know for sure he loved you very much. Take your time and let me know if you need anything."

He then slowly made his way to the other end of the hallway. A full bathroom sat between Bella's bedroom and the next bedroom. Luke peeked into the bedroom. It was painted white and included a bed with blue and black sheets, a black chest of drawers, and a desk and gaming chair. Above the desk was a framed poster of a green plumbob from *The Sims*.

This is definitely Danny's room.

Then, he entered the bedroom at the end of the hallway closest to the stairs. This room was large and painted pale green, with a queen-sized plush bed in pastel green with pink pillows on the right side of the bedroom. The bed was adorned with a half-moon shaped mirrored headboard and framed with two white-framed glass nightstands. Large potted ferns accentuated the space. A white dresser, desk with desktop computer, and an ergonomic black office chair were also in the room.

What in the Miami Vice is this shit?

Luke stepped towards the desk and noticed a corkboard on the wall next to the computer table by the closet. Pinned to the corkboard were several photos. These pictures included a family photo with Paul, Alyssa, Bella, and Danny when the children were young, an old black and white portrait of Paul's parents, another photo he was in with his parents and siblings, a snapshot of him with Rina, and several pictures of friends, including some with Luke in it. He reached into his small camera bag and got out his GoPro, filming the photos on the corkboard.

As he recorded, he noticed a photo sitting on the keyboard. He took a closer look. It was a photo from college over twenty years ago featuring three people in semi-formal attire. Luke was dressed in a purple dress top and lavender tie and was seated next to Ann, who was wearing a long-sleeved purple chiffon wrap dress. Paul, who was wearing a navy sports jacket, pink shirt, and navy tie, stood between them. His hands rested on each of their shoulders, and he was leaning over with his face between theirs. All were smiling.

I have this picture!

He picked up the snapshot.

It's in the box at home. I forgot I made copies, haha.

He could not remember the context in which it was taken, but it was his favorite photo, and also the very one that ended his marriage.

The next morning, Luke woke up in Danny's bed. He peered at his phone.

Oh shit, it's eleven AM, I didn't mean to sleep that late.

Luke climbed out of bed and headed to the bathroom. After showering and readying himself for the day, he took the linens off the bed, along with the towels he used, and started them in the washer located in the hallway closet. He packed his bags, grabbed his luggage and headed downstairs.

In the kitchen, Bella had made breakfast, including bacon, eggs and biscuits. Piping hot coffee was in the coffee pot. She was sitting on the couch with her hair in a messy top bun and black oval glasses on her face, wearing orange plaid pajama pants and a matching sleeveless orange top. Her lean legs were crossed in front of her as she watched TV and enjoyed her meal.

"G'morning Luke! Food's on the counter. You're welcome to it."

"Thanks, Bella, I appreciate it." He plated up a biscuit, eggs, and bacon, and poured himself a black coffee.

"Did your dad leave all this food behind?"

"Oh, no. He was my dad, but he was still a guy. He didn't leave much in the way of noms, so I walked to the grocery store around the corner and picked up some things."

"I could've taken you,"

Bella shook her head. "You drove all the way here. I wasn't gonna wake you, you needed your rest."

He sat on the edge of the recliner and began eating. "This is delicious!"

"Thanks. It's super basic, nothing amazing or anything."

"It hits the spot. So, anyway, how'd you sleep?" he asked.

"I actually slept okay. I shocked myself. I felt strangely at peace in my bed, even though it was the first time I slept in it. How about you?"

"Uh, I slept alright. I overslept a bit, but it's fine. Heads up that I placed the sheets and the towels I used in the washer and started them up for you."

"Awesome. I'll take get them dried and everything. Thanks, Luke."

"No problem. So, I'm about to take off here soon, but if you want, I can stay longer. Is there anything I can do to help? I don't have anywhere to be right away," Luke offered.

"Oh no, you're fine to head home. You've got a really long drive on top of what you've already done. Danny and Auntie Rina will be here later today. They'll be staying here awhile to help me get Dad's affairs cinched up here."

"Now, are you sure you don't want the truck?" Luke asked.

"I'm sure. I have my own little truck up in Michigan, I don't need a beast like that. And besides, my dad signed it over to you for a reason, I'm sure. Danny and I will be okay."

"Alright. You have my number – reach out to me if you change your mind."

"Sure, but I won't. Take it."

"Oh!" Luke remembered, "what about his guitar?"

"Nah. Neither me or Danny play. It should go to someone who'll appreciate it. I know Daddy would want that."

"'Kay."

Bella continued. "Anyway, I'll let you know when we're up in Losanti. I'm sure you're aware, but my dad didn't want a funeral or anything formal with lots of people. He just wanted his ashes scattered along the Ohio River. So, we're going to make it up there at some point soon, and we're gonna have a little ceremony. I'll give you a call when we have a date. You should be there when we do that

– I think so and so do Danny and Auntie Rina. You were his best friend."

Luke got choked up. "Thank you, Bella."

After breakfast, and after saying their goodbyes, Luke left the condo, packed his luggage in the Jeep, and got into the driver seat to start it. As he was setting up his music for the long drive back to Ohio, he searched through the dashboard monitor to set the GPS up for the trip home. He stumbled upon a section entitled "Saved Trips."

What's this?

He tapped on the screen to review the saved itineraries. One of the logged trips was the one he had been on with Paul prior to his untimely passing.

Where were we going?

Out of an abundance of curiosity, he scrolled through the itinerary. At last, he discovered the destination. He could not help but to laugh.

Are you fucking serious, Paulie?

BRIGHT LANE
September-November 2023

Staying up after his overnight shift at the Dairy Union, Luke showered and changed into a black button-up shirt with matching slacks
and boots. He then donned a porkpie hat, grabbed a bouquet of
mixed flowers waiting on the kitchen counter, and left his apartment.

It was a quarter till eight in the morning and Luke pulled into
Riverfront Park. Flowers in hand, he strolled across the park grounds
to the banks of the tranquil Ohio River. He sat on the grassy river
bank, taking in the clear sky, and listened to the melodies of the birds,
the flow of the water, and the blowing of the gentle wind.

"Luke!"

He turned around at the sound of his name. Behind him was
a long-legged, thick-bodied, peach-toned woman wearing a black
blouse, wide-leg pants, and kitten-heeled shoes. She held a handful
of roses.

"Oh my God – Alyssa!" Luke stood up, surprised to see her, and
they gave each other a huge hug.

"Luke! It's been too long," Alyssa said, her voluminous sandy
blonde locks flowing in the wind.

"It has. I'm so sorry we're meeting up under these circumstances."

"Me too. Yet, God has his way. Just have to trust him."

"How was your trip down here?"

"Oh, it went pretty smoothly. I came down through Indiana, and it was fine until I got to Indianapolis. Got lost for a while on that silly loop, but figured it out, obviously. I'm here."

"Glad you made it, Alyssa."

"Yeah, I felt I needed to be here to support the kids. However the relationship was between me and Paul, was their father. And honestly, I never stopped loving him."

A short time later, Bella, Danny, and Rina pulled into the park. They were carrying a black box with Paul's cremains, flowers, a small banner written in Hangul script, and a framed photo. All were dressed in ebony. Once they made it to the northern bank, everyone greeted each other and hugged.

Rina pulled Luke to the side. "Luke, I'm so very thankful you were there for my nephew in his last days. You were such a wonderful friend to him. The world needs more people like you."

"Of course, I love Paulie, couldn't let him take that journey by himself. Are his parents or his brothers and sisters coming?"

"No. They are grieving in their own way. We're it."

Luke and Rina returned to the group. They set up a small shrine near the edge of the water. The portrait of Paul was made the centerpiece and was framed with flowers. The banner was to the side. Danny held the box.

Danny spoke. "We're here to informally commemorate the life of Paul Chu and commit his earthly body to his home. Dad, you know, despite everything, you're still my dad, and I'm thankful for you. You taught me how to accept myself as I am, flaws and all, and who I am is because of you. I truly hope you're in a better place, and when it's my time, I can see you once again." He then announced to the group. "Before we spread Dad's cremains, anyone else who wants to may share remarks."

Rina spoke next. "Dear *joka*, you were such a free spirit. You were like a little brother to me, you were my shadow, and you couldn't be reined in. You took life by the horns, and you made the most of the short time you were here with us. May you be at peace."

Alyssa then spoke up. "Paul, you were my soulmate. Ever since we met in college, I knew you were the one for me. You were an amazing person, and you lived for the people in your life. No matter what, we loved each other very much. And your spirit still lives in the beautiful children we made together."

Bella was overcome with intense sadness, bawling and leaning into her mother's shoulder for comfort. After Alyssa finished speaking, she nodded to Luke.

He cleared his throat. "Paulie, you were my best friend, and the world loses because you're no longer in it. We met at Great Lakes, and you were so fun. I admired that you could make friends effortlessly, and you always saw the good in people. You were a true friend who looked out for me when I was at my lowest point, and you saved my life. I'll do what I can to be there for your family the way you were for me. And I'll finish what we started. I promise you that, brother." He wept.

Danny then stepped to the edge of the Ohio River with Bella walking beside him. He opened the box and carefully scattered the remains into the river as it flowed past them. Then, everyone took the display apart and placed the contents into the river to follow.

***

It was nearing seven o'clock on a Saturday morning in September, and Luke was a bit tired from a long, exhausting solo trip across the country. However, he felt a second wind as he passed the small roadside sign crossing into the destination city.

**Sunnyvale
City Limit**

He turned onto Bright Lane, a quiet cul-de-sac lined with well-maintained, mid-century modern homes complete with nicely manicured lawns in desert style. At the end of the block, he found the address, located on the right-hand side of the street.

175 Bright Lane. This is it.

The GPS voice announced, "You have arrived."

He sat in the Wrangler, completely worn out from travel, and stared at the modest yet fine home. It was a single-story ranch-style house like the others, painted in azure stucco with stark white trim. A cornflower blue Volkswagen Taos was sitting in the paved driveway in front of the white garage door trimmed in cerulean.

An hour later, the redwood door opened. A short, zaftig yet solidly built woman stepped out with a large, furry, well-groomed Newfoundland dog on a leather lead. The woman turned around briefly and locked her door. She then bounded down the driveway in dark grey form-fitting yoga pants and a fitted tee shirt of the same color with a cube graphic on the front, her full, curly brunette ponytail with auburn highlights bouncing behind her, whipped around by a small bit of wind.

She's just as gorgeous as I remember her.

She glanced at the truck only for a brief moment, then loaded up her dog, stepped into her crossover, and pulled out of the driveway.

Luke switched on the Jeep and followed the woman. After several minutes, the Taos turned into a parking lot. Luke followed her into the lot and noted the sign at the entrance.

Bean Hollow State Beach

The blue vehicle parked near the pathway to the beach. Luke slid the truck into a space next to it.

After a moment, he stepped out of the Wrangler, closed his door, and walked toward the Volkswagen.

"Dude, what do you want?" the woman yelled, facing Luke with a small canister attached to her keychain at the ready. The large, tense dog stared at him intently, only held back by the leash wrapped around the owner's left wrist.

"Ann..."

"Luke...is that you?"

"Yeah."

"Oh my God...what are you doing here?"

"AC, I...I needed to see you."

Ann's facial expression then softened, and she relaxed, pocketing her keychain. She reached over to pet her giant dog. "It's okay, Alexis." The dog then sat, wagging her tail. "Good girl."

Relieved that she finally recognized him, Luke smiled.

She took a deep breath and then started walking towards the beach, motioning him to come along. He strolled alongside her.

"Just so you know, I already heard about Paul. Alyssa called me."

"Yeah. I was there when he went."

"Oh wow, I'm so sorry. God, that sucks. This loss really hurts, not gonna lie."

"Yeah. It does."

"He was truly a good dude. He was so damn funny, and he was such a loyal guy who would go to hell and back for his friends." Ann's eyes welled up with tears as she continued. "I feel so bad for his kids. He was way too young."

"He was."

She stopped along the shoreline. He could feel the intensity of her slate grey eyes locked onto his. "Well, uh, not to be mean or anything, but you really didn't need to come all this way to tell me about Paul. And how did you figure out where I was, anyway?"

"Uh...we were driving out here right before he died. He told me where you were...well, sorta."

"What? Are you for real?"

"Yeah, I am."

"Damn it, Paul...he *would*." She chuckled sarcastically.

He smiled a bit. "For what it's worth, he didn't tell me directly, but he made it pretty easy to figure out."

She shook her head.

He continued. "Eh, look AC, you see, I didn't come out here to tell you about Paulie. I came out here 'cause I need to see *you*. I meant what I said."

Her face contorted. "Why?"

"Huh?"

"Luke – don't you remember? You wanted to 'distance' yourself from me. I was too embarrassing to be with, I was too clingy, too fat, don't...don't you remember that? Because I sure do."

"Yeah, I do. I...I was young and stupid. Really fucking stupid. I am so, very sorry."

Ann sighed, her voice cracking. "I don't think you understand, Luke. There are people here who want to be around me, who want to be seen with me, who don't send their friends to do their dirty work. Nowadays, I surround myself with those people. I've made a good life here. I am happy here. You are not going to ruin this f—"

"I love you."

She was stunned into momentary silence. Upon regaining her voice, she responded hesitantly, "What? Uh...are you serious?"

"I'm so fucking serious. I love you, AC. When I said all that awful shit to you in Losanti, when I complained about you to Paulie, when I said I wanted us to just be friends, I was a fucking liar. The truth is, I knew as soon as you said 'goodbye' to me that I made the biggest mistake of my life, but I was too much of a coward to make things right in the moment."

She listened, her expression softening slightly.

"I have lived just about all my life as a coward. And I regret every minute of that, because at the end of the day, I still lost everything. Everything." Luke paused for a moment, then continued. "But what I realized is I can't live like that anymore."

She looked at him, then stared out into the ocean.

He continued, emotion welling up inside of him. "I have always thought you were an amazing woman. From the time I first met you. Beautiful and unique. One of a kind. And God, you're just as stunning now. You have always unapologetically been yourself. You could've done the things you were expected to do, but instead you sought the kind of life you wanted. You faced the hard parts of life instead of running away from them. You began to question what you believed way before I ever did, and you took leaps of faith even when nobody around us understood it. That makes you amazing and I have always admired that about you."

She sat down on a beach rock, and her dog lay comfortably on the sand beside her. She rested her chin in her hands.

He sat beside her and looked into her sparkling grey eyes. "Ann Leigh Corbin, I know I can't fix the past, but I want to make things right with you in the now. I want you back in my life and not just as a friend. I want you to b—"

Ann put her finger up to his lips. "Luke, *you* may want that, and don't get me wrong, I appreciate that you came all this way to find me. But it's not just about you and what you want. It's been twenty years since I've last seen you."

"I know it's been a long time, AC, but..."

She held her hand up. "No, Luke. You don't get it. Things are different now. *I* am different now. I'm not the same as I was back when we were in college, or even when I was living in Losanti. I have gone through therapy, I take care of my body, and I don't hurt myself anymore, and I treat my soul well. I've done the work, and it was fucking hard, but I did the work. I know the past several years haven't been too kind to you..."

"How...how do you..."

"Dude, you know Paul told me. He said he had a feeling you were having a hard time."

Luke sighed. "Figures."

She then squeezed his hand and spoke to him softly. "Luke, you and I being together will not improve your life. I am not the answer to your problems. I can't fix you. You have to do the work to fix yourself."

Ann stood up with Alexis, leather lead in hand, and walked away, leaving Luke sitting on the edge of the water alone.

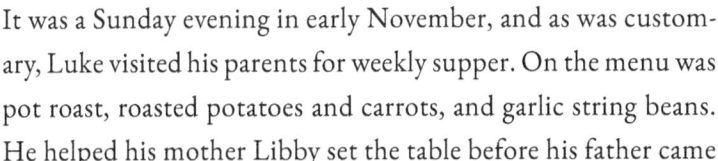

It was a Sunday evening in early November, and as was customary, Luke visited his parents for weekly supper. On the menu was pot roast, roasted potatoes and carrots, and garlic string beans. He helped his mother Libby set the table before his father came downstairs to eat.

"Luke, I'm glad you were able to finish up the road trip you and your friend started," Libby remarked. "I'm sorry he couldn't be there with you."

"Thanks, Mom. It was bittersweet for obvious reasons, but I'm glad I did it." Luke responded somberly. "Paul was a good guy. I really do miss him."

"I'm sure you do. Losing a friend is difficult, especially since he was so young."

"Yeah, I didn't see it coming. I don't think he did either."

She was quiet for a moment, then said, "I'm not so sure about that, dear."

"What do you mean?" he asked, while arranging the utensils and drink glasses on the table.

"Well, obviously you couldn't have known, but maybe he knew. Not consciously. I mean, how could you possibly know you're going to come down with a deadly bout of pneumonia?"

Luke nodded. He told his parents few details of Paul's cause of death, so as to keep his late friend's confidence.

Libby continued, "But, maybe his spirit knew. As you know, I lost my mother pretty young. I was a teenager, I was thirteen. At a certain point, I remember her talking to me and your uncles a bit differently than she once did. She would try to impart life lessons, life advice, and she kept telling us she wouldn't be around forever, and to cherish our lives, live them to the fullest."

"Oh wow, Mom, I didn't know that, but it makes sense. Didn't she die of terminal cancer?"

"She did, but she wasn't told. In those days, if you got a diagnosis like that, they'd tell your family, but not you. The doctors thought you would be better off living your life and not knowing, because they were afraid you would give up and die more quickly. Eventually, she ended up in the hospital and passed away shortly after."

"Aww."

"Things are a lot different now, but sometimes, I believe you might get a sense you don't have long. Or at least your spirit knows. Your friend had a pretty important job, right?"

"Yes, he was a city engineer."

"And he decided to take a long vacation just to come get you, drive cross-country, and visit the people important to him. Maybe that was his spirit's way of saying goodbye."

"I've never thought of it that way, but maybe you're right."

"Perhaps so. Anyway, I notice you seem different."

"Maybe a bit. I'm taking my medication every day and I've been back to seeing my therapist regularly."

"That's good, but you know, Luke, when I say you seem different, I don't mean sad or depressed. I mean you don't seem so on edge. You seem more at peace with yourself than I've seen you in a very long time."

"Thanks, Mom. I do."

"Oh, looks like we're done with the table. Call your dad down."

Once everyone was at the table, Cam recited a small prayer over the food, then they began to serve themselves and eat. He had his favorite, Guinness, beside him, while Libby had a glass of Riesling and Luke drank a cup of tap water on ice.

"No wine for you tonight, son?"

"No, sir."

"Pregnant?" Cam quipped.

Luke chuckled. "I decided it's not for me these days. Trying to take better care of myself."

"Looks like losing your buddy really spooked you."

"Yes...you could say that."

As they were finishing their meal, Libby asked, "So, Luke, since you've finished your trip, what are you planning to do with your life? Have you thought about applying for another researcher job? I'm sure they're hiring at other places besides Ohio Valley Ranch."

Cam added, "Or, have you looked into going back to school? You can apply to med school, or, y'know, maybe enough time has passed that they might let you back into vet school."

"Uh, about that – there's something I need to talk to you both about," Luke declared.

"Alright, go ahead," Libby said.

"On the cross-country trip I took with Paul, and the follow-up trip I made out to California, I did some filming, y'know, documentary-style. Since I've been back, I've been uploading those videos to YouTube for posterity. Apparently, people really like the videos, and a few of them went viral."

"'Viral?'"

"'Viral' means very popular. A lot of people watched them. I was able to accumulate enough channel subscribers and views to become monetized."

"Monetized? What does that mean?" Libby asked.

Luke explained. "It means YouTube pays me when people watch the videos, and for the ads they play on them. It's a fair amount of money coming in. My subscriber and view counts are going up, so that just means I'll make more from the videos."

"That's...new," Libby remarked. "I guess I don't get it, but it sounds nice."

"You know that making videos on the internet isn't a consistent or sustainable way to make a living," Cam warned.

"Yessir. I'm not depending on it, but it is a little extra income besides what I make at the Dairy Union."

"I'm still shocked they hired you back," Libby said.

"Nobody wants to work the hours I was working, and it's not like I was stealing from them or anything, so they brought me back on, no problem. But anyway, my lease is up soon. I'm already moving my things into storage for the time being. I've sold the Kia and I'm keeping the Jeep. And..." Luke took a deep breath, "I'm moving."

Cam was shocked. "What?"

"Where are you going, dear?" Libby asked.

"I'm moving out to California, San Jose. I need a clean start."

His mother cautioned, "This isn't a good idea, Luke. I know you miss your friend and you're disappointed with the way your life has turned out, with failing out of veterinary school, your career, and your divorce. But you're in your forties now. You need to pull yourself together and focus on making a good living and saving for retirement. It'll be here before you know it."

"I understand that, Mom. I'm already sending out applications and I've got a couple interviews lined up. I even have some leads on a place to live."

Cam sat back in his chair. "That's a bit impulsive, son...and it's very expensive. The cost of living is much higher in California than here in Ohio. You should really think long and hard about this."

"Dad, I have. I've had quite a while to think this through and research things there. I have a game plan and I'm already putting it into action. If all goes well, I'll be living out in San Jose before Thanksgiving."

"Well, you're on your own. Sink or swim. Your mother and I will not be paying your rent out there."

"And don't expect your brother to bail you out, either," Libby added.

"That's fine," Luke assured them. "I had no intention of asking you or anybody else for money. You've done more than enough for me, and I appreciate it very much, but I need to do this. And I'll be supporting myself – as I said, my plan is already in motion."

After a silent moment at the table, Libby replied, "We'll miss you, dear."

Cam took a deep breath. "Son, you're making this decision like a man, and you're taking on a man's responsibility. I respect that." He stood up from the table and held out his right hand. Luke got up as well and shook his hand firmly. He then told his son, "Good luck and Godspeed, Luke."

"Thank you, sir."

Libby then stood up and gave her son a long hug.

"I'll be okay, Mom," Luke promised her.

"I sure hope so, dear."

STEVIE
August-September 2024

"Stevie, what are you looking at?"

Luke stood up and stared out the window of his cozy one-bedroom apartment near San Jose's Santana Row. He noticed a squirrel running up a palm tree nearby, but otherwise, the street below was relatively quiet.

"You're not gonna catch that squirrel, kitty," he noted as he began to pet his grey and white long-haired cat. "Let me get you some food, so you'll be fine when I'm out today."

As he sat out a plate of cat food for Stevie, he heard a knock at his front door. He opened the door to see a lean middle-aged man looking up at him.

"Ready to go out on the trail?"

"Yeah, Mark. Lemme get my shoes on, and we'll get the bikes strapped to the truck. Have a seat."

Luke's neighbor and friend Mark, who was wearing tight black shorts and a yellow top, sat on the burgundy couch in the living room. Luke was sitting on the matching recliner, wearing similar shorts and a light green top, tying up his white and black Hokas. Stevie perched herself on the windowsill watching the men with apparent curiosity.

"Who's all coming?" Luke asked.

"Just us. Lamar's got work and it's Pete's weekend with the kids. But that'll be fine. It's quite a nice September day."

"That's for sure. Y'know, it's great that the weather has calmed down at least a little bit. It's been so hot all summer."

"Yeah, that's 2024 for you."

Luke nodded. "Alright, I'll grab my helmet and we can get the bikes loaded."

A half hour later, the men arrived at Coyote Creek Trail, a scenic bike trail on the southern edge of San Jose. There, they began their day of riding together, covering much of the path. Luke marveled at the diversity of sights along the trail, including arid grasslands, forests of redwoods and oak trees, and small lakes. He enjoyed taking in the beauty of nature in his new state, and being one with his environment gave him a sense of peace.

After the bike ride, the friends went to the Bayside Cafe, a popular restaurant nearby. As they sat in a plush beige booth and ate lunch, they chatted about their lives.

"How's the new job, Mark?"

"I can't complain. It's nice to be back to work after being unemployed for the past few months. Tech is a rough industry right now, so glad I got hired on. I'm making more than I did at my last job, and what we sell is always in demand."

"TechTrod makes computer processors and other internal hardware, right?"

"Yeah, we do, and our products are competitive with Intel, Nvidia, and AMD. The projections are looking great for our business. How's everything going at the zoo?"

"I love it," Luke responded. "With the social media campaigns we're running right now, we're getting a lot more visitors, and vendor sales have gone up over the past few months."

"What social media are you using?"

"Uh, the big ones – TikTok, Facebook, Instagram, X, Threads."

"Which social media outlet is performing the best?"

Luke stopped to think for a moment. "Y'know, that's a good question. I really don't know."

"Have you guys gotten granular and run the numbers based on ad buys for each social media outlet?"

"We've done the overall numbers, but it's hard to sort out which of them is doing the heavy lifting. I'm a hard sciences guy – this is a bit out of my depth, and it's not like we have a flushed-out department of statisticians or anything."

"Okay Luke, so if you don't have a data analytics department or a financial planning and analysis team, it might be worth outsourcing that function to a market research firm. It's a bit of a cost upfront but it'll save you in the long run. Lamar's company does that type of work. You might want to reach out to him about it."

"Sure, I'll reach out to him. Sounds like a great idea." Luke then changed the subject. "Mark, I can't believe that as of two weeks ago, I've been sober for a whole year. I really appreciate your help and guidance, man."

"Thanks Luke, but it wasn't me. The thing about being a sponsor is, my sponsees help me stay sober too. I'm just walking this road with you. It's your relationship with your higher power, and your willingness to diligently work the program. You're living in freedom. One day at a time."

"Yes, one day at a time."

———◆◇◆———

Two weeks later, Luke met up with his friend Lamar at the local animal shelter, where they volunteered regularly. It was a Sunday afternoon, and they went out for a walk with a few of the shelter dogs. Luke had a Doberman and a pit bull mix, while Lamar was walking a pit bull and a German shepherd. All the dogs were well-behaved and got along.

"These dogs are great, aren't they, Luke?" Lamar remarked.

"Oh, for sure. Good boys. I love spending time with them. I hope they get adopted soon."

"Yeah. You know Ayesha and I foster, and I'm not ashamed to say we've had a couple 'foster fails.' Rescue dogs are so great."

"They are. I would like to have dogs, but my apartment wouldn't accommodate one. But, y'know, cats are great companions too."

"Not as affectionate, though."

"Eh, it depends on the cat. Stevie, my cat, she likes to be cuddled, and she's always there checking on me, especially when I'm not in a great mood."

"That's dope. I grew up around dogs, not so much cats. My bad for the assumption."

"Don't worry about it. To be fair, I grew up around neither. My mom is into extreme cleanliness. I wonder if she has OCD like I do, but she'll never get checked out."

"Makes sense. I bet it's a generational thing. A lot of older folks were taught to tough things out and aren't really into getting help."

"Yeah, that's for sure. I love that my mental health is managed enough at this point to comfortably have pets."

"For sure. They're awesome."

The friends rounded the corner and continued walking with the dogs, who were all energetic.

"I'm glad you called me up about the needs you have for your job. I'm sure we can help y'all. Did you give your boss the proposal I drew up?" Lamar asked.

"Yeah, I did," Luke answered. "Donna was really excited to hear The California Republic Agency wanted on board. Said y'all are the best marketing firm in the Bay, and she said she was impressed that I could get something set up. I have her buy-in, and I believe the other executives on the board. Looks like they'll be signing the contract soon and we'll get the ball rolling. They were very impressed with the proposal — thanks for drafting that up, man."

"No problem. Glad we'll be able to help y'all out. I already put a word in to get our best team to work on your project. As soon as I told them that it was for the San Jose Zoo, they got excited."

"That's great to hear. Looking forward to this."

"For sure. Now, how do you think the Warriors will do this year?"

"You know what, man?" Luke replied, half laughing. "I have no idea. Couldn't even tell you anything about basketball or most sports for that matter."

"That's fair. Did you ever get into sports back in your hometown?"

"Kinda. I would go to the ballpark and watch baseball with my dad and my brother growing up. That was their thing, not so much mine. I was more into singing along during the seventh-inning stretch and eating mini helmet sundaes."

"That's cool. My dad and I went to basketball games a lot when I was a kid. It was something that bonded us, and we still shoot the shit about it when we talk, which is pretty much every day. I didn't have any kind of talent to play, though. I'm the one black man in America who can't jump," Lamar joked. "By the way, are you close with your family, if you don't mind me asking?"

"Eh, it's fine. Honestly, not really. I think they're shocked I'm doing well out here. My dad's a Vietnam vet. He came back from the war and worked in a steel mill, back when working blue-collar jobs like that supported a whole family. He worked there for something like twenty, twenty-five years, until they closed up shop in the late nineties."

"That's tough."

"Yeah, it was. Fortunately, he had some money put away, and he ended up becoming a civil servant and did that until he retired. Overall, he provided well for our family, but I think he always had ambition for more. He's one of those guys who hates his life and tries to live vicariously through their kids."

"Ah, I see. I can't imagine."

"It's alright. I've come to terms with it. We're not close, but these days, we're okay as we can be. At least he has some respect for me. My mom and I are a bit closer. Not super close, but she's easier to talk to than my dad. She worries a lot. My brother – he's out here too, he's up in Pacifica."

"How close are you and him?"

"We're not. We've never gotten along. Our relationship has always been competitive, but not a lot of parity. He's done quite well for himself. He's a dean over at Berkeley, and he was responsible for developing GPS for the civilian market."

"GPS, like the online maps?"

"Yep."

"Ooh, that *is* a pretty big deal."

"For sure – try competing with that."

The men laughed.

"So, it's only been since I've moved out here that I've gotten a fresh start and things are looking up," Luke added.

"They're more than looking up, Luke. You're the marketing director for a world-class institution. You live in a nice part of town. You're fit, you look great. That's not nothing."

"Eh, that's true. I used to resent him, big time. These days, I've let it go. We have our own race to run."

"Have you and your brother met up since you moved here?"

"Nah. Y'know, sometimes I wonder if the time for us to reconcile has passed us by."

"Not as long as you're both still breathing, but time waits for nobody."

I've got this. I've got this.

It was a sunny Tuesday morning, and Luke studied himself in the mirror as he prepared to head to the California Republic Agency, the premier marketing agency in the Bay area. Stevie lay curled into a loaf on the bed, staring at her guardian's image. He straightened his blue striped tie, fastened his navy suit jacket, and shook out his muscled legs, loosening his crisp matching pants.

Glad I took my meds last night. I can't imagine doing this if I wasn't regularly taking them.

After tidying himself up, he placed his laptop into his computer bag. He then stood over Stevie and petted her furry head. "Well, even if I bomb this presentation, at least when I get home, you'll be here staring me down for food. I'll still be your servant and at least that won't change."

She purred contently.

Once Luke arrived at the agency office in nearby Santa Clara, he stopped, breathed deeply, and took in the lobby. It was adorned in dark blue, white, and maroon, with a gold "California Republic Agency" logo emblazoned on the wall opposite the door. A fresh scent with a hint of hibiscus filled the air. He walked to the receptionist, who smiled invitingly at a mahogany desk in front of the logo.

"Good morning!" the young man greeted Luke. "Welcome to the California Republic Agency. How may I help you?"

"Yes, good morning. I'm here to meet Lamar Porter for a nine o'clock meeting. I'm Luke Phillips with the San Jose Zoo."

"One moment, I'll let Lamar know. Please have a seat anywhere you'd like."

Luke chose a plush royal blue chair close to the reception desk, his leg sitting atop his knee.

Wow, this place is super fancy and modern. Do I belong here?

This is so far off from working thirds at the Dairy Union.

Can't believe this is my life now. I just have to remind myself I worked hard for this.

Lamar, clad in a blue button-down shirt and tie, navy blue pants, and matching shined shoes, walked out of a solid white door on one side of the lobby that closed behind him. When he saw Luke, he greeted him, shaking his hand and clasping it with his free hand.

"Hey, Luke! Today's the day."

"For sure, Lamar," he responded while standing up. "Everything's ready to go."

"Sounds good. Our best data science team will join us in one of our meeting rooms. They'll get to hear more about what the zoo needs for the project, and I'm sure they'll ask you any questions they may have. Just remember that they're looking for all the information they need so they can do the best work for you guys."

"Yeah, for sure."

"Alright, let's go."

Lamar opened the security door with a key fob, and then Luke followed him past the barrier through the busy, open-concept office. The men entered an empty meeting room walled on three sides with glass.

Luke sat his black bag at one end of the long wooden conference table and began to set up the laptop for his presentation. Lamar helped him with the inputs and getting him logged into the network and the virtual meeting space, as some team members worked remotely.

A few minutes later, three members of the team filed in and took seats around the table. Lamar also took a seat as well. When it was time to begin, he introduced Luke to the group.

"Hi everyone, today we're going to hear a presentation from Luke Phillips. He is the marketing director for the San Jose Zoo, which is a new client for us. As you know, we typically send out a small group to visit clients and discuss our plans. However, due to the nature of the project and the client, we decided instead to invite him in and have him present the work he has done so far, and we can discuss what we can do to build on it and best meet the Zoo's needs. Before we have you begin, Luke, I'll have you meet the group that will be working on your project. Go ahead and introduce yourselves, starting with the in-office folks."

A young woman with long, ebony Senegalese twists started off the introductions. "Hi, I'm Tonya Johnson, and I'm a senior data scientist. I've been here at CRA for five years."

A man with short blond hair spoke next. "Hi, I'm Jared Richardson, and I'm a data scientist. I've worked here for, uh, four years."

Then, a middle-aged woman with bobbed brunette hair with blonde highlights gave her introduction. "Hello, I'm Juanita Jimenez, I'm a senior data analyst and I started here in 2021, so it's been three years."

Once they introduced themselves, virtual team members made their introductions.

Then, Luke spoke. "I'm glad you all could come out. We'll go ahead and get started..."

Lamar interrupted, cell phone in hand. "It looks like the executive vice president of research wants to join in on this meeting. She just texted me. She'll be in here shortly, in about a minute or so."

"Wow, this must be a very big deal," Luke remarked.

"Yeah. I told you, and I wasn't kidding, but don't worry. She's one of the smartest people I know. I have to warn you – she's very direct, but she's nice."

As Luke waited, paying attention to his laptop in anticipation for the meeting, the glass door opened. He looked up to see the executive vice president, who was wearing a fitted grey pantsuit with a maroon camisole, looking up at him.

What the...

Lamar spoke up. "Hi, Ann!"

"Hi, Lamar! Hi, everyone!"

"Ann, this is Luke Phillips, he's the marketing director for the San Jose Zoo. Luke, this is Ann Evans, she's the executive vice president of research here at the CRA."

"Ann Evans?" AC's married?

Fuck.

"Hi, Luke," Ann greeted him, holding out her hand for a handshake.

Luke took a deep breath. "Uh...hello, Ann."

Why didn't she tell me she's married? Why didn't Paulie tell me? Dammit!

Ann sat amongst the team. She adjusted her soft, textured hair, which was corralled in a French braid tied into a bun at the nape of her neck.

"Lamar, you didn't have to wait on me."

"Sure, but we couldn't get started without the head honcho!" Lamar joked.

Everyone laughed but Luke, who looked as if he had seen a ghost.

Lamar tapped on his friend's hand. "Okay, Luke, we're ready to start now."

Alright, I can't worry about AC right now. It's go time.

He pulled up the slideshow presentation on his computer and spoke to the group. "Hi, I'm Luke Phillips, marketing director for the San Jose Zoo. We have been running a robust social media marketing campaign for the past six months, using several outlets, with video and photo visuals. Here are a couple of examples."

A slide with two visuals flashed on the screen, including one with an elephant blowing water and another with children pointing at peacocks. The group watched intently and took careful notes.

"I've also sent over a portfolio with the campaigns we've used in greater detail. We have seen a significant increase in zoo attendance, but we would like to be able to get more granular. We would like to have a better idea of what and here's where I'll need your expertise."

Ann nodded and smiled briefly. Luke locked eyes with her, nodded back, and continued the presentation.

After the meeting concluded, everyone left the room except for Luke and Lamar.

"You were fantastic, Luke. You don't give yourself enough credit."

"Thanks, man."

"Listen, this is very much your wheelhouse. Have you ever thought about a future in data science?"

"Eh, no."

"Why not?"

Luke explained as he packed up his computer. "Not my thing. Don't get me wrong, I'm pretty decent at statistics and math in general, and I did quite a bit of it back in college. Did I tell you I was once in veterinary school?"

"No, it never came up, I guess. What happened?"

"Y'know, it wasn't really what I wanted to do. I love animals, but I am more an admirer of their beauty and their instincts. I enjoy their company. But the nitty-gritty of it all, the sickness and the death, it takes away from it. I'm capable of doing it, but I don't have the passion for it, y'know? So, it didn't work out...I failed out."

"Oh, man, I'm sorry about that."

"It's fine. If that didn't happen, I wouldn't be doing what I'm doing now. I love this shit."

"I can tell. The zoo is lucky to have you. And you gave our team the information they needed in a clear, concise way. I'm sure they appreciate that, it's more than what we normally get from clients."

"I've been working on this for a while, so I'm glad I could give them what they need. And I'll tell you what – the zoo board is just as excited as I am."

"Now I hope you weren't thrown off by our executive vice president sitting in on the meeting. That seemed to catch you by surprise, but you took it in stride and your presentation was on point," Lamar encouraged him.

"Appreciate it. Y'know, funny thing is...I actually know her...well, I *knew* her."

"Really? Why didn't you tell me?"

"No...see...I didn't know she works here. I knew her as Ann Corbin and this was a long time ago, like twenty, twenty-five years ago. She and I went to college together in Michigan."

"I knew she went to The University of the Great Lakes, and I know that's where you went, too, but never thought to ask you if you knew her."

"It's fine. We were old college friends. Then, I moved back to my hometown once I graduated, and she came down to start her career, but we lost touch not long after that. Didn't know she was out here, and I'm sure she didn't know I moved out here, either."

"Yeah, I hear you. Small world, huh?"

"For sure."

Lamar looked down at his vibrating phone on the table. "Looks like Ann wants you to stop by her office on your way out. Do you have time? I don't know what your schedule looks like."

Luke took a deep breath. "Yeah, I've got some time."

After he finished packing up his laptop, they left the meeting room and strode through the illuminated office, climbing up a flight of floating stairs to the executive offices. He then led him to a glass door with a gold nameplate next to it labeled "A. L. Evans." Ann's eyes met Luke's, and she motioned him to enter.

He walked into the well-lit office, the door closing behind him. He placed his laptop bag in the corner and sat in a grey felt chair facing the stark white desk. On the other side, she was reclining in an office chair with a slight smirk. Behind her was a wall of windows to the sunny day outside. On the desk and shelves to the right side of the room were a few photos, books, and two small plants.

"Didn't expect to see you, Luke," she commented. "You *moved* out here?"

"Yeah. I needed a fresh start. Honestly, I didn't think I would run into you, at least not like this."

"Did you know I work here?"

"No, not at all. I swear. Lamar's a friend of mine, we're in the same cycling club."

"Huh...small world."

"Yeah. He said the same thing when I told him I know you."

"Want something to drink? I've got water and Diet Coke."

"Eh, water sounds good."

She retrieved a bottle of water from a microfridge behind the desk, gave it to him, then sat atop her desk.

Luke took the bottle and sipped. "Ann *Evans*, huh?"

"Yeah."

"AC...why didn't you tell me when I came out here to see you last year that you're married?"

"I'm not, and even if I was, why would I tell you? You didn't bother to ask. You just assumed I was single."

"No, I was just hoping you were. You're not married, though?"

"Not anymore. I'm surprised Paul didn't fill you in before he died."

"Nah, he really didn't tell me anything. He just said he was in touch with you, but he wouldn't go into it any further."

"I'm surprised. So, uh...I *was* married. My ex and I met in Losanti, but we got together some time after you and I stopped talking. We got married, and we decided to move out here."

"Oh – no wonder I never ran into you."

"Yeah. I was outta there maybe a year or so after we stopped talking."

"Can't blame you one bit."

She nodded. "So, when we first moved out here, we lived over in San Francisco. He wanted to pursue his dreams of being a full-time artist, and I was willing to support him. It went okay. Not spectacular, but we survived."

"Oh, wow. So, what happened?"

Ann shrugged. "You know, it wasn't anything crazy. We just wanted different things."

"I get it."

"So, my ex had strong feelings about me working in corporate America. He didn't like it, even though I was working in the private sector when we met. Then, I had the offer of a lifetime down here, it was at a tech firm I worked at before CRA. He insisted I not take the job. He hates everything Silicon Valley, so he told me if I took the position, I would be 'selling out' to tech-bro hypercapitalist interests."

"Y'know, it sounds like he's got his convictions."

"Totally. I don't fault him, he really is a good person. And, uh...I have my own feelings about capitalism, so I get it. But I also need my peace."

"You've always been so headstrong."

"You're not wrong. I enjoy this work, and I'm damn good at it. And yes, I love being creative, too – that's what initially brought my ex and I together. I started acting in community theater back in Losanti, and I've continued that out here, but I can't make it my entire life. It stops being fun when I'm forced to live by my art. I need the balance. He couldn't live with that, and we decided to end the marriage."

Luke took a swig of water. "That makes complete sense."

Her legs gently swung over the edge of the desk. "The divorce was amicable. We didn't have kids, thank God. It was almost ten years ago...my ex and I are still good friends. We make much better friends than lovers, truth be told. And I guess I haven't changed my name back because it was enough of a pain to change it to begin with."

"That makes sense. I was married for a while too, but we divorced a few years ago. I'm sure Paulie told you all about it."

"Uh...no, not really. He just said he had a feeling you were struggling. I take it you ended up not becoming a veterinarian?"

"Nope. I failed out of school, I worked as a lab researcher for Ohio Valley Ranch for a while, and then my career just went downhill from there. I didn't deal with my failures in a healthy way. I stopped taking care of my mental health, and I coped with the bottle."

"Oof."

"Yeah, I know. Not the best choices."

"Welp, we all make mistakes, Luke. "

"That's true. Eventually, my ex-wife was over it and she filed for divorce. It went pretty smoothly, but we didn't stay friends. To be completely honest, we weren't friends during the marriage either."

"Must've been pretty isolating."

He nodded.

"Um...so why did you move out here?" she inquired.

"Like I said, I needed a fresh start. See, what you said to me last year made a lot of sense. Y'know, I finished the trip that Paulie and I started, and I drove out here to see you. At the time, though, I guess the way I looked at it, he had just died, and I thought to myself I couldn't keep living in regret."

"I understand...grief can make us do strange things."

"Oh, for sure. It wasn't fair to expect you to say yes to being with me or even resuming our friendship. We ended badly, and I hadn't shown you anything at that point to make you believe I actually changed because I hadn't done anything to take control of my own life."

"Yeah, sounds about right."

"So, I finally decided to live the life I wanted to live, and I needed to do that independent of my parents and everything in Losanti. I sobered up, got the help I needed, and started putting effort into my online nature videos and vlogs on YouTube."

"Uh...that's cool. What's the channel?"

"'Cross Country with Carter.'"

"Carter...like, your middle name?"

"Yeah. Figured it would make a cool YouTube name."

"I can see that. Nice alliteration. Let me pull up your channel." She placed her computer on her lap and found his channel.

"Which one should I watch?"

He stood next to her and pointed out a video showcasing the Arizona desert and the south side of the Grand Canyon.

As she watched, she lit up. "You're damn good at this."

"Thanks. That means a lot coming from you. My channel was what got me the position at the San Jose Zoo. I've been out here for close to a year. For once, I'm living life on my own terms."

"That's awesome. You definitely kicked ass during your presentation, and you've given my team a solid foundation they can run with."

"I'm glad to hear it."

"I get the feeling you're passionate about your work. All I ever wanted for you was to do what made you truly happy."

He smiled. "I am. I love what I do for a living, I live in a nice apartment in San Jose with my cat, I've made friends, and I'm living a clean, healthy life. I can truly say at this point that I'm living well and I'm in a good place."

"Wonderful." She placed the laptop on her desk, then pivoted. "So, you say you have a cat?"

"Yep. My first pet. Finally managing well enough to have one living with me."

"That's awesome. Tell me more."

"She's a domestic long-haired cat, grey and white. Very friendly and chill, really curious. I could talk about her forever." He took out his cell phone and found a photo of his feline to show her.

"She's so adorbs, so fluffy."

"Yeah, that she is. And did I tell you her name is Stevie?"

Ann lit up. "Stevie? Like Stevie Nicks?"

"Of course. Some things never change."

"Fleetwood Mac...that was our thing, wasn't it?"

"Sure was. So, do you think your dog would get along with a cat?"

"Alexis is the gentlest of giants. Why?"

"Hmm, just...thinking," he smiled wryly.

She cocked her head to the side, her slate eyes penetrating his soul. "Luke, are you trying to ask me something?"

"Here's the thing, AC. When I came out to see you last year, I meant everything I said, and I still feel the same way. But, it's not just about what I want."

She smirked. "It's not. I don't play house, but I'll tell you what."

"I'm all ears."

"Let's live in the now. We can take it day by day and see where this goes."

With that, he leaned in and tenderly kissed her soft lips.

THE BEGINNING
November 27, 2025

"AC, girl...you're so hot."

Ann, dressed in a maroon long-sleeved, button-up blouse and blue jeans, blushed and waved at the GoPro, as she stirred a pot of fresh collard greens on the black electric stovetop. "Of course I am – I'm minding the stove!" she joked.

"What are you making?" Luke asked.

"Um...greens."

"That's a bit strange for Thanksgiving."

"It's not strange for *my* family. And eh, yours can try something new." Then, she broke concentration. "No, Alexis, greens are not for Alexises," she gently admonished the long-haired black pooch, who was jumping up and down on the linoleum floor trying to reach for her stirring fork.

Luke panned over to the dog with his camera. "Alexis, sit," he said. Alexis sat with her bushy tail wagging. "Good girl," he said, giving her a banana and bacon dog treat.

"Babe, don't forget your mashed potatoes," Ann reminded him.

He sat the GoPro down on the counter and stirred the potato pot on the shiny retro stove while rubbing her back. "It'll be nice having Monday and Tuesday off too, on top of the Thanksgiving holiday.

It's a nice-sized break from spending time at the zoo. I love the work, and the work-life balance is pretty surprising."

"Oh, yeah. I was wondering about your work-life balance when you accepted that promotion."

"Yeah, the new position has a lot of responsibility. You get it."

"For sure. In any case, I'm thankful for the ability to do what I love, and then having time to be with who I love."

Luke lit up.

"Speaking of," Ann continued, "how are things going there?"

"Excellent. The recent marketing push I'm leading for the zoo, which your people were so helpful with, has paid off dividends."

"I'm not surprised. We have great folks at Cal Republic."

"For sure – y'all have the reputation as the best marketing firm in California for a reason."

She nodded while tending to the pot.

He continued. "The board is very impressed. The CEO pulled me aside to tell me they're seeing a significant increase in daily attendance and patron donations, and to keep it coming."

"Nice! Sounds like you have their ear. Two years there and you've got in really good with them. Impressive."

"Thanks, AC. I appreciate the new position, and how I'm still free to vlog and work on my other side projects. The work-life balance is amazing for that kind of role."

"Sounds like the best kind of job, the kind that pays you and gives you the time to do the other things you're passionate about."

"That's for sure."

"Babe, these are almost done. I'll finish up your potatoes and get them tinned. Go ahead and get ready. I think it's just about time for your alarm to go off for your pills, right?"

"Yeah, of course." He kissed her forehead and left the kitchen.

Fifteen minutes later, Luke called out to Ann from her bedroom down the hall. "AC!"

"What's up?" she yelled back.

"Is the food ready yet?"

"Yeah. I'm about to pack it up."

"Put it all in the oven and turn it to warm, then come in here," Luke said.

A few minutes later, Ann entered her bedroom. As soon as she walked past the threshold, Luke clutched her arm and gently placed her against the wood-paneled wall, where they began to make out.

He whispered in her ear, "I've been dying to make the most passionate love to you, girl."

"How long have you wanted to do that, babe?" she asked softly.

"All week long...I've longed to have *you*." He led her to the lavender-adorned queen bed, and as she lay on her back with a small smile, he pulled off his white tee and stepped out of his grey sweatpants, throwing the articles of clothing onto the felt purple chair in the corner of the room. He then reclined next to her, slowly unbuttoning her top and separating the front clasps on her black lace bra. He then kissed her soft, beige skin. "You're so beautiful."

She giggled playfully, as her brilliant grey eyes met his shimmering ocean blues. "You are absolutely incredible."

He worshiped her perky bosom, and a short time later, slipped off her jeans. He then straddled her and kissed her on her pillowy lips, as he ran his fingers through her auburn-streaked brunette locks. "Ann Leigh, I love you so much."

"I love you too, Luke Carter."

He gently parted her legs and made his grand entrance, which she responded to with mellow moans. An hour of passionate and vigorous lovemaking ensued.

Afterwards, they showered and dressed. Luke wore a turquoise polo shirt and khaki shorts, while Ann donned a fuchsia flowing top covered by a jean jacket, and a pair of beige capris.

"Babe, you might want a hoodie," she advised. "It could get cold."

"I've got one in the truck."

They then climbed into Luke's Wrangler, bag of greens and mashed potatoes in tow, and headed out.

"Did you call your family earlier?" Luke asked while driving.

"Yeah, I did."

"How are they?"

"They're good. Mom's doing great. She loves her job," Ann recalled.

"Court reporter, right?"

"Yeah. She says to tell you 'hi.'"

"Cool, let her know I say 'hi' back, and I look forward to us visiting her this summer."

"For sure."

"How's your birth mom?"

"Well...she's been sick, but she said she was glad to hear from me."

"Aww, that's tough. I hope she gets better soon."

"Yeah, me too. Um...I talked briefly to Lionel and Keonna. They're good, and so are the kids."

"Good to hear. Have you talked to your sister?"

"Yeah, Michelle and I spoke this morning. She's doing great. She's coming out with a new graphic novel in January."

"I saw the announcement on her Instagram page – she's really got talent."

"Totally. Just so you know, she and her wife are looking to fly out here to visit over Christmas."

"That'll be a lot of fun. God, I haven't seen your sister since we were at Great Lakes."

"Damn, it really has been that long, huh? She was a bratty teenager back then. Now, she's married and living in Baltimore."

"Time flies, doesn't it?"

"It sure does."

"So, how are your parents?"

"They're alright, just as crazy as ever. My mom's asking me when we're gonna have kids."

"Wow – she's asking about kids? We're not even married."

"Yeah…it's a bit weird. When I talked to her yesterday, she just had to remind me some women have them in their fifties."

"True enough, but you know, that ain't happening!"

Luke smiled. "I'm fine with that."

"Uh…honestly," Ann confessed, "I never felt ready to have kids. I know they say no one's ever 'ready,' but I dunno. Then, at a certain point, I had to tell myself that if I'm in my forties and I still don't feel the call to be a mother, then it's probably not for me."

"I get it. For the longest time, I wasn't mentally prepared for fatherhood. At this point, I'm not expecting for us to become parents, but if it happens, it happens."

"Yeah, I'm there with you. I'm not looking for it, but let's be real, it's not like we're trying to prevent it."

"Y'know, AC, I'm so glad you're coming with me."

"Of course. Why wouldn't I?"

"I know, but please be aware that my brother's a bit of a dick," he warned.

She looked at him. "I work in tech. Tech in Silicon Valley. I doubt your brother's a bigger dick than some of the guys I work with."

The couple headed up Interstate 280 towards the San Francisco area.

"Babe," she spoke, "I don't know if I've said this already, but I'm super proud of you."

"Huh? Why?"

"You took a chance and moved all the way out here, and you made a clean start. You decided to make a go of it without your parents' support. You got a job that makes you enough to live comfortably on your own, which is really saying something for California, and you worked yourself into a promotion. And you're pursuing your dream, what you really want to do. You're living the kind of life you always wanted to live since I've known you. More than anything you've done, you're finally living for you. You're *free*."

He smiled and breathed deeply. "Y'know, AC...having you back in my life motivates me, to be honest."

She reminded him, "But babe, *you* did this, not me. You chose to do what you needed to do to be whole. You're putting in the work, and I admire you for that. And now, you're actually going to visit your brother and his family for the first time. That's a hell of a step."

"Don't get too proud yet, AC. There's a good chance he could say something stupid, and I might have to choke him out."

She chuckled. "You know what? I just have this feeling things will be alright."

———◆◆◆———

It was a quarter to four in the afternoon, and Luke and Ann arrived at a wood-paneled two-story custom home in the enclave of Pacifica, outside San Francisco. The retro-style house sat on an incline near the beach and boasted of a misty view of the Pacific Ocean. They parked in the driveway and stepped out of the truck. After she grabbed the bag with the dishes, they walked to the door and he rang the doorbell.

Sandy, in a cream-colored sleeveless turtleneck top, answered. In the background, the screaming of a young child could be heard. "Hi Luke!" she said, "and this must be your girlfriend Ann – hi! We've heard so much about you. Great to finally meet you!"

"Hi, Sandy!" Luke said. "Yeah – AC, this is my sister-in-law, Sandy."

"Hi, I'm Ann, it's nice to meet you too!"

"Are you a hugger?" Sandy asked.

"Yeah, hugs are great."

"You'll fit right in." She hugged them both and took the bag from her. "Oh, this is heavy. It smells good. What is it?"

"It's collard greens and mashed potatoes."

"Oh wow, thank you very much. Glad you brought the collard greens. I haven't had them in years. My grandma on my dad's side, God rest her soul, she was from the South, Mississippi, and she would make 'em for Thanksgiving dinner. I loved them growing up."

Ann glanced at Luke with a sparkle in her eye.

Sandy continued. "And are these Luke's famous mashed pota-toes?"

He bragged, "Of course!"

"This will be delicious, I'm sure. C'mon in guys!"

"Thanks! Sandy – where's Trey?" Luke asked.

"Oh, he's in the study."

"Where's that?"

"Go right around the staircase and down the hall, it's the last door on the left."

"Thanks." He turned to Ann. "AC, I'll be right back. Hang tight."

"Sure, of course, babe."

Luke walked past the floating staircase and down the dark paneled hallway to the double doors of the study complement-ing the wood finish of the walls. The doors were glass-paneled, and he could see Trey sitting on an ergonomic office chair smok-ing an opaque green glass pipe, facing at an angle slightly away from the door. He softly knocked.

"Sandy?"

"No, it's Luke."

"Oh, come on in, asshole."

He opened the door, and the earthy scent filled his nostrils. Trey, who was wearing a blue argyle cardigan sweater over a tee shirt, pleated khaki pants, and Birkenstocks, turned around to face his brother.

"Looking a little taller, huh?" Trey quipped.

Luke shrugged.

"Sit down."

Trey guided his brother to a chocolate leather couch.

"So, you fuckin' did it. You came out to Cali, and you made something of yourself."

"I did," Luke responded confidently.

"President of marketing and communications for the San Jose Zoo. I'm impressed."

Luke stared at his brother suspiciously.

"I'm serious. That's a very big deal. It's one of the best zoos in the world."

"Thanks, Trey."

"I know Mom and Dad were pissed as hell when you told them you were moving out here."

"Eh, not really."

"Wow...I'm surprised by that."

"Well, when I told them I was moving out here, they said I was being impulsive yet again and I was on my own financially. They even told me not to expect you to bail me out."

"So, they even had to bring me into it. That's *them*."

"It was weird because I've never asked you for money, but y'know, that was fine with me. When I made it clear I had a practical plan in place and it was already in motion, they kind of had to let it go. Even Dad said he respected it."

"You grew some balls, huh?"

"I suppose so."

"Wow, by God, you figured it out," Trey declared. "You got your ass out of fuckin' Losanti, you came out here, got into a great career where you can support yourself comfortably, and you have your own place nobody else is paying for. Santana Row...that's pretty nice."

"Yeah. It's a great place, renovated, lots of room, it's close to work, and it's maybe like fifteen minutes away from my girlfriend's house."

"Shit, Luke. I'm truly proud of you."

Trey then took a long puff on his pipe and handed it to his younger brother. He tried to take a hit, but lacking prior experience, he instead coughed.

"Noob." Trey poked, taking back his pipe. "Just fuckin' with you. First time for everything."

Luke caught his breath, eking out a "yeah."

"So, is your girlfriend here?"

"Yeah. She's out there talking to Sandy."

"That's great. I've been looking forward to meeting her. Ann, right?"

"Yeah."

"I've seen pictures of you two on Facebook. You make a fine couple, you match well. You look *happy*. Nothing like how you were with your ex."

"Thanks...that's because I'm truly happy with her. She's amazing – the best thing that ever happened to me."

"That's great. Any thoughts about marriage?"

"Good question. We'll see, but I will say this: I can't imagine my life without her."

"Playing that one close to the vest. Smart. Just don't wait too long. Women like her aren't gonna wait around forever."

"Very true."

Anyway, I was talking to Mom, and she said that y'all knew each other from college or something?"

"Yeah, Ann and I met at UGL, and we were good friends. We lost touch, and then we reconnected out here after my friend Paul died."

"Oh wow, I'm sorry to hear about your friend. But it's great that you and Ann were able to get back in touch. Sometimes the best relationships grow from friendships."

"Oh, for sure."

Trey's tone shifted slightly. "Does Dad know about her?"

Luke smiled sardonically. "He knows."

"You know why I hardly go back home to Losanti?"

"No, but to be honest, I never got it. Mom and Dad love you, you're their favorite. You're their rockstar. They treat you like a king every time you visit."

Trey shook his head. "It's funny, because I don't see it that way. I know what you're saying, but when I go home, all I feel is pressure. I get slotted into a spot, the same spot I've had as long as I can remember, and I have my part to play. We both do. I'm fifty years old, and every time I go home, it's like I'm still six trying to impress Dad. If I stayed there too long, either I would become a hard man like him, or crumple under the pressure." He took a hit. "The distance helps."

"Yeah, I'm starting to see that myself."

"Now, it doesn't mean all my problems were fixed by moving. Far from it. Sandy could probably tell you. We've gone through a lot together. I still have my problems."

"But you're so successful, Trey. Something you had a hand in is part of most people's way of life nowadays. I dunno...if I did something like that, my ego could not be contained."

"Eh, you'd think so. But that's not how it works. There's this saying, 'Wherever you go, there you are.' And it's true. There are times I sense I'm becoming like Mom and Dad, Dad especially. I recently had to quit drinking because of it."

"Same. Two years and four months."

"Good, good, Luke. You're doing the damn thing." Trey smiled. "But yeah, I found myself becoming like Dad and I had to stop."

"I get it."

"I've been Cali sober since February. I still smoke cannabis, that's natural and it relaxes me. But it doesn't make me mean the way alcohol does. That had to go."

"I'm glad to hear it."

"Thanks, but don't get me wrong, Luke, I still struggle in other ways. Like, I don't want to make differences between my kids, and I love them both the same, but I get Braiden in a way that I don't get Shane. Braiden's a lot like me. He's excitable, he's very active and boyish, he likes sports, and he loves school. You can really see it in his grades. Shane's shyer and more artistic. He's not into school so much, but he's still a smart kid, he's into music and shit. You know what his favorite thing in the whole world is, Luke?"

Luke shrugged.

"Remember that guitar you gave him the last time we flew out to Losanti? He fuckin' loves that thing."

"Really?"

"Yeah, really. He's self-taught, he practices all the time, and he and his friends from school started a garage band a few months back."

"Wow, he's a smart kid."

"For sure. Sky's the limit when he applies himself. See, I don't know how to connect with him. I'm a pragmatic man. I know the arts are hard to make a living with, but I don't want to crush his spirit. It's what I hated the most about visiting Losanti. Every time I'd be there, I'd see it happening to you."

Luke nodded.

"So yeah, coming out here didn't make me a better man. I'm still a fuckin' Phillips. But being away from Losanti, being away from our hometown, being away from our parents, it gave me the distance to work through my problems and to build that self-awareness I wouldn't have had if I stayed." Trey looked at his brother, his expression softened. "I was scared you were gonna die there. Glad you're here, little brother."

There was a knock at the door.

"You can open it," Trey called out.

The door cracked. "Mom said to come get you for dinner," Shane said. He then looked over to the sofa and smiled from ear to ear. "Hi, Uncle Luke!"

"Hi, Shane!" Luke got up and faced his nephew. Shane ran over and gave him a huge hug.

"Shane – tell your mother we'll be in there in just a second," Trey instructed him.

"Okay, Dad." He left the room excitedly.

Trey got up and shut the door. "I swear," he confessed, "I have never seen Shane light up like that in my life. So glad you finally made it out here." He gave Luke a hearty and heartfelt hug.

The men left the study and entered the dining room. The mint green room was adorned with Southwest-inspired artwork. The circular pine table in the middle was simple and surrounded by matching pine chairs with felt burnt orange seats. The table polish was worn with the imprints of cup rings, but the set was sturdy and clearly well-loved.

The food graced the middle of the table, and clear glass plates with forks, knives, and matching glass tumblers were placed in front of each seat. Sides, which encircled the golden turkey, already pre-carved, in the center, included dressing, green bean casse-role, and dinner rolls, as well as Ann's collards and Luke's mashed potatoes. A carafe of ice water was sitting alongside the spread. In addition, a double chocolate cake was displayed on a side table.

Luke brought Trey over to Ann. "AC, this is my brother Trey. Trey, this is my wonderful girlfriend Ann."

"Hi Ann, it's a pleasure to meet you."

"Likewise, Trey."

Everyone grabbed seats around the table. Trey had Braiden to his right and Shane to his left. Sandy sat on the other side of the hyperactive child, and Luke sat between Ann and Shane.

Sandy spoke up. "Luke, I remember always telling you that you should come out here to visit us. I'm beyond thrilled you finally made it."

"I'm glad too."

Trey then spoke up. "Ann," She looked towards him, and he took a deep breath and continued. "Thank you for getting my little brother out here to Cali." He got choked up. "It means a lot to me, a lot to us."

Ann blushed. "Uh, it wasn't me, I didn't make him. He chose to be here. And he had help from a dear friend." She squeezed Luke's hand under the table.

"I'm hungry!" Braiden said excitedly.

"Okay, okay!" Trey laughed. "Let's dig in."

The plates got passed around the table as food was served.

"Shane, what sides do you want?" Sandy asked.

"Um, I'll have turkey and rolls. And I'll try the green stuff."

"Those are collard greens."

"Oh okay, Mom. I'll have that. The potatoes, are those Uncle Luke's?"

"Yes, they are."

"I'll have those, too. Just make sure my food isn't touching."

Sandy started scooping.

"More."

She gave him one last scoop. "Save some for everybody else, bud." She sent his filled plate over to him. She then spoke to the table. "We have water on the table. If you want soda, we have Coke and Sprite in the fridge."

"Water's fine for me, thanks," Ann said.

Trey got up to go to the kitchen. "I'm getting myself a Sprite. Luke, you want something?"

"I'll take a Coke." Trey went into the kitchen, got two cans of soft drinks, then came back out to the dining room. "Here you go."

"Thanks, brother."

After everyone was served Thanksgiving dinner, they started to dig in, enjoying the food and cherishing each other's company.

———◆———

On the sealed redwood balcony of Trey's home stood Luke and Ann. They leaned against the railing, watching the immense ocean against the darkening horizon.

"The sunset is beautiful, isn't it?" Ann marveled.

"It sure is," Luke agreed. "I've never seen anything so breathtaking. Y'know, AC...it's funny, we've been together now for over a year, but I've never asked you this. What made you decide to give me a second chance?"

She looked at him perplexed.

"Back when you were living in Losanti," he explained, "I took you being there for granted, and I didn't do right by you. And you walked away from me, as well you should've. You didn't owe me a second chance. Nothing I had ever shown you back then said that anything would change. How did you know I would?"

"I didn't."

"What do you mean?"

"So, back when we were at Great Lakes, I had it in my mind that you were my soulmate. That uh, it was a God-willed thing."

He was a bit taken aback. "Really?"

"Yeah. For real. Why the hell do you think I would ever decide to move to *Losanti* of all places?"

Luke shrugged. "It's not that bad."

Ann gave him the side eye.

"Okay, it *is* that bad."

"But yeah, a part of me knew that sounded batshit insane. And you know, uh...it kind of was. And let's be real, if I had told you that back then, what would you have thought?"

"Yeah, probably that you were batshit insane."

"And I can't say I'd blame you. But after a certain point, I knew that for myself, I had to let that shit go. I had to begin living in the present. I walked away to take care of me, to find a different way to understand God, and what it means to live. At the end of the day, I had to become comfortable with myself and accept myself for who I was, even if no one else did."

"I get that, AC."

"And as you know, I was married for a while, I was in other relationships after that. I made friends, I legit moved on and lived my life. The way I looked at it, if it was meant for you to come back into my life, it would happen. There was no deity that could make it happen, one way or the other. You had to want it of your own free will. I had to accept the possibility, the probability, it would never be the case, and I had to live with that."

He nodded.

"But it's funny," she recalled. "I moved out here to California for a fresh start, and ultimately, that's what happened. Things were different and sometimes complicated, but at the end of the day, I got the peace of mind I needed. I put the Midwest in my rearview, and I was happy with that. Then I got a call."

"Hmm?"

"Yeah, I sure did. Paul gave me a call out of the blue, this was maybe a couple of months before he died. It was the last time I spoke to him. It was so weird. He said he was thinking about heading out this way. And after we got off the phone, he texted me this picture."

Ann took her cell phone out of her pocket, and after flipping through her photo album, she stopped. "'Kay, here it is." She held up the picture. It was the photo of Ann and Luke with Paul leaned in between them, the same one Luke found in Paul's bedroom, and the same one in Luke's wooden box.

"You know what's crazy? I remember the picture, but not that particular night," he said.

"Funny thing is, I don't remember either. But Paul...he sure did."

The two looked up at the darkened sky with both grief and gratitude.

"Thank you, Paulie. You're my guardian angel, man."

"*Our* guardian angel," she added.

Taking in the beautiful surroundings, they silently remembered their late friend.

"One more thing I gotta do, AC. I'll be right back."

Luke reentered the house. In the living room, Braiden was running around with his arms out to his sides pretending to fly, while Trey and Sandy conversed and laughed on the couch. Shane was lying on the floor writing in a notebook.

"Shane, come with me."

The teenager got up from the floor and followed Luke out the front door. They headed to the back of the Jeep parked in the driveway.

"I wanna show you something that's really important to me." He opened up the back on the truck. He carefully pulled out the guitar case.

"Oh, cool."

"This is an acoustic guitar, but it's not just any acoustic guitar." Luke opened the case to reveal the instrument.

"Wow, amazing! That's a Taylor, isn't it?"

"Yes. Yes it is."

"Ooh, that's spendy."

"Sure, but it's special too. This guitar belonged to my best friend in the whole world. His name was Paul. He died over a year ago, but I still miss him every day. I was holding onto this, even though I can't play it. Y'know, I couldn't part with it, but now I can. If anybody should have it, it should be you, Shane."

The boy stepped back. "Uncle Luke, wow, I...I can't..."

"No, you can. You have talent, and music is what you love. Paul ie...my friend...he was like that too. The guitar, he named her Katie, and Katie needs to go where she'll be loved and appreciated and well taken care of."

Shane smiled broadly and hugged his uncle. "Thank you, Unc. I'll take very good care of her. I really will. I promise."

"Good."

Now, she's home.

Also by Jaye Pool

The Losantiverse Duology
Book One: *Make Me Free*

———◦———

Short Stories and Poetry
http://www.jayepool.com/blog

———◦———

Love *Make Me Free*? Leave a review on your favorite review site or social media!

———◦———

Subscribe to Jaye's newsletter for new releases, sales, in-person and virtual events, and more!
http://www.jayepool.com/newsletter